A Willow Tate Novel

Celia Jerome

DAW BOOKS, INC.
DONALD A. WOLLHEIM, FOUNDER
375 Hudson Street, New York, NY 10014

ELIZABETH R. WOLLHEIM
SHEILA E. GILBERT
PUBLISHERS
www.dawbooks.com

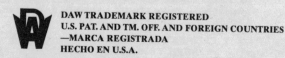

Raves fo...

"This is a fun zany rom... ...ple (Willy and Grant) he... ...y to keep Long Island warm in the winter." — *Midwest Book Review*

"Willow Tate is back with another crazy adventure. You'll love her feisty attitude as she tries to stick to her 'no men' creed with her newest partner. Laugh-out-loud funny! Readers will be in stitches." — *RT Book Reviews* (RT top pick)

"Fans of Jerome's Willow Tate, a cheerfully melodramatic writer and Visualizer, will find much to enjoy in her fourth adventure.... Willow is an unlikely but affable protagonist, undercutting her neurotic self-absorption with cheerful humor and a strong desire to perform good deeds." — *Publishers Weekly*

"This is a fresh new take on the fantasy world mingling with our own, with a bit of supervillains and true love thrown in. For someone who likes paranormal, but wants a new twist, this is the perfect read." — *Parkersburg News and Sentinel*

"This light-hearted urban fantasy series, which is what used to be known as the Unknown style of fantasy adventure, stood out for me with the very first book and the third is the best yet. Willow Tate is an illustrator who can bring magical creatures into our world by drawing them, in both senses of the word. Her latest is a fire wizard, which leads to a series of magical mishaps involving fire, until the secretive organization that deals with these things sends a man whose presence suppresses fire. But that leads to all sorts of new complications. There's a bunch of quirky subsidiary characters, amusing plot twists, and Keystone Kops type mayhem. This is definitely not a series you want to lump in with the majority of recent urban fantasy, and it's guaranteed to bring a smile to your face." — *Critical Mass*

"The world-building is the best part of *Trolls*. The people and places come alive; the fantastical back-story is unusual and fascinating; and the whole of it is definitely something new and extraordinary, and a welcome break from vampires and were-creatures." — *Errant Dreams*

"In fine, small-town mystery fashion, Paumanok Harbor is full of quirky people, many with odd little magic talents.... It's a fun adventure; Willow's an engaging character ... charming series." — *Locus*

"This is a well-written, cute series that is on the very lightest side of the urban fantasy genre—almost chick-lit light, really (but without the shoe shopping).... The author definitely captures the sense of place in both Manhattan and the Hamptons. This is an entertaining and amusing series that would make a perfect beach read." — *Fang-tastic Fiction*

To Carole, and everyone else who believes in magic and laughter, small treasures and small dogs.

ACKNOWLEDGMENTS

To all the usual suspects, with love and gratitude for your support and good ideas.

And to Robert Parker.

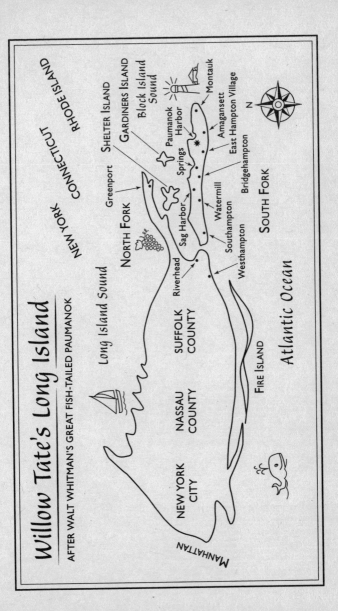

Willow Tate's Long Island

AFTER WALT WHITMAN'S GREAT FISH-TAILED PAUMANOK

CONNECTICUT

RHODE ISLAND

NEW YORK

Long Island Sound

SHELTER ISLAND

GARDINERS ISLAND

Block Island Sound

Greenport

NORTH FORK

Paumanok Harbor

Springs

Montauk

Amagansett

East Hampton Village

Sag Harbor

Watermill

Bridgehampton

Southampton

SOUTH FORK

Riverhead

Westhampton

SUFFOLK COUNTY

NASSAU COUNTY

FIRE ISLAND

Atlantic Ocean

NEW YORK CITY

MANHATTAN

Celia Jerome lives in Paumanok Harbor toward the east end of Long Island. She believes in magic, True Love, small dogs, and yard sales.

You can visit Celia at www.celiajerome.com

CHAPTER ONE

I had a new fan. And a nosebleed.

Part of being a writer like me is promoting yourself, creating a fan base, getting your name out. In my case, I push Willy Tate's name. My own Willow Tate is too girly for some of my audience, so I try for androgyny or ambiguity.

For better or worse, book tours, store signings, and library talks have mostly given way to online social networking sites like Facebook. A lot of the kids who read my YA graphic novels aren't old enough for Facebook, not legally anyway, though some of them find Willy Tate there. I automatically accept Friend requests because that's part of selling books, showing the new covers, announcing publishing dates and book conventions, connecting with the people who actually pay my rent.

For the same reasons, I keep a weekly blog and fan page for the younger readers, mostly about my writing progress and Little Red, my six-pound, three-legged Pomeranian. I often ask them for character name suggestions — they love that — and about their own pets. Sometimes the threads go on for pages.

Then there's my website, where visitors can look at covers, read excerpts, check the backlist. They can post comments about my books or whatever they want there, or write to me directly at Willy Tate's dedicated email account, as opposed to my own personal addy, for friends and family.

Maybe three times a year I get a real letter, in a real envelope, with a stamp even, forwarded from my publisher. Wow.

I try to write back to everyone, online or those three snails. It's the courteous thing to do, and good PR, even if it takes hours a day, hours I could spend writing. Sometimes the kids are sweet and charming and ask intelligent questions, which makes it all worthwhile and gratifying. Sometimes the need to be cheery and chirpy and polite to some teenaged twit who finds fault with one of my books is enough to piss me off. It's not like I can't handle criticism—What author can't? What author likes it?—but if I don't like a writer, I don't buy another of their books. I don't write a diatribe about what they did wrong and how they should stick to writing orders at Applebee's. I don't enjoy giving up precious hours for a brat's ego trip.

Deni wasn't that bad, just a pain in the neck. She showed up everywhere, leaving effusive comments at every site, ones that required an answer.

LV LV LV YR BOOKS!!! RED EM ALL 2X. WHEN'S THE NEXT 1 OUT?

I wrote back with the date and title, then mentioned the meeting that afternoon to finalize the cover. I'd post the artwork as soon as it became final.

Not good enough. She—Denise?—switched to instant message: WHASSIT ABOUT?

I replied it was a secret for now, she should have a great day and thanks for writing.

ANY BKSIGNINGS SOON?

Damn. I could shut off the computer or make a ttyl excuse, but I felt bad since the kid had to be a good customer. So I wasted more time explaining that I didn't do many bookstore appearances anymore, but I'd let her know if I'd be at ComicCon or any science fiction/fantasy conventions, maybe the one at Stony Brook on Long Island. Bye.

She must type a lot faster than I do.

IF ITS CAUSE YR NOT A DUDE, THAT'S OK. I ALREADY KNOW. +I LIVE IN NYC LKE U. WE CLD MEET 4 COF AND U CLD SIGN MY COPIES.

The pain in the neck radiated to my skull, the kind of headache that sat over your temples and played bongos. SORRY, I wrote. TOO BUSY. MEETINGS, AND WRITING, ETC.

PLS. I WANT TO BE A CARTOON ARTIST 2. NEED YR ADVICE ON MY PORTFOLIO.

Worse and worse, a wannabe. I didn't have any magic words to pull a publishing contract out of my hat, or the heart to tell someone their work wasn't professional enough or creative enough. The drums went right to my sinuses. I told her about all the on-line courses and wished her good luck, then said I had to get to that meeting. I signed out.

I pressed my fingers to the bridge of my nose. That didn't help so I went to see if I had any painkillers that hadn't expired.

Holy hell. The bathroom mirror showed blood dripping down my nose and upper lip. I swiped at it with a tissue, but more kept coming. Don't panic, I told myself, wiping it off my chin, my fingers. Too late. I really hated the sight of blood, especially mine. I tried to convince myself it was only a nosebleed, not a brain hemorrhage. Except I'd never had a nosebleed before in my life. Was I supposed to put my head back? Or lie down? Pack my nose with cotton balls—yeck—or put an ice cube on the back of my neck? Meanwhile, a red Rorschach spatter bloomed on the blue man-tailored shirt I'd intended to wear to the sales meeting at my publisher's office, because it matched my eyes and I had a nice navy wool blazer perfect for the end of September and a new silk scarf with batiked blue butterflies. That and jeans, and I'd appear mature and competent and artsy. Perfect, except for looking like a mugging victim.

Don't panic. I had lots of shirts, lots of time to get downtown. A simple bloody nose had to stop soon, didn't it?

It didn't.

Like millions of mature, competent, independent women before me, I called my mother.

"Mom, my nose won't stop bleeding. What do I do?"

"How am I supposed to know? If one of my dogs bled from the nose, I'd rush it to the vet."

My mother was a renowned dog whisperer. After thirty-five years, I should have known that nothing without four feet and a tail registered on her radar. Except my single state.

"That's what you should do. Call that nice Dr. Spenser you've been seeing."

"Mom, Matt is a veterinarian! And he's out in Paumanok Harbor. I'm in Manhattan."

She sniffed, which is my mother's way of saying a toothless Chihuahua had more sense than her only daughter. And she'd like the dog more. "Well, I'm in Arkansas and you called me. I'll be up north for Halloween and we can talk about it when I get there."

"My nosebleed? I'll be dead by then!"

"For heaven's sake, Willow, stop being so dramatic, but I suppose you can't help it, being your father's daughter. The jackass most likely gave you thin blood, too."

The divorce was decades ago, the rancor remained. She sniffed again. "We need to talk about sharing the Manhattan apartment if you're not going to move in with Dr. Spenser. My new TV show starts taping in November."

Could stress cause nosebleeds? I went through another box of tissues. "Yeah, Mom, we'll talk when you get here. Remember they don't allow dogs in the apartment." I had to sneak Little Red in and out, but he was tiny. My mother tended to rescue greyhounds and pit bulls, which could eat the Pomeranian, as if I didn't have enough to worry about. "I've got to go stop this bleeding and get downtown by noon for an important meeting."

"Call your grandmother."

My grandmother was a renowned herbalist whose potions and powders could cure almost anything. She also ran Paumanok Harbor's All Hallow's women's celebration. Like any elder witch would, she terrified me. Call her and her crone coven cronies? My nose could fall off first. Or maybe later, if I let her experiment on me. Besides, whatever Grandma Eve recommended couldn't be found in the city, like dried toad skin. I shuddered and grabbed some paper towels.

The other reason I wouldn't call my grandmother was that she firmly believed I held the responsibility for keeping all of Paumanok Harbor safe, its crazy people with their crazy talents, its secrets, its connection to another universe where magic ruled, and its future filled with infant espers. Yeah, like I wanted that load on my shoulders.

My mother's sister wrangled children for a living, as assistant principal of the Paumanok Harbor school. She'd know all about nosebleeds, but I hated to bother her during school hours. My cousin Susan could cook, not cure, and my father in Florida would only tell me about some awful premonition of danger that no one could figure out. They all had psychic talent, like most people born or bred in Paumanok Harbor, but magic couldn't help me now. I did not need someone to control the weather or talk to dead people.

Matt? I couldn't think about him now, unless I wanted a bleeding ulcer, too.

So I went across the hall to Mrs. Abbottini, whose apartment took up the other half of the third floor of the brownstone we lived in.

I knew to knock loudly over the noise from the TV that filled the hall. "It's Willow, Mrs. A. I have a nosebleed." Of course it came out like a cow's mooing, with the wad under my nose.

Mrs. Abbottini opened the door an inch, on the chain, to make sure I wasn't some thug about to knock her down, have my evil way with her, and steal her Yankee memorabilia. I repeated my problem, in case she missed the stains on my shirt and the sodden paper towels.

"Don't bleed on the carpet," was all she said.

"What do I do about it?" I shouted.

She nodded on her chicken-skin neck, barely moving the dyed-black helmet hair, like a geriatric bobblehead. "My Antony got the nosebleed a lot." She shuffled her pink slippers over to find the remote and turned the TV volume down a notch.

I still had to yell. "What did you do for Antony?"

"The nosebleeds stopped after my husband hit him on the side of the head."

"A physical blow stopped the bleeding?"

"No, it stopped him from shoving things up his nose. I always had to take him to the emergency room before that. Of course, they had to stick a long tweezery thing up his nose to get whatever he shoved up there. What did you do?"

"I didn't do anything, I swear. And I'm not going to the emergency room for a nosebleed."

She didn't hear me. Or didn't want to. "So when are you going to marry that nice vet from the Hamptons?"

I bled red, not gray matter, the way I'd have to before I discussed my love life with my mother's old friend. "It's nothing like that. We're just dating."

"Hating? That's not what I heard, the two of you screwing like bunnies on the beach."

"We did not!" Well, maybe a little. "Dating," I shouted at her. "We are dating."

"How can you date with you in the city and him in the country?"

That was a damned good question, and another headache. I'd gone back to the Harbor a couple of weekends ago, but Matt had two emergency surgeries, so we didn't spend a lot of time together. Then he had to cancel his turn to come into the city. His ex-wife's father died suddenly, and he had to go to the funeral in Connecticut. Not that I expected to be invited—how tacky would that be, bringing your new girlfriend to your former wife's grieving family?—but I wished he'd sounded more sincere about regretting missing the museums and shows

I'd planned. Then last weekend he made some excuse about a cat scratch that sounded lame. "I don't want to talk about Matt."

Or think about him getting back with his ex in her moment of need. I had a bad taste in my mouth. Maybe the blood from my poor nose.

"Your mother thinks he's a good match."

At this point in my thirty-fifth year, my mother thought Donald Trump was a good match. But she did like Matt and trusted him . . . with her dogs. "Should I put ice on it?"

"Freeze your eggs? Mightn't be a bad idea, you wait any longer."

"On my nose!"

"Oh, stop whining. I'm missing my game, and you don't hear me complaining."

I was not whining. And her game was a rerun of an old Yankee classic. The team never lost in the replays.

"Come here." She gestured for me to sit in a chair—not her favorite, I noted.

Then she reached over and pinched my nose between her fingers, tightly. How could a little old lady with arthritic joints squeeze so hard? "Hey, are you trying to kill me?"

"Sure, then I can finally have the front apartment with the view."

Hers faced the building behind us, overlooking a tiny space for the garbage cans. She thought she should have the front unit after my mother decided to live full time in Paumanok Harbor, other than her dog-rescue work around the country. I took the rent-controlled apartment for myself, instead. Mrs. Abbottini squeezed harder.

I jumped up and ran for the door before my poor proboscis broke. "You wouldn't like it. We get all the street noise."

"What did you say?"

Chapter Two

I had a meeting, and misgivings.

When I fled Mrs. Abbottini's apartment and got back to my own, the answering machine light flashed. Deni had found a new way to annoy me.

"I hope this is the right number for Willow Tate even though it says Rose Tate. She's the famous dog trainer, isn't she? Her website says her daughter is a famous author, so I'm guessing it's you, Willy. This is Deni. I thought I could catch you before you left and ride to your meeting with you."

Oh, boy.

"Maybe you left already. I'll meet you. You can call me on my cell. Or tweet me."

I did not tweet with twits who intruded on a person's private life. I did not return calls from unwanted admirers. I definitely did not give my cell phone number to strangers, and this kid with her high voice and artificial, nervous giggle was sounding stranger and stranger. At least my nose had stopped bleeding, though it was red and swollen and sore from Mrs. Abbottini's vise grip. The skin on my upper lip was rough from the paper towels and now itched. I did such a Lady Macbeth trying to scrub the dried blood off my hands that they itched, too. What bothered me most was that some kid with no life of her own kept trying to shove herself into mine. I cursed Google. If Deni found my mother's phone number—still listed because of her dog-training business—she'd know the address. She couldn't know I lived here, though—hell, just thinking of living with my mother made my fingers itch more—so I didn't really worry that she'd be waiting around the corner with a stack of sketches. I hated them already.

I was so aggravated at the nerve of some people that I didn't have time to fret about my red clown nose or my ruined shirt. I grabbed a new top, slapped some concealer on my upper lip, and stuffed tissues in my pocket. I gave Little Red a good-bye cookie, shut all the closet doors tightly so he wouldn't chew up my shoes in revenge for being left, and still had time to call my father in Florida.

After hearing about his golf game and his poker buddies and the new woman in his condo who made him a cheesecake, I asked if he had any bad vibes lately. His talent was foreseeing menace to his loved ones.

"I have a couple of regrets I need to talk to you about, baby girl. And a favor to ask for a friend."

"Sure, whatever he needs if I can help. But I meant your bad feelings of danger. Presentiments, I guess they're called. A fan is being a pest, and I wondered if you thought I should worry."

"My daughter, the celebrity. With groupies of her own."

"No, it's nothing like that. Just a kid who thinks I can help her career. I never should have rented that Stephen King movie last year, you know, the one about the author. And I just had a bad nosebleed."

"It can happen more if you take a lot of aspirin."

"I don't take any."

"Good. Now that you mention it, I did have a quick shiver this morning, not a fist-to-the-gut kind of feeling, like if you were in real trouble, but just a glimpse of an Irish tenor singing to you. That didn't seem right."

Or likely. "I don't know any Irish tenors. Or anyone who'd sing to me." Except that haunted house on Shearwater Street in Paumanok Harbor that played music, and Matt in the car. "A tenor doesn't sound dangerous."

"That's what I thought, why I didn't bother calling to warn you."

"Are you sure? You've got no twinges about an adolescent psycho, no hints of a hemophilia plague?"

"Nothing like that. And I'm as sure as I ever am about these things. You know how it works. I'm fast asleep, taking a shower, or waiting to tee off, and there it is—a sound, an image, a creepy sensation that someone I love is threatened. A guy with an Irish accent and a nice voice serenaded you. That's all."

"Okay." I knew exactly how my father's precog ability worked: inscrutably, like the Oracle at Delphi or the Sphinx. His premonitions often proved true, but usually after the peril was past and I had time to interpret the warnings or backtrack the clues. Like the time he warned me of a creature, but the true danger was a teacher. His green-eyed mouser wasn't a cat at all but jealousy, the green-eyed monster. Other times he was dead-on, like his warnings about boats. Every time I got near one, I almost died. And got seasick, too. "I'll stay out of O'Murphy's Pub for awhile. Thanks."

"Sure. About my friend, though . . ."

"Sorry, I don't have time right now. I have a big meeting downtown, but I'll talk to you later. Okay?"

"It's comedy night at the clubhouse, but I'll try to call before if we finish dinner in time. Lucille is making lasagna."

"Don't eat a lot of it, or the cheesecake. It's not good for your heart."

Neither were all the women my father dated, too few months since bypass surgery, but I refused to be a nag like my mother. "Be careful."

"And you. Love you, baby girl."

"Love you, too, Dad."

The trip downtown turned out to be uneventful.

I didn't take subways if I could help it. Or tunnels, taxis

with one-eyed drivers, or planes. Escalators and elevators were problematic but conquerable if I kept my eyes shut and told myself I'd lived through worse, like lightning storms and kidnappings and fire-breathing babies.

I never said I was brave.

I got the bus, transferred to another one, and walked. Nice fall day, not too much pollution, good exercise. And I could keep my eyes out for street singers, pubs, and teenagers with satchels full of manuscripts and drawings instead of being trapped inside a thundering metal roller coaster underground.

The offices of DCP, my publishers, were in the financial district, where people walked a little faster and dressed a little better than uptown. The bars had names like The Old Brokers' Inn, the Bulls and Bears, and the Speculator, not an O'Anything in sight.

"I love, love, love your new book, Willy."

Oh, God, she found me.

No, the speaker was DCP's latest twenty-something receptionist, editorial assistant, and proofreader. In other words, Sandy — Mandy? Randy? — an overworked, underpaid English major with aspirations, was the small company's gofer.

I said thanks, and she told me to go on to the conference room. Everyone was waiting.

Everyone consisted of Don Carr, the owner, founder, and editor in chief of DCP, Don Carr Publishing, three other writers who doubled as senior editor, managing editor, and art director, two staff graphics artists, the sales manager, and three men and one woman introduced as sales reps and distributors. The last group could make or break a book by pushing it to buyers or burying it under other, favored titles. The men favored books with bare bosomed women on the covers. Content didn't matter as much to them as the artwork and the author's track record of previous sales. Their opinions at these marketing meetings decided how many of each book was actually printed.

So I smiled and shook hands all around, hoping no one noticed my raw, tender skin or how I rubbed my itchy fingers together afterward.

While Sandy served coffee and bottled water and muffins, I dabbed at my nose with a tissue to check for disaster. Fine so far.

So was the response to my new book and the proposed cover, now that my illustration had the title in bold colors and my name along with "Award winner."

The sales people smiled around their muffins. I had good sell-throughs, which meant they got rid of most of the Willy Tate books we published.

"It's another winner, Willy," Don said. "A lot stronger than your last couple. Better plotted, better characters."

"I'm glad you think so, Don. I was a little worried."

"Yeah, me, too. That sea monster was pretty scary."

And he hadn't seen the real thing the way I did. "I was afraid it was too scary."

"I ran it by my daughter and some of her friends in our focus age group."

I held my breath, waiting for him to tell me I had to tone down the paralyzing, petrifying horror of the waterspout serpent that swallowed ships. "Did they have nightmares?"

"Who cares? They all gave it a ten. My kid adored the parrot."

I did, too. It helped save my friends and helped vanquish the kraken.

"She fell in love with the hero."

Me, too.

"I thought it was a great touch, having him own a pet shop. Kids love that, even when they're trying to be tough."

"He's a vet."

Don flipped pages. "No, I'm sure you had him in a store."

"You're right. I, ah, changed my mind halfway through."

No, I didn't. Spenser Matthews, the superhero sea god whose alter ego ran a pet shop, starred in my latest book.

Matt Spenser, veterinarian and altogether super guy, starred in my life. Or he would if he met me halfway, and I don't mean some motel midway on the Long Island Expressway.

Mrs. Abbottini was right: you can't build a relationship from three hours away. Absence might make the heart grow fonder, but it also led to frustration, loneliness, and doubts. How could I think about the future when we couldn't work out a weekend? We both had commitments, careers, and dogs. We both liked our chosen locales and our homes, although my apartment suddenly felt cold and empty, especially at night.

I've met some amazing men recently and loved all of them a little, or a lot. I even thought about marrying a handsome, wealthy, brilliant British lord. I didn't want to live in England, though, or learn to curtsy to the queen. I didn't want to follow the world's finest, and nicest, equestrian on his rodeo rounds, either. And I didn't consider for an instant building a life with the wonderful man who saved lives by running into burning buildings.

The Royce Institute for Psionic Research and its Department of Unexplained Events sent them all to me. The people there—and everyone in Paumanok Harbor—hoped one or the other dude would be a match, helping me face the challenges of my own knack for getting into trouble with the trespassers from another world. They also wanted my children to expand the gene pool of talented espers.

I chose Matt for myself. He didn't have a drop of psychic powers until we got involved. He didn't have wanderlust and wasn't a daredevil. He was solid, steady, and caring, with enough bravery for the two of us. If I were a willow tree, swaying with the slightest breeze, Matt was an oak. I didn't care that he didn't have Paumanok Harbor blood in his veins; I wanted to be with him. I wanted a nice, normal life like his, without serpents or trolls or spectral horses that caused nightmares. I wasn't certain about kids, but if I had any, I wanted them to be ordinary, not empaths or telepaths or any kind of oddball psychopaths. Like half the residents of Paumanok Harbor.

I loved Matt. I'm pretty certain of that, anyway. Marriage didn't scare me anymore like snakes and going crazy like my father's mother did. Not that Matt had asked me yet, but I did not want to be his little wife who helped run his little veterinary practice, kept his tidy little house, raised his little children, and lived the rest of her life in the isolated, inbred, idiosyncratic little village of Paumanok Harbor.

The Harbor was great for summer weekends, the beach, the clear skies, the sounds of surf and seagulls. I did not want to live there.

Or here in Manhattan, with my mother.

Or anywhere, without Matt.

All of which made my head spin, which, naturally, made my nose bleed again.

CHAPTER THREE

I had more blood and mortification.

Contrary to popular expectations and opinions and any hopes a person might have, one did not die of embarrassment. I learned that a long time ago as a shy teenager when a snake ran over my foot during a tryst in a secluded area of Paumanok Harbor. Unfortunately, that secluded area was on an estate, during a fancy charity gala. The entire party—including the mayor, the chief of police, and my own parents—saw me run shrieking across the lawns, buck naked.

I did not die then. Or last month, when the Hispanic dishwasher at my uncle's restaurant caught Matt and me naked. At least I had clothes on today.

So I did not expire on the spot, not even when the twenty-something offered me two junior tampons to shove up my nose in front of the people whose respect my career most depended upon.

Sure, sit around continuing the sales meeting with white strings hanging out of my nostrils? Sure, they were the most absorbent items on hand, but what happened when they absorbed and expanded? My nose exploded, like a potato in the microwave when I forgot to punch holes in it?

I politely refused, meanwhile offering prayers to whatever gods were listening, of this world or that other one, to have the floor open up and swallow me. When it didn't, I accepted a box of tissues and Don's offer to call a town car to drive me home.

He didn't offer to pay for it. He was as glad to get rid of me, itching and bleeding and stammering in embarrassment, as I was to take my now empty portfolio and be gone.

While I waited for the car, I kept telling myself the indelible, blood-spattered impression I made on these people did not matter. I'd written a good book, with vivid graphics and dramatic scenes. Besides, I hated dealing with middle-aged men with soup stains on their ties asking if I could add a mermaid to the cover. A bare-breasted one, of course.

At least I wouldn't have to see these people any time soon, although I'd be seeing their looks of horror in my nightmares. Sure there'd been a lot of concern mixed with the usual aversion to gore, but mostly everyone stepped back, in case they caught whatever malady I had.

They could kiss my sore nose and itchy skin—and all the money I brought in—good-bye. I loved my Willy Tate novels and illustrations, but my next project paid better, carried more prestige, and challenged me in a hundred new, exciting ways. I'm illustrating Professor James Everett Harmon's *Bestiary of Fantastical Creatures*, a coffee-table art book. My art, my name under his. My pride.

I'd be happy to get home to my work, my dog, my apartment. The town car driver drove like he couldn't wait to get rid of me either, the leper in the back seat, so I got to my street in a third of the time it took me to get downtown. The nosebleed stopped under the force of the car's velocity.

Better yet, I found flowers outside my door.

Matt loved me! He missed me. He was sorry he couldn't come into the city.

No. The enclosed note said Deni was sorry I'd left before she could meet me. Next time? She'd call tomorrow.

I bet illustrators of fancy books by famous scholars didn't get harassed by obnoxious readers.

Packages for my brownstone had to be left with the building manager next door, not carried past the two sets of locked doors unless one of the residents gave permission. Too many city apartments without doormen had been robbed by bogus delivery people to let strangers wander up the stairs. Sometimes the mailman left boxes in the vestibule with his key, and sometimes they disappeared.

Yet here were flowers, daisies dyed ugly, unnatural colors like electric blue and kelly green, and a computer printout of an amateurish, sloppy cartoon.

Hell, the cartoon was one of mine. Most of it, anyway. Deni'd taken a page from one of my books, then altered it to put neon-tinted flowers in the hands of my hero.

That made me maddest of all. You can insult my writing, invade my privacy, give me a headache, but steal my ideas? Copy my drawings? Over my dead body, and my copyright attorney's.

I stomped across the hall.

"Mrs. Abbottini, did you see who delivered these flowers? She had to be buzzed in."

"Aren't they beautiful?"

No, and yes, she'd seen them. "Who brought them? There's no florist card."

"A nice young man. He said he had flowers from an admirer of yours. I thought they came from your veterinarian, the one you're not bonking with like bunnies on the beach."

"I'm not . . . So you let him come upstairs? You could have been robbed."

"Oh, no. I wouldn't have done that. I was coming home from bingo and saw him pushing all the call buttons. You know, like those upstairs tenants do when one of them forgets his keys."

"That should have told you he didn't belong here.

You should have called the police, or the manager. What if he were dangerous?"

"I had my mace can, like always."

Which, in the shaking hands of a half-deaf old woman would not have discouraged anyone intent on mayhem. "So you told him you'd bring the flowers upstairs, to Willy Tate's apartment?"

"Well, they weren't for me, were they?"

She looked at the horrid flowers with longing, so I shoved them into her arms. "If you like them, you can have them. Just don't do that again."

She grabbed the flowers and bobbed her head. "That's what I get for trying to be nice to some people."

She got the flowers; I got Deni knowing where I lived. Damn.

I tried to explain that I didn't want to encourage strangers to call at my door or annoy my neighbors, but Mrs. Abbottini didn't hear me. She didn't try to. She stepped closer and peered at my face.

"What's that on your lip? You're too young to grow a mustache."

A mustache? I ran to the mirror over Mrs. Abbottini's couch, figuring I hadn't wiped all the dried blood away. No blood, but little red raised blisters. I rubbed the area, then realized I had the same spots on my itchy fingers.

"I've been scrubbing at that spot to mop up the nose-bleed, that's all, and scouring my hands. My skin is irritated, I guess, like diaper rash."

She backed away. "I never heard of a bloody nose causing any kind of rash. Could be desert fever."

"I don't have a fever, haven't been near a desert, and never heard of such a thing."

"Well, I saw it on the news. Those poor soldiers coming back with scrambled brains and dramatic syndromes and desert flu. And no jobs."

"That's from bombs and traumatic stress and the economy."

"Could be a virus."

Mrs. Abbottini tottered away to get antibacterial

soap, spray germ killer, and alcohol to wipe the door-knob. "Can't afford the flu at my age."

"I don't have the flu. And I am not contagious."

She narrowed her eyes. "Auto impunity, I bet, when your body turns on itself."

"It's nothing! Go back to your ball game. Enjoy the flowers."

"I'll make chicken soup. You'll feel better."

How could I feel better when I had the printout of my butchered drawing and the worry that Deni'd be waiting at my front door every time I went out?

"No, we can't go for a walk," I told Little Red, back in my own apartment. "Use your papers. It's raining and you don't like it out there anyway."

Little Red didn't like much, including the carrier I had to use to sneak him in and out of the apartment, the noise and traffic of the streets, the other dogs we passed everywhere, being left alone, or lied to. My shoes didn't smell of rain, my jeans weren't wet. So he raised his leg on the portfolio I put down.

"Bad dog!"

The Pomeranian could be as selectively deaf as my neighbor. He went back to the couch and curled into a furry red ball with his plume of a tail wrapped around his nose like a squirrel, content he'd made his point.

We had to work on his attitude.

When I got the paper towels and disinfectant spray, I noticed the answering machine light flashing. If that little bitch called once more, I'd—

The phone rang before I could check the messages. I stomped over to it, ready to do battle. "Hello," I snarled.

"Uh, this is Sandy, from DCP. We wanted to know if you were all right."

That deflated my anger. "I'm fine, thanks. Just a nose-bleed. They say once you get one, they come in clusters. Weakened blood vessels or something. It's real nice of you to care, though."

"Well, Don worried you wouldn't be able to add the mermaid to the cover."

I should have known. "Tell him the cover is fine the way it is. There is no mermaid in the book and there's not going to be one on the front. You ask him if he wants to be sued for false advertising, bait and switch tactics, or bad taste. I'm going to put my head back now so I don't get another bloody nose. Thanks for calling."

The first message was from my father. "I really need to talk to you about my friend, but Lucille and I are going to a cooking class before dinner, so I won't be home long after golf. Tomorrow, okay? Oh, and watch out for that singer. I heard him again this morning. Love you."

The second message was also from Dad. "I forgot. Watch out for mustangs too."

Mustangs? My horse-whisperer friend, Ty Farrington, rescued wild horses, but he hadn't called in weeks, and not many mustangs ran around Manhattan. Or Paumanok Harbor . . . yet. Ty and his foundation were working to establish a horse ranch on the old Bayview property there, but they hadn't moved any animals in so far. Ty would never be a danger to me, either.

And I doubt many singing cowboys had Irish accents.

I filed the warnings away for when I had less on my mind, like adult acne, stressed skin, or Deni on my doorstep.

She had to be stopped. I went to my laptop, signed on, deleted her from my Friends list, blocked her IMs, and sent a short email. YOU HAVE GONE BEYOND THE LINE. MY PERSONAL LIFE IS PRIVATE. MY ARTWORK IS LEGALLY PROTECTED. PLEASE REFRAIN FROM CONTACTING ME IN THE FUTURE.

So there.

Next I sent a message to Matt. I knew he'd still be at the vet clinic, so I didn't want to call or text his cell. Besides, I didn't want to hear him make some lame excuse for not coming into the city this weekend again. Cat scratch fever, my ass. If he could claim that, I could say I had the desert flu. And too much work.

So there.

What I had was a rash I didn't want anyone to see. I signed off with love and misses, which were true.

No sooner had I sent off the email to Matt than the new message dinger dang. BITCH. I THOUGHT WE WERE FRIENDS. YOU'LL BE SORRY.

I already was.

CHAPTER FOUR

I had a rash and a rabid reader. Hysteria hadn't set in yet, but panic was close, even with the laptop shut down. I checked the door locks, again, put some cortisone on my lip and hand, left over from when I had chiggers. The stuff hadn't worked then, but I had nothing to lose now. I made hot chocolate and found the Oreos I'd been saving for a rainy day. Fear counted, didn't it?

I sat at my drawing table, but no ideas came except Deni creeping up the three flights of stairs to my apartment, next to a redheaded, freckled guy with a shillelagh and a good voice. Irrational, but better than imagining her with a gun in her hand. Or a knife or a baseball bat or—

No, there was work to be done, hard work I'd been struggling with for days. Work could get my mind off the rest. I hoped.

More frustration. The professor whose book I was under contract to illustrate described his magical creatures for me to paint, but how do you draw beings who were more spirit than solid? Hard enough to get the colors right when I knew they were phosphorescent, scintillating, swirling rainbows that changed continuously. I'd been working with glitter pens and sparkle dust, even gold leaf, mixing styles to fit my usual cartoon efforts. Despite the hard work, I'd been having a wonderful time experimenting with watercolors, gouaches, and metallic paints on the usual fairies, elves, piskies, and selkies. The latest phantasms stumped me.

I reread Dr. Harmon's notes about the Andanstans. Their actions were amusing, how the tiny hominids kept stealing from each other, stealthily absconding with their sworn enemies' hoards of treasures, only to have the booty stolen back the next dark night or high tide. I knew what they *did*, how they used magnetics, telekinetics, and the strength of their numbers to shift whole piles of loot. I did not know how they looked. Jimmie Harmon was a dear man, the grandfather I wish I had, but his memories of what he'd written so many years ago had faded. If I asked too many times, in person or on the phone, his voice wavered and his eyes moistened. He did not need any more reminders of what had slipped away from him.

No way could I hassle the true gentleman who'd put his own life on the line to save hundreds of people on a sinking ship. He did it again, to save Paumanok Harbor.

Maybe I could paint the Andanstans as sentient water, gathering molecules at will to form arms and legs and—that stank. And they looked like wee leprechauns. Yeck. For sure Jimmie would have remembered if they were green. I tore the page off my sketch pad and turned the computer back on. I had to check on desert fever, didn't I? And cat scratch fever too, while I was at it.

Both of them really did exist. The health info site said cat scratch fever, Bartonella, was a bacterial infection caused by contact with an infected cat, which made sense in Matt's case. Vets must get scratched all the time. Symptoms were blisters at the site, fever, swelling of lymph nodes, fatigue, and malaise. No wonder he didn't want to schlep into Manhattan.

I felt terrible for doubting him. I should have jumped on the bus to the Hamptons and brought him chicken soup, if they sold it at the deli in town.

Desert fever didn't fit my symptoms so well. A bacteria from mold, it caused lung infections, not bloody noses and rashes. Most references were to miners in California and the American West, though I suppose it could exist in any desert, infecting the soldiers fighting there, but not with a flu-like bug.

They'd think I was crazy if I went to the doc-in-a-box at the big drugstore on Third Avenue. I've never been wandering in a desert, and I didn't have any of the chest pains, swelling in extremities, or coughing the references described.

And the police would think I was crazy if I went to them with my problems with Deni. Another email from Denidenis lurked in my inbox. Open it or not? How could I know if she apologized or threatened me if I didn't read it? I watched the new mail list like an idiot, the way you'd watch a grizzly, wondering what the bear would do next and if you could outrun it. The list looked just as lethal, harboring malice at the drop of a mouse button. Open it to check for hate mail? Ignore it and hope Deni found another hobby, another victim?

You could not outrun a grizzly bear.

Curiosity won over dread. Stupid, stupid, stupid. Now I couldn't convince myself Deni was just some maladjusted kid I'd disillusioned. She was a frigging sociopath. The email was another cartoon, a collage of my characters from four of my books, scanned or traced, copied, then photoshopped so their heads rolled at their feet. The message read: YOU ARE NEXT, BITCH.

No U R NXT, which I would have expected, as if Deni were a different person now, as if disappointment and rage made her more mature, more careful, studied almost, in her furious communications. Maybe I was prejudiced, but I felt a person who could spell posed more danger than some slapdash, corner-cutting, hasty tweeter.

Not wanting to touch it, but knowing I had to, I printed out a copy, and one of Deni's previous menacing email messages. Then I called my friend Van on his cell and left a callback number for him.

Officer Donovan Gregory had interviewed me when

the troll came to town, although he had no idea of Faf-hrd's existence, only the chaos the trespasser from Unity caused. Van and I became friends. We had dinner once and spent a day together when he came out to Montauk with some cop buddies and their families. Maybe more could have come from it, but then Grant came on the scene, the British agent from DUE that I almost got en-gaged to. Van disappeared from the case and from my thoughts, but I knew he'd still give me advice.

He sounded glad to hear from me when he called back ten minutes later. Until I explained the situation.

"What are you, a lodestone for trouble?"

"This one wasn't my fault."

"That's what they all say. Funny how all that trouble with the runaway truck we never found on your block and the broken toilets at the hospital where you took your cousin and the fallen crane across from the pub-lisher's office you visited all stopped when you left town for the Hamptons."

When the troll followed me to continue his mayhem there. "Yeah, but this is a kid, and my books."

He told me to forward the emails, so I did and waited. I heard him whistle when he saw the hacked-off heads. "Nasty stuff."

"And my drawings got ruined, too."

I thought I heard a smile when he said, "That's the least of our worries."

I liked the "our." Van was on my side.

"The problem is," he continued, "there's not enough to charge anyone, even if we could find the sender. You say you don't know her name?"

"She uses a screen name, which could be fake alto-gether. And her phone number shows up as unknown."

"A throwaway cell phone. You can get one anywhere. We can trace where the call came from, maybe where the phone was bought, but most times people pay cash at those no-name stores. No credit card receipt we can get the ID from. Our cyber guys can track down an In-ternet address, but we'd need to work with her server, and I just don't think there's enough evidence for them to kick it up so far. I mean, it's not like this is some kind of terrorism. Without that, they're all afraid of being sued on a freedom of speech charge or invasion of privacy."

"So they won't look until she cuts off my head?"

"I'm not saying that, Willy. I know a couple of the guys who work Internet crimes, and I'll ask one of them to take a look, see if he can come up with a name we can cross-reference. If there's a prior, then we can move in. Or if the threats escalate."

Now that was something to look forward to.

"Do you think I have anything to be afraid of?"

"Honestly? Most times it's all bluff and bluster, but I think you need to be careful. If she knows where you live, maybe you ought to stay with a friend for a couple of days, see if things settle down."

"I have a dog and my work. Neither travels well."

"Then have someone stay with you. You still seeing the Brit?"

"No, he was at the space station last I heard."

"You putting me on?"

"No. He was chasing Abominable Snowmen in the Himalayas before that."

"Man, and I only get to chase pimps and gangbangers."

"You get to help me."

"We live to serve. Want to have dinner tonight?"

"Um, I have . . ." I couldn't come out and say I had an ugly rash on my lip.

"I understand. You're seeing someone. Good. Ask him to stay with you."

Matt was a better excuse than desert fever. "He's not in town right now. He's from Paumanok Harbor, actually."

"Then why don't you go out there? I doubt a kid will follow you, or know where you are."

She'd guess if she read my mother's website again. Mom listed the Harbor phone number there, too; a lot of her wealthy clients traveled to the Hamptons for the summer. They called the house all the time, looking for help with their unruly trophy dogs.

"Maybe I will go in a couple of days. I'll think about it. What do you think I should do in the meantime?"

"Monitor your calls, keep a tape of the messages, save all emails and notes if they come to your door, but do not answer. That's important, Willy. What you do not want is a confrontation with a nut job. No telling what they're capable of. You'll only throw fuel on the fire if you sound scared or angry. They feed on that. Sometimes these cranks just want to vent. They find another target when they don't get a response. "

And sometimes, I figured, they got madder when they got ignored. I thanked Van, wrote down all the contact numbers he gave me, and promised to forward any more emails to him.

"Don't worry. It's probably nothing. But I'll ask the guys to drive by your building a couple of times extra. Okay?"

"You're a prince, Officer."

"So put me in one of your books."

I laughed and told him I would. And I drew an Andanstan as a tiny, well-muscled, handsome Black man. Van Andanstan.

Nope, I couldn't see Officer Gregory stealing anything. I threw that page out, too. Then I retrieved it and filed the sketch for another time. You never knew when you were going to need a new hero.

Speaking of heroes, Matt called during office hours, he was so worried about me.

"It's only a nosebleed and a stupid kid."

"What nosebleed? What kid?"

"If you didn't know about the nosebleed or the kid, why did you worry?"

"I got a bad feeling."

God, was he getting to be like my father, sensing doom for his loved ones? Now that Matt had been touched by the beings from Unity, no one knew what talents or powers he had. I knew he could sometimes see the Others now, the way I did. Maybe he became a telepath or an empath or a precog, too. For sure, he knew what I needed him to say:

"And I miss you."

Ah. "I miss you, too. And worry about you. I looked up cat scratch fever and it sounds terrible."

"Antibiotics can fix it. But the medical clinic in Amagansett sent a blood sample out. It's not Bartonella, or anything else they could find. Just a rash where the cat scratched me. I guess he knew I was going to neuter him. They don't think it's contagious. I was afraid of giving you something."

"That's weird, I have a rash, too. That's why I didn't want to come out." I did not admit I worried more about letting him see me this way than letting him catch whatever I had. Now it seemed he had it, too, whatever it was.

I could hear him let out a long breath. "I thought you were giving up on us."

"I thought you were, too."

"Never."

Did the sun just come out? Or had that one word warmed the chill in my heart? We had issues, but we could work on fixing them. I didn't know how, but I'd try, if he would.

Then Matt wanted to know about Deni. Then he got pissed that I called a cop friend instead of him. Then I told him I hadn't wanted to bother him, that I thought I could handle it on my own. That it was a city problem, not a psychic one.

Silence. Then: "I thought we were partners."

When it came to facing sea serpents and saving Newfoundland puppies, we did fine together. Guarding a metamorphing sea creature and its symbiotic fireflies, no problem. Bridging that distance between Manhattan and the East End of Long Island? The gap didn't get any narrower, no matter our good intentions. I sighed.

He said he thought I should come out to the Island.

I sighed again. That's what Van said, too. I was scared.

Hell, hearing the gravity in Matt's voice made Deni loom larger. But I couldn't run away, could I? I'd spent years—and a small fortune on therapy—learning to overcome my fears, becoming my own person, not the horse the phobias rode in on. I trusted Matt, loved him, but I did not want to become dependent on him or any man. Maybe if I'd met him in my twenties, before I became content with my life the way it was. Maybe if my parents' marriage hadn't been such a bad example.

Maybe if I loved him more.

Crap.

"I'll think about it. I'm working hard on Dr. Harmon's book, though, and I hate to lose my train of thought. I'm stuck on one of the chapters, but—"

"Come talk to Jimmie. He misses you, too, and he knows the book better than anyone."

"His memory isn't as good as it used to be, and I hate to push him."

"I wouldn't worry about his memory. He still beat us all at poker last week."

Since half the players could tell truth from lies, that said a lot. "I'm glad you let him play."

"Hey, he hosts at Rosehill, your cousin Lily cooks gourmet style, and both refrigerators are full of beer. There's the hot tub, the sauna, the exercise room, and the entertainment center. The guys love to play there. And Moses"—Matt's Newfie puppy—"is more at home at Rosehill than he is at the vet clinic. And we all feel kind of bad that the parrot flew off. Dr. Harmon really misses the bird, or whatever it is."

"Oey? She's gone?"

"For a week now. No one's seen or heard anything of her. The poor old guy spends hours on his deck, calling for her. I know he'd be happy if you came back, even for a short visit."

Now I had to worry about the professor, too. Jimmie didn't know a lot of people in Paumanok Harbor yet, and Rosehill, where he lived, still hadn't opened for business as the Royce Institute's outreach center. I know

Cousin Lily, the housekeeper there, looked after him, but he'd been so pleased to have Oey as a companion. Oey didn't belong to our world, though, being half bird and half fish, half male, half female, with the halves changing places continually, to say nothing of how the whole creature could vanish in an eye blink. I guess she went home, which meant I couldn't ask her about the Andanstans. Bummer. I'd miss Oey, too, so I could imagine how Dr. Harmon felt.

"Tell him I'll come as soon as I figure out what to do about Deni."

"There is nothing to do except get out of her territory. Besides, I think your grandmother needs you."

"Grandma Eve needs me to have someone to pick on."

"No, she's not looking well. And I hear she and some of the others are worried about the Halloween bash they put on. Why don't you call her?"

Because she's a witch, for heaven's sake! Doesn't anyone else worry about that?

CHAPTER FIVE

I had a grandmother who had a grimoire. The original old volume of enchantments, incantations, and herbal concoctions is kept locked under glass in a climate-controlled room at the library, but Grandma Eve had a copy transcribed, translated into modern English, annotated, and indexed. That one stays in a safe at the farm house, and on her computer. She adds to it constantly. People think she uses parts of Garland Farms to experiment with rare and exotic plants for their curative powers, cheap energy, or to feed the hungry.

I know better.

I know for a fact she caused genital warts in some boys who trashed her pumpkin patch one year. And when a bigger girl shoved my cousin Susan down the school steps, that girl's eyebrows fell out. The fly-by-night driveway paver who took senior citizens' deposits, then disappeared? He really, really disappeared. And that summer we had all those frogs? A neighbor's loud, annoying, and water-fouling flock of geese went missing.

Grandma Eve also mixed potions and read tea leaves. People came to her for headaches, infertility, indecision, and how to invest their IRAs.

I never drank tea at her house unless it was iced, from a pitcher. Before I learned better, I had to listen to her "read" my future, which was all wrong the way I planned it, in her opinion. According to her "gift," I should avoid a dicey middle age by traveling to England to study at Royce University instead of going to art school. Instead of facing certain misery in Manhattan, I should move to Paumanok Harbor with my mother. And children? She always saw three, perfect little specimens of Paumanok Harbor psi-sters.

Wishful thinking, Gran. Your goals, not mine. Besides, I liked coffee better.

Which is not to say I wouldn't do everything I could to help her. According to my mother, who'd been traveling for months now, looking after Grandma Eve was my duty, even though her other daughter, son-in-law, other granddaughter, and a niece lived minutes away. My mother believes that family watches out for family. That's why she went to Florida to take care of my father after his heart surgery, despite their decades-ago divorce.

So why didn't she come back to look after own mother? Because I could do a better job, she said. And a lot of dogs in the South needed her. I didn't.

Oh, boy.

While my mother thought I was responsible for Grandma Eve, her health and happiness, Grandma Eve believed I was responsible for Paumanok Harbor, its prosperity and preservation. And its population, naturally, both the current residents and my three future children.

A crock. My grandmother was the strongest woman I knew. She half ran the entire village, and everyone in it would gladly eat worms for her. She did not need me. As for Paumanok Harbor itself, the place existed since the Indians—involuntarily—gave way to the British settlers, the ones who left England, then New England, before they got burned at the stake as witches and warlocks. I did not make the tiny village a secret center of paranormal activity, or open the gates between the Harbor and a parallel universe. So how could I have its future in my hands or unfertilized in my womb?

To be honest, some of the weird happenings there did have a hazy connection to what I drew, but not on purpose. I thought I had a great imagination, not that I was a Visualizer, seeing the trespassers from Unity and sometimes communicating with them through my art. I did *not* call them forth to wreak havoc in the Harbor. And I'd done my best to keep the damage to a minimum.

So maybe now I shouldn't go there, in case Deni followed me. Not that there was anything otherworldly about the nasty piece of adolescence, I just saw no need to bring danger to Grandma Eve's front door.

Conscience called on me to call my grandmother. She'd mention my inadequacies; I'd remember why I liked New York City so much. Times like this, I wish I drank. Instead, I decided to fortify myself with a diet soda and a chocolate bar. With nuts, fittingly.

While I nibbled so the treat lasted longer, I thought more about the Andanstans, idly tapping a drawing pen on my sketch pad, in random dots like pointillism, or rain. Pok pok pok. Why couldn't I get a grip on these beings? Pok pok pok. I was the Visualizer, after all.

Professor Harmon's book sat right next to me on the desk, open to the page I had memorized by now. He'd written the slender volume of magical beast stories long ago to show the creative writing students of Royce University in England how far imagination could carry them. He'd quietly published the vignettes under his first and middle names, James Everett, and never took credit for the charming work. Now retired and reestablished in Royce's new outreach center in the Harbor, Jimmie felt able to claim his work, to expand the contents, and have the supposedly fictional creatures illustrated—by me.

His offer thrilled me. His stories awed me. His fooling the entire world amused me. Those wondrous, colorful, universally telepathic beings he wrote of were not from his imagination at all. They were from the magical world of Unity, from his trances, from a hole in the fabric that kept our two worlds apart. Dr. Harmon never spoke to his visions, never knew their real names, so he made them up and wrote Tolkienesque tales about them. Maybe Tolkien went off in trances, too.

I didn't, but I got to illustrate the marvelous creatures he'd seen and remembered with joy and wonder. I'd seen some of them, too, when no one else could. Pok pok pok.

I couldn't see *these.*

So I called my grandmother.

Matt was right: Grandma Eve sounded tired, worried, maybe old, which I had a hard time accepting. I couldn't face her, but I couldn't face a world without her in it. "You feeling okay, Gran?"

"Fine, fine, except for a bothersome rash."

Uh-oh. "A rash?"

"It's nothing. I pruned a rosebush and got scratched by the thorns. Poison ivy, I suppose."

"Um, anyone else have a rash?"

"Now that you mention it, Doc Lassiter cut himself shaving and his cheek broke out. I told him being a psychiatrist didn't count. He had to go to a real doctor."

"What did the doctor say?"

"That it wasn't Lyme disease, psoriasis, shingles, or my poison ivy. He has an appointment with a dermatologist he knows on Shelter Island. Jasmine got a paper cut that turned blistery, but the school nurse couldn't say why, just told her to get antibiotics. Susan cut a finger slicing onions. She's always doing that."

I rubbed my upper lip. "But she got a rash this time, didn't she?"

Pause.

In a frailer sounding voice, my grandmother added, "And Janie at the salon nicked a mole on the back of Joe the plumber's head when she buzz-cut his hair, and both of them got the rash. Young Kelvin Junior at the garage broke out after football scrimmage, but the team doctor called it early acne."

Everyone in the village had a rash? Pokpokpok. I didn't want to start any Paumanok Harbor hysteria, not yet. "Why don't you ask around, see if anyone else has a suspicious skin condition?"

"I don't have time for that. We have worse problems."

I wasn't sure what was worse than an outbreak of blood-borne irritations, but I asked anyway. "What now?" Last time she had a rare bird at the farm and bird watchers trampling her fields.

"The All Hallow's ceremonies might have to be called off."

Sure, like a canceled witches' convention at a pagan holiday mattered more than an unknown epidemic. So what if they called it a fall festival and held it the night before Halloween. "It's weeks away. A rash isn't going to keep your friends from coming. Mom swears she'll be back in time to help."

"That's not it." Her voice trembled. "We have no place to hold it."

"Of course you do. The village green, the firehouse, the school parking lot. Even the bowling alley ought to be big enough. Uh, how many wit— That is, how many guests are you expecting?"

"Don't be foolish. We live in Paumanok Harbor. We always hold it on the beach where we can make a big fire."

So they could dance naked under the full moon? I knew better than to ask.

I didn't have to. "Which you'd know if you ever spent enough time here the way you should have. We need the beach for the fire and the water to float our blessings."

My pen ran out of ink. I grabbed two new ones so I could pok twice as fast. "What's wrong with the beach, then?"

"There is no beach!"

"Come on, we have lots of beaches. The one a block away from Garland Drive is perfect. People can park at the farm stand and walk in. I'll put up signs so they can park in Mom's yard, too."

"That's what we always did, but the beach isn't there anymore. There's a couple of feet of sand at low tide, but that's it, just a drop-off to deep water."

"That can't be. I walked the dogs on that beach all summer. And there were still tourists and swimmers and sunbathers and joggers past Labor Day."

"Now there's swimming, nothing else. As you'd know if you spent any time here."

Poketapoketapoketa. That wasn't fair. I'd been out just a few weeks ago. Granted, Matt and I hadn't left the house much. Or the bedroom, for that matter, but it rained a lot. We had a great time. We'd made plans to go away for Thanksgiving, just the two of us, no dogs, no issues, maybe somewhere rainy.

"It's that last hurricane," Grandma Eve went on. "Desi, the one that brought the huge tidal wave."

We both knew the hurricane didn't do it, the sea monster N'fwend did. It sucked all the water out of the bay so it could rise up, and up, and up, a vast fluid tornado ready to rush back in and swallow first the cruise ship we used as a war command post, then the whole town.

Except we vanquished N'fwend before it came to shore.

"The water came back."

"But the sand did not. It's out there somewhere, where your dragon swept it, clogging the outer harbor. We don't have the funds to dredge all the way across to Gardiner's Bay to reclaim the sand and barge it to shore. The experts natter on about inevitable erosion. We cannot tell them the truth, for obvious reasons."

They'd put straitjackets on everyone. I added a yellow marker to the pens in my hand. Plok.

"The Engineer Corps claim that more beachfront washed away on the south, oceanfront shore than ours, so they won't help. They predicted the next storm would bring the sand back, but it didn't."

That had to be the weekend Matt and I stayed inside, which I would not think about right now. "There's always another storm out there."

"But no sand for the winds and the tides to carry ashore. If we cannot get our beaches back, we have no tourism. No tourists means no money for the school or the streets or the police. Not the arts center or the library. No jobs, either. And no sand means we have no protection from the next hurricane or nor'easter. Any storm surge could flood half the village."

I knew she was right, but I had to try: "We lose some sand every winter."

"And gain it back when the storm patterns shift, but not like this. Besides, every other beach up and down the bay coast is fine. Three Mile Harbor, Louse Point, Noyac. The North Fork of the Island barely got Desi's wind or high tide."

No, the sea serpent came right here, after trying to capsize the ship with the professor on it off Montauk.

If it weren't for help from other beings from the world of Unity, which incidentally banished the kraken to our world in the first place, the ship would have sunk. Instead, a new breed of dolphins pulled the ship's passengers from the cold water, a disappearing parrot guided rescuers to other victims onboard, odd lantern beetles lit the way through the ship's dark corridors . . . and a tall underwater sandbar held it up.

A sandbar that wasn't there the week before.

A sandbar that we blew up to get the cruise ship off.

I threw the pens across the room. Little Red picked one up and ran under the couch. It was too late to take back what I'd unconsciously drawn. Not too late to curse and stomp my foot and bite my lip and scratch at the rash on my fingers. And curse some more.

Dots filled my sketch pad, dots in different colors, dots in loose, random configurations. So loose I could just make out the shapes of tiny people if I squinted sideways, people made of grains of sand. Ann. Dan. Stan. Sand.

Now I knew what the Andanstans were and what they stole.

My life.

CHAPTER SIX

I had a mission. And a migraine.

The mission: get the sand back, get rid of the Andanstans, cure the rash. Desert fever? Hah. Revenge of the Andanstans, more likely, for miners digging holes, for terrorists and their land mines, for us blowing them and their sandbar to smithereens.

The migraine: why was I in charge? I didn't bring them here. I couldn't talk to them. I never saw them. I had no idea how to proceed, except buy stock in hydrocortisone cream. The simple thought of them tapped inside my skull with sandy sledgehammers.

That's assuming the missing sand, the rashes, and the minuscule thieves were all connected, of course. The odds of there being that many oddball occurrences were as small as the Andanstans. Every cop show and detective novel says coincidences are rare and suspicious. Cops and writers never came to Paumanok Harbor, where situations like this are commonplace.

There were two possibilities. One, the Andanstans had been around our world forever, spreading disease. Two, if mold spores or fungi or naturally occurring toxins truly caused the early documented infections, the Andanstans did not arrive here until last month, at some higher power's bidding, not mine. Sure I'd asked for help to fight the sea monster. How could mere mortals destroy a creature of magic on our own?

I did not ask for nasty, gritty little beings who'd stay here and start rashes. They'd done us a favor, but now they and their plagues weren't welcome.

I had to talk to Oey, the male/female parrot/fish who came to warn us about the kraken and ended up adopting Professor Harmon . . . or vice versa. Like all otherworldly creatures, Oey could communicate telepathically with any other species of them. So I'd talk to Oey in English, she/he would talk to the Andanstans in Unity-speak, and we could light the bonfire on the beach. With luck, the rashes would leave when the Andanstans did.

The problem, of course, other than I never seemed to have such luck, was that Oey'd gone missing. If the feathered fish didn't come back, we were sunk. Literally. Unless someone else could speak the mental tongue.

How many people on our Earth could translate a language that was half telepathic? Less than a handful, and I knew one of them. Talk about coincidences.

Grant is the leading xenolinguist from the covert Royce Institute for Psionic Research, as opposed to the overt and respected Royce University, which he'd also attended and where his father was dean. He is also the man I'd almost married.

Sometimes I felt guilty about breaking up and maybe breaking his heart. Sometimes I wondered what if . . .

Most times, like now, I felt awkward calling him, not out of love and affection, but out of need.

As they say, needs must when the devil drives, whatever that means. Someone had to talk to the Andanstans and get them to leave, without taking our sand with them. Someone else. I could not do this on my own.

I had finally visualized the sand folk; now Grant had to translate. That's what he did, when he wasn't being a viscount chatting with the queen or a top DUE agent chasing rumors of ETs across the globe. Well, he could damn straight get his tight linguist butt over here and talk to the tiny thieves.

I left a message, a bit more polite than what I was thinking. Then I took two Tylenols and the last of the Oreos while I waited for him to call back on what I knew to be a more secure, "Men in Black" line. Answering these kinds of calls was part of his job.

He didn't sound happy about it. In fact, he sounded annoyed, exhausted, and ill. Or maybe the satellite communication had interference.

I asked where he was. He'd been at the space station last time I needed him.

"Ireland."

Oh, no. They had a million Irish tenors, and they raised racehorses, too. "What are you doing in Ireland?"

"I *was* tracking a bogwilly."

"You had to track a bog? Do they move? Aren't there maps?"

"Not a bog, Willy. A bogwilly, some supposedly hideous beast they use to frighten children into behaving. They should fear the shaggy local ponies instead. I fell off the blasted animal they swore couldn't be spooked by any, ah, spook."

I knew there was a horse. My father'd said so. "Did it sing?"

"The pony? Bloody thing fainted! Keeled right over on top of me before I could jump off."

"No, the bogwilly, with which, incidentally, I have no connection except a shared name. What is it?"

"I still do not know."

"Does it sing?"

"Not that I heard. I didn't pick up any psychic sendings, either, just the light. You know, that peculiar iridescence like a hundred prisms reflecting moonlight."

I knew it well. I'd been trying to capture it on paper for the professor's book. "Did you find the, ah, willy?"

"With two broken legs and a cracked skull from the rock the deuced pony dumped me against?"

Oh. "Are you all right now?"

He wasn't, and he wasn't pleased about it. "Concussed, seeing double, with an inflammation of the lungs from lying in the blasted bog until they could get a rescue team in."

Suddenly the rash did not seem as urgent. I told him about it anyway, and asked if he had any idea when he could travel, by wheelchair if necessary. We needed him to get rid of the sand thieves.

He cursed. I couldn't tell if he hated the idea of the wheelchair, or the fact that I only called when I had trouble. Turned out that what he hated, which he expressed in many short words, was missing all the fun.

"Fun? Everyone has a rash, and the beach erosion is at crisis point."

He didn't care. "If you married me, we could be together on these adventures."

Like riding a small freaking horse at night through a bogeyman-inhabited Irish bog? Man, did I not regret breaking our almost engagement. How could I have ever thought our personalities or lifestyles matched?

I wished him a quick recuperation and promised to call with updates.

So much for my linguist.

I tried the professor next. Cousin Lily, the housekeeper at Rosehill, answered the phone instead. Jimmie was out, she told me. He'd been out all day, walking the grounds, calling for Oey. Now he'd gone over to Grandma Eve's farm, the first place people had spotted the rare pink-toed oiaca bird, not knowing how rare it was.

"I'm worried," Cousin Lily said. "Your uncle promised to drive him back before dark, but Jimmie refused to have dinner at the farm. He hardly eats when he is here, no matter what I cook. He comes back drained and damp, all scratched up, with poison ivy. Then he sits on the balcony outside his bedroom in the cold night air, with a bottle or two, which cannot be good for his lungs, either. He stays out there all night. I can hear him calling and coughing. It's enough to break my heart."

Mine, too. "But he has other friends now."

"Yes, Chief Haverhill and the mayor are always calling, the other poker players too, and every widow in the vicinity. Matt brings Moses whenever he can. The dog drools and sheds, but I put up with it, hoping Jimmie will not feel so melancholy and lonely."

"You say he has poison ivy?"

"I haven't seen it, but he asked what we use here for a blistering itch. They have nettles in England."

Which was another reason for being glad I didn't marry Grant. "Um, do you have a rash, too?"

"Not poison ivy. I did get a bad reaction at the site of my flu shot, though. So did a bunch of others from the Harbor. The weird thing is, we all had different batches of the vaccine. Some from the senior center, some from the drugstores in East Hampton and Bridgehampton. A lot of people went to their own doctors for the shots. I understand the County Health Department is looking into it. Why did you ask?"

"Just a thought, that's all."

"Well, think about getting out here soon. Jimmie needs you. And Eve is running herself ragged about the erosion."

"I'm working on—"

She didn't let me finish. "Now that you mention it, I think she had a rash, too, from the rosebushes, she told me. And Joanne at the deli had her arm bandaged when I went in for potato salad the other day. She said she scratched a mosquito bite and it turned lumpy. She had it checked out, so she could keep serving food. The physician's assistant said it didn't seem contagious, but to keep her arm covered. And Alan from the liquor store closed early yesterday. He's diabetic, you know. Said he got something wrong when he tested his blood sugar last week, now his finger's all puffy and sore. His doctor sent his testing kit back to the manufacturer to test for bacteria. Then there's— Wait. Willy, you know something more about the rashes, don't you?"

I rubbed my itchy lip with my itchy forefinger. "Nothing certain yet. I hoped the professor could help."

"You do know! You've brought something else dreadful here, haven't you?"

"No! I'm not there, I'm in New York. And I didn't draw them"—until an hour ago—"and I'm not sure they caused the problem in the first place."

"You do know!" she yelled. "You've gone and done something awful again, and we'll all have to suffer, then wade into ugly, impossible situations to pull you out."

"No, I didn't—"

"And now that dear old man is losing his will to live and you give him a cough and rash?"

"I didn't—"

"You get out here and fix it, damn you, Willow Tate, or I am calling your grandmother."

"I already spoke to her. I'll be there tomorrow, if I can."

"You can't not."

My next call was to Oey. I'm no telepath, but she is. I did not know how far away she was, or how far away her powers worked. I tried anyway. *ET, phone home. We need you.*

Stupid. I'm no telepath but I am the Visualizer. So I grabbed a pencil and a fresh sheet of paper, drew a willow tree, a weeping willow, then added three little people made of dot sand. They wore scraps of seaweed to hide their privates. They carried shell hatchets and rock hammers in their tiny hands, battering at the tree. I fixed the image in my head, then silently called, *Help!* I added a magnificent parrot with a forked, scaled fish tail and shouted in my head, *Come back.* Then I drew a handsome glittering fish with a long feathered tail, swimming in the water that lapped at the tree. *Please, Oey.*

No response reverberated in my head or in my thoughts, just that painful pounding. Shell hatchets and stone hammers, all right. I was out of Tylenol and didn't know if I could mix them with the Advil I had, whose expiration date was long past. Worse, I was out of candy and cookies. If I was leaving tomorrow, I needed snacks for the three-hour bus ride, too. Maybe Mallomars to get me through the night. And treats for Little Red so he'd stay quiet on the Jitney. The dog needed to go out before September's early dark, too.

I packed him in the carrier, went to the drugstore on Third Avenue, bought enough goodies for a week, unless I got desperate, and then freed Little Red to do his stuff near some sidewalk trees.

I put down my bags and his carrier to pick up his leavings. He walked on the leash nicely until we neared our building, where I put down my bags, his cleanup bag and his carrier. He got in without protest for once, because he knew it was suppertime and we'd get home sooner that way. So I picked everything up again and went home, cursing the need to hide a six-pound dog from the building manager.

Then I cursed the man and his custodial staff some more when I saw garbage on the building's doorstep. No, that wasn't garbage; it was a big rat, as common in Manhattan as taxis. This one was dead, though, with its head cut off.

Anybody would have freaked out. I screamed and dropped all the bags, except Little Red in his carrier, thank goodness. Between the missing sand, the missing bird, and the bogwilly, I'd completely forgotten about Deni.

She hadn't forgotten about me.

Chapter Seven

I had a decapitated rat and a deranged reader. I also had a pissed-off Pomeranian and a panic attack. Anyone would.

I rushed inside the building and slammed the door behind me, as if the dead rat could get in and go for my throat. Little Red snarled at being shaken up and kept in his carrier. I ignored him and leaned against the inside wall, catching my breath. Then I realized I had to go back outside to get my shopping bags. I really needed those painkillers, and the Mallomars. Anyone would.

The rat was still dead. Both pieces. People walking past averted their eyes, the way New Yorkers did when confronted with crazy bag ladies. I looked around. I was the crazy bag lady.

I gathered my broken cookies and stepped-on candy bars. Everything was in pieces, including the rat. The only item intact was the Tylenol bottle, which no one could open at the best of times. This was not one of them.

I gathered my stuff into one bag and covered the psycho's victim with the other. I stopped gasping and shaking and whimpering. My shock turned into anger.

How dare that . . . that person lurk at my building, waiting for me to leave, just so she could terrify me with a mangled corpse? What kind of person thrives on mutilating animals, or scaring people? Not the kind I wanted to meet.

I looked around but spotted no one suspicious, no one hiding behind a parked car or in a basement stairwell.

I didn't look too hard, just clutched my stuff and keyed the door open again. Little Red yipped in his carrier, between growls. "Hush up. You can't climb the stairs to the third floor by yourself anyway," I told the three-legged dog. The first-floor renters yelled so loudly at each other, maybe they wouldn't hear him. I hustled up the stairs, talking to calm both of us.

"Easy, good boy. The rat is dead. We're safe. For now. And we're getting out of Dodge in the morning."

I eyed my door to see if anyone had broken the locks. That's what all the good detectives did, wasn't it? Nothing looked different, and nothing waited on my doormat. I breathed easier.

As soon as Red scrambled out of his container, I called the manager to get rid of the rodent before any of the other tenants saw it. I did not say I had anything whatsoever to do with its presence.

Then I called Van at the police station. He told me rats died all the time.

Not with their heads cut off, they didn't.

"Get out of town. Escalation is never a good sign."

"Neither is animal torture. That's how serial killers start, right?"

"You don't know if the unsub killed the animal herself or simply butchered an already dead one to get your attention."

"It got my attention, all right." An unsub is an un-identified suspect, which I knew from those same cop shows on TV. "And I know precisely who did this. You've got to find her."

"I'll get my guys tracking this Deni person. Save the rat."

"You've got to be kidding."

He thought about it. "I guess not. If you can't do that, at least get out of town."

I looked out the window at the fading twilight. "It's too late. I'm not going outside at night, when I couldn't tell if she's waiting for me. Even if I took a cab to the Hampton Jitney bus stop, she could follow me. I'd be waiting there by myself, in the dark." With Little Red, my laptop, a suitcase, and tote bag of drawing supplies and broken cookies. I'd eaten a flattened Cadbury bar while I talked.

"Okay, I'll be off duty in an hour. I'll bring a pizza, sleep on your couch, then put you on the bus in the morning. How's that sound?"

I'd lived alone for years, until Little Red this spring. I was good at it, came and went when I wanted, ate cereal for supper if I wished, left the bed unmade sometimes. Solitude worked better for my work, with few distractions. I had my books, my friends, lots to do and see in the city, and Paumanok Harbor for when I wanted, rarely, to have my family's company. Of all the things I feared—and the list suddenly kept growing by the minute—staying alone in my apartment had never been one of them.

I almost wept in gratitude that Van offered to stay the night. "Sounds like heaven." I started hiding the cookies and candy and dirty dishes and my washed bras hanging from the shower curtain. "Thank you for being such a good friend."

I felt so much better I decided to check for phone messages after I fed the dog, while I cleaned the apartment and waited for Van. Another threat from Deni wouldn't bother me now, not when a policeman was on his way. He'd hear it, get the call traced, nab the bad guy, or girl, like they did in books, and I could go back to worrying about the Andanstans and the rash.

Oh, my god, the rash. And Van was coming. I raced to the mirror to look and lather on concealer, bronzer, a flesh-colored Band-Aid under my nose. Now I'd pass for someone with a bad reaction to a botox injection. Or a battered wife.

Deni hadn't called. Sure, she didn't have time, watching the apartment, catching rats.

My father had. "I'm on my way out of the house, baby girl, but I got a whiff of someone telling secrets, something bad."

As in I smell a rat? Thanks, Dad. You're too late.

". . . And I need to make sure you won't go anywhere in the morning until I call before my tee time. I won't be home tonight, but I really need you to do this favor for my friend. Unless that's the secret. Maybe. No, it doesn't smell."

I ignored my father's mental wanderings. His friend was going to be out of luck if he needed me to show him around town or let him sleep in the spare bedroom. I hated to disappoint my father, but he'd understand. He'd be a hell of a lot more disappointed if I ended up like the rat. And if his friend's problem was so critical, Dad could have canceled his date for tonight.

I kept cleaning and packing and looking out the window.

The downstairs buzzer went off, too soon to be Van. I didn't answer it, but someone else in the building could buzz the door open, like Mrs. Abbottini did with the flowers.

I got my pepper spray out of my purse and dragged the love seat in front of my apartment door. Of course I had to stand on the cushions to reach the peephole to see who knocked on it.

Deni might have been better than the person on the other side, banging on the door with a heavy, double-sized fist.

"Who is it?" I called out, stalling for time while I pushed the furniture back into place.

"You know damn well who it is, Willy, so let me in."

"Who called you?" I sure as hell didn't call Lou the Lout, Lou from DUE, Lou who was hard, ruthless, with a sense of duty as oversized as his meaty paws. The older man's duty these days appeared to consist of eliminating threats to paranormals everywhere, but to Paumanok Harbor psychics in particular. I lived in dread he'd find me more of a menace than a benefit because his methods did not bear considering. His means encompassed magic, and his modus operandi had nothing whatsoever to do with the Bill of Rights. His saving grace, and my continued existence, I felt, was that he liked to stay in my grandmother's good graces. I think so he could stay at her house. Or in her bed, which did not bear considering either.

"Everyone called. Your grandmother, your cousin Lily, your friend at the police station, his lordship in Ireland, Chief Haversmith at the Harbor. Oh, and Mrs. Abbottini next door."

"I told her to stop buzzing in strangers."

"I'm not a stranger, and she didn't have to let me in. I have a key."

Great. The scariest man I knew had a key to my building. He was big and mean and wore disguises. I'd seen him pretend to be a janitor, a farmhand, a limo driver, and a wealthy man about town. Today he had on biker leather, complete with a helmet in his hand, which did not give me confidence in his friendly intentions. "Well, everything is fine now. You didn't need to check on me."

He lifted a plastic bag with my drugstore's logo on it out of his helmet and held it up so I could see it through the tiny viewer. The rat. Both of them.

I opened the door, in time to watch him put a key in my bottom lock. "You have a key for my door, too?"

He didn't answer, just stared at my face. "What the hell happened to you? No one said the berserker gave you a fat lip."

So much for the concealer and the Band-Aid.

"It's an allergy, nothing else. An allergy to, um, strawberries."

"If you're allergic to strawberries, why do you eat them?"

"Listen, I am fine. So you can take your friend"—I

gestured toward the plastic bag—"and go. Van is coming."

"He can't get here for an hour or more. That's why he called me. And I want to look at the emails and notes myself."

"Van's men are looking into them."

"My guys can go places the cops can't. Or the Feebies, for that matter."

Lou and DUE could break any law they wanted, or make up their own. That's why Lou scared me to death, no matter how many people told me he'd been my bodyguard, watching over me for months. Like now, when he pushed right past me without an invitation to come in. At least he left the rat outside the door.

So I made copies of the emails and gave him the note that came with the flowers and explained how Deni'd used my own drawings to send her nasty messages.

"I don't suppose you'd let me take the whole computer to my cyber department, would you?"

"With all my notes and sketches and drawing programs? No way."

"All right, don't get bent out of shape. We'll take it to Russ at the Harbor. He's as good as my guys anyway."

"Better."

"Yeah, he's got cyberpsi talent like we've never seen. They tried to get him to London, too."

I knew by the "too" he meant me. I refused to go get indoctrinated or whatever they did at the secret Royce. I might have been more prepared for all the woo-woo stuff, but I'd have been their puppet, not myself. Then it occurred to me: "What do you mean, *we'll* take it to Russ?"

"Everything centers there lately, and it's too dangerous for you in the city until we get rid of these threats. So you'll leave after Van brings the pizza. I'll get there tomorrow, once I make sure no one follows you. Are you packed?"

He had to have noticed the suitcase out, and Little Red's traveling case by the front door. "Van said he'd drop me at the bus stop in the morning and see that I got on okay."

"That's not soon enough."

"Well, that's when it will be. I need to speak to my father in the morning."

That got his attention. "What did he say?"

"A friend needs a favor. Oh, you mean what did he foresee? He smelled a rat, but he heard an Irish tenor, and a horse."

Lou rubbed his chin, all stubbly today in keeping with his rough appearance, not that he needed a scruffy beard to look menacing. "An Irish singer and a horse, huh? Not much to go on, is it?"

"It never is."

"But he felt a threat?"

"I guess."

"And he nailed the rat."

"There's that, even if the thing already arrived. And I couldn't have done anything about it, no matter when or what I knew."

"You could have left Manhattan."

"I'm leaving as soon as I speak to him. He's not home now and doesn't put his cell phone on when he's on a date, but he said he really needs to talk to me."

Lou looked out the window, searching for spies. Then he pulled the curtains closed. What, did he think Deni'd be shooting at me from a roof across the street? "Listen, my father's warnings are always vague. This time he's right. That rat will be smelling soon if you don't take it away."

"Yeah, I'll get it to the lab, try to figure out what the thing actually died of. See if the techs can guess at a weapon or find fingerprints on the note. Maybe send a sketch artist to Mrs. Abbottini for a better description of the delivery kid. Meantime, I'll have someone watching the building until you leave with Van in the morning."

For a minute I'd been afraid he'd insist on staying, too. "Thanks. That'll be great."

"And do not go out until then, hear me?" He looked

down at the dog, who had one of my shoes in his mouth and was shaking it, pretending the shoe was a dangerous rat. I grabbed my sneaker. If he couldn't kill it, Little Red would pee on it.

"Red can use his papers until then. Or the garbage alley by the back exit."

"Good. It's too easy for someone to follow your patterns if they know you have a pet to walk."

"His picture's on my website, so she didn't need to be any genius sleuth."

He gave one more look around, searching for heaven knew what, nodded when he didn't find it, then headed for the door. I felt safer, knowing he'd have the place watched, knowing the guard would be someone else. I started to say good-bye, but I had to ask, "Um, you don't happen to have any kind of rash, do you?"

"Yeah, on my . . . ." He turned in the doorway, staring as if he could see into my head, wondering if I'd developed new talent the people at Royce could use and manipulate. "How'd you know about that?"

"A wild guess. There's a lot going around."

"Lily mentioned something about that, but she said the Health Department was on it."

"They think it has something to do with the flu shots, but it doesn't. It's blood that brings it on, the pinprick, a rose thorn, a paper cut, a nosebleed, not the serum. And as far as I can figure, the only people getting the rash are those who were on the cruise ship the night of the storm."

He shook his head. "The ship was full of sand and water and muck from being tipped over before we got on board. Maybe the floors and walls got filled with a brown tide thing or started growing black mold. Something toxic in the carpets."

I hated to say it, but knew I had to. "No, it's the sand. They're mad."

"They who? Mad about what?"

"The sandmen."

"Come on, Willy, I have crotch rot, not insomnia."

He wasn't going to sleep well tonight, not after I showed him my drawings and the professor's story.

"I can't be certain, of course."

He scratched his head, then scratched his ass. "Why am I not surprised?"

Then Van arrived. Lou gave me a look that warned me not to talk of sandmen, rashes, or the capsized ship. He drew a finger across his throat to reinforce his message. As if I needed his warning.

The two men spoke quietly in the hall while I put paper plates and napkins on the table. Lou didn't accept Van's invitation to stay, thank goodness.

Van closed the door behind Lou and turned to me, his brows lowered. "You look terrible, Willy," he said after Lou left. "What's on your face?"

"It's just a rash. At least it's not on my cr— That is, too many strawberries."

"No, it's blood. Your nose is bleeding."

He reached out to touch it, to show me. I batted his hand away. And grabbed for the napkins. "Don't touch it! You'll get the plague, too."

He edged toward the door. "You have HIV?"

"No, another plague. But you weren't there. You didn't, ah, eat the strawberries. So you can't catch it."

His brow stayed wrinkled. "You sure no one hit you in the head?"

CHAPTER EIGHT

I had reservations. And reservations.

The early Jitney bus would get me to the Harbor midday, get Van to work almost on time, and get my father home after his hot date. That was the best I could do for him until I got off the bus. Whatever he wanted couldn't be discussed in the three-minute limit the bus company requested. I hated when people spoke on their cell phones, right next to me, interfering with a nap or note taking or a good book. I would not abuse the rules for courtesy, not even for my father and his friend.

I finished packing after dinner, with pieces of tissue stuffed in my nose. How embarrassing was that? Van said he saw worse every day on the job. And I still looked adorable. How nice was that?

We took Little Red down the stairs, under my sweatshirt jacket, to the back door, the fire door that stayed locked. Van checked the area first, and the security camera over the door before letting me step outside. I felt safe. And safer, knowing Mrs. Abbottini kept watch, too.

"Who's there?" she called down from her open window. "I'll call the police."

"It's all right, ma'am," Van shouted. "I am the police. I'm with Ms. Tate."

She poked a flashlight through her window. "Oh, it's

that nice Black officer. Your mother won't be happy, Willow."

Before I could apologize to Van, or claim my mother was not a bigot, that she preferred dogs to men, all men, the old lady went on, loudly, the way hard of hearing people did: "She wants that vet in the family. Thinks she'll get a discount on expenses for her rescued dogs, I guess. And then you'll go out to the Island, Willy, so she can have the apartment back."

Great. Why didn't she tell Van and the downstairs neighbors my bra size while she was at it? And mention how my mother offered to get me a boob job as a college graduation gift?

"I am going out to the Harbor in the morning, but I'll be back. And Mother won't stay here long, not with the apartment rules banning dogs."

"What's that sniffing around the garbage, then?" she shouted.

"A big ra—" I caught myself before I mentioned the *R* word. She must have heard about the dead rat by now, but I did not want to remind her or give her nightmares. I figured I'd have enough for the whole apartment.

"Good night, Mrs. Abbottini. I'll let you know when I'm coming home." I stressed the *home*. This is where I lived, not that scrap of land hours away from everything. Except Matt. The hours away from Deni mattered more right now.

"Will you water my plants?" They lived at her house, I'd been gone so frequently. Mrs. Abbottini still considered them mine so she could complain about the extra work, for a jade plant and two violets. I always brought her a thank-you gift when I got back, a jar of jam from Grandma Eve's farm stand, some ripe tomatoes, or a pretty shell or a smooth piece of driftglass from the beach. She had a whole collection in a jar.

She raised the flashlight to my face and raised the decibel level. "Why do you have toilet paper hanging out of your nose?"

Yup, safe from the menace, but not the mortification.

Van chuckled. "Being around you is better than Comedy Central."

"We live to serve," I muttered.

When we went back upstairs, I took a shower, once I was certain there'd be no more blood to spread the rash all over my body, if that was the causative irritant. It seemed to be, what with the rashes coming after paper cuts, cat scratches, razor burn, and needle pricks. Thank God I didn't expect my period soon.

When I got out of the shower and dressed in unsuggestive sweatpants and a long T-shirt, Van was hanging up the phone.

"The vet called. At least I guess Dr. Matt Spenser is the vet your mother wants you to marry."

I glared at him while I spread crumbs from the broken cookies on top of chocolate fudge ice cream. Never waste food, right? "You didn't check the caller ID? Or let the machine pick up?"

He shrugged. "I answered in case it was your hinky admirer. Sometimes letting the crazies know their victim has protection is enough to discourage them. They'd rather prey on vulnerable targets."

"Just doing your job, huh?"

Now he grinned. "And satisfying my curiosity. The dude didn't sound happy you had company."

Damn. "I hope you explained."

"Sure, I explained that you were passed out after steamy sex in the shower. And, gee, you hadn't called out 'Matt' when you came, just some other guy's name. Harry? No, it might have been a Hail, Mary."

They gave the death penalty for killing a cop, didn't they? It might be worth it.

Van laughed and held his hand up when I came at him with the ice cream scoop. "Just kidding. I told him about the rat and said you'd call him back, that's all."

I waited for Van to take his turn in the shower before I dialed Matt's number. I opened my email while I waited for him to pick up.

DID YOU LIKE MY PRESENT, BITCH?

This time the email came from Loves2read837, which sounded innocuous enough. Hah. It contained a picture from my own website, Little Red at the beach. But the photo had been photoshopped in two, so his head was separate from his body. I dropped the phone and screamed.

"Willy? Willy? What is it? What's wrong, sweetheart? Did that stranger break in? Was that guy really a cop or just pretending to be one?"

I picked up the phone in shaking hands, gasping. "No, he is a cop and he's right—Good grief, put on some clothes and put down the gun!"

"Sorry. You okay?" Van lowered the gun, strategically, except it wasn't that big a gun.

"Willy? What the hell is going on? Why is the cop naked?"

"I got another email from that psycho. Van got out of the shower when I screamed."

Van left and came back with a towel, not the gun, and looked over my shoulder and cursed.

Matt heard him and cursed louder. "Tell me what's happening, damn it! And that guy better have his clothes on now, cop or not."

"It was another email. From a different name. You don't want to see it." Or Van in a smallish towel.

I had to look at him, his sleek, wet back with its well defined muscles, while he forwarded the horror to police headquarters and to Lou so they could try tracing this new screen name. Yummy. Not that Matt didn't keep in shape, but Van was younger and had more time to work out. Not that I was the least bit tempted, not when I had a madwoman after me and a mad Matt on the line.

Van said he'd go get dressed while I talked to Matt. He did turn the computer away before he went, but I saw it and moaned.

Matt sounded frantic. "Are you okay?"

"No! She left a dead rat and now pictures of my dog with his head torn off! And my nose is bleeding again!"

I held the bottom of my T-shirt to it, until I could grab a handful of paper towels, half cursing, half crying.

"Calm down, Willy, and tell me what's going on."

If there was anything I hated worse, it was someone telling me to calm down when I had every right to have hysterics. It did no good, and didn't solve the original problem. I wouldn't be this frantic without damn good cause, would I? "I told you what happened."

"No, your naked buddy with the gun told me about the rat first. You didn't."

His tone was accusative, as if I'd withheld evidence. Or been disloyal. "I didn't have time. Lou came and then Van came and a message from my father about smelling a rat and Mrs. Abbottini saw us in the alley."

"What the hell were you doing in the alley with the cop?"

"Forget about the cop already!"

"Why? You called him and that weird guy Lou you think is some kind of terminator, instead of me. For all I know you called the firefighter and the Brit and the cowboy, too."

"No, neither Piet nor Ty could deal with this, and Grant was no help at all. He's got two broken legs and a concussion."

"But you called him, your ex-fiancé, before you called me?"

"For crying out loud"—which I was trying not to do—"we weren't officially engaged. And I called the professor, too."

Silence across the line, Van whistling in the guest bedroom.

"Listen, I wouldn't have called any of you if I could speak with Oey. The bird has flown the coop, though, so I called whoever I thought could get here fastest and do the most good. Van's police station is right in the city, in this very district, and Lou seems to be everywhere. You weren't."

"Are you blaming me? If you'd come to the Harbor when I asked you to . . ."

"Are you blaming me for having a life of my own?"

"I thought I was part of your life."

I heard the unspoken sounds of betrayal, sorrow, distrust. And jealousy.

I understood jealousy. I hated every woman who looked at Matt in speculation or the way I'd looked at Van. And every woman he looked at, period. But tonight was not the time. "I do not need this now. I'll be there tomorrow. I thought I'd stay at your house, in case the nut job figures I went to Paumanok Harbor."

"With your posse?"

"With my dog. On second thought, maybe we'll be fine at my house. Little Red still isn't all that comfortable around your Newfie. And Susan'll be there with the big dogs, and Uncle Roger is just across the street."

"But the cop is staying at your apartment tonight?"

"Yes. Him and his gun. You have a problem with that?"

"No," he snapped, an obvious lie. "You have a problem with me caring?"

"No," I snapped right back, furious at both of us now for acting like teenagers, when I should have been angry at Deni, the teenager. "He's a friend, that's all."

"Where's he sleeping?"

"What does it matter? The guest room or the sleep sofa, he is not sleeping in my bed! Are you satisfied now?"

"What's he wearing?"

A big grin, but I didn't tell Matt that. I made shoo-ing gestures to Van, who went toward the kitchen to get more ice cream. I handed him my dish, too.

"He is wearing one of my dresses and high heels, okay? He's gay."

Something crashed in the kitchen.

"Listen, I've got to go finish packing. I'll call tomorrow when I get in."

We left it at that. No fervent invitation to stay with him tomorrow or forever, no tender words of apology for doubting my fidelity, no blowing kisses through the phone lines. I told myself the reason I didn't say I love you, I'm sorry we argued, I can't wait to see you, was because Van could hear every word.

That wasn't the reason.

I had reservations, all right.

CHAPTER NINE

I had no sleep, and no solutions. What could I do about the Andanstans and the beach, the rash and the blood? What should I do about Deni and my dog, my mother and moving to Paumanok Harbor, the missing bird and missing Matt? The senior citizens getting older? I hope to hell no one expected me to do anything about that! And I prayed my father's favor could be handled easily. Easier than dealing with Matt and my mixed emotions.

Van checked my computer for me, saw nothing suspicious, then went out to get us breakfast. He ordered me to stay put, as if I'd think of going anywhere with Deni and her accomplice on the loose.

I waited for my father's call. Instead, sirens blared, not unusual for the city, but awfully loud and close. I looked out the window to see a cop car coming straight up my block. I doubted Van decided to take me to the bus stop in style.

I had to crane my neck to see down where the black and white stopped: right at my apartment, at the hydrant. A crowd gathered in the street, reminding me of when the troll came to town. That time no one saw him but me. Today, everyone was looking and pointing at the front of my building. I swear I had nothing to do with whatever happened. I hadn't visualized anything but my own f-ed up life.

No way was I staying in the apartment when something way more interesting was going on. We could be under attack for all I knew. And I'd be safe enough, with the police already there. If Van could answer my phone, I could check out his crime scene, if that's what it was.

When I got downstairs, I saw the noisy first-floor tenants in a huddle right outside the front door. I didn't know them well, but I nodded and started to ask them what happened when I saw Mrs. Abbottini, on the ground. I ran toward her, pushing aside a florid-faced, heavyset policeman who kept asking if she needed an ambulance, where did it hurt, did she know her attacker. He wouldn't let her get up from the pavement until he was sure nothing was broken.

She looked old and small and frightened, not like the battleax with dyed black hair I'd known forever. She grabbed onto my hand.

"It was him, Willy."

"Him, who?" The cop nodded at me to continue, to get her to talk. "Somebody from the neighborhood?"

"No, the punk who brought the flowers. The ones you didn't want."

The cop mouthed, "Get his name," but I shook my head. We didn't know the kid. "Did he bring more flowers?" I looked around without seeing anything, except another, younger officer asking if anyone in the crowd had seen the attack. "Or another dead rat?"

The first cop raised his eyebrows. "You Willow Tate?"

I didn't ask how he knew. I guess Van put in a police alert for the neighborhood. Either that or I was famous for being a troublemaker. I squeezed Mrs. Abbottini's hand. "What did he want this time? Did he say anything?"

"He wanted my purse." She held up the suitcase-sized black bag, the strap still clutched in her fingers. "That's what I thought at first, anyway. But I held on tight. He knocked me down then. I still held on. No nasty delivery kid was getting my bingo money."

The first cop shook his head in frustration. No matter how many times they told the old folks to give up their valuables and don't get hurt, some codger tried to be a hero. "Tell your granny to give the mugger whatever he wants, nothing's worth dying for."

"She's not my granny. My grandmother would have stopped the thief in his tracks, turned him into a frog, or set his hair on fire, wouldn't she, Mrs. Abbottini?"

Everyone laughed, not knowing I meant it. Mrs. Abbottini smiled, to my relief. "That she would." Then the smile faded. "She wouldn't be lying on the street with everyone gawking at her."

"They're just concerned for you. But the officer is right. It's only money. You should have let him have it."

"No, Willow, he didn't want the money or the credit cards. He reached for the keys. The keys to the apartment, the front door, the back door, my apartment, and yours, too." They were all on a long chain clipped to the zipper pull of her pocketbook. She pulled it out to show me and the cop and the people circled around. "That's what he wanted, Willy. To get in."

Mr. Rashmanjari from the first-floor unit clapped. His wife bowed her head. "You saved us all, brave madam. We could all have been robbed or murdered in our beds. My daughters . . ." He let the thought fade away. "Such evil should not exist."

Amen to that.

He whispered something to his wife and she pulled two young girls closer to her side. I did not think she spoke English. I knew the children did, because I'd heard them screaming at each other. The Rashmanjaris had only been here since June, and I'd been in Paumanok Harbor a lot of the months between. All I knew of them was they were a large, multigenerational family, with large lungs and loud voices.

Then Van appeared, kneeling at Mrs. Abbottini's other side after a quick conference with the first responders, all of whom he called by name. He set down a large bag from the deli and took the shaking hand I wasn't holding, prying her fingers off the purse. "Maybe he left fingerprints we can trace." The older cop nodded and went back to his car to get a crime scene kit.

Van assured Mrs. Abbottini they wouldn't take her pocketbook as evidence, then asked if she was injured. She said no and tried to get up.

He gently pushed her back. "I heard you put up a good fight, ma'am, saved the day, but you need to stay down until the EMTs get here to make sure."

"No, I cannot stay here. I was on my way to church, where I go every morning. I need to light an extra candle today, in thanks that the motherf—"

Mr. Rashmanjari clapped a hand over a young boy's ears. Van laughed and said, "I'm sure you can say your prayers in the emergency room."

"Those places try to kill you so that you don't bother them anymore." She tried to shove Van's hand away and sit up again, then groaned. "What if I broke my hip? Old ladies die of that. How'll I get up the three flights of stairs? My sons'll put me in a home, and never come visit. Ingrates don't come now. What will I do?"

"You'll be fine. You're too tough an old bird to slow down," I lied before she started to get weepy on me. "You saved the keys, didn't you?"

That was all bull. She had a hard time with the third floor now. I never thought about what would happen when she couldn't navigate the stairs. I guess I supposed her sons would take her to live with one of them. As for the keys she fought to keep, we could have changed the locks easily enough or put in a modern pass card system.

The heavyset cop huffed back and started dusting the pocketbook, over Mrs. Abbottini's complaints that he was ruining her good bag. Van reassured her the black stuff could be wiped off. The younger policeman had a bullhorn out now and tried to get everyone to leave the area so the emergency squad could get through, but if anyone heard or saw anything, they should step forward now. No one moved except Mr. Rashmanjari, who said he'd heard the screaming and called 911. He only saw the back of a thin youth in jeans and denim jacket.

The younger cop came closer and looked over Van's shoulder. "The ambulance is on the way, ma'am," he said in a Hispanic accent. "Five minutes more." Then he asked Van if she'd given a description of her attacker.

Van and the older cop shook their heads. "Vague, only. Young, white, evil eyes, pointy chin."

"Please, ma'am, can you give us anything else? You said you'd seen him before. Does he live in the neighborhood?"

"Ask Willy. He brought her flowers."

Everyone looked at me. "I never saw him. And the flowers started a lot of trouble. They had no florist card or anything to say where he got them, either."

The Hispanic officer nodded. "We've been watching, keeping an eye out. Willow Tate."

He said it the way you'd say registered sex offender. But I guess my name or reputation got them here so fast, which had to be a good thing. "Did he say anything?"

"Yes, he said, 'Give me the fucking keys.' Not that I use words like that, you know."

The cop's lips twitched. "No, ma'am, I'm sure you don't." We'd all heard what she started to call the mugger.

"I didn't hear him at first, too busy screaming at him to let go of my purse." And she was hard of hearing, but I didn't interrupt. "He yelled it real loud the second time." Now she raised her voice to show us: "Give me the fucking keys!"

Mr. Rashmanjari urged his wife and children back into the apartment.

"Right. Got it. High voice? Low voice? Accent?"

"Not like yours." She pointed toward the Rashmanjaris. "Or theirs."

While the cop kept asking questions and getting unhelpful answers, I checked my watch. The bus I'd planned on taking had come and gone. There'd be another one in an hour or so, most likely with an empty seat, but I couldn't leave my old neighbor lying on the sidewalk. Besides, those emergency rooms could be daunting. And someone had to call her sons.

And it was all my fault.

We could hear the sirens now. Mrs. Abbottini started crying and saying she didn't want to go. Just help her up the stairs.

I choked back a tear or two myself. "I'll go with you to the hospital, okay?"

She sighed and relaxed. Then she patted my hand. "I knew you'd do the right thing, no matter what your mother says."

Van consulted with the other policemen, then reported to me, "The perp's long gone, but there's definitely a connection to your stalker. You've got to get out of here."

"I can't leave her. I promised."

The older cop shook his head. "We can't keep you in sight twenty-four/seven."

"I know."

"Lou ain't going to be happy," Van muttered.

Hell, I wasn't happy.

I raced upstairs, got my cell phone, a pad, a book to read, and a good-bye treat to leave Little Red. I forgot about my father, breakfast, and the rash that was twice as red as it was yesterday. When I got back to the street, the EMTs wanted to put me on a stretcher, too.

The triage doctor at the emergency room didn't think Mrs. Abbottini had broken bones, but ordered X-rays to be sure. While we waited our turn for that, I sketched what Mrs. Abbottini described.

I'm no police artist, and I understand they use computer programs to do this faster and more accurately, but the effort kept us busy for the seemingly endless hours we sat in dreary, crowded corridors and waiting rooms.

According to my neighbor, the mugger was short and thin. Not so much effeminate as wimpy, with long dark hair, not much of a chin, a nose stud, and small, squinty eyes, my interpretation of Mrs. Abbottini's evil eyes. He wasn't as young as I would have guessed. Mid-twenties, she thought, maybe, and stronger than he looked.

Of course anyone appeared strong to a little old lady.

We kicked around theories, that he was Deni's boyfriend or brother, avenging the slight she imagined, or trying to please her by harassing me. I had no idea why he'd want to hurt me or Mrs. Abbottini.

The doctor we finally saw wanted to keep Mrs. Abbottini overnight, despite not finding any broken bones or irregular heartbeat. She refused. I tried to convince her, mostly because she looked frail and shaky and how the hell could I get her up the stairs? Ask the neighbors?

She thought the unmarried lawyers on the second floor were living in sin. The gay couple on the fourth floor definitely were. The way she spoke her mind, loudly, meant they'd drop her on the stairs. Besides, they all worked during the day. And Mr. Rashmanjari might have gone to work by now, also, and the children I saw appeared too small to be much help.

I left Mrs. Abbottini in a wheelchair by the hospital exit while I went to flag down a taxi, but Lou waited there, with an illegally parked silver Beemer. I never thought I'd be so glad to see him. This time he looked like a successful executive in an expensive suit and Gucci loafers. The man with him looked like a CIA operative, all muscle and dark glasses, buzz-cut hair, and phone wires in his ear. So what if he never smiled, I was happy to see him, too.

I told Lou I'd take Mrs. Abbottini to Paumanok Harbor with me as soon as she was well enough to travel. "She can't stay here, for sure."

Lou rubbed his recently shaved jaw and looked to see no one could hear us. "I'm not sure about that. Bringing a non-talent to the Harbor is never a good idea."

Especially if there's an epidemic. I saw no choice. I couldn't go without her, not while she was on painkillers and told to stay off her feet and see her own doctor if she felt dizzy, out of breath, or got a headache. I had all three, plus horror at being responsible for the old lady. Maybe I could get one of her sons to come take care of her tomorrow.

I wasn't getting on the bus today.

She was pale and stiff, obviously in pain trying to get out of the car. Lou declared he and his associate, Harris, would carry her up. And Lou would stay.

Fine, he could make her soup and see she had her pills on time. I'd try to get some work done.

I went ahead to open the front door while Lou argued with Mrs. Abbottini about picking her up.

Before I reached the vestibule, though, Mr. Rashmanjari and his wife and two young sons and two little girls stepped out of their apartment.

He bowed slightly. "The brave lady can stay with us. On the first floor."

"That's very kind of you," I said. "But Mrs. Abbottini will be more comfortable in her own surroundings." And not among dark-skinned strangers of a different religion and culture. If you didn't go to her church and speak her language, with an Italian accent, you were a heathen, if not a sinner. I know, because she considered me a limb of Satan, and I'd been born right here in Manhattan. Mr. Rashmanjari did not need to hear a slight to his family and gracious offer, though, so I added that he already had a full house.

"My oldest daughter is away at college. Harvard," he said.

"How wonderful, you must be proud."

"And my oldest son and his wife and children moved to New Jersey where they have a backyard."

"Great for the kids. But . . ."

He held his hand up and smiled. "And my esteemed mother-in-law returned to India last week."

Ah. Maybe that's why it seemed quieter. But Mrs. Abbottini and the Rashmanjaris? I was ashamed I didn't know much about my new neighbors, their religion, their ways. That shame was nothing to getting my old neighbor hurt by someone with a grudge against me. What I did know was that with Mrs. Abbottini's narrow mind and ungoverned tongue, she could start a range war right here on the East Side, by God.

"We would be honored to have Nonna Maria to stay with us. That means grandmother in Italian. She taught us."

Nonna Maria? I'd known her forever and she never said to call her anything but Mrs. Abbottini. "You know her?"

"Of course. She passes every day for church. Such a devout woman is much respected. My youngest son helps carry her groceries and takes her garbage out. My third daughter learns to knit from her."

I never knew that either. "But the imposition . . ."

"She can help my wife learn English and teach my sons about Yankee baseball. And show my second daughter how to cook American."

American-Italian. "But she's used to having a room of her own."

"Of course. Nonna Maria can have the very valuable front room, where my esteemed mother-in-law stayed. We have already prepared it for an honored guest."

"Did you say the front room?" Supported by Harris, Mrs. Abbottini showed more life than I'd seen in years.

"It might be noisy, so close to the road."

Mr. Rashmanjari was already directing Lou, Harris, and the old lady to the room, which had *two* windows facing the street. They had security bars on them, but nice curving ones, and window boxes planted with fall chrysanthemums. The room was small but clean, with a flat-screen TV.

Mrs. Abbottini had tears in her eyes. "I accept, with pleasure. Temporarily, of course. The doctor said a week."

Mr. Rashmanjari bowed. "Of course."

Except I doubted she'd give up that front view, if she didn't insult the family into throwing her out. I was

already wondering if I could get my mother to sublet
Mrs. Abbottini's rooms on the third floor when she came
for her TV show, so I wouldn't have to move or share my
apartment with her.

Too soon and too much to hope for. I went upstairs
to find Mrs. Abbottini's nightgowns and pills and
spare glasses. One of the Rashmanjari girls followed
me to help carry some of her clothes and her jewelry
box.

Then Nonna Maria wanted me to fetch the eggplant
parmigiana from her freezer, so she wouldn't feel so
beholden. "And the olives and the bowl of antipasto."

I didn't know what dietary rules the family followed,
but they could work that out themselves.

I found her address book and called one of her sons
before I went back down the stairs that seemed steeper
and longer with every trip. I found a listing for Antony
at work, the one who used to shove things up his nose.
He didn't show his love by visiting, but let him find the
scum who knocked down his mother, he swore, and the
bastard'd be a stain on the street.

"The police are looking. But the reason I'm calling is
that your mother is staying with the first-floor neighbors
for now, the Rashmanjaris. She couldn't manage the
stairs, and I have to leave."

I waited for Antony to make some comment about
foreigners, but all he said was he'd been begging her to
come stay with his family for years. Maybe now she
would.

I doubted it, knowing what she thought of Antony's
wife and unruly children. I gave him the phone number,
my cell phone, and he said he'd come by in the morning
to try to convince his mother to move.

"If she's staying with a frigging family, it should be
her own."

They'd have to work that out, too.

I'd never had breakfast or lunch. I thought about going
to the sandwich shop on the corner, until I remembered

Deni and the delivery kid. Luckily, I also remembered seeing some baked ziti in Mrs. Abbottini's refrigerator.

Lou was already heating it up in her microwave. "I'll stay here tonight, with the door open. Harris will hang out in the vestibule, and I've got a guy watching the alley. Van sent a copy of the fingerprints, so my people will work on them and the Internet stuff. I'll drive you to the Harbor tomorrow."

Ding went the microwave. Lou's dinner was ready, end of discussion.

What could I say? "Great. Thanks."

I had a bowl of cereal.

CHAPTER TEN

I had the offer of a ride. With an off-putting, old-time
Rambo.

Going out to Paumanok Harbor with Lou in the silver sedan had to be better than taking a bus with the
dog and all my stuff: faster, cheaper, with a lot fewer
hassles. If I had to take Mrs. Abbottini after all, if she
forgot about having a view of the street and remembered her picky prejudices, a private car was the only
way to go. But Lou's?

He'd want better explanations, which I did not have.
And he'd want to know my plans for dealing with the
issues, which I did not have. What if I had another nose-
bleed, which he wouldn't want on his leather seats?
Would he shoot me or leave me on the side of the Long
Island Expressway?

Even if I did not mess up his car—or if Little Red did
not—we'd have nothing to talk about during a three-
hour car ride, nothing I wanted to hear or say, anyway.

That was for tomorrow. We both knew I had to stay in
Manhattan tonight to make sure Mrs. Abbottini stayed
with the Rashmanjaris, or left with her son in the morning. If I had to remain here, with two crazy kids coming
after me and my dog, I guess I was happy Lou was across
the hall.

For now, I had about fifty phone messages to answer,

a lot from the same people. When they couldn't get me on my cell, they tried the apartment land line, or vice versa. I made a list while I ate my cereal.

My father sounded anxious in his first three messages. Annoyed in the next two. Furious in the ones I stopped tallying. Every half hour since nine this morning. Hadn't I promised to be home today? Didn't I understand how important this was to him and his friend?

Susan told me Matt would meet my bus instead of her. Later, she got aggravated when he called her to say I wasn't on the damned bus, had she gotten the schedule wrong. "What the hell have you done now, Willy? And why am I in the middle of it again? Call me. No, call Matt."

Matt's first message was just what I'd wanted. He regretted any harsh words between us, knew we could work things out. He'd been upset, that's all, that I was in danger, that I had problems he couldn't solve for me, that we were so far apart. His second said he'd meet me in Amagansett at the Jitney stop, take me for lunch at one of the clam bars along the Nappeague stretch headed to Montauk, where they had outdoor seating for us and Little Red. His new receptionist had almost quit when he asked her to juggle six appointments so he could spend time with me, but he had three hours free. We could plan our getaway vacation for November.

His third call, to my cell from his cell, asked if I missed the bus, and should he wait for the next one? His receptionist could move two more appointments. Why hadn't I called, though? If I was too mad at him to go for lunch, I should say so, so he could reschedule his patients.

His fourth call sounded frantic. Had something happened to me? Why didn't I answer the phone? Where was I?

Damn. I never knew he knew what bus, so how could I know he'd be waiting and worrying? That was Susan's fault, not mine.

I waded through more messages, and added raisins and cookie crumbs to my cereal before calling him back.

I barely recognized Professor Harmon's voice, it was so raspy. Between coughs, he wanted to know where I was and why I hadn't called yet to discuss my new thoughts about his Andanstans. Jimmie and the housekeeper, my mother's cousin Lily, had planned a lovely tea for us on his deck as soon as he heard I'd be returning to the Harbor.

Lily snarled that she'd spent the morning baking and cutting crusts off bread for the stupid tea sandwiches, happy to see the professor looking forward to a meal. How could I simply not show up?

My grandmother was her usual surly self. First I'd disappointed Jimmie, upset Lily, put Susan in an awkward position with *my* gentleman friend (heaven forfend Susan's feathers got ruffled, while mine could be plucked out at the roots) and missed the emergency meeting she'd called for me to address the Paumanok Harbor special council between lunch with Matt and tea with the professor. We'd have dinner at her place later. Her second message complained that the least I could do was return the calls.

Mrs. Terwilliger at the Paumanok Harbor Library reminded me that I had a book waiting for me at the front desk. If I did not intend to come take it out, she would have to give other patrons the opportunity.

I hadn't ordered any books. Mrs. Terwilliger always selected what she thought people should read. For that matter, I never arranged for Matt to pick me up, to have tea with the professor, or to attend any of my grandmother's secret council meetings, or dinners. The fact that everyone else had plans for me, my life, even my reading material, was beginning to rub me the wrong way. Deni and her delivery boy were bad enough. I ate the rest of the cookie crumbs with a spoon while I listened to more unhappy voices.

Matt's new receptionist did walk out when he asked her to rebook the missed appointments. And three customers threatened to take their pets to another vet. If he didn't hear from me soon, he'd call the police.

My father, again. He'd dreamed of gossip and slander and double-crossing. He never expected his own daughter to be the one backstabbing.

And again, Dad on the other phone. How could I do this to him? The damned Irish tenor kept singing in his head, and I couldn't bother calling him?

My publisher left a message about the cover. If they couldn't have a mermaid, how did I feel about a girlfriend for the pet store owner?

I felt they should stop trying to make my book something it wasn't. The goddamn hero had a goddamn parrot for companion, not Lois Lane.

My dentist's office called, reminding me about my appointment tomorrow, which I'd meant to cancel as soon as they opened this morning, before Mrs. Abbottini got mugged.

Two friends wanted to get together in the city this weekend for a film festival. It sounded great. Paumanok Harbor didn't even have a movie theater of its own.

Another friend wondered when I was going out to the Hamptons. Any chance she could come along? It sounded like all the hunky men gravitated there. I'd had more than my fair share, from what she'd heard.

Not on your life, sister. I made a mental note to keep that huntress two hundred miles away from Matt.

Of course, my mother added her two cents. She didn't know what was going on, but I seemed to be upsetting a lot of people, from the six phone calls she'd received.

"Even your father called, the jackass. As if I know where you are every minute of every day. The old fool spouted his usual gibberish about a rat and a horse and an Irishman. At first I thought he was starting a really bad joke, then he added crap about a knife in the back." She sniffed in disgust. "And what's this about an angry fan calling you? It's still my name in the phone book, right? Are you certain it wasn't one of my readers? Do not offend the paying public, Willy."

Sure, Mom, it had to be about you, didn't it? You want Deni? You can have her. Maybe my mother's skills at training difficult dogs could carry over to a nasty, aggressive kid.

As if I'd conjured her up, Deni's high-pitched voice screeched out the next message: "I'm sorry I didn't knock the old lady's teeth out. Maybe next time."

Which made no sense at all. She wasn't the one to push Mrs. Abbottini down, the messenger was.

I called Lou to tell him about the message. He already knew, from the tap he had on the line.

"Is that legal? I didn't sign any papers or give my permission."

"You want to catch the bastards or not? And I called your grandmother and told her about Mrs. Abbottini so she stops worrying."

"Grandma Eve worried about me? Hah. She was pissed I'd missed her meeting, which I incidentally did not know about."

"That's her way of worrying. She said she'd call Susan and Lily, the professor, and your mother, but you better get to your father."

"It can't be all that important, or he would have told me last night. It's something about a favor for a friend."

I guess Lou hadn't put a bug on my cell phone because he didn't mention Matt. Deni never had that number, thank God, so Lou had no reason to screen those calls. I made a note to myself to buy a cheap prepaid phone so I'd have some privacy, somewhere.

I called Matt first. He had two minutes between irritated patients—the owners, not the pets—so I hurried to explain about Mrs. Abbottini, how I'd spent all day in the hospital where cell phones were not allowed, and how I couldn't leave her to go outside or find a pay phone. Then what with bringing her home and getting her settled, this was the first chance I had to call. And I did not know Susan had asked him to pick me up at the bus stop, so why would I call him?

"She'll be all right?"

"Susan? Not once I get my hands on her."

"Your neighbor."

"Oh, yes, unless she starts a diplomatic incident. And Lou is going to drive me out tomorrow. He's in her apartment right now, keeping me safe by listening to my phone calls and organizing my life like everyone else."

"Then I guess I won't ask what you're wearing."

I looked down at the crumbs on my sweatpants, the dog hair on my ragged old men's shirt. "Not a good idea."

"I'm worried."

"Yeah. Me, too. I'll be glad to get out of here. I'm sorry I missed the lunch. Steamers would have been nice."

"Steamy sex would be better."

"Can't we do both?"

"Ask Lou."

I went across the hall. "I do not want you listening to my calls."

"We're screening, not listening. The tap lets us know who the calls come from, and the numbers. We only listen to the unknowns, like your dentist. Better call. They charge if you don't show up. Your fan doesn't stay on long enough to get a trace going." He growled. "Damn cop shows. Now everyone's an expert criminal."

I went back to my apartment, found a freezer-burned fudgesicle behind the ice cube tray, and called my father.

He started ranting before I said hello.

"Finally you call? Finally?"

I tried to explain about cell phones in the hospital and Mrs. Abbottini and the mugger, without saying I never once thought about him.

He didn't listen. "I worry about you all the time, try to keep you safe, warn you away from danger, and all I ask is one little favor. You can't be there for me, when you said you would?"

"I'm here now, Dad."

"It might be too late, after I sat by the phone all day, waiting for your call."

"You had your cell. You could have been between tennis matches, for all I knew."

"No, I said I'd call this morning, so I canceled. For nothing."

Now I got as angry as he was. I'd spent the day with people coughing and bleeding and moaning and trying to avoid me, with the rash on my lip. Now I was stuck here for another day while I waited for Antony Abbottini while Bonnie and Clyde plotted to steal my peace of mind and my apartment keys. I had Lou next door, and everyone else in the world, it seemed, telling me what to do, where to go. Fix this, solve that, don't let us down, again, Willy.

Enough.

So I ranted right back. How my father could have given up his golf game yesterday, skipped dinner with his latest Lucille last night, and stayed in his own condo in his own bed for a change, to talk to me. I was in all last night, and could have talked to him then. Today I'd spent the entire day at the hospital, if he cared, with nothing to eat but guilt-bile and crap from the vending machines. My dog had missed the pee-pee pads, by two rooms, and used my slippers as a potty. My boyfriend threw a fit because I missed a bus, and my grandmother thinks I can stop beach erosion single-handedly. So what was his damn emergency?

I never yelled at my father. He must have been shocked, by the silence at the other end of the line. "I'm sorry, Dad. It's been a dreadful day."

"I'm sorry, too, baby girl. You're right. I should have stayed home and worked this out while I had the chance yesterday. And I am sorry about Mrs. Abbottini, even if she is an old bat. And your slippers. But I've been so upset by all this. And I hate having to involve you, so I put it off as long as I could. It's about Shirley's daughter."

I never heard of any Shirley. "Another of your chippies?" That's what my mother called his heart attacks in high heels. "That is, your lady friends?"

"Stop sounding like your mother. Shirley is a friend, all right? I've known her for years."

"Okay. So what's her problem?"

"They're going to commit her daughter, Carinne, for psychiatric evaluation, involuntarily, if I can't get her help."

Oh, shit. "From me?"

"You and your friends at Royce. She hears voices."

Double shit. "Like your mother did? Those kind of voices?" The voices weren't caused by psychosis or a chemical imbalance in the brain, but breaches in the gates between worlds, between us and the beings of Unity. I know that now, but when I was a kid, I thought I had two crazy grandmothers, not just the witch. I always worried I'd go bonkers like my father's mother.

Dad took his mother to Royce Institute, where she died, at peace, he always said. They were used to things like that, at Royce. What they couldn't cure they accepted as normal, special even, worthy of study.

"How weird is it that she has the same, ah, trait—not a gift, surely, if this girl is to be locked away—as your mother."

"Carinne's not a girl. She's two years older than you are. And it's, um, not that uncommon a problem. She has other talents, practical magic, a kind of career foretelling. But it's the voices that drive her crazy with headaches. She yells at them to leave her alone, which is why people think she's gone off the deep end. A danger to herself and others, they say. They'll fill her with dope and lock her away. She's already lost her job and her friends."

"What job did she do?"

"She was a guidance counselor for high school kids. She knew what they'd be doing when they reached whatever age Carinne was at the time, so she could point them in the right direction."

"Oh, boy. That's Royce stuff, all right. So get her on a plane to England."

"I can't. She's afraid to fly."

I understood. I hated planes, too.

"And what if she starts shouting at the voices in her head or yelling at creatures that aren't on the plane?"

"So have her mother drive her up."

"Shirley had a stroke a few years ago. She's in assisted living and doesn't know how bad Carinne's situation is getting, thank goodness."

"Her mother isn't a Royce alumna? She can't call them and ask for help?"

"No, and no. Carinne never got registered with them, either. And before you suggest I drive her up, my doctors say I shouldn't. The whole thing has raised my blood pressure and . . ."

"Don't say it, Dad. We just have to find another way. Does she have other family?"

"She had a stepfather, but he died ten years ago, and that's all. There's no one but me to help. Who else could understand?"

"What I don't understand is how you got involved."

"She needs help. Isn't that enough?"

"You're not, ah, shtupping her, are you?"

"Willow Tate, bite your tongue. And stop listening to your mother. I am not a dirty old man, just old. I'm too old and sickly to bring her to you and that new Royce outreach center at the Harbor."

They could help her, once they had a full staff. The professor already had rooms and an office there, so he could show her how to cope. Maybe they could put together what he saw in his trances with what she heard. For that matter, if she heard any of the Unity speech, Grant would love to talk to her. "Yeah," I told my father, "that's the right place for her. We just have to get her there. I'm on my way tomorrow, but that won't help. I know, Mom's on her way back for the Halloween thing. She can bring Carinne. She'll be happy for the company. And if I know Mom, she'll be carting dogs to shelters along the way and she can use the help. If you call her, she'll come get Carinne. Or I'll call if you want."

"No, that won't work. I keep seeing gossip and rumors and backstabbing."

"Mom's not like that."

"She will be, this time."

Hmm. "You sure this Carinne isn't your mistress?"

"Willow!"

"Then there's something else you're not telling me, isn't there?"

"Um, uh, ah."

"Wait. She's two years older than me. She has your mother's problem, plus a knack for foretelling. And her mother has no talent, right?"

He sputtered some more.

"So what you're not saying is that you have a secret brother, a desperate criminal, and that's the friend who asked for your help?"

"No."

"A sister you never knew who got put out for adoption at birth?"

"Uh, no. Stop letting your imagination run wild."

"So what's left? You care so much about this Carinne because . . ."

He sighed. "She's my daughter."

Chapter Eleven

I had a stalker and a skin condition and, holy shitolly, a sister!

"Dad, stay right where you are. Do not move. I'll call you back in ten minutes after I catch my breath."

"Good. I need a drink."

"You're not supposed to drink."

"I'm not supposed to have two oddball daughters, either."

Oh, boy. I had ten minutes to rearrange my worldview and my place in that world. My father? Hell, my mother! Where do you start when a tornado rips your house apart? You have a cigarette, a bottle, a prayer—whatever crutch you need to help you limp on.

I hugged my dog.

"Okay, Dad," I said a few minutes later. Maybe I misunderstood. Maybe he said he had a dilemma. "Start at the beginning, only slower this time, with a few more details. True ones."

"What, now you're with the Royce truth squad?"

"No, I trust you to tell me the whole story. You have to, after dropping a bombshell like that in my lap." Where my iced tea also landed.

He said all right and started. I tried not to interrupt.

He never lied to me, he swore. Sure, he never needed to. Why would I ask if he had another family somewhere? How many kids think their fathers are bigamists or philanderers?

And he was faithful to my mother, he also swore, no matter what she always thought. Which was that he screwed around every chance he got, like he did now. According to him, he never did, not while they were married.

"Did Mom know about you and Shirley?"

"Hell, no. She would have cut off my— That is, we would have been divorced years earlier."

"Does she know about Sister Carrie?"

"No, again. Nor about the money I sent."

"Whoa. You haven't mentioned money before. I'm sorry for getting sidetracked. Start over."

"That's what I am trying to do."

By my father's standards, he had not committed adultery. He and my mother were engaged at the time, but the wedding kept being postponed, canceled, or rescheduled so many times neither of them were certain it could ever take place. Or should.

"Kind of like you and that Grant fellow."

Nothing like Grant and me. We had never been officially engaged, and I never would have slept with another man if we were. In fact, I broke off with Grant before I dated anyone else. I believed in old-fashioned honor. If you said I do, you damned well better don't mess around. Get a divorce, like my parents. Don't lie, like my parents.

"Go on, but leave me and my boyfriends out of your story."

Dad had to go on a business trip, he told me, an important convention in Florida. Mom refused to go with him, even though his company was paying all expenses.

"She was minding a pregnant dog. She wouldn't leave it with the vet or a kennel. No, she chose a goddamned pregnant dog instead of me, my career, my wanting to be someone, wanting to be a success, for her. So I went, but with a mad on. Not crazy mad, more a disappointed, jealous, hopeless mad."

I knew the feeling.

"Shirley lived in Florida, but she attended the convention. She was single, pretty, and had none of your mother's hang-ups, that I could see. None of her amazing talents or great intellect, either, but we had a lot in common. We talked, had a couple of drinks, dinner, and went back to my room. That's all there was. Nothing more, I swear. It was the Seventies, so no big thing."

Leaving out what they did in that hotel room, which produced Carinne.

"I loved your mother, thorns and all. Being with another woman only made me see it better."

So he came back and convinced Mom to get married a week later. They produced me and lived semi-happily for a decade or so.

Shortly after the wedding, though, he received a letter at his office—people still wrote letters then—from Shirley, announcing her pregnancy.

"What could I do? I was recently married, hardly knew the woman in Florida, but knew your mother's attitude toward loyalty and faithfulness. She judged everyone by dog standards. I sent Shirley money to help, to fulfill my responsibilities as much as I could. And I set up a separate bank account your mother never found."

"She always knew you were keeping something from her." I wondered now if we'd had to go without luxuries or niceties, so that Carinne could have them. "She assumed it was another woman, not the money."

"There was no other woman!"

He said he had nothing to do with either the woman or her child, except sending the checks and receiving an occasional picture Shirley sent to his office. And a wedding announcement to Harry O'Dell, who adopted little Carinne and took good care of her and Shirley until he died.

By then, my parents had divorced and my father had moved to Florida, so he called Shirley to see if she needed help. He met Carinne for the first time.

"How did you know she was yours? Maybe Shirley'd

been stringing you along all those years, for the money. Maybe she was already pregnant when she came to your hotel room. Did you do a DNA test?"

"There was no need."

Carinne had talent. My father recognized it right away, how she tried to warn younger kids not to ride their bikes in the street, kids that a year or so later got hit by cars. Her mother had a lot of such stories, and seemed proud. My father was appalled. How could he get Carinne to Royce without admitting whose child she was? They'd know. My mother would know. Grandma Eve would know.

I could hear the fear and trembling in his voice.

So he kept quiet. And agreed with Shirley that Carinne had a bit of Irish blood in her—from Harry O'Dell?—and everyone knew the Irish often had The Sight, or some such bullshit.

Carinne got better at the prescience as she grew older.

"She had a talent I never heard of. A kind of a fore-telling, but way better than I can do, and not only for danger, not only for her loved ones. She can look at a person, any person as long as they are younger than she is, and know what they are going to be doing when they reach her age."

"Say that again?"

"I know, it's complicated. But it worked fine for her. She went to college for an education degree, got her master's in adolescent psychology, and became a high school guidance counselor. She knew what direction the kids should take to reach what she'd seen when they were her age, twenty-something by then. You know, if she saw them as a cook, she'd suggest culinary classes. A doctor, they better take science courses. The kids appreciated her encouragement, and most followed through. They came back to thank her. It's all documented in a journal she kept."

"What if they became criminals, or died? Or if she saw them miserable, washing dishes in a diner?"

"She didn't tell them anything, just that the vocational and aptitude tests were inconclusive. I think that's what made her hear the voices, shouting over the lies she had to tell. It drove her crazy. Not true crazy, of course."

"Of course. So what did she do about it?"

"She got a job at a senior center, where everyone was older than she was."

"Good. But . . . ?"

"But they had young aides, and they brought in the Girl Scouts once a week. And the residents always had grandkids visiting. She started yelling at the girls not to follow the path they were on, they'd end up as hookers or addicts or night shift counter clerks. Some of the boys would grow up to be wife beaters or carjackers or wretched executives. She saw them, their futures, the way I see danger sometimes. It was too much for her. And for the Girl Scouts. And the senior center. She lost her job, her friends, her savings. And she kept hearing voices, telling her people's fates that she didn't know how to change or if she should try. I mean, what if, when Carinne turned thirty, she met a younger waitress, call her Hope, because she hoped to be a singer. Only Carinne sensed her still waiting on tables when Hope turned thirty. That didn't mean Hope couldn't get a big break when she was thirty-two, or wasn't saving money to study with a voice coach, or a hundred other reasons. Carinne couldn't interfere, but the voices shouted too loudly."

And I thought I carried a heavy burden being the Visualizer.

"She managed to hide her problems for awhile, claiming migraines, her mother's stroke, all kinds of anxiety. I didn't know how bad it got until some social worker called me, as a friend of Shirley's. I went to Carinne and had to explain to her that she wasn't insane, she was normal for who she was."

"Your daughter."

"Yes."

"She wasn't surprised?"

"She always knew she wasn't Harry O'Dell's kid. I think she was happy knowing her real father instead of wondering. And she liked me. She was relieved at my explanation, even if she only half believed me, but she was better for awhile."

"Why didn't you get her more help? Your friends in Paumanok Harbor would have known what to do. Someone could have gone to talk to her. Police Chief Haversmith, the mayor. Any of the others."

"I was going to invite a couple of them down here for the golfing, and see what they thought. Maybe they could convince her to get on a plane. But, hell, what if she started telling the younger passengers they'd be in a plane crash or something? I figured I'd fly to England with her, myself. Keep her calm and distracted. Or drugged. Then I had the heart attack and the surgery. And your mother arrived."

"Mom would have helped. She can't walk away from a creature in need."

"Carinne's not a dog."

"Okay, Mom mightn't feel so strongly about wounded people, but she'd know what to do. She always does, or she'd ask her mother. And neither of them had to know Carinne's parentage, just her talent."

"They'd know. She kind of looks like me. Or you."

"She looks like me? Enough that Mom would know?"

"You know the way your mother can look at a mutt in the pound and rattle off its ancestors' breeds?"

"Carinne's not a dog!" I threw his words back at him. "Mom would have helped. She came to take care of you after the bypass, didn't she?"

"And almost killed me with her nagging."

"Irrelevant. But, all right, if you won't call Mom, then call the people at Royce. You know they'll send someone to help her. I can give you numbers for people right in this country, so there'd be no planes. One of them is in the apartment next door." I didn't know what Lou could accomplish, but he'd do something, for sure.

"No, once I heard about Royce opening a branch in

Paumanok Harbor, I knew that's where she had to go.
With you, baby girl. You're the only one I can trust."

"Trust? I wouldn't have the slightest idea what to do
for her."

"No, but you'd make sure to find the right people, and
keep her safe until then."

I tried to tell him about Deni, and how I couldn't
keep myself or my neighbor safe. He didn't listen.

"You fought like hell to save that kidnapped boy, and
the injured colt that caused all the nightmares. They say
you did everything but burn up the whole village trying
to keep that sea creature and its arsonist firefly friends
alive. And you wouldn't give up till you found the professor who's there now, then almost got everyone
drowned in helping him banish that sea monster. You've
got a staunch heart, Willy. You care."

I grasped at straws. "That doesn't make me an expert
on espers."

"You do not need to be. I checked. Your Dr. Harmon
is one powerful wizard, and he's used to advising younger
talents."

"He's a retired professor of creative writing!"

"Who stood up to a kraken and got it locked in the
center of the earth. Who knows more about the Others
than anyone else in our world. Who's too old to come
here, so Carinne has to get to him. People in London
might be more familiar with her problem, they did fine
with my mother, didn't they? But now there's help on
your doorstep. It's like fate sent you the troll so DUE
sent Grant, whose father's a big shot at the University,
who saw a vacant estate suitable for the outreach center,
where the professor can live, so Carinne has a place to
go, where she won't be alone."

I didn't think fate planned so far in advance, but I'd
seen so much strange crap recently, I could believe anything. "So I'm supposed to play camp counselor to her in
Paumanok Harbor?"

"You're the only one who can do it, who can protect her from all the dangers, all the pettiness of that foolish little town that keeps its secrets hidden, all the backbiting."

"But what danger, Dad? Do you sense anything?"

"Nothing specific. Just a lot of menace."

"For her or for me?"

He sighed. "I wish I could tell. Maybe both. You know my thing only works for people I care for. I love both of you."

My father loved his other daughter? I'm a big girl. I could handle that. I had to. Or not. "But you love me better, don't you?"

"Of course. You're my baby girl; the one I bottle-fed and taught Beatles songs to. The one I took to the park every Saturday while your mother held obedience classes."

He taught me to be afraid of the dark and riptides and electric storms and a hundred other things, with all his warnings and worries, too. Because he cared.

And she was my sister. "Okay, Dad. Matt and I are planning a vacation for November. Maybe we can drive down to Florida and bring her back with us. He's great, calm and steady and understanding. And he wants to meet you anyway."

"Aren't you listening, Willy? They want Carinne locked up. She told some people on line at the unemployment office that they'd OD before their thirty-seventh birthdays. Another that she'd die of AIDs. She started a riot there. When they sent for some junior bureaucrat to take charge, she told him he'd be in the same cubicle in five years. He freaked out, called for security."

"But what do you expect me to do? I hate planes as much as she does, it sounds like, and I can't drive to Florida to get her. You know how I am with bridges and tunnels and getting lost. I don't even have a car!"

"I've got that covered. I've reserved a compartment on a train with a sleeping car. They'll bring her meals and she won't have to see anyone."

"That sounds great. Maybe next week, if this mess with Deni gets straightened out."

"Carinne's train gets into Penn Station the day after tomorrow. I told her you'd meet her there."

Oh, boy.

Chapter Twelve

I had dread. And hair dye.

How was I supposed to handle this? I wasn't worried about the paranormal parts, not with the pros in Paumanok Harbor. They'd teach her control, like someone had taught Connor Redstone, the Native American who could diagnose mortal illnesses without being able to cure them. Carinne had to suffer the same agonies and frustrations, besides the voices in her head.

And getting a loony through Penn Station didn't faze me. Half the people who hung out there would have been hospitalized a couple of decades ago.

But how could I manage the personal side, bringing a stranger who looked like me to the Harbor? Or getting Carinne past my mother, without humiliating Mom in her hometown? Or letting my mother vent her anger at Carinne, who hadn't committed any crime? I'd guess she was the victim in all this, except she had a mother and father who loved her and stayed together for most of her life, and she also had my father's love and money.

The first thing I did after taking a shower to wash away the nervous sweat from my conversation with my father was Google Carinne O'Dell. She had citations for journal articles, speeches at colleges, appearances at conferences for school psychologists. And—aha!—she had a website.

The site included an impressive résumé and a discreet mention that Ms. O'Dell was now available for private counseling in career management and life.

A photograph accompanied the bio. I studied it carefully, and my dread morphed into despair. She had a narrow face with a straight nose like mine, sandy blonde hair cut short like mine, and big blue eyes. Like mine.

Crap, I never counseled anyone about anything, yet here I was, looking for a job as a life coach. Any thoughts of passing Carinne off as a friend from college, as a chance-met train-station stranger, as an anonymous person in need, just evaporated.

She could have been my twin. A little older, a little thinner, hair smooth where mine wanted to frizz. Maybe she had it straightened. She looked serious, but maybe because she was looking for a job. Or thinking she was a nut job.

The second thing I did after my shower—I needed another one already—was pull apart the cabinet under my bathroom sink. Somewhere I had a box of hair color from years ago, when I felt dull and dreary. My books hadn't caught on, the men I dated were losers, and my hair made dirty dishwater look appealing. I'd decided to become a redhead, or a strawberry blonde at the least, to add spice to my blah existence, to change my appearance and, hopefully, my life.

I chickened out and took a karate course instead.

I did it now, before I had second thoughts. I was *not* going to parade around Paumanok Harbor as part of a surprise twinhood. Or the butter-stamp sister of an illegitimate sibling.

While timing the gunk on my hair, I called Lou.

"We have a problem. I can't leave the city for at least two days."

"Listen, kiddo, I'd have you out of here and on the road in an hour if I had the backup in place. People to follow us, to make sure no one was on our tail, and people to stay in the building in case your stalkers show up again. That's our best bet for nailing the bastards."

I wished he hadn't used that word. "You don't understand."

"Sure I do. They'll be in place in the morning, with the usual traffic giving us additional cover."

"No, we cannot leave until Saturday. We—that is, I; you don't need to come"—I wished he wouldn't—"have to meet someone at the train. I have the schedule and the gate. Then I'll take her to Paumanok Harbor, to the professor. If you cannot drive us," I prayed so, "I'll rent a car, I suppose."

"It's not that parrot come back as something else you're bringing Dr. Harmon, is it?"

"On the train? No, I haven't heard anything about the bird. This is a woman of amazing talent that Royce will be interested in. I'm hoping the professor can relieve some of her anxiety."

"You say she has talent? Undocumented talent?"

"Yes, and she needs help."

"And you just found her today, when two psychos are leaving warnings and escalating their attacks? You don't think this could possibly be a trap to get you out in the open, vulnerable to anything their warped minds think up?"

"No, she's, um, someone my father knows. That's what all his urgent messages were about."

"If she's a friend of your father's, you better ask if she's been tested for STDs."

"No, she's not one of those friends. She's, um, a distant relative, some branch of the family I never knew existed." No lie, there. "Dad and her mother met through business years ago and discovered the, um, connection." Whew. Not lying was harder than lying. I never knew who could recognize a falsehood when they heard one, though.

"So the mother has talent, too?"

"The mother is ill and Carinne can't cope, so Dad's trying to help. She's in big trouble, hearing voices."

"We can't chance it. I'll try to get an agent to meet the train, but no promises."

"That's not good enough. She's already traumatized. In a strange city, one as chaotic as Manhattan, heaven knows what will happen. You wouldn't want that on your conscience." If he had one. "Or her yipping to some cops or a judge about going to Paumanok Harbor, where she can get help for her delusions because everyone there is blessed with paranormal skills. I'm guessing that's what my father told her."

"Damn. But you're still too valuable to leave exposed in the middle of Manhattan. In Paumanok Harbor at this time of year, I can count the strangers on two hands, and have fifty pairs of gifted eyes watching them. I'll have the woman picked up, for sure, before she can get us all into trouble."

That wouldn't work, not when I promised my father. And what happened after he had her "picked up" at the station? Lou believed in expediency, not compassion.

Before getting into that, I had to ask, "What do you mean, I'm valuable? What are you going to do, sell me to the highest bidder?"

"No, I'm going to keep you alive and healthy. You're valuable to your grandmother and the professor, for starters. And you're the only Visualizer we know of. No one can figure if you call the trouble or just attract it, but you're the only person who's had any luck getting rid of the trespassers when they do come. So we are leaving in the morning, before the whole town falls into the sea, or comes down with leprosy or nosebleeds."

I grabbed my nose. Was it bleeding again? How could Lou know, unless he had one of those tiny spy cameras set up somewhere in my apartment?

I checked the mirror over the sofa . . . and got reminded of the slop on my head. "Eek!" Oh, shit, the timer must not be working. I shouted "Gotta go," and slammed the phone down.

I raced toward the kitchen sink with its water hose spritzer thing. The dye rinsed off, the neutralizing conditioner went on. My sleep shirt went in the trash, with ominous stains on it. I went back to the mirror and stared, horrified, at the color of my hair. Maybe I should have checked the expiration date on the box, or the color I'd picked so long ago. Maybe I should be the one institutionalized instead of Carinne. Maybe I—

"What the hell happened?" There was Lou bursting through my apartment door, gun in one hand, taser in the other. There was I, naked except for a clown's wig that wasn't a wig. I scrambled to wrap the kitchen table's tablecloth around me.

Apparently Lou hadn't noticed my naked body, which said a lot about Lou, or my flat-chested, puffy-bellied, jiggle-thigh body. He pointed to my head. "Is that blood?"

"Uh, no. I'm altering my appearance, that's all."

He nodded and put down the weapons. "That's not a bad idea, with stalkers out there. Except now you look like Little Orphan Annie with a fat lip, and you'll be easier to spot in a crowd. Any crowd. We could have bought you a mousy brown wig, or a hat."

"Maybe it'll dry lighter."

And maybe pigs'll fly.

I showed great restraint and patience in not calling Janie, the owner of Paumanok Harbor's beauty salon, and begging for help as soon as I got rid of Lou. I called Matt first. No way was I going to make the mistake of leaving him out of the loop again.

No way was I going to admit I looked like Lucille Ball or a ball of fire. "How do you feel about redheads?" I asked subtly.

"Is this a trick question? Or did you already hear that my ex-wife might be coming to the Harbor for the weekend?"

"What?!" The thud was my heart hitting the ground.

"Well, Marion is a redhead."

"Who left you and bled you dry in the divorce and stole your dog and—"

"And her father just died. She wants to take her mother away for awhile, and she has no one to leave the dog with. He's a great pup. A rescue mutt, smart and sweet. Moses will love him, and Red . . . Well, Red hates everyone."

My heart started beating again. "So she'll come and drop the dog off and leave the same day?"

"Not exactly. We decided she ought to come Friday and stay till Monday to help acclimate the dogs. But you and I will have tomorrow when you get here to get reacclimated ourselves. I've been thinking about that hot tub at Rosehill, when we go to visit the professor."

"That's why I'm calling. I can't get there until Saturday." When his wife, his ex-wife, a natural redhead from the pictures I'd seen, would be staying at his house.

"I thought Lou was bringing you tomorrow to get you away from danger."

I was going to unburden my soul to him, admit how the stalkers terrified me by threatening innocents like my neighbors and my dog. Then I'd tell him the truth about my father and his other daughter, how I felt that my birthright had been stolen, my foundation shaken. How I felt disloyal not telling my mother. How telling my mother would kill her, then she'd kill me. Instead I said, "A many-times-removed relative of my father's has an aura." He'd understand what I wasn't saying, now that he understood about Paumanok Harbor psi. "And it's causing a mental breakdown. I promised I'd help get her to the Harbor. Her train arrives Saturday morning."

"Oh, so I won't see you until then?" He sounded gratifyingly disappointed.

"Not until I get her settled, hopefully under Professor Harmon's wing." And not until the former Mrs. Matt Spenser slithered away.

"I'm sorry. I miss you. Oh, and I like blondes better than redheads. Ones with gold and pale yellow and dark honey streaks in their hair, so I can run my fingers through it and find all the colors."

I called Janie.

*   *   *

"You did what? Without me? Now you want me to do what? From three hours away?"

"How's your niece's baby, Elladaire?" I asked. Subtle was becoming my middle name. "You remember, the one I took care of after she ate a lightning bug and set her own house on fire?"

"That's low, even for you."

Yeah, but it worked. Janie consented to give advice, after the lecture.

"You can have an accident with your car. You can have an accident with scissors. You could even have an accident when you sneeze. But an accident with your hair color? No, that's stupidity, plain and simple. You don't take out your own appendix, do you? And you wouldn't take a pill without reading the expiration date or checking the dosage."

She came up with a possible rescue and recovery, from the drugstore. I knew Lou wouldn't let me leave, and in truth, I didn't want to go outside. Deni and her delivery boy loomed, of course, but so did strangers seeing the burning bush on my head. So I called the drugstore and paid twice the price to have blonde dye delivered. Janie said that would tone down the red and leave me a nice strawberry blonde, which she'd wanted to do for ages, but I always refused. And she'd save me an appointment for Saturday afternoon. "You and your new cousin. On the house."

The drugstore didn't carry any of the brands or colors Janie mentioned, so the telephone lady and I guessed. I gave her Mrs. Abbottini's apartment number, so Lou could answer the door. And I told him it was an item of feminine necessity to stop him from asking questions.

I called the professor while I waited for the package. At first he was disappointed I'd be delayed again. He'd been hoping I'd be there to communicate with the missing parrotfish through the ether the way I once had. I explained I'd be there Saturday, but that I needed to ask if a room at Rosehill could be prepared. I knew the old mansion had dozens, but I didn't know how far along the renovations had come. I needed one for my troubled cousin, I told him.

"Susan?" he rasped.

"No, a new, way-distant relation. My father discovered her and realized she belongs with you, before she draws too much of the wrong kind of publicity."

"I should think the young woman would do better staying with you, rather than with an old man. You could get acquainted. One can never have too much family."

Oh, no? Try mine.

"And Susan might enjoy having another relative."

Which meant another snakepit. Susan was younger, and had cancer last year. What if Carinne saw her future and it stank? Or worse, if she did not see any future at all? Connor Redstone had declared Susan cancer free now, but what about when she turned Carinne's age? I meant to keep the two of them as far apart as possible.

"Um, Susan is a lot younger. I doubt they have much in common."

"Well, think about it, my dear. We have a spot of difficulty here. With so many decisions to be made about construction and curriculum, Royce has sent a director, a young gentleman with definite opinions on how Rosehill should be utilized."

"He's not bothering you, is he?"

Jimmie had what was the former master bedroom suite, with its own balcony, hot tub, kitchenette, and elevator. If anyone tried to move the fine old gentleman to lesser quarters, he'd have me to answer to. Me and my connections to the big shots at Royce, i.e., Grant and his father, the Earl of Grantham.

"Oh, he would not dare. I'd simply call Royce."

I forgot. Dr. Harmon's connections were better than mine, with the current Duke of Royce a second cousin and a close friend.

"No, the young simpleton they sent does not like what he calls a party atmosphere, with my new friends calling at odd times. I think his knickers twisted when I did not invite him to the last poker night." He lowered his already whispery voice. "And I have my suspicions the nodcock had something to do with Oey's disappearance. Master Monteith does not believe pets have a place in an institute of learning."

"Does he have any idea how much we have already learned from the parrotfish?"

"He could not see Oey for what she or he is. Many cannot, you know."

Most could not. "Well, we'll see about that when I get there. But Carinne is coming as a talent in need of guidance, precisely the mission envisioned for Rosehill."

"Ah, yes, excellent argument. Perhaps you should mention that to Miss Lily. She is on better terms with the gudgeon than I."

But Cousin Lily definitely had a bit of the original Royce ability to tell truth from lies. No way could I explain Carinne to her. "I was hoping you could call her. It's awfully complicated here right now. In fact, someone is knocking on my door."

"I'll try, my dear. But I do feel your cousin would be happier at your house."

Sure, but would my mother be happy to have her? Had hell frozen over when I wasn't looking?

Chapter Thirteen

I had palpitations. And pink hair. The timing was right, the expiration date was years away, but the color I'd chosen was wrong. Dead wrong. Like the dead pinkish pigeon left in the back alley where Lou let me walk Little Red.

The bird had its head on, so maybe it wasn't Deni's handiwork. On the other hand, the left one still shaking, how many pinkish pigeons from someone's coop dropped dead on top of my building's dumpster?

My right hand had a death grip on Little Red, as if that could keep him safe from some maniac who butchered small creatures.

Lou said we didn't have enough people to keep watch twenty-four hours a day. He called for more agents. And tried to get me to leave town before Saturday again.

Van said the police simply couldn't exhaust their limited manpower on a dead pigeon and a decapitated rat, no matter how scary they were. Did I want him to spend the night? I said thanks, but Lou was enough if I never left the apartment. Which I wouldn't, no matter how much Red complained. Neither one of us could wait to get to Paumanok Harbor.

Janie said if I tried one more processing, my hair could turn to straw. Or it could all fall out.

Okay, I had pink hair. I'd get used to it, just like I had

a day and a half to get used to having a sister. Or a distant cousin, which is what I intended to call Carinne for as long as I could get away with it.

My mother called. "I don't believe what Lily told me for a second. The jackass never mentioned any missing branch of his family."

"Maybe he didn't know until recently. I'll find out more when she gets here Saturday."

"Find out if he's passing off one of his chippies as a Royce candidate. I don't want her in my house."

I felt bad for thinking the same when I spoke to my father. "He's not dating her and she's not staying at your house. She'll go to Rosehill, to be near people who can help her."

"Lily doesn't want any loose women at Rosehill either. And don't let her near your Matt to screw up that relationship, too."

Lily didn't want whatever my mother didn't want. They must speak to each other three times a day, usually competing over whose children showed less respect and filial devotion. Lily's daughter lived in New Jersey and seldom came to visit, but she had presented Lily with two grandchildren. My mother never let me forget that.

"Sorry, Mom, I'm writing now. You know how I hate to be interrupted while the creative juices are flowing well."

She sniffed. "I know when I'm being scammed. Do you?"

All I knew is my mother once got asked to train a standard poodle someone had dyed pink. She tried to have the dog taken away from the owners on a cruelty charge. I did not mention my current color. I did mention the stalkers. "But there is no need for you to come back to the Harbor sooner than you planned."

Not that she'd offered, thank God.

Susan called. "What have you done now?"

Why was it always my fault? "You're the one with all

the body piercings. If I wanted pink hair, that's no one's business but mine."

"Who's talking about pink hair?"

Oh.

Predictably, Grandma Eve called. I'd expected her lecture sooner. "How could you go off on tangents like this . . . this person when we need you to address the sand problem. And the skin condition."

I'd forgotten about that, except when Lou noted how my hair still matched my lip, which had faded some, along with the flaming red curls. I took that as a good sign the rash must be getting better. At least it wasn't worse, and I hadn't had a nosebleed recently. I told Grandma Eve.

"Better? How could it be better when the government sent some nosy female from the Centers for Disease Control in Atlanta to survey the entire town? There have been so many reports from so many different sources the CDC took notice."

"Can't you do something about it?"

"About what? The government, Ms. Garcia, or the rashes?"

Not even I thought my grandmother could keep the Feds out of Paumanok Harbor if they got a whiff of something weird, dangerous, or profitable. I figured they'd send someone else if this Garcia woman disappeared off the face of the Earth, or started croaking like a frog. That left the rashes. "Can you cure them?"

"No." She sounded bitter. Grandma Eve did not like to fail. I guess it ran in the family. "So what I and the council are trying to do is make sure everyone in town has a touch of it, especially the people who weren't onboard the *Nova Pride*."

"You mean ordinary citizens?"

"I mean we cannot afford to have the gifted residents singled out, or some snoop inquiring why so many of us were on that ship during a predicted hurricane. Or why we're the only ones to suffer with the epidemic."

"So you're giving innocent people a skin disease to protect the Harbor's secrets?"

"No one dies of the itch." She sniffed. That ran in my family, too. "Or would you have the place overrun with ghost hunters, UFO trackers, and paranormal fanatics? And more government acronyms than anyone can keep track of? Or maybe you'd like to be interrogated about your own recent activities? I'm sure some obscure congressional committee would be interested in trolls and night mares and sea gods."

Gulp. "So how do you give people the rash?"

"I am not poisoning anyone, if that's what you're thinking. We're merely exposing as many people as we can to your sand. We've had sand castle contests for the children, sand-candle making at the senior center, a beach clean up, on what beach there is."

"What's the epidemic lady think about that?

"That we're all crazy, what else? At least now, if she can trace the condition to the sand, it won't be just us."

"Um, I don't think you've thought this through enough. What if the government and Ms. Garcia decide the sand is the cause, so it's some kind of health hazard? They'll shut the beaches, for one. And truck away the sand, for another. There goes the tourist season next year, on either count. Worse, heaven knows what the Andanstans will do if someone spreads chemicals on the beach or carts off the top three feet of sand."

"That's irrelevant. No one new is getting hives or itches or any kind of dermatitis."

"I think it's tied to the blood and being at the scene of the tidal wave. I get the feeling the Andanstans are mad at us."

"But we didn't blow up any sandbars! The Coast Guard from Montauk did. Why aren't they getting suspicious rashes?"

"They didn't ask for help. We did."

"You did, you mean."

"Yes, to save all those lives, and then to get rid of the

tornado-tsunami. Which would have wiped out the whole village."

She cleared her throat, in acknowledgment of my necessary contribution, I suppose. "So what do you suggest we do?" she asked. "From your comfortable little nest miles away?"

"I'll be there Saturday, I swear. And I'll try to talk to them." Shit, now I had to talk to sand? "Or find Oey to talk for me."

"I'll make that squash soup you like so much."

Maybe she had a heart after all.

Matt called. How would I like to come to dinner Saturday night? He thought he'd take his former wife and me and my guest from the train station to dinner at the Breakaway.

I'd like that about as much as I'd like to have my hair fall out.

I told him I thought dinner among strangers, with a young wait staff, might be too much for Carinne for her first day in the Harbor. Besides, she was staying with the professor. Jimmie'd arrange something with Lily, for sure. And Grandma Eve was expecting me.

But the ex wanted to meet me.

With pink hair and a pink rash and a peculiar relative? I'm sure she would.

He'd told her all about me. "She sounded happy for both of us."

Then she was a better man than I, Gunga Din. "I hope you didn't tell her too much, like all the stuff no one is supposed to know."

"Of course not. I had to tell her about the shipwreck—she heard all about it in the news—to explain how I got Moses. Just your ordinary sea rescue, right?"

I knew I could trust him. And the secret council's threats to wipe out his memory.

"I miss you."

"Me, too."

"Soon."

"Uh, Marion's decided to stay another day. To avoid the weekend traffic."

I thought I could trust him. Now I wasn't so sure.

Mr. Rashmanjari called. Uh-oh again.

He merely wanted to reassure me that Nonna Maria had a good night, with no pain or problems, and they were all delighted to have her, except what should they do about church?

I told him to find a Mass on TV. I know Mrs. Abbottini tuned in sometimes when the roads were too icy or snowy. "Unless that offends you?"

It didn't, bless his tolerant heart.

Half an hour later, Antony Abbottini called, not quite as tolerant. "Those damned foreigners have brainwashed my mother. She won't come home with me."

Let's see. They waited on her hand and foot, showed her respect and affection, gave her the coveted front bedroom, and let her pray to whatever god she chose.

"Gee, Antony, I wouldn't take it personally. Your mother's at home here in the apartment. And they're taking such good care of her, making her feel important to them."

"She says the food is better than my wife's cooking and the children are better behaved."

Okay, he could take that personally. "It's just the pain meds talking. I bet she'll want to come visit when she feels better."

Or when Antony moved into a mansion with a guest house, servants, and a view.

The bright spot of the delay in leaving the city was that Deni did not call, come, or leave any more messages. Reinforcements did arrive from DUE, though, so I felt safer anyway.

I knew a couple of the agents from when they patrolled Paumanok Harbor. Kenneth was a precog; Colin had extraordinary eyesight and weapons skills. Together, they'd keep the whole block safe. Together, they made a great couple.

And they loved my hair. According to Kenneth, bright streaks and happy color hair weavings were all the rage. Maybe I'd take the fad a step farther.

Of course, Kenneth's hair stood up in magenta spikes. Colin had a blue Mohawk. They might be the best security a girl could want, but maybe they didn't have the best taste.

But I was in fashion. The second Rashmanjari daughter adored my hair, too, when I went to visit. She wished she could dye her hair like mine, but her father said he'd disown her. The next time I checked on Mrs. Abbottini, the girl had one long pink hair extension, the kind they handed out for breast cancer awareness month. It looked nice with her dark hair, slightly swarthy skin, and the pink sweatshirt she wore. I wanted to borrow the sweatshirt to match my hair. It had a hood.

Mrs. Abbottini clucked her tongue, shook her head, and went back to explaining the ground rule double to one of the younger boys.

Late Friday night a strange cell phone number showed up on my caller ID. Lou nodded for me to pick up; he was listening.

. . . To Carinne, weeping. She was on the train, in a tiny compartment with all her baggage, afraid to order supper because the server might be younger than her.

Her voice was low, tremulous, sad. I guess mine would be, too, leaving my home for who-knew-what.

"Is it okay for me to come? I know you'd do anything for Uncle Sam."

No, I wouldn't join the army— "Oh, you mean my father." No one called him anything but Tate, or Jackass, as long as I could remember. "Uh, our father."

"I'm so sorry," she said on a sob. "That's what I call him. Harry O'Dell was my father. I know Sam asked and you couldn't say no. But I don't want to come where I'm not wanted. My own mother asked me to leave. I was embarrassing her in front of her friends at the nursing home. I can't help it. I see things, and I have to say what I see, or the voices shout in my head until I think my skull will split with the pounding to get out."

"No, it's fine."

"But I don't have to come, Willow. Truly."

"You have other choices? Dad, ah, Sam didn't mention any."

"I can get off the train in Washington, DC. I have some money. I can get a room, maybe look for a job."

While she acted crazy? What kind of job could she get without references? That plan sounded like one of my nightmares: being lost in a strange city, money running out, no friends, no family, no job. And aberrations.

Her voice grew thready, scared. "I can stay inside."

"Forever?" She couldn't even go to the dinner car on the train. "No, this is the place for you. Not this place, Manhattan, but Paumanok Harbor. You'll see. And maybe you won't hear all the voices or the warnings. Some scumbag tried to hypnotize a bunch of espers last month to take over the town. It wouldn't work."

"Really?" Hope blossomed in the word. "Why?"

"No one is sure. Maybe protection comes with the talent. But you can't count on it. A psychic diagnostician could read my cousin's health, the mayor can wipe out memories in ordinary citizens and psychics both, and the truth-seers aren't stopped by anything or anybody. Remember that."

"Yes, Un—Sam warned me. But you might be immune to me?"

"We can keep our fingers crossed. But, if not, we've got a precog coming to Paumanok Harbor with us. He'll help. And Professor Harmon knows everything about talent and training." Unless the elderly gentleman had forgotten.

"Do you think they can get rid of the voices?"

"I don't know." I was pretty sure Lou could, if he saw Carinne as a threat. I decided instantly that I'd protect her from him, no matter what. The foretelling was part of her. No one had the right to wipe away her talent, and what made her special. "But it doesn't matter. We need you here. We need all the psychics we can get to help solve bigger problems, like saving the entire village. I'll explain on the ride home."

"You're sure?"

"I'm positive. I want you on my side."

CHAPTER FOURTEEN

I had a half sister. And a hat.
 I still intended to keep her connection to me and
my father private, or as private as anything could be in
Paumanok Harbor where people had eidetic memories,
built-in lie detectors, pride in their ancestry, and eyes to
see for themselves. To myself, though, Carinne was family.

Maybe I had a strong sense of kinship and loyalty because of my parents' split. A shrink could explain it better, if I ever went again. The last one cost a lot of time
and money, and we both still thought I was crazy.

I knew there was a lot of my mother in me, wanting to
rescue needy creatures. Maybe I was a glutton for pun-
ishment, like the way I'd adopted Little Red. The Pomeranian was a royal pain in the ass, snippy and snarly
and decidedly unconcerned with notions of loyalty, obedience, or housebreaking. But he was mine, and I'd protect him from harm or Deni or going back to the pound,
unloved and unwanted.

Just so Carinne. Maybe she wasn't a lost dog that'd
been abused and abandoned. Maybe she represented a
horrid mistake in my father's past, a humiliating episode
in my mother's future, but right now Carinne needed
me. Dad was right about the gossip and backbiting and
general unpleasantness facing her. Who else amid the
close-knit community would stand by her but her sister?

So I put on a Yankees cap over my pink hair and went to meet her train.

The good thing about having death threats, if there was a good thing, was the ease of accomplishing stuff a person on her own could not do without a retinue of big, tough, armed bodyguards. Like having Colin go find a parking spot while Kenneth the precog and Lou walked beside me, ready to nab evil-doers or carry Carinne's luggage. Harris got to stay outside with Little Red in the other car, both of them on the alert for suspicious characters.

Ken wanted to know which train car Ms. O'Dell was on. Or how we'd recognize her when she got off.

"Trust me, we'll know."

She had a Florida Marlins cap over red hair, but she looked like me, a little taller, a little thinner, but enough that Kenneth let out a gasp.

Lou gave me a dirty look for not warning him, then said, "The shit's going to hit the fan for sure, now."

That's how you recognize a half sister.

We'd be almost identical, except she had red hair where I had pink. I guess we thought alike, too, because I fingered my Easter-eggy hair and said, "I thought you were blonde. I thought it best if we didn't appear so obviously related."

Carinne touched her red curls and said, "You're blonde in all the pictures Un— Sam Tate had of you. I thought we should look less like sisters."

Then we laughed, as she pulled a wig off her head to reveal my usual sandy blonde hair. And we hugged, right in the middle of hurrying passengers towing their luggage. Kenneth and Lou formed a barrier around us. Hell, Lou could have kept people away with one of his glowers.

We embraced awkwardly at first, not knowing if it could be misconstrued or bring insult if we didn't. No etiquette books covered this situation.

Then she started to cry. "I saw your future, when you're my age, thirty-seven."

Lou frowned harder, if possible. "Ladies, can we take this out to the cars, in private?"

"No," we both shouted, Carinne through her tears. "I saw you."

"And it's so horrible?" I felt like crying, too. "Was I dead? Decapitated like the rat?"

Kenneth handed her a tissue so she blew her nose. "What rat?"

"What future?" I demanded. "What's so bad that you saw it and cried?"

"I saw it, that's what. You were wrong, that your talent protected you. It's not what I saw, but that I hoped the future thing wouldn't work around you. It does. For him, too."

She pointed at Kenneth, who had to be in his late twenties, and said, "When you are thirty-seven like me, you'll be in charge of ten other agents, in an underground office. And you're wearing a wedding ring."

Kenneth grinned. "I can't wait to tell Colin. We've been looking forward to it being legal. And my own squad, huh? And an office at HQ, besides. That's great."

I wanted to strangle both of them. "What about me? What did you see?"

She wiped her eyes. "Oh, you're reading a picture book. With your name on the cover. You're reading it to a baby."

"You know, I always wanted to write a children's book. Maybe after people see my illustrations for the professor's book, they'll pay me to do one." I felt a nice glow at the idea.

"What about the baby?" Lou wanted to know. "Her grandmother is anxious."

"I have no idea if it's Willow's baby or not, but she loves it. I can tell from her smile."

I was more excited about the book. It'd be about Little Red and his sad life until he came to Paumanok Harbor and—

"All this luggage belongs to you?" Lou said with a growl.

Carinne started weeping again.

"Ignore him," I said. "He's always grouchy."

"He's scary," she whispered, close to my ear.

"Yeah, but he'll lay down his life for us. Or maybe he'll lay down my life."

She went white.

"Just kidding." I hoped. "For now, he'll keep us safe. And we have two cars, so all your stuff will fit."

"I didn't know what to bring for northern weather, so I brought most of my clothes."

She had a nice southern drawl. Not a y'all accent, but softer, slower than New Yorkese. "That's fine," I told her. "The weather changes every hour at this time of year. But what's in the carry case?" I had a bad feeling about the familiar-looking bag at her feet.

"It's my cat. I couldn't leave her behind, could I?"

Oh, lord, a cat. With that new director at Royce-Rosehill already on the warpath about the parrot, and Matt's dog coming to stay sometimes, and me and Little Red visiting, he'd have a cat fit. Literally.

We'd face that later. First, we had to get Carinne and her bags out of the train station. Kenneth located a red-cap, or whatever you called a train porter these days. He got everything onto a rolling cart and asked where we were headed. Lou spoke into a hidden mike to alert Colin and Harris, then led us in the right direction in that vast warren. We tried to cordon Carinne off from families with children, teenagers with earbuds, and young executives in a rush. The baggage cart piled high helped some, and Kenneth and I at either side blocked her view more. We could still hear her mutter "school teacher, dentist, shop clerk, prisoner, janitor. Oh, no, don't keep smoking. Please." And she started to cry again.

No wonder she was having a breakdown. So I talked to distract her, telling about Deni and Paumanok Harbor and Little Red, who did not like cats any more than he liked dogs. Or strangers. Oh, boy.

Outside, she told Colin he'd have a wedding band to match Kenneth's, but Harris would be in a jungle, chasing rumors of a creature that was supposed to be half man, half jaguar. They were both happy.

We loaded the cars, while Lou grumbled because I'd brought a lot of suitcases too, besides my computer and reference books and art supplies. I didn't know how long I'd be staying, or if I needed fancy clothes if Matt and I went out, after his ex left. Little Red had his carrying case, of course, and another tote bag filled with his food, toys, bowls, leashes, and a new sweater I bought him, for when it got cooler.

Each of the men had a duffel bag, plus computers and electronic gear. They had two large metal boxes, presumably for weapons, and a larger cooler, hopefully for food, because I'd eaten all my traveling snacks days ago. Both cars got crowded. Carinne and I sat in the back seat of the Beemer, Red trembling on my lap because of all the commotion, the cat yowling in its carrier on Carinne's lap because it wanted to get out. Or to get at Little Red.

Kenneth drove; Lou rode shotgun, or light saber. One never knew about him. Colin and Harris followed in a big white Jeep. Lou murmured to them and his headquarters constantly through his walkie-talkie and cell, running license plates on any car that got too close, having the guys behind us check on any drivers who seemed suspicious.

While he was busy, and to get my mind off the seemingly endless Midtown Tunnel—with water pressing down on it—I asked Kenneth to describe his precog ability to Carinne, to help her get a handle on her own.

"Please. I've never spoken to another psychic except, um, Sam Tate. I didn't really believe in such things until he explained my own ESP to me."

Ken told us that he only saw danger, like my father, but his was immediate, not miles or days away, and not necessarily focused on himself or people he loved. He called it a soldier's sixth sense, a survival instinct, only more so. His sensations of imminent peril weren't ambiguous like Dad's doom-saying, just not pinpoint specific. He didn't get mental signals of which weapon or what assailant, but when he got the feeling, he knew what direction it came from. That's why he and Colin made such good partners. He pointed, Colin aimed.

Ken explained how he'd learned not to yell "Danger, everyone down." Like shouting "fire" in a movie theater, it just caused panic, with no one listening. The innocent bystanders were more liable to trample each other getting away. Besides, he needed a moment to figure out if the menace were coming from the air, the street, the very ground. His para-intuition encompassed earthquakes, fires, venomous snakes, drunk drivers, runaway autos, and bad guys with evil intentions. So far.

Right now he was relaxed, or as relaxed as anyone could be driving on the Long Island Expressway with four eastbound lanes of cars going eighty and trucks as long as a house. "The trick is to stay calm," he told Carinne. "And not give people more information than they need."

She nodded, and I could see her trying to figure out how to apply his advice to her situation. "So I don't have to tell some teenager pumping gas that he'll be dead before he reaches thirty-seven? Just that he should take better care of himself and stay away from drugs?"

"He won't listen. But maybe that'll shut up the clamor in your head."

I asked about that. Were the voices in English? Sometimes, she said. Were they gibberish? Sometimes, too. With pictures? She saw the people at her age, but nothing afterward. And the sight, how close did she have to be?

"Close enough to see their eyes. I don't need to look into them, just be that near. Like that little boy in the car seat in the SUV beside us. He'll be a Japanese scholar. Maybe Chinese. I can't tell what language he is translating, but a lot of books are on the shelf behind him, all with the same author, him."

I looked over. The kid kept banging a plastic truck on the back of his father's seat. He'd be lucky to reach seven, much less thirty-seven.

"So you look at someone younger than you and see them at your age, with enough detail for you to guess what they're doing?"

"It's no guess. I'm a hundred percent certain, and don't ask, because I have no idea how."

"Okay, but where do the voices come in?"

"When there's no future, or a terrible one. I don't want to see the picture. I don't want to tell some young soldier he'll be grievously injured in Afghanistan and spend the rest of his life in a wheelchair. So I try to ignore it. That's when the shouting in my head starts, as if the bad news wants to get out, wants to yell at him to be careful, wants me to use what I've been given. I have to try to change his future, try with all my might to get him to watch out for bombs, to shoot himself in the foot before he is blown up. If I don't try, the noise gets worse. If I do try, people want to lock me away. I don't know if I can ever alter a person's future, only see it, then hear the noise in my skull."

We were all quiet. What do you say to someone carrying such a heavy burden? Little Red moved over to lick her hand. Kenneth offered her another tissue.

CHAPTER FIFTEEN

I had an idea. And a new itch.

Carinne's cat had fleas. Everything in Florida does, she said. She couldn't go to the local pet store for a new batch of flea and tick killer drops, because the store only hired kids to work, for cheap. And the security guards at all the malls had her name and photo on their lists of undesirables. One more incident and she'd be sent to the psych ward.

Maybe we could pass the cat around to the non-talents, I suggested, half in jest, and confuse Ms. Garcia of the CDC. That got vetoed when Lou started itching and cursing that his entire car would have to be fumigated. I worried he'd toss the cat out of it, but I didn't mention that to Carinne, who had enough worries.

Thinking about her difficulties, I wondered why Lou hadn't offered to fix Carinne's problem. I know he could wipe out an esper's talent because he'd threatened the evil hypnotist, the last villain to jeopardize the safety of Paumanok Harbor. I did not know how it worked, or the cost in collateral damage, but I thought Carrine might consider a cure at any price; she was that desperate to reclaim her life. Lou did not suggest any such drastic solution. He got busy finding the nearest pet store on his GPS.

I figured he wanted Carinne to be studied, surveyed,

and scrutinized to see if her talent could be used for the good of Royce and Paumanok Harbor before he wiped out part of her mind. I'd warn her later, when we were alone. Lou wouldn't like it, but my sympathies lay with my half sister, not my wholly scary bodyguard. Any messing with her head had to be her choice, not Lou's.

We got the drops on the cat with only a few scratches. Of the car's leather seats. The cat should have shriveled up from the glare Lou sent its way.

We also got more anti-itch creams and slices of pizza and soda. I walked Little Red, Lou vacuumed out the car at the nearby gas station, and Carinne sat on a bench outside the strip mall, cat carrier at her feet. Colin and Kenneth and Harris formed a circle around her, so she didn't have to see any of the other shoppers. She smiled at the guys and I could see them melting, the big, muscled DUE agents. They were on her side. I relaxed a little and told her about my idea.

First, I scrounged through my pocketbook for the small sketch pad and pencil I always carried. I handed them to Carinne. "My idea mightn't work, and someone at Rosehill will have a better plan, but maybe if you draw what you see, instead of having to say it, the clamor in your head would die down."

Colin agreed. "She's the Visualizer. It's worth a try."

"But I don't have a drop of your talent, Willow. I couldn't make an accurate picture of what I see, especially not the horrible scenes."

"That doesn't matter. You only have to make it real and recognizable to you. Use stick figures if you want, just so you get the bad stuff out of your mind without distressing the poor person in trouble, or causing yourself more harm."

Lou came back and nodded. "It'll be a good way to research, too. We can get names from the license plates, and see what comes of your prognostications. Not that I'm doubting you, just that we should have records." He looked around, spotted a gym.

"Let's sit on the bench over there. There's bound to be some thirty-something coming out and getting into a car. Any older and it won't work, if I understand your gift right. Any younger and it'll take too long to verify."

I protested: "For Pete's sake, Lou. Carinne's not a gypsy fortune-teller in a circus tent! Don't ask her to perform, especially if it can upset her. We can experiment with the sketches at Rosehill, where Dr. Harmon can help, or maybe we can get Doc Lassiter to come with his mental soothing skills. Or even Grandma Eve's rescue remedy teas. Just not in public, where people will freak out if she shouts their futures."

"No, Willow. It's fine. I want to try the drawing thing. I never thought of that. And yes, you should have proof of what happens. Otherwise I'm just a delusional psychotic. Why should you believe me?"

I took another sip of my Diet Coke and fed Little Red the last scrap of pizza crust I'd saved for him. "Because Sam Tate said you had talent. And he wouldn't have sent you to Paumanok Harbor where a lie could be detected before you could learn to spell the village name. And because we've seen weirder magic than yours could ever be. Magic, not insanity."

No one came out of the gym. Carinne doodled on the pad. "People always think I'm crazy. When I was ten and saw a younger kid who was going to break his arm in two years, I tried to warn him. I went from Carinne O'Dell to crackpot in the dell, to Ding-dong Dell to plain Dingaling. It got worse all through school, until I went away to college. The first year was great. Almost everyone was older than me. The second year, not so much. I tried to keep away from all the incoming freshmen, but most were healthy, so I did okay. I saw a few overdoses, a couple of drunk driving accidents. Not enough to cause me major issues. And I kept my head down, buried in my books, so I didn't have to see their eyes. The headaches started as I got older and so many more people were younger. Then the voices got louder."

"So why in the world did you decide to become a school guidance counselor?"

She set the pad aside on the bench and knelt to check on the cat, reaching in to stroke it and whisper that Puss'd be out of the carrier soon. "All I'd ever wanted to do was help children. I thought I could do it with my wacky intuitions. I didn't know how bad the headaches and voices could get."

"You had great intentions. And Dad said you did help a lot of students. That's a good thing."

Three people walked out of the gym, two women and a man in spandex and jogging suits. They all looked about my age, and they looked right at us before heading for three different cars. Carinne closed her eyes and started reciting, as if she were giving the make and models of the vehicles. "A wife, a bank teller and uh-oh. Him."

"What about him? What's going to happen to him?"

She scrunched her face up, obviously in pain.

"No!" I yelled, shoving the pad into her hands. "Draw it!"

She started sketching, pressing so hard she broke off the point on the pencil. I tossed her another one. Lou dictated notes into his Blackberry while she concentrated on the scribbled picture taking shape.

We all looked at what she'd drawn. All three people, recognizable by their hair and the man's mustache. But the guy was in bed with the bank teller, and the housewife had a gun in her hand.

"He's dead."

Colin whistled. Harris handed all three license plate numbers to Kenneth, who called them in somewhere. As the information came through, Lou wrote names and addresses and birthdays on the sketch, then added today's date and his own initials.

Carinne asked why.

"Maybe we can change the future after all. If we find them, and figure out the date you saw, maybe we can head the wife off, or the girlfriend. Or take the gun away. Anything that changes the components."

Carinne looked at him as if he'd handed her the moon. "You really think we can save his life?"

"Not by warning him to keep his zipper closed. But hell, we can try to get him transferred to another state."

"He'll still be a sleazy philanderer," I said. "He'll still cheat on his wife." I tried not to look at Carinne when I said it, thinking of my father. Her father.

Lou didn't notice. "Yeah, but he might live to tomcat past his thirty-seventh birthday. I'm not condoning cheating, but don't forget the bank teller isn't pure as snow either. She had to know he's married. And the wife could have gone to a lawyer instead of a gun dealer. No one's without fault here, but maybe we can keep it from turning tragic. Carinne, did you see the wife in jail when she's thirty-seven?"

"No, just at home, making beds."

"So maybe we do stop it. Or maybe she's out on bail. But now we have a yardstick for what we can try to do, what you can do. Just think what good we can put your gift to if this works."

"Wait a second," I said. "You can't drag Carinne around like a counting pig or something, telling futures for you to change. Maybe she doesn't want to be a celebrity seer. And think how much publicity you'll stir up for Paumanok Harbor or DUE."

Colin laughed. "You think we'd give Carinne's name to anyone? Or let the police or Feebies work these cases? On what? Suspicion of a crime taking place two years in the future or something? Give us a little credit, Willow. We've kept DUE and Paumanok Harbor secret for over two hundred years."

True. "But you'll give her migraines, or worse."

Lou stooped down to look at Carinne, on the bench. "Are any voices shouting at you now?"

Carinne took the sketch back from Lou and stared at it. As bad as it was, the drawing still made her wince. "No, I have a slight headache, that's all. Maybe Willow's idea of drawing what I see will be enough. And, Willow, I'd be looking at the futures anyway. What's the difference if I send the information where it can do some good? Besides, we don't even know if the future can be changed. I mean, if it's not like this"—she tapped the drawing—"why did I see it?"

Now I was getting a headache. But my idea worked. She wasn't screaming or carrying on. I clapped my hands. Little Red bit my ankle. "Let's not worry about the 'whys' now. Or what we can do about drug ODs and wars when you see them, or those kids you want to help. But it's a start that you're not raving or in agony after what you just predicted. The drawing worked."

She studied the pencil in her hand as if it were some magical device. Then she studied the three men and me. "Maybe I'm better because you've all been so supportive, surrounding me with good feelings, instead of the usual fear and horror at my rantings. You won't be around me all the time."

"But the pencil can be. That's the joy of something so simple. Heck, we can hang one on a ribbon around your neck and sew pockets on all your clothes for a pad. Give it a chance, Carinne. Maybe it'll help."

Lou shrugged. "It can't hurt. And we can try to change the pictures. What's your birthday, kiddo? Maybe you're looking at people when they're exactly your age, like thirty-seven and three months and two days. Maybe even down to the minute you were born. That will make our job a lot easier."

He wrote down her birthday and the hospital where she was born, so he could check the time of day.

Harris brought him a plastic bag to keep the drawing safe.

We got back on the road with an hour to go and a lot to think about.

Little Red belched.

"If that dog pukes in my car, you're walking home."

Sure, Lou had Carinne now. He didn't need me.

CHAPTER SIXTEEN

I had introductions to make. And injustices to make
right.

We decided to stop at my house first to leave Little
Red there, so I warned Carinne about my cousin Susan,
who was about ten years younger than our new relative.
I explained how she'd been sick, but was declared
cancer-free by her doctors and Connor Redstone. Which
did not mean something dire couldn't happen to her before her thirty-seventh birthday.

"She's the baby of the family and everyone dotes on
her, so please, please, do not tell us her future if it's sad
or ugly. Draw it and throw it away, swallow it, burn it,
anything."

Carinne took a death grip on the pencil, her eyebrows
tight together as we drove up the dirt road toward Garland Farms.

Susan had already left for work at the restaurant,
thank goodness. She'd taken my mother's old white Outback, which meant I'd need a ride home later, adding to
the complications.

I did not invite Carinne into my mother's house. That
felt disloyal to me. The invitation had to come from
Mom. Besides, that poor cat had been kept caged for so
long, it had stopped meowing and just moaned occa-
sionally. I tried not to look at Carinne's face at the lack

of hospitality. I'm sure she needed a bathroom as much as I did, so I didn't use one either. Fair is fair.

I greeted Mom's senior rescue dogs that had been left in Susan's care, gave them and Red dog biscuits, and got back in Lou's car to drive to Rosehill. I still had trouble thinking of it as Royce now, but that's what it was, an enclave of the extrasensory, and where Carinne belonged.

Lou called ahead to alert Lily, my mother's cousin and housekeeper there. We bypassed the downtown streets of Paumanok Harbor village and drove around to the long private driveway up to the old estate. Carinne was speechless at the sight of the huge mansion on acres of grounds, now turning into a study center and research facility. We could see the construction vans and piles of lumber. The workers must have gone home for the day.

"Are you sure I should be here? I mean, it's so luxurious. I thought the facility would be like a private school or something small and rustic, in a quiet little village. Maybe rooms in someone's house."

"The village is quiet, all right. It's almost dead in winter. And this *was* someone's house. Then it got rented out to movie moguls and such. If Royce hadn't purchased it, the whole huge plot of land might have been divided up for mini-mansions and no one could have appreciated its views and grandeur."

"It's grand, all right," Kenneth said. "Wait till you see the gardens and the pools and tennis courts."

Wait till you see Cousin Lily, I thought, dreading the moment.

Lou directed Kenneth to drive around back to the service entrance and the rear doors that led to the kitchens and Lily's own apartment. Maybe he wanted to shelter Carinne from the intimidating formal entry, which could hold my entire Manhattan apartment. Maybe he wanted to avoid Monteith, the newly appointed director, a grim despot, according to everyone who'd met the new Brit overseer.

I held the back door open for Carinne, who clutched
the cat carrier in front of her like a shield.

"What are you dragging home now, Willy?" Lily
started. Then she saw me, behind Carinne. Her head
swiveled from one of us to the other.

"Oh. My. God. Your mother was right after all. Tate
cheated on her."

"No, he did not," I snapped. "Carinne was conceived
before they were married. And we will not discuss this,
not in front of Carinne or the people from DUE, and
definitely not with my mother. Do you hear me? There
is no reason to upset her before she arrives. And no reason to make Carinne feel unwelcome."

Cousin Lily's official title was housekeeper, with a
large staff of cooks, maids, and handymen—the grounds-
keeper had his own crew—but she looked on herself as
hostess of the place. As such, she would never be rude to
a guest. I hoped.

She bit her lip, but gestured to the platters of sandwiches she'd prepared, the pitchers of iced tea and cider.
Kenneth snagged a half sandwich and a napkin before
going back out to help sort the luggage. He and Colin
were to have the same rooms at the gatehouse they'd had
when we chased down a kidnapper. Lou would stay at
Grandma Eve's, as usual, and Harris got assigned to me.

"I don't need a bodyguard," I tried to tell Lou, who
had filled a plate and sat at the table. "Not with you right
down the street at the farmhouse."

"Yeah, but I need a man to listen to the phone, check
the security, watch out for stalkers. You get Harris." No
discussion. No arguments.

I tried anyway. "It'll be crowded when Mom gets back."

"We'll have the perps behind bars before then."

I started to lead Carinne to the nearest bathroom, an
elegant affair toward the front of the house, but the professor stepped out of what had been the servants' elevator, right into the large kitchen area. He looked pale and
thinner, but his eyes lit up when he saw me. Or Carinne.

"Ah, Willow, my dear. At last. You must do something

about finding poor Oey. Then we can speak about the Andanstans."

I cleared my throat, behind Carinne.

He adjusted his glasses. "Ah, what a lovely surprise. You must be our new guest, Miss O'Dell. Charmed to meet you."

Carinne didn't seem to know whether to curtsy or offer her hand. I kissed the old dear's cheek and said, "I am happy to see you, too."

He patted my shoulder, peered at my pink hair without commenting, then turned back to Carinne. "I hope you do not mind, but I have hired you on as my assistant. That's to satisfy our resident cabbagehead, Monteith, who wanted to house you in the students' dormitories in the attics. I work odd hours, so you'll have a room next to mine, with your own bath, of course, but sharing my balcony and the hot tub. There will be a small monthly stipend, with room and board included. Is that agreeable to you, my dear?"

"I never expected . . . That is, how can I ever repay . . . I have a cat," she babbled, overcome.

"Excellent. I adore cats. Please call me Jimmie. Oh, do you play chess?"

"Yes, but I may be rusty. My father was state collegiate chess champion in Florida, and I managed to defeat him several times before he passed on."

"Better and better. Come, we'll show your furry friend its new residence and allow you to refresh yourself. Then we can return for Miss Lily's excellent tea."

But I needed to talk to him. And I needed a bathroom, too, and some of Lily's oatmeal cookies. "You'll be happy to know we might have solved some of Carinne's problems already. She can explain later."

"Excellent. I cannot wait to hear about it." Professor Harmon smiled at her, then at me. "I am so glad you brought Miss O'Dell to us."

"Well, I am not," came from a newcomer striding down the hall. "Especially if that is an animal in that carrier case."

"Milo Monteith," my old friend said on a sigh, before making the formal introductions.

Monteith was tall and lanky and needed to have his brown curls trimmed and styled. He obviously hadn't been eating Lily's cooking for long, or been introduced to Janie at the hair salon or Vincent the barber. Perhaps the gardener had cut his hair last. He did have nice blue eyes, except for the cold glare in them. Worst of all, he wore a suit.

Nothing marked a man as an alien to Paumanok Harbor, an outsider, more than a suit. No one around here ever wore them except lawyers and undertakers. Even Mr. Whitside at the bank stuck to a bow tie and a vest.

On one memorable occasion, when a local fisherman died, his friends and prospective pallbearers discovered they had one jacket between them. They gave it to the dead guy to wear.

Monteith's suit did not even fit properly, with the coat lopsided and the pockets baggy. I was not impressed.

Carinne stepped closer to me.

Monteith crossed his arms over his chest, barring the elevator. "We do not permit animals. Not for the ancient mariner"—he jerked his head toward the professor—"and not for a person with no credentials or documented history."

Carinne gave me a beseeching look. We both knew the cat wouldn't be happy at my house, and Carinne wouldn't be happy without the cat. Saggy suit and stiff posture aside, Monteith annoyed me. Pick on Jimmie, intimidate my sister? I'd had a bad enough day and I needed to pee. So I crossed my arms over my own chest and let him have a piece of my mind, one of the few I could spare. "What's with the royal we, Monteith, eh? Who made you commandant of this outpost?"

"The directors at—"

I didn't let him finish. "The directors at Royce wanted this place to serve and protect the uniquely gifted and talented. Well, Carinne O'Dell is both. In fact, Lou is thinking this very minute of how her skills can save lives."

"Not this minute," Lou grumbled from across the room. "Right now I'm eating Miss Lily's amazing rice pudding."

I ignored him, after checking to see he'd left some oatmeal cookies. "Have you met Lou? Heard his reputation? You wouldn't want to mess with him, trust me."

The ruthless DUE agent spooned more pudding into his mouth, then grinned. "You tell him, Willy."

"And trying to deny Dr. Harmon an assistant? Do you know how valuable his work is? Priceless, that's what. The whole village would be underwater if not for him."

The professor blushed.

"If he wants to keep a parrot or a . . . pet goldfish, that's his business. And I'll bet the powers that be at Royce care more for his contentment than they do for yours."

"Please, Willow, don't yell at Mr. Monteith," Carinne pleaded. "He's only doing his job."

"No, his job is to meet our needs. We need you, you need the cat." I turned back to Monteith. "She has no other family nearby." Lily and Lou, Harris, Colin, and Kenneth all cleared their throats or coughed or clattered their silverware. "The cat stays. Do you understand?"

Carinne promised the cat would never leave her room. "And she won't hurt anything either. She's fastidious about her litter box, and I change it twice a day. I wouldn't expect anyone to clean up after me," she told Lily, "and I'd be happy to help in the kitchen or whatever else you need."

Lily smiled at her and dished out another serving of pudding. "I'll save it from the ravening hordes for after you get settled."

Monteith fumbled in his baggy jacket pocket and took out a heavy silver yo-yo that had ball bearings spinning on the outside. No wonder his clothes did not fall right. A freaking yo-yo. That made me angrier than ever. "See? She's willing to do anything. What are you willing to do except make people miserable? From what I hear, that's your only talent, aside from crunching numbers. And now you're playing with a toy?"

"It soothes me. So I don't lose my temper, like an intemperate, spoiled child."

"Who are you calling an intemperate, spoiled child?"

Carinne touched my shoulder and whispered in my ear: "Willow, his yo-yo has no string."

"Of course it has a string. It wouldn't come back and circle and land on his finger and . . ." Bloody hell, the yo-yo had no string. Nor did the other one he took out of another pocket and had spinning and doing tricks in perfect unison with the first.

"Okay, you're a wizard. But that doesn't give you the right to run ragged over everyone else. You are supposed to be furthering the cause, discovering and developing unknown talents. Protecting them, encouraging them, using them to benefit people everywhere."

"Hear, hear," Dr. Harmon said, bringing me a glass of cider and a cookie. "I did not want to throw my own weight around, but you have put the blighter in his place nicely. Too bad Monte's my godson."

"Your godson?"

"I'm not proud of it either," Monteith said, making one yo-yo whiz around his head, the other around his shoulders. "And yes, one of my duties is to see the old codger is safe and not jauntering off to face down monsters by himself, or following some otherworld avian into the unknown."

"You should have told me," I said to Jimmie.

He shrugged his narrow shoulders. "You didn't tell me about Miss O'Dell, did you?"

Hmpph. "That's not the point. He has to treat you better. And Carinne, too."

Monteith replied to that: "I should think it might be a great deal easier than dealing with you. Miss O'Dell appears quite agreeable, except for the cat."

Carinne stared at her toes, bright color in her cheeks. "Willow's had a hard day. She's really very kind."

The blasted yo-yos rolled up his arm, across his neck and down the other side. If he was trying to distract me, it was working.

"And Carinne's had a hard time, too. But not as hard as you'll have if you keep picking on senior citizens and women in awkward circumstances. She's been picked on all her life and it stops now, this instant. Her own mother did not understand. We do. She is one of us. You treat her like the treasure she is or . . . or I'll sic Lou on you."

Lou was pushing me out the door. "You've done enough for now. Carinne will do fine, won't you, kiddo?"

Carinne nodded and smiled at him, and at Monteith.

"Monte and Lily and Jimmie will take good care of her," Lou told me. "And her cat. You'll see her in the morning. Right now your grandmother is waiting for us. She and I are headed for dinner on Shelter Island. She wants to ask Doc Lassiter to come back and work with Carinne."

But I was supposed to have supper with my grandmother. Squash soup and cornbread and apple pie on her hand-thrown pottery dishes.

Instead she handed me a recycled plastic ice cream tub on her way out the door.

"Two minutes in the microwave. Even someone dumb enough to dye her hair pink should be able to get that right."

CHAPTER SEVENTEEN

I had Harris, and a heavy heart.

I got the idea he'd rather be at Rosehill with everyone else and Lily's cooking. So would I.

He stayed polite, but aloof and efficient, setting perimeter alarms and listening devices and security cameras. I made up the bed in the guest room. We both figured he was wasting his time and DUE's money. Deni'd never know where I'd gone, so I was safe. Except from my own insecurities.

He made test runs. I made phone calls.

The first was to Susan, warning her of the alarms.

"Won't the deer set them off?"

"I tried to tell him how many creatures ramble through the backyard every night. He says his technical gadgets are advanced way past that. Infrared, sonic, electromagnetic, body temperature."

"Is he hot?"

"No, I haven't turned the heat up yet. Oh. He's good-looking, I guess, in a rugged military way. You know the type, all muscle and perfect posture, ready for action. He's nice, but he doesn't smile much."

"Bet I can make him smile."

Just what I needed, Susan coming on to the bodyguard.

"Yes, I'll bring home the leftover brownies."

That was better. "But don't get cozy with him. Carinne says he'll be off chasing aliens across the globe, like Grant."

"I don't believe all that crap. Word is she looks like you."

Lou must have given Grandma Eve advance warning. Now every person in Paumanok Harbor knew.

"I guess so."

"You guess? They say Cousin Lily mistook her for you. Is it true?"

"I suppose."

"I've got to see this for myself. Why don't you bring her and the hunk over for dinner? We're pretty full, but I'll save you a table."

"No, I'm exhausted. And Carinne's at Rosehill with Lily and the professor. Grandma Eve gave us some squash soup for supper." Nothing else. The restaurant sounded good, except that Matt was going to be there, with his ex. "Maybe tomorrow."

Maybe never, if I could keep Susan and Carinne apart.

Speaking of Matt, I decided to call him before he left for dinner. Just to tell him I'd arrived safely, of course. I asked if he could go to the beach with me tomorrow morning to look for Andanstans. It was too late today, with the sun setting so early, but I wanted his opinion. And the reassurance of his company.

He couldn't go with me. He'd promised to show Marion around the Hamptons on his day off. She was in the shower, but he knew she'd be happy for me to come along.

No, I did not wish to go sightseeing and shopping with them. I'd spent most of my summers out here, seen it all, and still couldn't afford the Hamptons prices.

"Oh, and I have pink hair."

"Bubble gum pink," Harris called out when he came into the room with a tool box in his hand.

"Who the hell is that?"

"Harris, a kind of bodyguard."

"Another one? Does he have his clothes on?"

"Of course he does. Does your ex-wife?"

The call ended, abruptly. Harris disappeared, wisely. He didn't like squash soup, but he'd eaten enough of Lily's sandwiches to hold him. And he had the cooler in the car for later.

He didn't offer to share.

My father wanted to know if Carinne arrived safely, if people were being mean to her. Did she have a decent place to stay and what about her pet? The cat meant a lot to her.

I assured him she was fine, the cat was fine. The professor adored her, and Lily had started fattening her up. Even Milo Monteith showed an unexpected gentler side. Carinne seemed to bring that out in people.

"And we may have found a remedy, if not a cure, for her headaches and brainstorms." I explained my suggestion about the drawing.

"I knew sending her north was a good idea."

Yeah, sending her was his idea. Putting the voices in her head on paper was mine. He didn't mention that.

"Tell her to call me tomorrow. I'll be home after tennis."

"Tennis? What about your blood pressure? You know, the reason you could not bring her here yourself."

"You're sounding like your mother."

Yikes.

"The important thing is that Carinne is safe."

"But what about me, Dad?"

"Oh, you can take care of yourself. Except for the damned Irish tenor on his mustang. I just worry Carinne might backslide into depression or go bonkers from the stress. You'll look after her, right?"

Right, Dad. Better than you did.

"And you'll watch her back?"

Carinne had Colin and Kenneth and Lily and Milo and Professor Harmon. I had Harris and a three-legged Pomeranian. "Got it."

Russell, the computer genius, came over after calling, on Lou's orders. Russ was suitably impressed with Harris' gizmos, and Harris appreciated the tweaks Russell made to the security system now taking up half the dining room and the guest room.

Then Russell asked for my passwords. "You might as well write them out for me. Save me about fifteen minutes. You can change them later."

"That's all it would take to open my programs and read my email? Steal my credit card numbers and my identity?"

"Unless you got real creative. Then it'll take twenty. I bet you use one of your dog's names. Or a character from one of your books."

Shit. "Iverthehero1. My first title."

"Cute." He copied my hard drive, accessed all my Internet files, including the messages from Deni. "Lou wants the source of these found tonight. His people said they need two days."

"The sooner the better, so I can go home."

"The sooner the better, so I can get back to the new game system I'm developing. Hey, do you think that new esper you brought in can tell if I make it big before I'm forty?"

"What if she tells you you're broke and living on the streets?"

He grinned. "Then she's bogus. I can't miss. And don't use Little Red for your new password." He left.

For once, my mother didn't know everything going on in my life. "What's this about pink hair? And all the paramilitary types invading the Harbor? And that woman you brought with you. No one is saying who she is. And how could you leave Mrs. Abbottini with strangers?"

"She's fine. I called. She's teaching the Rashmanjaris blackjack for when they all go to Atlantic City as soon as she recovers."

"They're going to want to move more of their family into her apartment."

Which was fair, if she stayed in theirs. But then my mother couldn't sublet Mrs. Abbottini's rooms. Which meant she'd stay in mine. Ugh. "Maybe you should start thinking about looking for a short-term rental?"

"Pay rent when my daughter lives in my old apartment?" She sniffed. "Did I charge you rent for staying in my house in Paumanok Harbor all summer?"

"You insisted I come to take care of your old dogs!"

She sniffed again. "And now?"

"Now Grandma Eve demanded I come help with the beach erosion and the rashes."

Now that I thought about it, my rash was almost gone, and no one else had complained about theirs or showed signs of allergic reactions. "Besides, I had to help get Carinne here. Dad asked—"

"I knew it! You'd bend over backward for the jackass, and you get all huffy when I ask to share my own apartment! I don't see why you can't move in with Matt the vet like any reasonable woman would do. He'll get tired of waiting, Willow."

Like my father had? "He hasn't asked me. Besides, his former wife is here this weekend."

"And you have pink hair. Well, I have to find homes for ten pit bulls before I can think about where I'm going to stay when I get to New York."

What about me? Living with my mother was not an option. So where was I going to stay, and who cared?

Here I was, having microwaved soup with three dogs staring at me.

My supposed bodyguard was upstairs, watching TV and checking his security monitors for deer.

My new half sister was Dr. Harmon's new best friend, sharing Jimmie's balcony, hot tub, Lily's biscuits, and his wonderful stories, that should have been mine.

And Lou called her kiddo. But *I* was kiddo.

Grandma Eve was out having a *ménage à trois argenté*, after dumping a missing shitload of sand in my lap.

My father only wanted to know if his other, older, firstborn daughter was all right.

Even Monteith had smiled at Carinne and carried the cat into the elevator. I bet he was showing her new tricks. With the yo-yo.

And Matt . . .

Yeah, what about me? I mean, things weren't always all about me, but it wouldn't hurt if sometimes I starred in my own life.

I wandered around the house, after looking in every cupboard for something sweet. I doubted if Harris had any chocolate in his cooler, so I didn't ask. Instead I shouted up the stairs that I'd be outside, looking for the professor's parrot.

He wanted to go with me. I said no. I'd be in plain sight, on the property, within calling distance. Mostly I did not know if Oey would come if a stranger with a gun loomed in the shadows. I doubted she'd show on the cameras in her true guise; creatures from Unity never did.

I told Harris he could watch from the windows, but no closer. He reluctantly turned off the alarms, but not the boundary sensors or the motion detectors. He'd watch them instead of me, he said. Lou's orders.

I found a heavier sweatshirt and turned the porch lights on, then I dragged the plastic kiddie pool out of the shed and filled it. Next I pulled one of the wicker chairs off the porch, made sure my flashlight had working batteries and my drawing pencils had sharp points.

I sat and waited. That got boring after five minutes, and the insects found me. So I got up and paced around the side of the house, still in Harris' view. Feeling foolish, a not unusual experience for me, I squawked like Oey, loudly, harshly, but distinctly recognizable as the parrotfish's call.

Nothing. So I switched to words I knew she understood in parrot mode. I'd never heard the fish, the male part, say anything but "glub."

"Come on, pretty bird. We need to talk. And I miss you. I'm all alone out here, with no one for company.

Your Jimmie misses you, too. I filled the pool, if you want to swim. Jimmie still keeps the hot tub uncovered for you. Come on, lovey, come to Willow."

Nothing. I heard something scurry in the shrubs, a sound that hadn't come from any parrot. Or any fish. Harris didn't rap on the window or come flying out with a weapon in hand, but I retreated to the safety of the porch anyway.

"Come on, Oey," I begged, wishing Harris were in sight instead of peering at his various screens. Then I wished I had a chocolate bar. Mostly I wished Matt were here with me again. Nothing scared him, especially not a critter in the woods. He stood firm in any crisis, and kept me from panic. If I were a willow, he was an oak that kept me from being battered by storms.

Nothing answered my wishes.

I started drawing. The light from the house windows and the bulb on the porch wasn't great, but I'd made the same sketch so often, I didn't bother with the flashlight.

First came the willow tree. My willow tree. With a beautiful big parrot in its gracefully arching branches, forked fish tail dangling beneath its perch. I stared at the picture and concentrated on sending my thoughts and the image and my emotions, all at the same time, because that is how the creatures of Unity communicate with each other.

Hey, no one might want me around tonight, but I was still the Visualizer. That's what I did. I held up the drawing and scrunched my eyes shut and projected: *Love. Friendship. Loneliness. Pets. Come, Oey, talk. Need, want, help. Warm, smooth feathers, smooth skin, Willow. Shiny scales, glub.*

I changed the drawing to the same tree, with bare branches. This time I tried to express urgency: *Winter coming, ice, snow. Oey cold. Come back to the warmth of Rosehill and Jimmie. Alone, lonely, sick at heart. You? Me? Come back, Oey. Come warm my heart.*

Nothing.

I stank at that, too.

CHAPTER EIGHTEEN

I had bad dreams. But I had brownies.

Susan came home to find me asleep on the porch, huddled in a blanket Harris had brought me. Poor guy was so afraid of Lou, he couldn't go to sleep until I went inside, locked the doors, and reset the alarms, which I couldn't do till Susan got in anyway.

She brought the leftover bottoms from the Breakaway Restaurant's bestselling dessert, hot fudge sundaes over chocolate brownies. We ate in the kitchen.

She'd brought milk home, too, knowing the refrigerator here was empty, knowing my tastes. "Although I never thought you ballsy enough to go for pink punker hair."

"It was an accident."

She looked more closely. "Uh-oh. You've really messed up this time."

"I told you, the color was an accident."

"No, there's something else. You're definitely hiding something bad."

Susan always knew when I was in trouble, and always tattled. As soon as she learned to talk, she knew when I tried my mother's makeup or robbed the cookie jar at Grandma Eve's . . . and she always sold me out. The less she knew now, the safer my secrets.

"I am protecting the innocent," I said, pouring on the

pomposity with a glass of milk. "Besides, you'll find out soon enough."

Harris came down from his room then with his laptop. He showed a bunch of hieroglyphics he considered a computer profile of Susan: voice recognition, facial features, patterns of talk, walk and posture, plus body shape and weight. He and his machines could identify her again and not set off warnings when she approached the house. I wondered if he could recognize the speculative look in her eyes. I could: good-looking dude, no ring, staying right in the guest room.

I cleared my throat and gave her the same narrow-eyed look she'd given me. I didn't need her psychic talent to notice trouble or guilt. I didn't need to watch Harris check out her skimpy shirt and low jeans that left her belly bare. His sensors couldn't tell him my cousin had flexible standards. The navel ring might.

I offered him a brownie to get his mind off Susan's body.

I lost the bet about Susan getting him to smile. He grinned after the first bite. "You can cook, too?"

We all laughed, then talked about the restaurant business, favorite foods, awful customers. Things were looking up, until Susan mentioned that Matt and a woman had come into the restaurant. Did that have anything to do with my hair? she asked. A lot of dumped women cut theirs off, as if getting rid of a bad memory. Mine was already too short for that.

"I swear I didn't mean to go pink. I was aiming for strawberry blonde, instead of my own streaky sandy."

"Hm. You didn't mean to go red like the woman Matt brought in!"

"Definitely not. Uh, was she good-looking?"

"Not unless you go for tall, thin redheads with a toned body and high cheekbones."

"Sounds hot to me," Harris put in, unhelpfully.

I had to ask: "Was she hot for Matt?"

"For anything in pants, according to Uncle Bernie. She held his hand too long during intros."

"Ginny would kill him."

"No, she'd kill the bitch."

Which reminded me of the scene at the gym. So I had to warn Susan about Carinne and her talent. Susan might hear something unpleasant.

"I still don't know if I believe all that crap."

"Well, she said she saw me with a children's book I'd written." I left out the baby part.

Susan let the old German shepherd lick crumbs off her fingers. "That's how they get you, carnival fortune-tellers and Vegas acts. They find out enough about you to guess your dreams and ambitions."

"But I always wanted to write and illustrate a kids' book."

"Of course you did. You're an artist and a writer. She guessed, and your imagination supplied the rest. That doesn't make it real."

She didn't bother with the fact that my imagination provided a troll, magic horses, and sea gods, all of which turned out to be real.

"So if your dreams are going to come true, why do you look like a little kid after some bully dumped cotton candy on her head?"

I touched my poor hair. It felt like a pot scrubber. "It's the humidity in this wretched place."

"Not the woman with Matt?"

"She's not a woman. She's his ex-wife."

"I would have gone for black hair. You know, to contrast with her red."

I slammed my glass of milk down on the table so hard a lot of it sloshed on the floor. Little Red growled the big dogs away then lapped it up. Now he'd be sick. "My hair has nothing to do with Matt's ex-wife!"

"Sure," Susan said. She didn't believe me.

Harris shrugged. "I'm no truth-knower." Which meant he didn't believe me, either.

I tried to change the subject to what he *was*, if not a Royce-Harmon descended psychic lie detector. Kenneth was a precog and Colin had dead-eye aim. Harris had to have some talent to qualify for DUE.

All he said was, "I'm a bodyguard," and dipped his brownie in a saucer of milk.

Speaking of talents, Susan wanted to know when she got to meet the new woman.

"Matt's wife? Oh, Carinne. She's working for the professor now. I don't know when she'll have free time."

"Then I guess I'll have to go visit Cousin Lily."

"No! That is, Lily's already got Colin and Kenneth and all those workers to manage. She doesn't need more company."

"It's Sunday. I'll bring scones."

Susan was as stubborn as three mules. She'd go, one way or another. And who knew what Carinne would see, or what seeing it would do to both of them.

I felt another headache coming on. Maybe a nosebleed, with my luck. "Well, I'm leaving early tomorrow morning to look at what has Grandma Eve in such a snit. I might have to walk for miles once I get to the beach, or get someone to take me out in a boat"—heaven forbid—"to look at the shore from that angle. So I'll need the car all day." That wouldn't stop her, but it might slow her down until I could think of something else, like taking her with me.

She wouldn't go. She needed more sleep than that, she claimed, to work the rest of the weekend. Besides, there was nothing to see, with hardly any beach left. She ate the last brownie. "I don't see what you can do about the erosion anyway."

Me neither.

"Grandma is the one who has a bug up her ass that you can do something. I don't have much hope, but maybe you can get rid of the rash lady."

"You still have a rash?"

She held up both hands. I couldn't see anything. Neither could Ms. Garcia, Susan said. "But the woman took apart my kitchen. Seems we supplied a lot of the food for the ship rescue and after the hurricane. Ms. Garcia thinks my ingredients were contaminated. She took samples of everything."

"That's bull."

"Of course it is. But how could I stop her? She had a board of health inspector with her, and a bunch of official looking documents with seals on them."

"They won't find anything."

"Will you?"

I had no idea.

Since there were no brownies left, we decided to go to bed. First Harris explained the security system to Susan, how to override it or deactivate it. He warned her not to, though.

Susan stopped on her way upstairs. "You take those threats so seriously?"

"Not necessarily," Harris told her. "Lou's just hedging his bets. Anything happens to Pinky here, he has to face the grandmother."

Susan tapped her own chest. "And me."

See? I did have people on my side.

Harris went into the yard with me for the dogs' last outing. I silently called Oey, in my head, with pictures and pleas, but the birdfish did not answer, not from in a tree, in the kiddie pool, or in my mind. We went back inside, turned on the alarms, and went to bed. Separately. Or so I supposed, but, knowing Susan, I couldn't be sure. At least that was one thing I could not be held responsible for.

I thought I'd have trouble nodding off with so much on my mind, but I was fast asleep when the phone rang.

A phone call in the middle of the night could only be a disaster, or a crank. My stomach clenched as I fumbled for the bedside lamp. I heard Harris get out of bed and hurry toward his equipment in the guest room next door. "It's your father," he yelled out before I could check the caller ID.

"Dad? What's wrong? Are you okay? You aren't in the hospital or anything, are you?"

"Your mother is going to have a heart attack."

"Oh, no! When? How bad? How soon? Maybe I can

warn her and get her to a doctor before it's too late. Should she take aspirin or go to the emergency room?"

"It's not that kind of heart attack. It's figurative. I was lying here trying to fall asleep when I realized she was going to have a fit when she discovered the truth about Carinne."

He should have thought of that thirty-seven years ago. "I could have told you she'd be mad, Dad. During the day."

"But she'll hate Carinne for existing and you for hiding her. The fit she'll throw will be worse than that hurricane you had last month."

"That's why I'm not going to tell her. She won't be staying here long, not with filming her new TV show in Manhattan. And we'll keep Carinne busy and out of the way."

"No, you'll never be able to hide it. She has to be told before she gets to Paumanok Harbor. Or hears from her sister or cousin or the whole grapevine they've got going there."

"Fine. You tell her." I got ready to hang up the phone. "I'd wait for the morning if I were you."

"Oh, I can't tell her. I tried for years and never could. I think it'll be better coming from you."

"Me? Not on your life. I had nothing to do with this mess. You straighten it out. Besides, what can she do? Divorce you again? She can't murder you either, if you stay in Florida, so you're safe."

"But she'll take it out on Carinne. I've got a bad feeling about that."

"Is that one of your presentiments or just common sense?"

"I don't know. I'm concerned Rose will push Carinne out of Paumanok Harbor and not let her back."

"How can she do that? Carinne is safe at Royce's Rosehill. They'll keep her as long as she wants."

"I don't know, baby girl. It's a worry."

"But not the worst worry, so go to sleep already. Unless you can tell me about Deni or the sand people or Matt."

"Did you say Matt? That's it!"

"No, he won't tell her either."

"I need a new mattress. That's why I can't sleep. It's killing my back. You have to tell your mother. And watch out for wives."

"Yeah, I'm already avoiding Matt's ex."

"Or is it chives?"

"You must mean hives. I've got that covered, too, Dad. Almost gone. Good night."

That's when I had the nightmares.

First, I was buried under a ton of sand. I was trapped and couldn't dig myself out. I called for Matt and Oey and Susan and my mother. Even Lou. I gasped frantically—and realized Little Red was lying on my chest, his fluffy tail covering my nose.

I rolled over.

This time I was lost in a swamp full of quicksand, alligators, snakes, and spiders. I was all alone, but not alone. Someone followed me. With chives in her hand, like Grandma Eve collecting her herbs. She didn't hear me call out to her, or else she didn't listen. "Help," I cried. "I cannot find my way back."

Back. That was it.

I jerked awake, my heart pounding, Little Red snarling at being disturbed again. I took deep breaths, realizing that I couldn't sleep because my father's words had kept nagging at me. Like a name you know but can't locate in the back of your mind.

Back. Like backbiting, backstabbing, backsliding, watching Carinne's back, not letting her back, even my mother jumping into the mix by saying I'd lean over backward for Dad, his bad back, my not finding a way back home.

I finally understood what he'd been subconsciously trying to tell me: The Andanstans wanted their sand back, so they were stealing ours.

I had no idea how we were supposed to replace the sandbar they'd built, or restore the grains blown to dust in the explosion, or even return what the tidal wave had washed out to sea. I had to talk to them. And my mother. And Oey and the professor. Definitely Matt. Maybe the mayor and the police chief and the rest of Grandma Eve's council.

I tossed and turned for hours without falling back to sleep.

Too many problems.

Or too many brownies.

CHAPTER NINETEEN

I had to talk to sand? I had to have my head examined.
Since I couldn't sleep, I figured I'd get a head start
on what looked to be a long day. I tiptoed around washing, getting dressed, and letting the two big dogs out into
the fenced front yard.

Which set off the alarms, of course.

Harris flew out the door with a gun in his hand, un-
zipped jeans and no shirt. Susan followed, with a golf
club and a short nightshirt. Since when did she play golf?
Then I remembered the golf pro who hung out here last
spring. I looked past Susan to see if some stud in a
Lacoste shirt came out, too. Nope. He must have left her
a souvenir.

"Sorry, sorry. I couldn't sleep. I forgot about the
alarms. Sorry. I told you we didn't need all the bells and
whistles."

"Good thing they're not tied to the police station."

Oh, lord. I could just imagine Big Eddie or Baitfish
Barry driving up, sirens blasting, to find me, pink fuzzy
hair and pink rubber Crocs, with an old Hunter College
sweatshirt over Hello Kitty flannel pajamas. Worse, the
first responder could have been Uncle Henry Haversmith, the Chief of Police, one of Paumanok Harbor's
best truth-knowers.

"I'll, uh, put on coffee?"

"Not for me," Susan said. "I'm going back to bed. If you can manage to give me a couple of hours with no phone calls or alarms."

"I said I was sorry. And the call was from my father with an important message, he thought."

"A warning?" Susan brought the golf club up, like a baseball bat, ready for trouble.

"No, nothing like that. Go back to sleep."

Back, again.

"What about you, Willow? You going back to sleep, to work, what?" Harris asked, trying to hide a yawn.

Now that I was up, I thought I'd swing by the deli for a buttered roll and coffee to go, then head for the beach. Or what was left of it. "But you don't need to tag along." I did not want anyone see me trying to call up sentient rock shavings. "I might stay awhile drawing, too."

I call it Visualizing. Sometimes it bridged worlds of differences, forming a thread of communication. I didn't know how much Harris knew or suspected, but I wasn't ready to demonstrate my talent, or my craziness, in public. Besides, I half-intended to stop by Matt's house to inspect—that is, to introduce myself to Marion if they hadn't left yet on their Hamptons-hopping. She said she wanted to meet me, right? It was the only friendly thing to do, right? I wasn't a sneaky jealous shrew, right? Wrong.

Harris said he'd be ready in fifteen minutes.

I said that was ridiculous. No one knew I was here in Paumanok Harbor, so how could they follow me to the beach? At seven in the morning? If Deni suspected I came here, she'd be watching the house. Susan was in more danger than I was.

"Not if she has the alarms set." He gave me a disgusted look. "And the cameras will record every car that drives by in case anyone's scouting the vicinity."

"There'll be a lot of traffic past the house later. It's Sunday in pumpkin season. The farm stand does a big business when families come to pick their jack-o'-lanterns. Garland Farms grow cool-weather fall veggies, too. God, I could remember slicing Brussels sprouts off the thick stems for hours when I got volunteered to help. I never eat them, to this day."

Harris looked back at the house where Susan, with her short nightshirt and long legs, was warm and cozy. I don't know if he thought of the woman or just the warmth. The air outside had a definite autumn chill. He stayed put. "My job is to go where you go. I'll drive, so you can leave the Outback for your cousin."

"No, I'm bringing the dogs." It was a sudden decision, but a good one. I'd look like a typical early morning dog-walker if anyone saw me, not a nut case talking to the beach. Even better, Susan couldn't get to Rosehill and Carinne if I had the car. "They love the beach, but you wouldn't want three wet, sandy animals in your car. My mother bought the Outback because there's enough room for them, and they can't ruin the upholstery."

He still insisted on coming.

Joanne at the deli tsked her tongue at me. What did she mind more, the pink hair or the good-looking outsider dude with me? "He's one of the guys Lou brought."

"That's all right, then, I suppose. Not great, mind you." She handed me my coffee, light, and a blueberry muffin before I could order.

"I thought you wanted a buttered roll," Harris said.

"She changed her mind halfway here," Joanne told him, not exactly cold or rude, but not welcoming, either.

He looked at me. I shrugged. "She's right, as always."

She studied him, head cocked to one side. "Egg sandwich, over easy, Canadian bacon, black coffee."

"How did you . . .? Oh, we're in Paumanok Harbor."

Yeah, we were, with everyone who was up early watching me with a different man, not the local veterinarian they approved. Heads shook, eyes narrowed, lips puckered.

Vincent the barber out sweeping leaves from his sidewalk turned his back on us when we walked toward Harris' car. Not because Harris had his head shaved, either.

"They don't like strangers much, do they?"

"Half the time they don't like me, so don't worry about it. They'll be friendlier once Vincent informs them you have an aura. You know, talent."

"The barber can tell?"

"Hey, like you said, this is Paumanok Harbor. Where, incidentally, no one thinks I should be out enjoying myself instead of working on their problems."

"It's a strange town, all right, depending on an arty female to save their bacon."

"You don't know the half of it. Unless Lou told you."

"I know some. He said the rest was so bizarre I'd have to see for myself. All I know is Colin and Ken adore the place and were thrilled to be assigned back here."

"They like Rosehill and Lily's cooking. And they aren't related to half the residents the way I am." Some were only relatives by association and familiarity, like Uncle Henry at the police station, but they all thought the connection gave them the right to criticize, complain, and in general act like kin.

We headed toward the beach. He must have picked up on my bitterness about the tiny town. "You don't like it here?"

I looked at the view ahead of us, the sand, the sea, the sky. The endless waves, the constant murmur of pebbles shifting beneath them, the empty space, the salt smell mixed with seaweed, the breeze in my hair, and no one in sight to comment on its color. "This part I love."

So did the dogs. The two big old dogs ambled along, enjoying the scents and being off leash. Little Red chased everything from a migrating monarch to a bit of foam kicked up by the incoming tide. If the tide came in much more, it would be right up to the parking area. I could understand Grandma Eve's concern. One bad storm and water could wash through the paved area, flooding the streets, then the houses, then her farm. The downtown area might be okay, but the flatter land near here could be drowned and the docks in the harbor could be underwater. Feet, no, yards, had gone missing from this one beach since I was here a few weeks ago.

Paumanok Harbor had a long shoreline. If it was all like this, soon you couldn't walk from one boat launching ramp to a public beach to a sheltered bay. They'd all be gone.

I kept walking, while I could. Harris kept looking back toward the empty parking lot, then up at the shuttered summer cottages, sweeping the vicinity like a good bodyguard until I asked him to keep an eye on the dogs while I sketched. I handed him a tennis ball. Dobbin, Mom's ancient golden retriever, still liked to play fetch, if you didn't throw it past his poor eyesight. And he shouldn't let the German shepherd wander far because Buddy couldn't hear a call to come home. Little Red stayed with me. I had liver treats in my pocket.

I spread out a blanket and my pad and pencils, as far from Harris as he'd let me go. I looked at the narrow strip of sand around me, squinted at it, slit-eyed. No matter how hard I stared, I couldn't get anything to move or wave or call out a hello. Not that I expected the Andanstans to come for the liver treats or my company. Or to be dancing like angels on a head of a pin. If they were that obvious, someone would have spotted them by now.

So I drew. I sketched the usual willow tree. Then three tiny pointillism people. *Come, talk to me. Please.*

I heard nothing in my head, only two seagulls scrabbling over a dead crab in the tide line.

I added the fish-tailed parrot to the drawing, embraced by the branches. *Friend. All friends?*

I thought I heard car doors slam, so I hurried with my third attempt. This time I didn't draw. I simply pulled out the necklace I always wore around my neck. Its pendant had been crafted from my mother's wedding band, which had belonged to my father's mother before that, and back through generations. No one knew where it came from, but Grant, DUE's linguist, had been able to translate the inscription on the back with help from Colin, whose eyesight was about ten times better than a normal person's. Grant declared the language was Unity, which meant it had meanings and emotions and history tied to it, not just the words themselves. I held it out toward the water and recited out loud what he thought it said: "One life, one heart." I held it to the sun. "I and thou, one forever." Then I turned the pendant down toward the sand. *Friends*.

I quickly tucked the ancient piece back under my shirt when two people approached, with a scowling Harris and the two dogs. The newcomers, a middle-aged woman and a man young enough to be her son, both wore khaki windbreakers with CDC embroidered on their chests. The assistant, maybe a college intern, held a padded tray filled with stoppered vials.

"Hi," I started, standing up. "You must be—"

"Dogs do not belong on the beach. Especially now." She kicked up a cloud of sand. I cringed, thinking of angry Andanstans. Right now, I'd rather face them than Ms. Garcia. Hard to say which were more alien.

"They taint the samples," she ranted on. "And it's disgusting."

I held up two bags of dog poop. "I always clean up after them. And they are legal this time of year. I don't bring them when people are sunbathing. It's too hot for the dogs. And they are well trained." Except for Little Red, who kicked up some sand, too, in a show of male aggression and dominance, which was absurd when he already had to balance on three legs and he weighed six pounds.

Ms. Garcia, whose reputation preceded her like body odor and bad breath combined, frowned. Someone should have told her that made her thick eyebrows grow together.

"They also urinate. Where do you think that goes, miss? It gets absorbed in the sand, washed into the water, polluting both environments. It is a hazard to sea life and to children playing on the beach. They put their fingers in their mouths, you know."

They also put fingers up their noses, which I personally found disgusting, and no one passed legislation about that. I knew Ms. Garcia had no interest in my opinions, so I didn't give them. I did stare at the piles of seagull droppings. "Shit happens."

"That is natural and adds to the biosphere. Bringing dogs onto the beach does not."

In Paumanok Harbor, it did. I pointed to the occasional scrap of paper, an empty rusted soda can, plastic bottle caps, and other debris washed up by the waves or left by careless visitors. I always carried an empty bag to cart the trash away. "Sure, the world would be a cleaner place if humans didn't exist. But we do. So do our pets. Unless you people send us another plague."

She pulled herself straight and puffed out her chest. "Our job is to prevent epidemics, not cause them."

She sure caused an epidemic of hostility. I picked up my pad and the blanket, then Little Red, before he could be declared a hazard. Harris kept a hand on both of the big dogs' collars.

Ms. Garcia took out a notebook computer. "I need to ask some questions."

The assistant was filling vials from various areas on the beach: near the thin strip of beach grass, at the tide line, various spots between the water and the end of the sand. He meticulously labeled each one, placing an orange plastic flag at each place.

I could be as huffy as the next power-wielding petit tyrant. "I hope you do not intend to leave those flags here."

Harris grinned. The young man looked stricken at the idea.

"Of course not. We'll take photos, then gather them up."

Except the tide had come in and snatched one back out already. I helpfully pointed that out. Ms. Garcia glared at the assistant to go fetch it. Then she asked for my name.

"I don't see any reason for that."

One-brow again, she consulted her pad. "Do you live here?"

"No. Manhattan is where I reside and vote and pay taxes. That's where your salary comes from, I believe."

She ignored the implication that she worked for me.

"You are a tourist, then."

"No. I have family here." To my chagrin.

"Were you here at the time of the hurricane, the one called Desi? Or that shipwreck? Surely you heard of that."

Obviously, she believed all the dumb blonde jokes, and doubled her prejudice for pink. "Yes."

"Yes, you heard, or yes, you were here?"

"Yes, I am not sure why it's any of your business." I disliked being spoken down to, as much as I disliked dog-haters.

She turned the hostility up a notch. "I am trying to help this town, that's why, and investigate what may be a serious health issue for the entire region, if not the country. I am getting precious little cooperation, too."

With her attitude, I was not surprised. Besides, Paumanok Harbor held its cards closer to its chest than a one-eyed gambler in an Old West saloon. I shifted Little Red in my arms, prepared to leave.

"Wait. Do you have any unexplained rashes?"

Unexplained? I believed I knew exactly where they came from. "No."

She stepped closer, almost within Little Red's range. I stepped back. She put on a pair of black-rimmed glasses. "What's that on your upper lip?"

Damn, the rash was so faded I'd stopped putting on concealer. It didn't itch anymore, either, not since I decided to come back to Paumanok Harbor. I suspected the connection was not entirely coincidental, knowing how these things worked. Which I was not about to discuss it with this snarky, decidedly outsider scientist. "Must be beard burn. Isn't that right, sweetie?"

I batted my eyelashes at Harris. "You know, from before you shaved this morning."

Ms. Garcia pursed her thin lips. Maybe she didn't know about beard burn.

Harris turned as pink as my hair, but he played along. "Sorry 'bout that, Cupcake."

She turned away in disgust and shut down her hand-held, without thinking to interrogate Sweetie. "We have enough samples to work with. We already took the water and air."

"Did you check for ticks? They carry all kinds of diseases. Rashes, too. But you must know that. They're all over here, especially in those grasses you walked through."

Ms. Garcia jerked her head yes. The student started brushing at his pants. They left.

I picked up the garbage and handed it to Harris. He ought to do something to make up for laughing at how I'd handled the interview.

"Not enough sleep last night, huh?"

I told him to go on ahead with the dogs.

As soon as his back was turned, I knelt down and sifted a handful of sand through my fingers, peering at it. It still looked like sand. No tiny warriors with shells for shields or pointy shark teeth for swords. No minuscule people cursing at me for moving the sand or littering the beach. I squinted, I peered, I put my face an inch away from the sand.

Harris had come back, bodyguarding. "What the devil are you doing, Pinky?"

"I wish you'd stop calling me that."

"You like Cupcake better?"

I ignored him and fished a baggie from my pocket. I silently apologized to the Andanstans, if they were around, and promised to bring the sand back. I filled the baggie and sealed it up. I'd borrow a microscope from the school or a loupe from the local jeweler.

Harris shook his head. "How about Fruitcake?"

Chapter Twenty

I had a mission. Matt had a microscope.

Harris didn't understand why I wanted to go home to drop the dogs off. "I thought we were going to check other beaches. Maybe go out in a boat to look at the shore from another angle."

"There's a chop to the waves." Maybe a ripple, but my stomach did not do well in rougher water than a Jacuzzi. "The dogs don't go on boats, if that's what I decide to do." I held up the bag of sand. "First I want to look at this stuff up close. I know there's a microscope at the vet clinic. They check for worms all the time." Yeck. "I'm sure they keep it sterile."

Harris glanced at the bag. "You think you can find something the epidemics lady can't? She's got labs and scientists and the latest technology for testing something that sure looks like sand to me."

"Yeah, they're not talking to me."

Harris pulled as far away on the passenger seat as he could get from me, in case I sprouted horns and tail. "Please do not tell me you hear voices like Carinne. Lou should have warned me."

"Not exactly."

"How not exactly?"

Before I had to answer, we arrived back at the house. We bypassed the alarms, made sure the dogs had water and Susan still slept. Harris checked his monitors for anything suspicious, then we were off again. He wanted to take his car now that we had no dogs, and I let him. I was too nervous to argue, and Susan could sleep all day until time to go back to the restaurant.

I gave directions. And directed my heartbeat to stop fluttering. I needed to use the scope, that's all.

"Turn here."

Matt's SUV sat in the parking lot at the animal hospital, so maybe they hadn't left yet. "Drive around back to Matt's house." A black Lexus gleamed in the carport there.

I knocked on the door, but no one answered. We left the car at the house and walked back to the clinic.

"If you don't hear voices, how do you communicate with . . . with whatever you befriend? I know you're a Visualizer, but no one ever says what that means."

"I draw pictures, like how you'd try to connect to someone who doesn't speak your language and hand signals won't work. You draw objects. The rest is hard to explain. Especially since I don't understand half of what goes on. I think they do all the work, if they choose to. These guys aren't choosing. But you never told me what you do."

"Yes, I did. I'm a bodyguard."

I stopped walking. "There's nothing unexplained about that. You could be in the Secret Service or some private security thing, not working with Lou and DUE."

He picked up a small rock from the edge of the driveway. "Here, throw it at me."

"No, I can't do that."

"You have to, so you know how safe you are."

I lobbed the rock at him, softly so he could catch it without getting hurt. He didn't try. Instead Harris stood still and let the rock come at him, but it fell short.

"Come on, Cupcake. You can do better than that. That was a girly throw."

"I am a girl."

"No, you're magic. So am I. So throw."

I picked up a larger rock and threw it hard and straight. We were close enough that even a girly throw couldn't miss him. He wasn't ducking or dodging the way I expected. "Move! Move!" I yelled.

But the rock stopped within six inches of him and fell straight down to the ground. It dropped like . . . a rock. "Wow. Great trick. You must have been a star at dodge ball."

"And football, where no one could tackle or tag me, until they banned me from Pee Wee League. I stank at tennis, though. The ball dropped before I could hit it back. DUE found me before I ran into real trouble, or someone made a video of me playing. I had no idea I was so different until then."

We stopped outside the front of the animal hospital, which was closed. I thought about walking to the back door in case Matt was in the kennel area, checking on any overnight patients. First I pressed the doorbell. While we waited, I asked, "Have you ever met Piet Doorn?"

"The fire damp? Once. The guy's put out more fires than Smokey the Bear. If I had his range of protection, I could end wars."

"At least save a ton of lives. He was incredible when we had an arsonist here in town."

"I used to be jealous of him, until I saw all the scars and suffering. I'm content to keep one person safe at a time."

"But your anti-projectile talent guards your own body. What good does that do the person in danger, like me?"

"Well, say some evil dude pulls a weapon. I disarm him, without worrying about bullets or knives or fists. So you're safe. But what if Colin senses danger, unspecified? Then I fall on you, protecting you with my body. Or grab you and shield your body with mine. Like this."

He wrapped his arms around me. "Now you're in my circle of protection. Too bad we don't have anyone to throw rocks to prove it."

He didn't move his arms. Now if this were a novel, I'd feel heat and a rush of hormones. I'd be vibrating with electricity and anticipation. I'd take a deep breath of his scent, man and something spicy, with a little bit of Canadian bacon, which was a good turn-on for a Sunday morning. Nice.

And then, if this were a paperback romance, I'd step a half inch closer and he'd step a half inch closer and our lips would meet and the ground would shake and the kiss would go on and on and on. I'd feel safe and protected, by a man who would put himself or his magic in front of a runaway train for me. I'd feel my nipples harden, I'd feel his arousal. I'd feel like we had to get closer, physically and emotionally. Lust and longing. I'd be smitten. If this were a novel.

It was my life. No smits, no heat, no vibrations or electricity. No nothing. The ground didn't shake, the angels didn't sing. They cursed. No, that was Matt, coming around the corner from the rear of the animal hospital.

Harris dropped his arms but stayed close to me. "I guess we'll see if the magic works on magic folks. He looks ready to kill one of us. Maybe both."

"He'll be fine once I explain."

Harris leaned toward me. "He doesn't seem in the mood to listen."

He seemed ready to spit nails. "He'll be fine," I repeated, less sure now.

"Good thing I didn't knock you to the ground with me on top, huh?" Harris whispered.

"You're not helping." I jumped away from him, toward Matt. "It's not what you think. This is Harris, the bodyguard Lou sent. He's showing me how he'd protect me."

Harris coughed. "Let's not get too deep into the workings."

"It's all right. Matt has an aura." I didn't mean Matt had a halo glow like the pseudo-psychics say every living being has. Around here an aura meant a gift of power recognizable on sight by a few like Vincent the barber. "He's one of us now. He has talent."

"Matt has eyes in his head, damn it," Matt said. "I didn't spot any lurkers in the bushes, drive-by shooters, or stalkers with decapitated rats."

"I told you, he was demonstrating."

"Demonstrating what, his seduction technique? It's a hell of a thing, bringing you here to play grab ass on my doorstep."

"He never grabbed my ass! And I certainly never grabbed his. Yours is the only—That is, nothing happened."

He looked at Harris, who held both hands up in surrender. "Not even a quick feel."

Matt said, "Excuse us," to Harris, took my hand and pulled me, none too gently, inside the unlocked door to the waiting room.

"Hey, will she be safe?"

Matt slammed the door in his face.

The place was the quietest I've ever seen it. You couldn't even hear a dog barking in the back area. You couldn't hear anything but our breathing as Matt and I looked at each other. He was angry at what he'd seen. I was angry he didn't believe me, didn't trust me. Then again, I'd been thoroughly pissed about his ex-wife visiting, no matter what he said about separate bedrooms.

Then the heat of anger changed into the heat of the moment. I don't know who made the first move, but we were in each other's arms, chest to chest.

"Oh, God, I've missed you. And I got sick thinking of some crazy woman threatening you."

"Me, too," I said, inhaling the distinctive Matt aroma, him, his cologne, dog, and a tiny bit of disinfectant. People think disinfectant isn't sexy. What do they know? I reached up to feel his soft brown curls, his smooth cheek, his perfect ears. "Me, too." This time I whispered into one. And felt his body shiver.

He pulled me closer still, with only our clothes between us. I was already pulling his shirt out of his bulging jeans.

"No, we can't."

"Harris won't mind. If we hurry." I figured he'd burst

through the door in five minutes if I didn't come out. Five minutes ought to work, if we lasted that long. I looked around. An old leather bench for clients stretched against the wall. That worked for me.

"Your hired gun won't mind. Marion will."

Talk about a cold shower. This one rained sleet. I stepped back. "Where is dear Marion?"

"Getting ready to be seen in the Hamptons. I forgot how long she needs to prepare to face the day. Or how much hot water she uses up. Or how she's impossible before she has coffee. Fancy gourmet, safe trade stuff."

"Sounds like you two ought to get a divorce."

He laughed. "We did that. I just forgot what a good idea it was."

"I thought she left you for someone else. Where is he?"

"She left, with my blessings, but the guy is long gone. So is the one after, and the one after that. That's why she had no one to leave the dog with. She still doesn't. Beau isn't nearly as friendly as he used to be, thanks to her keeping him in the house all day, never seeing anyone else. In return, Moses doesn't like Beau getting anywhere near me. I'd have to keep them in separate rooms, or crated, which wouldn't be fair to either of them."

I couldn't blame Moses. I didn't like Marion anywhere near Matt, either. I hated the woman and I'd never met her. Maybe she wasn't so bad now though, now that Matt didn't seem hung up on her. Nobly, I told him we better go find her.

Not quite as nobly, but far more satisfying, he said we had three minutes more. And he kissed me. I still felt protected in a man's strong arms, but I felt wanted and needed and cherished and wanting some more. This time all the bells and whistles went off, the angels did sing, and the ground did tremble.

No, that was Moses, the Newfoundland pup, pushing his way into the waiting room, from the kennel area. He dashed between us, drooling on my shoes, wagging his tail hard enough to knock me over if Matt hadn't held me up, and whining to tell me how much he'd missed me, too.

I bent down, but not all that far because he'd grown another inch or five since I'd seen him, and kissed his sweet spot, right above the nose.

"Hey, what about me?"

So I kissed Matt on the nose, which led to a longer kiss, with tongues and moans and stroking hands and a hard weight against my belly. I'd missed this, too. Not so much the hard weight against the back of my legs, pinning me to Matt with a hundred pounds of dog that wanted to keep us together. Good dog, Moses. And he liked Little Red.

"Well, I guess that answers my question." A beautiful red-haired woman stood in the waiting room doorway, Harris behind her, looking sheepish because he couldn't protect me from her. Daggers maybe; daggered looks, no.

Matt made the introductions. He shook hands with Harris. I did not shake hands with Marion. She did not offer. "Um, what question was that, Marion?"

"Whether there was a chance of us getting back together."

"No," Matt answered.

"No," I seconded.

She turned to Harris. "You have an opinion, handsome?"

"Yeah, I'm fond of my privates, so I'll wait outside. Call if you need me, Willow."

"I'll be right out. They need to get going."

Marion was staring at my hair. "There's no hurry. But tell me, uh, Willy, is it?"

Which she knew damn well it was. "Is pink the new fashion statement in this funny little town?"

Paumanok Harbor was dead serious, not funny at all. And if she meant weird, which it was, that had nothing to do with her. She could just leave. I wished she would, so I said, "No, but pink is all the thing in the big city. I live there, you know."

"Do you?" As if I lived under a storm drain. "I visited Manhattan last month and the only persons over sixteen I saw with hair that shade were picketing for gay marriage."

"Oh, were you in that march?" Unworthy, I knew, but I hated her condescension.

Before she could meow back, Matt said he liked it.

"Gay marriage?"

"That's fine with me, but I meant Willy's hair. It reminds me of special sunsets over the bay here, where the horizon turns just that soft shade for an instant before the sun disappears entirely. And it's perfect with her sky-blue eyes. Besides, it's creative, like Willy, and full of life and spirit and independent thinking. Just like her."

Marion looked like she could cry—or puke—but me? I grinned from the inside out. I floated, I swooped, I didn't think of admitting the pink hair was an accident. It was a stroke of genius, a Picasso of hair color, a statement. I was special.

Then Matt winked at me. Okay, it was a mistake, but he'd stood up for me. I was still special to him, even if I didn't look like a sunset, but a baby shower run amok. He didn't let any former wife and lover send nasty digs my way. Matt mightn't be able to keep me from getting shot, like Harris, but this protection meant a whole lot more. I was safe, in my heart where it mattered.

Chapter Twenty-one

I had a good afternoon. And hopes for a better night.

Marion left with her dog. She'd seen enough sights in the clinic. That alone made my day. Then Harris agreed I'd be safe enough with Matt to be left on my own with him. Yes!

The DUE agent watching over my Manhattan apartment reported no suspicious mail, visitors, or phone calls. I had no disturbing messages online. Deni'd lost interest. Another weight rolled off my shoulders.

Lou's guy also kept tabs on Mrs. Abbottini and the Rashmanjaris. All was well on the first floor, and everyone knew not to give out information on my whereabouts, just in case. And Lou said Carinne was settling in fine with the professor and Lily: no kids, no voices.

I could almost relax and enjoy myself. Almost.

My father called, asking if I'd told my mother.

My mother called, asking what I wasn't telling her.

I decided to ask Grandma Eve to tell her. She was Mom's mother, right? Or maybe Aunt Jasmine, Mom's sister, could do it. I'd talk to them tomorrow, after a day with Matt. It had to be done soon, before too many people saw Carinne in person, but not right now. I deserved this time. Our relationship required it.

I told Harris to guard Susan with his life—and keep

her away from Carinne as long as possible, at least until Carinne learned to control her talent . . . or lie.

"Ask Susan to make you lunch, if she's awake. That'll take hours, but it'll be worth it. Then she'll go to work."

Harris waited to leave the clinic while we checked the bag of sand. Matt poured a sample in a little dish and focused the lens. It wasn't the highest magnification I'm sure Ms. Garcia had access to, but far better than the naked eye.

I thought about naked and nothing else.

"I don't see anything," Matt said after he stirred the sand a couple of times. "You look." He stepped back, but not far, so I had to stand in his embrace to look down at the eyepiece. What a sacrifice.

"What do you see?"

"Not much, individual grains." Harris might as well get going, thank goodness. I kept peering at the sand while Matt walked him out and locked the front door behind him.

"See anything?" he asked again, coming up close behind me.

"Nothing moving."

"Oh, yeah?"

I did feel something moving, but it had nothing to do with the sand. Either he really missed me, or the vet had a ferret in his pocket.

"What did you expect?"

"To wait until tonight."

He laughed, warm and rich and full of promise. "I meant in the sand. I'm not sure what we're looking for."

So I told him about the professor's notes and Ann, Dan, and Stan. How bellicose, how small, how powerful. How they wanted the impossible from us.

He fiddled with the scope again. "So they're in the sand like microbes?"

"No. They're made of sand, like magic." I took out my sketch of the pointillism people and told him to concentrate on it, asking them to appear. "Close your eyes and see the picture, feel the question. Maybe our thoughts together can get them to talk to us."

"I don't know about that, Willy. I'm new to this kind of thing. You're the one who gets things to communicate."

"Only when they want." I took his hand and squeezed. "Just try."

Of course our eyes shut, our hands together, his hard but gentle at the same time, ruined my concentration. His, too, by the way his breaths came a little louder.

"Let me look through the microscope again."

I had a better idea. I took the little dish of sand away and set it on the floor. Then I called Moses. The young Newfoundland had been saved from drowning when the sandbar saved the cruise ship. Then he got rescued by Oey, a thoroughly magical creature who talked to me, Matt, the professor . . . and Moses. Now the Newfie was way wiser than any dog I knew. He didn't like Marion, did he? That's how wise he was.

He barked at the dish on the floor, but we couldn't tell if he saw something, heard something, or wanted something more palatable in the dish.

"I wish your mother were here," Matt said.

"Hell, no. I'm not ready for that."

"But maybe she could tell us what Moses sees."

"I doubt there's words in English for what I think Moses might see. But if he can convince the Andanstans we come in peace . . ."

Matt rubbed the back of my neck, right where the muscles were tight. "I think you're giving Moses too much credit. He's the most teachable dog I've ever had, with the best temperament. He knows where the biscuits are kept, and what time his dinner arrives, but he still bumps his head under the table when he forgets how big he is."

Moses got touched by magic, the same as Matt did. No one knew their potentials. For now, Moses wasn't talking and Matt wasn't seeing anything I didn't.

I patted his back. Moses', not Matt's. "You're a good dog anyway. You put up with Little Red, and you kept Matt safe."

Matt smiled. "I didn't know I was in danger."

He hadn't seen that speculative gleam in his ex-wife's eyes. I patted his cheek. "You're a good man."

He didn't understand, but he smiled and kissed me. Which was good, very good. Moses whined.

I looked at him. "See how smart? He knows we aren't going to figure this out unless we concentrate on it."

"I thought we were doing fine."

"Not that, the sand."

Matt sighed. "Yeah, the police chief and the mayor keep nagging at me to get you working on the problem."

My grandmother, too, I told him. And how they were having a big council meeting on Monday morning to hear what I'd discovered. Which was almost nothing, except how Matt's brown eyes had dancing gold flecks in them, and how his smile made me happy to be wherever he was. And how I thought the Andanstans caused the rashes, to get our attention so we'd give their sand back. "I just don't know where to start if I can't find Oey, and can't get these guys to talk." I poured the sand through my fingers and back into the plastic bag to return to the beach; I was *not* stealing any more of their turf.

"Let's start with lunch," Matt decided. He was always hungry, but I guess he'd missed breakfast, too.

Moses perked his ears up. He recognized the word "lunch," at least.

So we went into town to pick up sandwiches at Joanne's deli. We parked near the library, so we went in there first, to fectch whatever books old Mrs. Terwilliger had for us. You never knew what the eldritch elder librarian kept on reserve for you, or why, but you usually needed it. Today she had a stack of books about writing and illustrating children's stories for me. And one called *Whose House Is It?* which was about adult women living with their mothers. Nothing about sand, stalkers, or skin conditions. Her rash from a paper cut was all healed up. Matt's cat scratch dermatitis was barely visible. Or touchable. I checked. Twice.

Mrs. Terwilliger gave Matt a book about office man-

agement and three résumés from local people Mrs. Terwilliger personally recommended.

"But I just hired a new receptionist," he said. "I don't
need these."

Mrs. Terwilliger gave him a schoolmarm stare over
her reading glasses. "You will."

I had to agree. Matt seemed to go through office staff
like Donald Trump through apprentices. No one had
been there longer than a week or two since his niece left,
after helping hack into the village computers to embezzle the municipal funds. She might have been hypnotized at the time, but the hellcat wreaked havoc in
Paumanok Harbor and among Matt's clients. Part of the
problem since then was that Matt hired people he felt
sorry for, or wanted to help, not the most capable, most
dedicated, most loyal, or most knowledgeable about
small animals. And he never fired anyone. They got arrested or they quit, usually in a tantrum or in tears. In
desperation, he'd hired an outside bookkeeping company, but he still needed a front desk person.

I already figured I'd be helping out, since I'd contrib-
uted to his last receptionist's departure. I'd ask later who
he hired this time and read the résumés myself.

We walked past Vincent the barber's, who gave us a
thumbs up through his shop's glass front. Yes, we both
had clear auras; yes, Vincent thought we looked good
together.

Walter the pharmacist ran out of the drugstore to
hand us both small brown bags. "No charge," he yelled
as he ran back in to wait on the customer he'd left at the
counter. I knew without looking what the bag contained.
Walter always knew when a customer—or a couple—
needed protection. Matt peeked in his and grinned. Yup,
we were both going to get lucky tonight.

At the deli, Joanne gave me lentil soup and a muffin
instead of the healthy salad I thought I should have. The
soup was perfect for a mid-October day when the sky
clouded over, like now. Joanne handed Matt a turkey
salad sandwich, while he still contemplated the menu

board. That was Joanne's gift, to know what her customers wanted before they did, just like the librarian and the druggist. She wrapped up a hot dog for Moses.

No one else was in the store, so I could ask, "You know what the dog wants, too?"

"No, he always wants a hot dog."

"God, I love this town," Matt said when we left. "You never know what's around the corner, or on someone's mind. Life is an adventure here, not a ho-hum slog."

I could do with less adventure, myself, and a lot less of everyone knowing my business. I wish Matt didn't like the place so much. He'd never move, especially now that he could see the magic.

I hoped one of us could see the Andanstans.

Matt drove us to the same beach I'd been at this morning, to return the sand and see if he or Moses spotted anything I'd missed. They didn't, but Moses chased the seagulls away from our blanket before they could mooch any of our lunch.

After that, we tried several other beaches along the shoreline; all suddenly narrow, with sharp drop-offs in the water. Moses went swimming. He didn't report any conversations with the sandy bottom, just wanted another hot dog. I was glad we had Matt's car.

He was still glad he lived in such a marvelous place with the gorgeous scenery and open spaces, where he could spend time with his dog. And me. With the wind in his hair and the grin on his face, he looked like he belonged here. Rugged, a little uncivilized, but natural and unique and happy.

On the way back toward town we stopped at a house on Shearwater Street, usually referred to, in fear and avoidance, as the House. No one lived there, yet the lawn got mowed, the taxes got paid, and trespassers—be they kids selling Girl Scout cookies, Jehovah's Witnesses, census takers, or real estate agents—all got yelled at, insulted, or pummeled with junk catalogs through the mail slot.

But the House talked to me and Matt last month. Actually, it sang, giving helpful hints like where to look for the missing professor and how to stymie the hypnotist. But not today. The place looked as tidy as ever, yet somehow it felt less inhabited. No one answered Matt's knock on the door, or my shouted, "Hello." No one responded to the pictures I held up, the messages I tried to send mentally. On the other hand, no one threw things at us, set the shingles to shuddering, or caused the porch boards to collapse with us on them.

I kind of missed the weird, and the help. Matt muttered in disappointment. "Maybe we should try singing to it?"

Oh, yeah, stand on the sadistic porch serenading an empty house. At least no one could see us, since the houses on both sides were empty. No one wanted to live next door to a haunted Colonial. We tried "Home on the Range," "Walking My Baby Back Home," and "The House that Grew Me." The results had Moses yowling, but the House stayed silent. I pushed a card with my phone number on it through the mail slot, just in case.

After that, we tried a couple more beaches before driving east toward Montauk, where the sinking cruise ship had heeled over on its side. On the trip there, we talked. We really talked, not like on the phone or in a text message, but face-to-face. I could see his expression, knowing he listened, even when he watched the road instead of me. Maybe that made it easier to apologize again for the angry words, the jealousy, the resentments that surfaced when we were apart because neither of us wanted to give up our chosen lives.

Matt pulled over to the shoulder on the Nappeague strip, and pulled me over to his side of the car. He apologized, too, for the jealousy that ate at him when he thought of another man getting to hold me.

So I let him hold me, even if the shift knob jabbed into my hip. I mightn't belong to the short list of world-savers, but I knew I belonged right here, in Matt's arms. Except people beeped at us as they passed by, and someone shouted out to get a room, which wasn't a bad idea except Little Red was back at my house, and Lou and Harris would throw a fit.

So we drove on to Montauk, to the ocean beach nearest where the cruise ship had been storm-tossed onto a previously nonexistent sandbar at sea. We parked in the lot next to the supermarket on Main Street, bought some apples, then walked along the beach, holding hands. We kissed and shared the tart taste of the apples, and forgave each other . . . and ourselves. We gave Moses an apple to eat or bury, and tossed our cores into the waves for the seagulls. And we listened to the sand.

We lay down in it a minute, too, thinking if we were closer, maybe we'd get a response. We got cold and damp, that was all. My hair had to look like a fuzzy peach by now, in the humidity, but Matt said he didn't care if I had purple polka-dotted hair or none at all. He'd take me the way I was, or the way I wanted to be.

All I wanted right now was to be with him. But we had a job to do and air to clear between us. So we walked and talked and stopped to pick up handfuls of sand to examine.

I explained my theories about the Andanstans, from the professor's notes, from my father's cryptic warnings, maybe from my imagination or intuition. Then I explained about my father and Carinne, the true story this time, and about my parents' tenuous relationship.

Maybe their bad experience at the happily ever after business made it hard for me to trust men. Maybe because his wife had left him for another man, Matt had the same problem. He wanted to solve his issues by binding us together so tightly I'd never want to leave.

I was afraid of the bonds. I didn't want to wake up ten years down the line thinking I'd made a mistake like my parents. After all, I thought I loved Grant in the spring, and felt infatuation and more for Ty the horseman and Piet the firefighter. How could I trust my instincts now?

"You can trust me."

"But what if you change *your* mind? What if your new receptionist is perfect for your office and for your life? No comings and goings, no dragging you into impossible situations, no stupid fears and phobias." I kicked at the sand in frustration.

"It'll never happen. The woman I hired is fifty-nine and has four grandchildren. And you—"

"Shush! I think I hear them!" I kicked at the sand again, and sure enough, I heard voices. Not exactly out loud, and definitely not in any language I understood, but I sensed arguing and aggravation. I knelt down and patted the kicked sand back into place, then grabbed my pad and a marker pen out of my pocket and I drew. Dot dot dot. Willow tree. Dot dot dot. Matt's oak tree. Dot dot dot. I drew as if my life, or my town, depended on it.

Matt shook his head. No, he didn't hear anything, but he kept picking up handfuls of sand, studying them. I kept drawing, trying to fix the drawings in my head, along with offers of friendship and appreciation and how to make amends.

"Talk to me, damn it!"

Moses whined.

The tide came up, the sounds faded away, if they'd been anything more than pebbles shifting.

Matt said we'd try again later, at Paumanok Harbor's beach where all the woo-woo stuff happens. Maybe the little dudes only came out at night. We'd bring blankets and firewood, a thermos of coffee and warmer clothes. Maybe marshmallows and sleeping bags.

"What if they don't come?"

"Then we'll have the beach to ourselves. My sleeping bags zip together."

No way was I sleeping on the beach in the middle of October, especially a narrow strip of sand that sloped down to the rising tide. We could try to reach the Andanstans on the beach after dinner, but I was sleeping in a warm bed. Unspoken was that it would be Matt's bed, and we wouldn't do a lot of sleeping.

We stopped off at my mother's house to pick up Little Red and a tote bag filled with a change of clothes, my

new nightie, and a toothbrush. Marshmallows and sex. It
didn't get much better than that. I floated through the
front door after punching in the alarm code.

Harris must have driven Susan to work because the
Subaru was outside, but neither of them were inside,
only a note from my cousin that she'd see me in the
morning and she'd signed my name for the package I'd
sent.

A FedEx envelope, big enough for legal documents
or manuscript pages, sat on the little hall table where I
usually threw my keys. Sure enough, it was sent by Willow Tate from my Manhattan address to Willow Tate,
Garland Drive, Paumanok Harbor, with extra charges
for Sunday delivery.

The problem was, I never sent myself anything.

CHAPTER TWENTY-TWO

I had a good plan. But I also had a bad package. And I had half the Paumanok Harbor police department in my front yard.

Matt gingerly wrapped the package in one of the dog towels by the front door.

"Don't touch it!"

"The FedEx guy handled it, so did Susan. If there are any fingerprints, they're gone."

I wasn't worried about fingerprints, only about bombs or cyanide powder or radioactivity. The mailing envelope wasn't very thick, but I had no idea how small a detonator could be, or a timer. "Don't jiggle it!"

"It would have gone off before this." He carefully carried the thing outside to the paved walkway while I speed-dialed Lou, who cursed and said he'd be on the way, and to call 911.

I gave the address to the dispatcher. She didn't sound surprised. "Willy Tate, right?"

"Just send Chief Haversmith."

Then I called Harris, who was at the Breakaway with Colin and Kenneth, enjoying more of Susan's cooking. He cursed, too, but I couldn't tell which upset him more, my getting the package or him having to leave his dinner unfinished. He said they'd be here in fifteen minutes.

"Wait! Lou's closer. You stay and tell Susan not to

come home. Deni can track the package on the computer and even see who signed for it. Now she knows I'm here, even if it's not my signature."

"You don't know it's from the stalker."

"It sure as hell isn't from me."

"Okay, I'll take care of Susan, but I'm sending Colin and Kenneth right now."

We already heard the sirens coming from town. The old retriever howled. I put the dogs out in the fenced-in side yard, out of danger.

Uncle Henry Haversmith, who wasn't really my uncle but an old friend of the family's, got there first. He made Matt and me stay on the porch while he directed the next arrivals to stay back, keep other cars away, put on their bullet-proof vests. I called Aunt Jasmine to warn her not to come by when she heard the sirens, and to tell Grandma Eve we were all fine.

Soon the DUE agents arrived, taking up positions on either side of me and Matt. Finally the K-9 patrol car pulled up, right across the lawn. I guess we were all waiting for Big Eddie and Ranger, Paumanok Harbor's bomb-sniffing, drug-sniffing, cadaver-sniffing, and fugitive-tracking dog. The old dog was another one of my mother's rescues. He ate, he slept, and he looked suitably heroic in the orange K-9 vest. He couldn't smell anything.

Big Eddie could. Short and skinny, the young police officer looked anything but heroic, or big in his flak jacket. Except for his nose. That super-sensitive organ could detect animal, vegetable, or mineral, perfume, poison, perspiration, drugs. He could identify and follow thousands upon thousands of scents. The dog was window dressing for the outside world. In the world of Paumanok Harbor, Big Eddie was just another useful talent.

I wanted him to stay back, to wait for Harris with his circle of protection. "What if there are so many layers of plastic you can't smell what's inside?"

Big Eddie shook his head. That never happened. But the chief held up a hand and looked toward Lou, who looked toward Kenneth, the precog, who shrugged. "I don't sense any danger, but Pinky has a point."

"Pinky?" Uncle Henry looked at me for the first time. "Jeez, Willy. It's not even Halloween yet." Which had all the local cops staring at my cotton candy mop, instead of at the package.

One stepped forward, Robin Shaw, the only female on the force, and the best marksman in the county, if not the country. She winked at me, said my hair looked great, then waited for the chief's nod of approval. When he noticed her, not my hair, she slipped a knife from her sleeve, a long, thin knife, and sent it toward the package. The blade sliced neatly through a corner of the mailing envelope, exposing the contents to the air, if not our eyes. I guess her infallible aim worked for knives as well as bullets.

"Now?" Big Eddie asked.

"Now."

He stepped near the package, wrinkling his nostrils the way a rabbit did. "No metal or plastic. No suspicious chemicals. Paper. Um, Xerox toner. Blue, no, black Magic Marker. Real faint scent of, um, off-brand shampoo. Fried food. Dog turds. No, that's from the lawn. Hard to say if the shampoo smell or the fried stuff came from the perp or the FedEx driver. Definitely not Susan. I know all her scents. But there's nothing dangerous about whatever's inside."

Uncle Henry looked at me and shook his head. "Pink hair? If you got us all out here for another one of your crazy stunts, I'll send you back to Manhattan so fast your ears'll turn pink from the wind rushing past."

Lou grunted. "It's not a prank. Okay, Willy, you want to open it?"

"No, I don't want to touch anything from that female."

One of the cops shined a floodlight on the package, but no one offered to reach inside the envelope, no matter what Big Eddie said. The fact that he led Ranger farther away discouraged volunteers. Matt started to step toward it, but I grabbed his sleeve.

"You don't want to see the kind of things she sends."

Then Harris drove up in a storm of pebbles and dust, with Susan, damn it. I wanted my baby cousin safe. And safe from Harris the Hunk, who would never settle down. Lou called him over and told him to open the damn thing, with rubber gloves. Not to protect him, but to preserve any forensic evidence. Officer Shaw handed him the knife.

Harris slit the envelope and pulled out exactly what Big Eddie'd said, photocopied pages, rubber-banded together, with a message across the first page in blue marker. Once they saw nothing but a manuscript, the others crowded closer. Harris read the message:

"'You should have read my book, bitch. Now I'll publish this one myself. It'll be on the Internet in the morning.'"

Someone asked if that was possible. Susan said it was.

But not with my name on it. As soon as Harris read the title and author, I ran over and took it from him, forgetting about the gloves. *Little Ded* by Willow—not Willy—Tate. I flipped pages, saw that half were cartoon drawings—not mine, but a poor imitation of my style. And the storyline was nothing I'd have written in a million years. Or drawn. The woman pictured had my features, short curly hair, with blue eyes colored with the same marker pen. The dog looked like a fluffy Pomeranian, only twenty times bigger than Little Red, and empty-eyed, like a zombie dog. And they were—

"Oh, my God."

I hadn't noticed Susan behind me. Harris tried to lead her away. Matt took the pages from me, again without latex gloves. "She's crazy. No one will let her publish this filth."

Lou and Uncle Henry had the loose pages by now, the rubber band carefully placed in a clear evidence bag. In the light I could see Uncle Henry's face turning as pink as my hair.

Lou kept grunting as he flipped pages. "She's not crazy. She's a pervert. This is nothing but pornography.

We can get her put away for decades, if we find her. And we'll send out an alert to block any new mention of your name across the web. Anyone who puts this up'll be hit by a lawsuit so fast they won't know what hit them. Then we'll trace the sender and shut down the servers. We'll get her."

"Russ can take care of it, Willy. He's already working with your computer," the chief reminded me. "He can destroy any program that publishes this filth."

Yes, but my reputation would already be ruined. My books would be pulled from libraries, from bookstore shelves, from classrooms. I'd never publish a story again. Or hold my head up. My publisher could be destroyed. And Matt, Matt who kept his hand on my shoulder, would be tarred by the same horrible, hateful brush.

A man in a wool overcoat was studying the pages now. I didn't recognize him, so I went to grab the manuscript out of his hands, not wanting anyone else to see the disgusting images, but he held me off, with rubber gloves. "You know, I don't think a girl did this. It's really more a young male's style."

Lou introduced me. "Special Agent Krause here's a profiler. He's usually at Quantico helping the FBI, that's why you never saw him before. That's why he's dressed for winter, too. His blood thinned, hanging with the Feebies. I thought he'd be a help on this case."

I felt better knowing that Lou believed how serious the situation was, that he called in a Federal profiler. Until Krause said he was in town visiting his mother anyway. He read through the pages and said the writer was definitely a male. Twenties, middle class background, some drug use, most likely dropped out of college.

Okay, maybe the messenger who'd knocked over Mrs. Abbottini was the writer and Deni the illustrator. Or vice versa. "I know I heard a female voice on the phone messages."

"Voices can be disguised," Krause said. "Your senses can be fooled. My senses can't."

Oh, that kind of profiler.

Lou nodded. "He's one of ours."

"Wait a minute." I whipped out my cell phone and punched in my father's number. He answered at the first ring for once. "What did she say?"

"I haven't talked to her yet. We have a situation here. Dad, you know that Irish tenor you keep hearing?"

Uncle Henry groaned. "Not another one of Tate's blasted riddles, Willy. We've got enough to think about already."

I ignored him. "Dad, what song is he singing?"

"Damn, Willy, what do you think? The song every Irish tenor sings, endlessly. 'Danny Boy.'"

Of course. I thanked him and hung up. So maybe Deni was Denis or Danny, not Denise. Either way, the person was deranged and dangerous. And determined. He or she knew where I lived, knew what was important to me. "What did I ever do to deserve this piece of slime?"

Krause answered. "You're a success while he's a failure. And you're pretty and smart and so far above his touch that he wants to destroy you, or be you. He worshiped you like an idol, but you rejected his love when you rejected his advances, his creative work. Now you represent everything wrong with his life, including his sex life. And he's afraid you'll write about him, telling the world what a loser he is."

"What about the maimed animals?" Lou wanted to know.

"A lot of perversions first evidence themselves that way. Nothing unusual there. The fact that the guy tries to write graphic novels is. I'll check the sex crimes lists to see if anyone fits the pattern, but from the eyewitness physical descriptions, your guy might be too young to be registered. Or just starting out."

Not a good prospect.

"So what can I do?"

"You write back. You have email addresses for him, don't you?"

"That's what Russell's working on."

"Well, write back. Act humble. He'll like that, thinking he's won. Say you are sorry you didn't help him, but you were caught up in your own work. Now you'd look at his book, not this one, of course, but another. Maybe give him some hints. You could even tempt him to lay off spreading this one around by offering to ask your agent about representing him, or showing his manuscript to your editor."

"I would never—"

"He does not know that. He'll write back or call. He *wants* your reaction. He'll make a mistake. He'll do something to lead us right to him. With DUE on it, we can get better traces, quicker IDs."

Which meant they'd go outside regular channels. I didn't care as long as they got this dirtbag away from me. I hated the thought of encouraging a monster, but both Lou and the chief agreed that the more contact I had with Deni, the sooner we'd find him.

Krause brought one of the pages over to the light. "I think he's already made an error. Artists like to sign their work, right?"

I nodded. He called for a magnifying glass. Lou sent him Colin instead. Colin's esper eyes had found the symbols on my pendant. Now they found a tiny, nearly invisible autograph tucked in the dog's fur, *DF*. "It's a start."

Lou got on the phone. Krause got on the phone. The chief got on the phone. I went to free the dogs from the pen. "We're not staying here, guys."

So everyone gave their opinion about where we should go. Susan's father had arrived and insisted we both come to his house. They lived almost across the street, just down the dirt road. Harris didn't like it, which meant my intuition about Susan and the DUE agent was working fine. I agreed with Uncle George that Susan, at least, should go home.

Lou wanted everyone at Rosehill, where the entire place was wired and filled with guards. He'd be staying there, too, now that Doc Lassiter was at my grandmother's. So I was wrong about a threesome. Win some, lose some.

Matt still had his hand on my shoulder. "Willy stays with me."

Win some.

We still had the sacks from the drugstore. I didn't know about him, but I had no urge to use them, after seeing those drawings. Lose some.

"She'll be safe with me," Matt said. He gave a hand signal to Moses, who came and sat on my foot. "Guard, Mo."

The big dog growled so low in his throat I could feel it vibrate in my toes. Not to be upstaged, I said "Guard, Red." The Pom in my arms growled louder than Moses and showed his teeth. No one had to know I'd pinched his tail.

"Listen, we can't take any chances with Willy, especially now that this sand thing is going on," Uncle Henry said. "Why do you think she'd do better at your place than where we can have a score of guards around her?"

Matt pulled me closer. "Because to you she's a key that opens doors, or shuts them. If you find a better key, you don't need her. I'll always need her with me, safe and happy, because I love her."

Susan clapped. I blushed. Someone else shouted out, "This one's a keeper, Willy."

I already knew I'd hit the jackpot. "I am staying with Matt as long as he'll have me."

Now he blushed, but no one disputed my right to choose my own fortune, which had always been my goal all along. That and spending the night with Matt. Harris had to stay at my house with his surveillance equipment in case Deni came there. He'd be the best one to confront the stalker anyway.

"But what about the old dogs?" I could leave them here with Harris, but they could never go out in the yard, not when a maniac animal abuser could be lurking.

Lou said, "The boys and I will take them to Rosehill. It's all fenced in, and electrified. They'll be good for Jimmie. He still misses that damned parrot."

Lily wouldn't be happy, but Dobbin and Buddy were

no trouble, and she did have that smaller fenced-in area where the previous renter had kept his poodles. "What about Monteith? He'll hate having them there."

Lou grinned, something he seldom did. "He sure will."

We all laughed for the first time in hours. It felt good.

CHAPTER TWENTY-THREE

I had to tell my mother where her dogs were. And where her husband had been.

Oh, boy.

By the time I got the dogs packed up, food, bowls, meds, beds, and schedules, plus more clothes for me, my drawing supplies, my super high-res scanner and printer so I didn't have to return here while Deni was loose, we were in a hurry to leave. No time to call my mother. Whew.

I'd see Grandma Eve at the council meeting in the morning and ask her to do it. Maybe Doc Lassiter's calming influence could work over the phone. If not, maybe it'd work on Grandma Eve after the bound-to-be explosive conversation.

I decided to ask Carinne to the meeting, to let everyone see her at once and get it over with, so she could walk down Main Street without people gawking at her. Jimmie ought to come, too, because he knew as much about the Andanstans as I did, which wasn't nearly enough to develop a plan to reclaim our beaches.

Matt couldn't go with me to the meeting. He had too many patients waiting too long and the new receptionist to train, but he'd have Harris pick me up and bring me back to the vet clinic. We could have lunch together if no emergencies showed up. He made me promise not to strike out on my own, unprotected by anything bigger than a six-pound ankle-biter.

I wasn't worried about Deni, now that I was out of my mother's house. I had a lot of questions, like how he knew I left Manhattan, if he'd respond to the emails Special Agent Krause helped me write, and if I'd have nightmares about the story he'd sent. But worried about him showing up in Paumanok Harbor? Not much. Strangers stuck out in the village, especially at this time of year with fewer tourists around, and people would be on the alert for a suspicious looking young man. I'd bring the sketch of Deni I'd drawn from Mrs. Abbottini's description to the meeting and hand out copies, along with the picture I'd done of the Andanstans. I didn't know if anyone would ever see them but me and Jimmie, maybe Matt, but I was the Visualizer, wasn't I? And the picture was all I had, other than a half-assed theory about them stealing the sand.

That was tomorrow. Tonight we drove fifteen minutes to Amagansett and picked up Chinese takeout. I stayed in the car with Moses and Little Red. The Pom wore the doggie jacket I'd bought him in the city, with the hood up so he didn't look so fluffy or so fox-colored. We were both in disguise. I wore a baseball cap.

Moses drooled the whole way back to the Harbor, salivating at the smell of the food. He'd have eaten it, too, except Matt put it on the floor at my feet. I found the noodles and shared with everyone.

Matt's house was like him, attractive without being pretentious. The classic saltbox cottage had two small bedrooms with exposed beams under the slanted roof, a small home office, one and a half baths, a narrow deck out back and a tiny unfinished attic room Matt couldn't stand up in, but I could. It had a window and an old stuffed chair and a card table. I put my work things there.

The living/dining area had big, comfortable furniture, but not much of it, so Moses had enough open space to sprawl in.

Of course he sat on my feet during dinner. "You can tell him to stop guarding me now."

"He's guarding those vegetable dumplings."

We didn't talk much over dinner, until time for the fortune cookies. Mine read: *Trust your instincts*.

Matt's read: *Trust her instincts*.

Weird. What were the chances of those two fortunes appearing together out of the bin of cookies? Next to zero, I'd guess. Unless you lived in Paumanok Harbor.

After supper Matt offered to change the sheets in the guest room for me. He made a point of saying that Marion had slept there.

"I know."

"So you do trust me?"

"That, too, but I know that if she'd slept with you, she never would have left."

"That good, huh?" He smiled.

"From what I remember . . ."

"We better refresh your memory, then."

We would have started new memories to replace the sickening images still in my mind, but my damned nose started bleeding and my lip instantly started itching again. So did Matt's cat scratches. He found me ice cubes and towels and the cream my grandmother had made up for the townspeople. "That's pretty odd, both our rashes coming back, like the matching fortune cookies. Unless we're allergic to each other. Do you think that's possible?"

No, I thought the Andanstans were sending a message, a reminder of their presence. I don't know how I knew, but I just did. I saw it laid out, like a maze, one step leading to another. Everyone's hives started clearing up as soon as I planned to return to the Harbor. All the rashes diminished more or disappeared as soon as we went searching the beaches. Now, with my mind on other things, like Matt and sex, and everyone else concerned with Deni and Carinne, the itch was back. I tried not to scratch. I even tried Grandma Eve's lotion.

Trust your instincts. Mine said run in the opposite di-

rection, but that wouldn't help. Chances were, I'd bleed
to death from a nosebleed and Paumanok Harbor would
be swallowed by the sea.

"Does that make sense?" I asked Matt.

"I trust your instincts. You see the connections. So
let's go deal with the Andanstans."

We both knew we couldn't enjoy the evening with
that council meeting looming. We couldn't think about
the bag from the drugstore, the king-size bed in Matt's
room, the big soft sofa, not while knowing we should be
looking for possibly hostile beings, ones who could de-
termine the fate of the whole little town.

Even the rocky road ice cream Matt scooped out didn't
taste as good as usual, but my nose stopped bleeding.

We went.

I saw them. Matt didn't. I think maybe he tried too
hard, or was too empirical by nature. I mean, a sick dog
has symptoms, things you can see or test for. Or maybe
he kept thinking of me instead. I'd like to think so.

He didn't hear them either, not that I had any idea
what they were saying. They weren't talking to me, but
shouting at each other, just the way I'd drawn them, the
way I saw them in my head.

I used to think the characters in my books—the sea
serpents and trolls and magic horses—were just that, fig-
ments of my imagination that existed only in my mind.
Then they turned out to be real beings, just not of my
real world. Did I dream them up, call them here, or did
they intrude on my thoughts, tickling my creative im-
pulses, suggesting themes for my stories, heroes, and villains?

Which came first, the chicken or the egg? I did not
know. This time, though, the idea for the Andanstans
didn't come from me. They were in Professor Jimmie
Harmon's notes. I just drew them. Or brought them to
life. Or brought them here. Who knew which? Not I.

We'd gone to the beach near my mother's house and
Grandma Eve's farm, with sleeping bags and firewood,
as Matt promised. First, we dug a shallow pit. I kept

apologizing for disturbing the sand. "Sorry, sorry." Then we lined it with rocks. "Sorry if this hurts." And piled logs and kindling on top. "I promise we'll clean up." We carried a bucket of water back from the tide line, too, like good little campers, just in case.

We gave up on the marshmallows because we'd forgotten sticks and couldn't find any in the dark. Neither of us wanted to go searching among the beach grass and underbrush at the landward edge, not with ticks rampant and poison ivy possible, to say nothing of creepy crawlies who lived at the shore. I ate the marshmallows out of the bag. Matt had pretzels. I ate a handful of them, too, blaming the Chinese food for my appetite. Matt just smiled and handed me the bag again.

By now the fire caught, and I shifted my sleeping bag—"Sorry"— so the smoke didn't blow in my face. I crawled in for its warmth and because I didn't trust my concentration if I shared Matt's body heat instead. I rolled onto my stomach, leaning on my elbows, and I drew.

I used broad marker pens, so I could see what I was doing without the flashlights we'd brought. This time I didn't try to focus my thoughts on the alien sand-nappers, sending out images to them, trying to communicate. I used all my intensity creating a story I could tell to YA kids. I worked like I usually did, making it up as I went along, sketching in some of the action, a word or two here and there to indicate what had to come next, or should be put in sooner. Soon I had a storyboard, boxes of drawings and text, none finished or complete, but a tale of jealousy in a love triangle, made of grains of sand.

I didn't love it. So I flipped the page and drew three siblings, fighting for their father's crown. No, three banditos, falling out over the division of the loot. Three contentious neighbors, arguing about property lines and how loud this one's pool filter sounded, how that one's dog barked too much, how the third one threw wild parties and didn't invite the neighbors.

Matt fell asleep, but I had a great time, inventing

petty wars among half-inch-high folk who fell apart
when wounded, only to regroup later, ready for revenge.
I loved playing with the ideas, feeling that rush of possibilities, that euphoric high of creativity.

And there they were, in a bit of wind-blown foam
that drifted toward our site like tumbleweed. They
landed near our fire, inches from my nose, like Horton's
Whos on a flower head, amid the bubbles and sand.
Even as I watched, tiny bits of the seafoam broke apart,
letting the sand spill. Then individual grains gathered
again and coalesced into vague man-shapes, with the
fire's glow visible through their forms.

"Matt," I whispered, but he made a whuffling sound.
I refused to call it a snore. How could I move in with a
man who snored? How could I take my attention away
from the sand people to climb out of the sleeping bag,
crawl to the other side of the fire and nudge Matt awake?
I couldn't. I stayed right where I was, watching a minuscule melee while he slept.

"Hello," I tried. "I'm Willow."

They pushed and shoved and shouted at each other.
Contentious? The Hatfields and McCoys were pacifists
compared to these dudes. Now that I could see them, I
saw them everywhere. Trying to carry sand away, trying
to knock down the ones whose hands were full, using
shells to sweep sand away from their foes, making sand-
drip mountains from the damp area where our fire
bucket had sloshed, digging trenches to hide in ambush.
Everyone tried to defend something, steal something, or
just batter the nearest sand person. Some made tunnels,
or were tunnels, to funnel sand through on its way back
to the water. I found it hard to tell where inanimate sand
left off and sand warriors began, all in a few inches of
beach. Unless the entire beachfront consisted of Andanstans in various stages of cohesion or dissolution. What
if every single grain of sand had the potential to become
part of a temporary individual being? No one would
ever see them farther away than the tip of his nose. The
professor had never said anything about the size of the

creatures or the size of their population. Just small. He did say there were three varieties, and I could begin to see how some were darker in color than others, as if freshly cast up by a wave. Others had finer grains to them, from being older, more worn down. A third tribe, for want of a better word, had rougher edges.

The longer I watched, the better I could differentiate between the groups, although I had no idea if the individuals were male or female. The amazing thing, beyond seeing itty bitty soldiers wearing a scrap of seaweed here, a blade of dried grass there, was how they didn't form coalitions, or friends, it seemed, not even among their own kind. They fought each other as often as they fought the darker or the finer or the rougher. All they had in common was an effort to get the sand—Paumanok Harbor's sand—into the bay.

I watched as a glob of damp sand fell near the fire. I pushed it away. Fire couldn't hurt sand, could it? These guys must be nearly indestructible, the way they fell apart and regrouped.

Except they hadn't rebuilt the sandbar the Coast Guard blew up. They hadn't brought back the sand swept out in the tsunami. "How can we give back what we don't have?"

No one answered. Matt groaned in his sleep.

"Do you know how much money it would take to dredge out the Sound? Or the ocean near Montauk?" More than Paumanok Harbor has budgeted for the next five years. I had no idea if these beings understood budgets or money. What could they spend it on? How could they carry it? Maybe the single grains were their currency. They seemed to covet them and consider them worth fighting for. Oh, how I wished I could understand their talk. These guys didn't appear to be telepaths like the other beings from Unity I'd encountered. Or they chose not to talk to me in any manner. That didn't stop me from speaking.

"Why don't you go home to Unity?" Which would solve a lot of our problems. "Maybe you can go to an arbitrator or find an impartial umpire. You could call a truce while someone negotiates boundaries for you. War is no way for people to live."

They kept fighting and ignoring me. What terrible little creatures, battling their brethren over—"

"Eggth."

"Matt, wake up, they're talking to me! Together maybe we can reach out to them, start a dialogue to find out why they're still here."

"Eggth."

Damn, Matt did snore! The sound wasn't coming from the little folk, though now I could hear their tiny grunts and groans and battle cries.

I tried to send encouraging thoughts their way, to get their attention, but they were too busy trying to beat each other back from the brink. I was afraid to move, thinking how many millions of them I could wipe out with one footstep.

As fascinating as they were, watching their antics got tiresome. Didn't they ever quit fighting? Maybe they remained here because no one wanted them back in our parallel universe. The rulers or masters or gods of Unity banished a sea monster to the center of our world, after all. I couldn't think of another good reason why the Andanstans stayed here.

"Eggth."

Shit, that was Matt talking in his sleep, not snoring. I tossed a rock from under my elbow at him. "You better not be dreaming of your ex."

Then the voice came from behind me. "Petth have eggth!?"

CHAPTER TWENTY-FOUR

I had found my lost friend at last. My friend had a lithp. Oey also had the persistent notion that we humans from the mundane realm had to be cared for, tended, and taught. Like pets. No matter how many times I tried to explain that people had pets—dogs, cats, gerbils, and parrots—not the other way around, Oey claimed us. According to Oey's understanding of pethood, the master was the one with higher intelligence and greater skills, which I suppose defined any being from Unity who was telepathic, able to disappear at will, call forth superpowers we humans never dreamed of, and travel between universes.

Okay, we were Oey's pets. Which ought to mean she looked after us, guided us, protected us from sand-stealing, rash-inflicting Lilliputians. I was counting on it.

And there she was, finally, the feminine parrotlike side, perched atop our fire bucket, with the masculine fish side dangling in the water. Oey, which was the closest I could come to the given name of the magical hybrid, a name filled with mental images, emotions, heritage, history, and future expectations.

"Oey! I missed you! I am so happy you came back."

She swiveled her head to stare at me with round black eyes that gleamed in the fire's light. "Oey never left. You did."

I'd returned to the city, thinking all was well in Paumanok Harbor, that Oey'd be living with Professor
James Harmon at Rosehill, watching over the elderly
gentleman. "But Jimmie couldn't find you."

"Bithy."

What kind of responsible pet caretaker left their
charges to fend for themselves? "You could have called
or sent a message." Shoot, now I sounded like my mother.
"That is, we all worried about you. Jimmie got sick searching, then despondent that you were never coming back."

"Didn't thay good-bye, yeth?"

"I don't think so. He would have said."

"Then I didn't leave."

Here I was, speaking to a creature half bird and half
fish, and I was expecting it to follow our customs. I
crawled out of the sleeping bag and went over to Matt
and shook him awake.

"What? Did they come? Did I miss them?"

"Yes, and yes, they're all over the place. But it's Oey,
who didn't leave, because she didn't say good-bye."

He shook his head as if jostling his brains could make
my words make sense. "Am I still sleeping?"

"Look!"

He did. "I see sand."

I worried about that, that he couldn't see what I did.
His newfound ability gave me support and proof I wasn't
hallucinating, wasn't letting my imagination run amok,
wasn't crazy. "Not at the sand, at the bucket."

He looked. "Oh. Welcome back, Oey! Glad to see
you."

"Do you see his tail?"

"Sure, in the bucket, keeping the scales wet."

Whew. I exhaled in relief.

"But Oey doesn't look good."

In my excitement to see the birdfish, hoping she or he
could communicate with the Andanstans and solve our
sand problem, I hadn't really looked at the creature.
Now I found the flashlight and shined it at the bucket.
Matt was right. Oey's previously magnificent rainbow-

colored feathers seemed bedraggled and faded, with bare spots showing pale pink skin to match the pink toes the fake Oiaca always had. His fish tail hung limply, not glittery with iridescent, changeable hues, but dull, barely more shiny than a dead flounder's. Even Oey's eyes appeared tired, showing no sign of the spinning kaleidoscopes they sometimes resembled.

"Did these little bastards do that to you? Have they been attacking you the way they do each other?" I pounded the sand near my foot.

"Not hurt. Molt."

"Molt? Like dogs shed a couple of times a year? Then this is natural?"

The parrot head bobbed. "Natuwal. Thed happenth."

The vet in Matt took over. "We have vitamins for molting birds, skin lotions, too. One parrot breeder even made little sweaters for her birds so they didn't take chills."

Oey clacked her beaks together, her sign of disgust, like my mother's sniff.

Matt shrugged. "Yeah, I guess our stuff wouldn't help you. But you could come into the clinic to see. Or to Rosehill, where Jimmie'd look after you."

"Can't let Immie thee. He thinkth Oey ith beautiful."

I'd forgotten Oey's vanity and pride. "You are beautiful, even now. But he'd love you with no feathers, or faded colors on your tail. He loved you when he was a sickly boy, remember? And you saved his life."

"Pet."

Now it was my turn to shrug. "I suppose."

Oey tilted her head the way parrots did, as if their necks were on elastic bands. "Pink?"

"Yes, he'd love you if you were all pink, with no feathers."

Matt said, "I think Oey means your hair."

Damn, another critic. "Yes, it's pink. Matt likes it fine."

Matt coughed.

"Molt?"

"No. Nothing falls out." At least not yet. "Just a change."

"Eggth?"

Double damn. "Yes, she has red hair, but that has nothing to do with anything."

Those powerful beaks clacked again. "Eggth. Eggth. Eggth. Willow layth eggth, then moltth?"

"Oh, no. I am not pregnant. Are you? That is, did you lay eggs? Is that what you've been telling us?"

"Eggth."

I didn't know if it was proper to congratulate an avian for producing an omelette. That is, a clutch. I returned to Oey's question. "Human females do not lay eggs. We give birth to live babies, like dolphins and, um, dogs."

"No eggth?"

"We do have eggs, inside. The eggs form babies, with the help of male sperm."

"Waithful."

"Well, we cannot all be as versatile as you, with interchangeable male and female parts and shapes so we can do it ourselves. We manage."

"And I bet we have more fun," Matt put in, his hand around me.

Oey stared at us, deliberating. Then she bobbed her head. "Ith good."

"What's not good is these, uh, people." I waved my hand toward the sand at our feet and around our campfire. "We call them Andanstans. And they are stealing our sand."

Oey made a sound halfway between a chuckle and a cluck. "They can't thteal thand. They be thand."

"Yes, but they keep disappearing with ours." I pointed to the land side, getting closer all the time. "Soon the waves will wash over, if there is no sand."

"Thaved the thip."

"Yes, I know they did, and we are all grateful. But why don't they go home now?"

"Eggth."

"They lay eggs? But they're sand."

Clack. Clack. Yeah, I got it. Stupid humans.

"Your eggs? They stole your eggs?"

Oey puffed out her chest. "Many eggth."

"We'll get them back for you. The whole village will·help. We can get divers and diggers and, um, where would they hide your eggs, anyway?"

Matt rubbed my back. "I don't think Oey would let anyone steal her eggs. Would you, Oey?"

She clacked her beak, showed the talons on her toes. Then changed to a large fish, with razor sharp teeth. A lot of them.

"You gave them your eggs as a gift? They're going to eat your babies?"

Glub. That meant absolute frustration for all three of us. "Okay, please explain so we can understand."

Oey went back to her bird shape, the one that could talk to us. "Oey called on Thandmen for favow. Oey do favow in wetuwn."

"By handing over your next generation?"

She preened at her nearly bare chest feathers. "Thpethal. Ith gweat honow to hatch eggth of—" What followed was a mental picture, a wash of feelings and sensations, parrotfish as companions to sea gods, wisdom, beauty, rare eggs destined to become powerful allies.

Matt let his hand drop to his side. "Holy shit. What was that?"

"Oey's true essence." I turned to the feathered fish. "Thank you for sharing that. We are honored, too. But don't you miss your eggs?"

"Pain in the netht. Watew, aiw. Watew, aiw."

Now Matt and I both saw an image of the Andanstans rolling the eggs, more colorful than Ukrainian Easter eggs, toward deep water at night, toward instant dry sandbars by day for the sunlight. I supposed both sides had to be nurtured.

"What happens when they hatch?" I shivered at the thought of finding homes for the many eggs, when people only saw the bird part.

"Go home."

"The—" What? Chicks? Sprat? "You'll take the infants home to your world? We'll be sorry to see you go."

"Oey thtay. Oeineth go. Find own petth."

I'd have to think about that later. For now, I had to work on the sand issue. "What about the Andanstans? Will they go when the eggs hatch? Will they give back the sand?"

Oey's entire body swayed side to side. "Not without curtthy."

"They want me to curtsy to them?" I tried a Scarlett O'Hara deep bend at the knees. Matt had to grab my elbow before I fell over on the little bastards I could hear yelling beneath me.

"I think Oey means courtesy, not curtsy," Matt said.

Oey bobbed her head. "Big favov they did petth. M'ma thent. Oey told how. Petth got thaved."

They kept the cruise ship afloat, then helped with the tsunami. "Yes, and we are grateful. And sorry if any of them got hurt, but we need the sand back."

"Not without big favov. The way it thould be."

Oh, Dad. Not backstabbing, not backbiting. Not even wanting the sandbar back. They wanted *pay*back. A favor for a favor. Courtesy. "What in the world can we do for them?"

Oey raised her wings without answering. For once she did not know.

Matt wanted to know if that was how all of Unity operated, a favor for a favor.

"Honowable. Inthult othewwithe."

"Oh, boy, we've insulted an entire universe?"

Oey gave that gesture of unenlightenment.

"But you did us a bigger favor, many, many big favors. What was your payback?"

Oey considered the new word. "Payback. Good curtthy. Honowable."

"Yes, but what did you get?"

"Petth. Immie, you. Whole village. Petth."

Good grief. "And M'ma?" The magic dolphins who'd rescued drowning passengers, the fire lanterns who'd shown the way through the ship, they were all his creatures, his sendings. I supposed the Andanstans were his too.

"Payback, fow help M'ma molt."

"So now we are even with everyone except the Andanstans, even if we didn't ask for their help?"

"Oey even, with care of eggth. Big honow. Petth?" She flapped her wings again. A feather fell out.

I picked it up. "What could we possibly have that they'd want?"

"Not our babies!" Matt shouted. "I'm not letting any invisible midget creatures raise my children." He took my hand. "Our children."

We were having children? We hadn't had sex in a month.

Oey seemed as offended at the idea of giving my babies away as Matt was. "Not my petth!"

"Someone else's baby? Never!" I thought of my friend Louisa, who'd finally given birth to her third child, another daughter. I'd get to see the new infant this week. I already had a bib and a book to bring, but I promised a painting of her to add to the family portrait I'd done. I could not imagine doing a Moses in the bulrushes thing, letting grains of sand get near that baby, any baby. "What else? Do they want a virgin sacrifice like pagan gods? I doubt we have any in the harbor. Money? A temple to their worship?" I could see me trying to get that past the village board. All ridiculous ideas. "We have nothing they could want or use."

"Hath to be thpethial now. Inthult."

"An animal sacrifice? That's barbaric!" I thought about Little Red, about Moses, the Newfie pup that Oey—and the Andanstans—had helped save. "No, we are not giving up our pets, any more than you'd give up yours."

"Want thand back?"

"Oey, this is our world. They do not belong here, and must be breaking a hundred rules to stay. Besides, they cannot expect us to follow a code of behavior repugnant to our own beliefs."

Matt asked if Oey could find out what they would like from us.

"But what if they want us to clean up oil spills? Stop global warming? Good grief, the whole planet hasn't figured a way to do those things. How can we? Can't we just thank them?"

"When eggth hatch, they go home. With thand."

Shit. "When?"

"Full moon."

Halloween eve. When my mother will be here to hold the women's convention on the beach, if there was any beach by then. I thought briefly of offering up Mom to the Andanstans. Just briefly, of course.

"Can I talk to them myself? Maybe explain that we didn't know your traditions, but we are very, very grateful, for the professor and the other passengers they helped save, for the village."

"And Moses," Matt added.

"Too big."

"Yes, Moses is too big to bring, but I could apologize for not knowing they existed. But I didn't know, so I never asked for their help. It was you who called them, or M'ma, who wanted help to vanquish his own enemy. We cannot keep repaying favors forever, in circles."

"Oey athk."

"And tell them to stop with the rashes, too. They got our attention. Now we'll try to negotiate."

Matt jumped up as if something bit him. I knelt down to see about thirty sand people climbing his sneakers to get to his bare ankle, all with shell shards or tiny twigs. A bunch actually worked together to jab him again with the end of a horseshoe crab's tail. He jumped and cursed.

"I don't think they want to negotiate."

CHAPTER TWENTY-FIVE

I had another message from my father. Matt had another rash.

Dad told me to call him back.

I got the back crap, already, I told the voice mail.

Oey had disappeared, maybe to consult with the sand reallocation team or the honor system board, or whatever or whoever passed judgment among the Andanstans. I supposed they cooperated with each other long enough to form a government, maybe a war council. They united to build the sand bar, then steal it back. And to inflict a skin condition.

Oey, in fish form, didn't say good-bye, so I assumed we'd see him again.

I didn't see or hear any of the hordes of bitty barbarians. Neither did Matt. They might have shown up to talk to Oey about eggth, 'cause they sure as hell did not converse with me, too big or not. With no fishy parrot or sandmen or marshmallows, we decided to go home to Matt's house, to put something on the horseshoe spear puncture before it got infected. The rash already blossomed around it. Nasty little bastards.

I called the professor to tell him Oey'd be coming back as soon as her feathers grew in, implying her health or abilities suffered, not her vanity. He sounded relieved, excited about the molt and the eggs, asking questions in a stronger voice about gestation and nest-building, more answers I did not have. Then I told him the fledglings—or fingerlings—might be leaving in just a few weeks, possibly with our sand.

"What a loss, for our world and our research."

He meant the baby hermaphrodite hybrids. I thought Paumanok Harbor falling into the bay or going bankrupt with no tourists could be a pretty big loss, too. When he said he'd try to convince Oey to change the plan of sending the young ones away, I didn't bother to mention Oey's pet issue. Yes, I was a hypocrite, not liking the idea of being a magic bird's pet, yet at the same time hoping she'd solve our problems. Like Little Red hating being left home, but loving his regular meals and soft bed. Sometimes you just can't have it all.

Jimmie wanted to go back to his chess game with Carinne, a smashing good player, in his opinion. I said I'd see both of them tomorrow, at the council meeting.

"Is that a good idea?" the professor asked.

"It's the best one I can come up with, unless you can convince Carinne to get on a plane for Royce in London."

"Did I mention she enjoys the same telly programs as Lily. Her cat is sitting in my lap right now. They are both much calmer and more content."

So was Jimmie. He only coughed twice.

"And she is an excellent chess player."

I got the gist: no plane, no London. "Bring her to town hall in the morning, okay?"

Next I returned my father's call.

"Did you tell her?"

"No, I'll see Grandma Eve tomorrow and introduce her to Carinne. She'll have to tell Mom, out of loyalty and maternal feeling. There won't be as much yelling." Not at me, anyway. I knew my mother'd go ballistic. I intended to be in another county when she did.

"The longer you put it off, the madder she'll be."

"I just met Carinne yesterday." Lord, was it just Saturday when we set out? "You've known her for decades. Do you want Mom's cell number?"

Silence.

Had they named the gene for chickenshit, lily-livered cowardice? There must be one called Tate, 'cause I'd definitely inherited mine from my father. "So have you had any more dreams? Ideas? Worries?"

"Do you still have hives?"

I looked over at Matt soaking his foot and ankle in a tub of some greenish antiseptic solution he'd fetched from the vet clinic. The rash went halfway up his calf now. "Yup."

"I think I dreamed about them."

Matt's legs, that I couldn't help admire? Not too hairy, with great calf muscles. His knees weren't as ugly as most men's, except for a scar from high school football days. That only added to his masculine image, I figured. And figured I'd dream about them, too.

"Um, what did you dream, Dad, and does that mean there's a serious danger in having the rash?" I was ready to go pound the beach, demanding a cure, if Matt got seriously ill.

"I'm not sure. Burl Ives is singing along with the Irish guy."

"Who's Burl Ives?"

"He's an old country singer, way before you were born. Big and fat. I think he played Santa Claus somewhere. I just figured Ives, hives."

"Is he singing 'Danny Boy,' too?"

"No. He's singing something called 'The Wayfaring Stranger.' They're driving me nuts, trying to drown each other out, and the sound of the mustangs."

"Okay, I'll watch out for strangers." I always did, especially now, with Deni on the loose. "But did you get to the doctor? How is your heart?"

"Sad when I think your mother will never forgive me."

"But, Dad, she never forgave you before she ever knew what you'd done."

He sighed. "I guess so."

I didn't know what he had to be sad about. He had all his condo widows and golf course cougars. I was the one who'd gone to shrinks for years to recover from my par-

ents. I was the one who couldn't commit to a loving relationship, and the one he'd dumped his love child on.
"Gotta go, Dad. Love you."

"Love you back."

"Enough with the back."

"Huh?"

"Forget it. Just take care of yourself."

We walked the dogs later—after Matt and Moses checked for stalkers—and tried to think what we could give to the Andanstans that didn't involve sacrifices or lifetime servitude. I wanted some ideas to toss to the council tomorrow. Bring them rocks, to make more sand? Have everyone chip in a broken bit of jewelry in case they liked gold? Make tiny breechclouts and sports bras so they didn't dangle or jiggle? I wrote a couple down while Matt went across to do one last check on the two recuperating dogs in the clinic's kennel.

When he came back, he asked, "How about a shower?"

"Sounds good. You go first. I'm still thinking about repaying the sand people."

"I thought we could shower together. You know, save hot water. Do each other's backs. Get steamy."

Ahh. I forgot about the list. What were paybacks, in light of soapy, slidy, sexy backs?

Showering *a deux* was not as much fun as it sounded, not in Matt's shower at least. It wasn't huge, for starters, so we were kind of cramped, with my back against the cold tiles. When I wrapped my leg around his, he groaned, and not in ecstasy, either. His ankle throbbed. He dropped the soap and I jumped away, so the metal safety grab bar jammed into my ribs. Then I slipped on the soap, of course. And we bumped heads bending down to retrieve it. How did all those romance novel heroines pull it off?

I tried harder because I really wanted to make Matt happy. And me, too.

When we finally had it all together in the center of the shower, trading long, hot kisses under the hot water, we remembered the sack from the drugstore.

Matt swore. "Maybe we could work on making eggth?"

"I already have eggs, Ace. Put a sock on your swimmers."

"Let me taste you. I don't need a shower cap for that."

He did, and I would have slid to the bottom of the shower if he didn't hold me up. Then it was his turn, except I looked up to see his grin and swallowed about a gallon of water and almost choked to death. And it wasn't enough, for either of us. "I need you inside, now."

So he left to grab the condoms. And the hot water ran out.

Beds are better anyway, except for the two dogs sound asleep in Matt's big king size.

The bed in the guest room was smaller, but adequate until Matt misjudged the size and we rolled onto the floor, which wasn't half bad, especially when Matt let me be on top.

We laughed and sighed and urged each other higher, hotter, faster, deeper. Making love with Matt made the world shrink down to here and now and us and feeling, not thinking. Passion rose and ebbed and crescendoed, without a single care for pesky sand-nappers or stalkers, just wet bodies, slick and shiny with soap and sweat and arousal.

We got it right.

"I missed you."

"Me, too."

"Will you stay?"

I couldn't move if I wanted to.

"But after Halloween? Give your mother her apartment back. Stay with me."

I brushed his damp curls off his forehead. "It's not fair to ask now. I've got a limp body, a limp brain." I kissed him. "Thank you."

"Okay, I'll ask in the morning over pancakes."

"You'll make me pancakes?"

"I'd make you waffles with whipped cream and berries if I thought that would keep you here." He sat up. "Hey, I can put the whipped cream to a lot better use."

He shooed the dogs off the big bed. Little Red growled, but found my clothes to sleep on, maybe a shoe to piss on to show his disapproval. Matt lifted me onto it and pulled the sheets around me, then left.

I was half asleep when he came back with a bowl of strawberries, a spray can of whipped cream, and a tub of that chocolate you can melt in the microwave. And more condoms. "So soon?" I asked coming out of a satiated fog to note he was naked, and needy.

"I really missed you."

"Nah, you missed the sex."

Matt sat beside me, suddenly serious. "You don't actually believe that, do you?"

"No. Well, not entirely. Maybe a little."

He shoved me over to one side of the bed so he could lie down without our bodies touching. "Okay, no sex until you trust my love. If it takes abstinence to prove it, that I want to spend my life with you even if I cannot make love to you, that's what it'll be."

"Are you kidding?" He was obviously ready.

"Yes. I'll give you about ten minutes of abstinence. How's that?"

He put a chocolate-dipped strawberry in my mouth. When I bit down, he finished the rest. Then he kissed me, tasting of my two favorite things: chocolate and Matt. "Works for me."

The no-sex rule lasted about five minutes, not ten, unless you count seduction by strawberries as sex. That worked for me, too. And the chocolate sauce, and the whipped cream.

We needed another shower. And fresh sheets. And maybe mouth-to-mouth resuscitation.

"Mine," Matt said, when we could speak. His hand still cupped my breast, his thigh rested across my legs, pinning my lifeless body to the mattress. "Mine."

I roused enough to mumble that I was not a pet.

"Tell that to Oey."

"Oey's from another world. Heaven knows how her mind works."

"It works well enough to think we're good together."

"Mmm, we just proved that, didn't we?"

"But not enough to make it official? You know, planning for the future?"

That woke me up. "Like babies and weddings and moving in together?"

"Maybe not in that order, but yeah. I want you. I want it all."

Now I put distance between us, philosophically and physically. It was a really big bed. And I had a really big yellow streak. "I don't know if I'm ready for all that."

"When do you think you will be ready? When we're old and gray and shuttling between your rest home and mine because you won't move in?"

"I mean I'm not ready to say forever. Or to be a mother. I know you want kids, and I know I am getting to now or never in that category, but I might never be ready to juggle a baby and a career. Or to have a child with paranormal potential. How can I raise a kid without inflicting my own hang-ups on it, raise it right so he or she will be a good, happy person? Hell, I can't even get my dog to stop pissing on my shoes."

"I promise our kids won't piss on your shoes. And you'll be a great mother, simply because you care so much about doing it right. And because you can't help but love them, weird talents or none at all, your heart is so big. Besides, everyone in Paumanok Harbor will give us advice."

I pulled the sheets over my head. "That's worse than having a para-prodigy."

He laughed. "They'll all be honorary aunts and uncles. We'll never need to hire a babysitter."

"I haven't decided about moving here."

"You wouldn't want to raise kids in the city, would you? Breathing soot and smog, when we have oceans of clean air and open space to play?"

"We also have wizards and witches and otherworldy visitors."

"Isn't that great? Where else can a kid see fairy tales

come to life, know that true magic exists, that anything is possible?"

"You always look on the bright side of things. I tend to look for the danger, the difficulty."

"See? We complement each other. Rose-colored glasses and dark clouds. Just like life. You'll keep my feet on the ground, and I'll show you the heights."

"You make it sound so easy."

"You make it sound so hard. Chances are, we can find somewhere in the middle, like all compromises." He pulled me back to the middle of the disheveled bed. "But speaking of hard . . ."

CHAPTER TWENTY-SIX

I had empty arms, an empty bed, and an empty stomach. Matt had an emergency.

I'd have to think about that, when my brain wasn't mush. It wouldn't be as bad as engaging myself to Grant, who traipsed around the world at the drop of a Bigfoot's foot. Or Ty, who rode, rescued, and talked to horses across the globe. Nowhere as bad as getting attached to Piet, who raced off to fight wildfires. I never understood how the wives of policemen and firemen and soldiers lived through their partners' tours of duty or shifts. Matt wasn't going away or into danger. He just had a lot of patients who needed him, day and night. He'd be that kind of committed, caring veterinarian wherever he lived, which was good, right?

I told myself I could get used to it. Look at all the spouses of doctors and snowplow operators who get called out in the middle of the night. They rolled over and went back to sleep. I rolled over and bumped into Little Red licking chocolate off the pillow.

"No! Bad! Chocolate can kill you!"

Or me, if sex didn't. I staggered into the bathroom, which looked like baboons had partied there. With hot water and one of Matt's T-shirts, I woke up enough to make it down the stairs. I wandered around with time to kill before Harris arrived to take me to the council meeting. I knew I'd have to find clean sheets, find something to wear, figure out where to leave Red, straighten the bedroom, the guest room, and the bathroom before Matt's housekeeper arrived to see what a shameless shambles we'd made. First I found a yogurt in the fridge, likely left over from the ex. It wasn't pancakes, but it was a start, while the coffeemaker did its thing.

I checked my notes, then carried them upstairs to the attic room where I'd placed my computer and printer. The pitched roof really was too low. And the window looked out on a big tree, nothing else. The card table was rickety.

I couldn't share Matt's office, which was about as big as a closet and filled with technical veterinary medicine journals and reference books.

The spare bedroom faced the back of the vet clinic and the outdoor runs for the dogs, which I could hear barking. If I used it for an office, the noise would drive me crazy, and then there'd be no extra room. I was not thinking nursery, only guests, and the dogs.

Downstairs, the furniture fit Matt, big and sturdy, comfy. Someone had chosen nice enough colors, if you liked neutrals. I liked bold colors. And a yard and privacy and a short walk to the beach, like from my mother's house. Mom's place sat on a big lot on a secluded private drive that led to the farm stand. It had more rooms, more gardens, more color and more fenced-in areas for the dogs. Mom talked about putting in a pool, more for water therapy for dogs than for her own recreation and exercise, but she hadn't done it yet. Matt's house lot didn't have space for a kiddie pool or a hot tub.

Matt's back deck had a grill and an umbrella table, nothing else, while my mother had a wraparound porch so you could always find sun or shade, whichever you wanted.

Not that I wanted to live on Garland Drive near my grandmother, or share my mother's home. No way. But this house? That claustrophobic shower ran out of hot

water again, and the bathroom had nowhere for me to un-
pack my shampoo, conditioner, mousse, spray, et cetera, of
which I had a lot. And the sick dogs sounded distressed.
Red kept barking back at them, which did not help.

Neither of my Paumanok Harbor options had twenty
takeout choices in three blocks, or museums and shops
and strangers who didn't want me to fix their lives. They
didn't want anything from me except maybe my purse,
or to get out of their way.

No one in Manhattan gave a rat's ass about me.

Matt did. And I didn't want to live where he wasn't.

Even if his coffeemaker took forever.

Matt's new receptionist didn't. She dragged Moses
back to the house before my first cup was ready. The
older woman did not look grandmotherly to me, not
with her nostrils flaring and red spots of dudgeon on her
cheeks. Mrs. Hargrove didn't look like any dog lover, either, holding the Newfie's leash as tightly as she could,
with a paper towel in her other hand to wipe drool off
her tailored gray trousers.

"This dog does not belong in the office. It slobbers. It
will also intimidate people and small dogs."

I pointed to where Little Red and Moses were busy
greeting each other like long-lost buddies, instead of
bedmates last night. "Moses is the most gentle dog ever,
or you would not have been able to drag him away from
Matt. And he's the only dog Little Red tolerates."

Her nostrils widened even further. "I trust that unfortunate creature will not be in the office, either."

Unfortunate? All right, Red lacked a leg. He also
lacked doggish loyalty, a pleasant disposition, and any
belief that the rules of housebreaking pertained to him,
but he had my love and the best life I could give him. His
food cost more than mine. I bought him a coat. "He goes
where I go."

She stared at me. Up, down. Uncombed clown-wig pink
hair, barely decent big T-shirt. Down, up. Bare feet, no bra.

"What's that on your neck?"

I put my hand to where she pointed her perfectly

manicured, politely pink finger. "Most likely chocolate." A mirror hung over the sofa. I checked. Cripes, it looked like a hickey, with hives. "It's a rash. Matt has one on his leg. It has something to do with the sand. We went to the beach last night."

"I know a hickey when I see one. And I know a Bad Influence when I see one, too. I have heard all about you. Disruptive. Destructive. Unsettled and unsettling. They say trouble is your middle name."

"Actually, I don't have one. It's just Willow Tate. Pleased to meet you." I kind of hoped she had some of the truth-detecting talent, the kind that made the espers sick to their stomach when they heard a lie.

Psychic or not, she recognized the falsehood. The spots of color on her cheeks darkened. "You are not what Dr. Matt needs."

He needed to read those résumés Mrs. Terwilliger collected for him.

"Gee, do I hear a phone ringing?"

She looked around. "I don't hear anything."

"That's most likely because it's ringing at the vet clinic, where you are supposed to be answering the calls and running the office, not running Matt's life. But be my guest, you go tell him how you do not approve of his dog or his fiancée."

She gasped. "You're engaged?"

"That's actually none of your business, either. Good-bye, and you have a good day."

I *really* needed that coffee now. What I got was Harris, come to guard me before we left for the town hall meeting. He had two muffins.

I almost kissed him, until he asked, "Is it true you're engaged to the vet? Some lady slamming doors at the clinic desk said so."

"No, I told her that to shut her up. She must have an unmarried daughter or a couple of nieces." I snagged a blueberry muffin that looked like one of Susan's.

"You sure look engaged to me. A hickey that size . . ."

"It's a rash." I started up the stairs. I still had to

change the sheets and clean the bathroom. I needed to find a turtleneck, too.

Matt barreled through the door. Before I could swallow the first bite of my muffin, Harris clapped him on the back. "Congratulations, man."

"She told you? She didn't tell me. My receptionist did."

"I only said that to—"

He grinned, grabbed me up, and swung me around. My muffin went sailing. Moses caught it on the fly.

"I knew you'd see it my way after last night."

"What happened last night?" Harris asked.

We both ignored him.

"No," I told Matt. "I hated the woman and I'm tired and hungry, so I said the first thing I could think of."

"But now the whole town will know. She's related to the electrician, the school nurse, a guy with a wood chipper, and a bunch more. Do you know what they'll say if you break another engagement?"

"We're not engaged!"

He set me down and smiled. "You're the one who said it, not me."

"What happened last night?" Harris asked again. We both glared at him.

"Okay, we're engaged to become engaged. No ring, no date set. And I don't like your house."

That wiped the smile from Matt's face. "What's wrong with my house?"

"It's too small. Moses needs a room of his own, and I can't work in that attic. It's too close to the clinic where your employees come and go and it has no view. Besides, you didn't make pancakes."

"So you want to break the engagement? It's been what? Ten minutes? That must be a record, even for you."

"We are not engaged! And I told you, I am tired and hungry."

"And cranky," Harris added before Matt asked, "How can you be hungry after last night."

"What hap . . .?" Harris started, then thought better of it. He ate the second muffin.

Matt ignored both of us and headed toward the kitchen. "I came back here as soon as I could set that dog's leg, ready to make pancakes and help clean up before regular office hours. I had no idea Mrs. Hargrove would get to the office so early. She must have heard about the Dalmatian from someone in town."

"Unless she's a psychic."

Matt started taking stuff out of the kitchen cabinets. "I hadn't thought of that. I guess I'm not as used to the bewitched stuff as I thought I was. Speaking of witches, I hope you don't want me to move in with your mother and cousin?"

"Hell, no. I don't want to live with them, either."

Harris took a seat at the kitchen table. "You should have picked the cousin. She's a real sweetie and she cooks."

"And she screws around. You, out. You, pancakes. I will change the sheets."

Matt muttered under his breath, "Maybe I should break the engagement this time."

"We are not engaged!"

"You better tell your mother that. Mrs. Hargrove was calling her next, after your grandmother."

"I hate that woman."

"Your grandmother? You love her, or you would never have come back to the Harbor and we would never have met. I love her. And your mother. And your cousin, even if they can all run astral rings around me."

"Not my grandmother, but the officious, judgmental gossip you hired. I hate your new receptionist."

"She hates my dog. I already fired her, before office hours on her first day, so that's another new record."

I set the table. "Ask your kennel man about his wife. She's on Mrs. Terwilliger's list."

"She has three kids."

"Who have a doting grandmother who already watches them when Marta cleans houses. This is a better job. With benefits."

"Hmm. Maybe I'll keep you after all."

"Maybe I'll stay if the pancakes are any good."

I went to make beds and get dressed while Matt cooked. I found one of his ties to wrap around my neck like a feather boa. This one had pawprints all over it.

By the time I got down, Harris had a full plate in front of him. My pancakes were in the toaster oven, keeping warm.

"Sorry, but we ate all the strawberries. Or squashed them."

I thought that was more information than Harris needed, so I asked about news of my stalker.

They'd found nothing that matched his description, the prints on Mrs. Abbottini's pocketbook, the voice on the phone messages, or the MO. The agent at my apartment had nothing to add, except that the Rashmanjaris were going to roll Mrs. Abbottini in a wheelchair to her church for bingo this afternoon. There'd been no phone calls to the apartment, and no new mail or "gifts."

FedEx was no help, either. The last package got paid for with a money order, put in a drop box. The delivery guy checked out fine. Susan verified his description as big, blond, overweight.

Not Deni.

Russ at the police station had a monitor on my email accounts, but there'd been no suspicious incoming messages, no reply to the gag-worthy conciliatory note I'd sent Deni. We had nothing to go on.

"So we stick close to you."

"And Susan."

Harris winked. "No problem."

Matt wasn't happy. "So there's no way of getting this creep before he gets to Willy?"

Now I wasn't happy, either.

"The perv most likely has a juvenile file, but without a positive ID, we can't start digging through those sealed records. We're getting some of the clairvoyants to take a look."

"Modern science, huh?"

"Ancient, but effective," Harris answered, then

checked his watch. "I'll call Rosehill and tell them we're on our way."

"And I better get back to the office." Matt put the dishes in the sink, said the cleaning service arrived at ten, and kissed me good-bye. "You'll keep her safe?" he asked Harris.

The bodyguard pointed to my neck. "Better'n you."

Matt started to raise the tie, but I pulled away. "It's a rash!"

"And you guys aren't engaged," Harris said. "Got it. I'll check outside."

So Matt kissed me again. "We'll figure it all out. Don't worry."

Easy for him to say. He didn't know my mother the way I did.

"I knew there was something you weren't telling me! I said so, didn't I? But that I have to hear such news from Loretta Hargrove!" Sniff. "As if my own daughter couldn't call me first."

"Mom, we're not—"

"But no matter. I'll make plane reservations this afternoon and be there in a day or two, as soon as I place the last dog I've been training. Then we'll plan a big engagement party, maybe for Halloween while everyone's gathered together anyway."

Sure. I'd be the one dressed up as the bride of Frankenstein. "Listen, Mom, I have to tell you—"

"Now don't be difficult, darling. This is the best news I've heard in ages."

"But Dad—"

"We'll invite him if we have to, but I bet the jackass won't leave his playmates for his own daughter's engagement party. We'll send him the bill, though. Gotta go, Willy. That new dog isn't socialized enough yet."

Grr.

That was me. Not the new dog.

Chapter Twenty-seven

I had a big mouth and a bad reputation and goose bumps about walking into that council meeting.

So I let Carinne and Dr. James Everett Harmon go in first.

I heard all the greetings from the door. Congratulations, good wishes, about time. Carinne halted in front of me, bewildered. I hadn't spoken to her about the engagement, only that we were going to get her presence—and her obvious relationship to me—out in the open, all at once, then never again. I hoped.

Harris shoved me through the door. Now the good cheer turned to shock, confusion, and a little anger that they'd been shocked and confused and tricked. I stepped beside my half sister.

"Yes, Carinne O'Dell and I are related on my father's side. Yes, Matt and I have an understanding. Yes, I have pink hair. No, I am not going to speak further on any of these matters. None of which is this council's business." I headed toward the empty rows of chairs facing the council. "And no, my mother does not know. I was hoping you"—nodding toward my grandmother—"would speak with her."

My grandmother went pale, and I think she mumbled something about how nice Italy was at this time of year.

"Too late. She'll be here midweek."

Everyone knew who I meant. No one volunteered to pick Mom up at the airport. Mrs. Ralston, the village clerk, fanned herself. A few others had beads of sweat on their foreheads, despite the cool temperature in the meeting room.

Mayor Applebaum banged his gavel. "We have a great deal of business, people. I call this emergency session of the Paumanok Harbor village council to order."

I guess he forgot my mother's temper, or how she could have every dog in the Harbor running amok.

I hadn't realized this was to be an official local government meeting, thinking it was the para-council only. All the elected officials sat at the front table, though, being filmed by a video camera on a tripod as they gave their names and positions, which never would have been permitted by the espers, lest copies fall into the wrong hands. Maybe they didn't start filming until the mayor called everyone to order. I could hope.

Jimmie, Professor Harmon, sat between Carinne and me. "This should be informative. My first encounter with everyday American government, you know."

Lou sat behind us with old Doc Lassiter, the cyber shrink from Shelter Island who was staying at my grandmother's. Monteith from Rosehill sat nearby. Now I noticed Colin and Kenneth at opposite corners of the room. Harris stood at the door, checking IDs of anyone who entered, after they passed through a metal detector. Uniformed police guarded the other exits. This was not your everyday American town hall meeting. Or maybe it was, these days.

I saw why we were following more formal procedure this morning when a gray-haired man in a shiny gray suit stood up and carried a sheaf of notes to the speaker's lectern. The mayor introduced him as a representative of an independent contractor company, working with the Army Corps of Engineers, to see if Paumanok Harbor could be declared an emergency zone due to threats of loss of income and property from the beach erosion.

We could not. Therefore, he suggested, we should

consider hiring a dredging company—with which he was not and never had been affiliated—to remove the new shoal that impeded boat traffic from entering or exiting the harbor area, and use that sand to restore the beaches as protective barriers.

As if we hadn't considered that option, and how much it would cost. Paumanok Harbor simply did not have that kind of money or any way of borrowing it after the embezzlement scandals in the summer. Now the Feds wouldn't help us pay for the work. They might consider adding us to the list of areas needing attention, the man said. We might see them back here in three years, barring a catastrophic hurricane.

The speaker added that we could plant native grasses whose roots helped anchor the remaining sand, erect snow fences to trap it, or build revetments and rock-filled gabions to buffer it from the next storm. He referred to pages of research, with projections of tides and winds and damaging storms. He quoted statistics on ocean currents and rising water levels and damage to areas downwind of the barriers. Most people stopped listening as soon as he said no money was coming our way.

I'm sure he had graphs and charts and big scientific theories. What it all meant, I gathered from what I understood, was that we would be wasting our own time and money on a losing proposition. The ocean always won. We'd do better to think about moving the town to higher ground.

Angry mumblings came from the audience. Easy for him to say. He didn't have a home and a business, his parents' pasts and his children's futures here. Besides, the town needed the harbor and the beaches to survive economically. If they went, higher ground wasn't going to matter.

The mayor banged his fist on the table in front of him. I guess he forgot he had a gavel. The amazing thing was he remembered to come to the meeting at all. Mrs. Ralston must have felt the session important enough to send the police for him. Uncle Henry Haversmith, the chief of police, had a place at the front table, too, along with the village financial officer, its staff attorney, and several others whose functions I hadn't paid attention to. I could tell which ones were psychics because the Royce folk didn't look worried at the dire predictions. They mostly looked in my direction and smiled.

They thought I could fix what the Feds couldn't.

Next up was Ms. Garcia of the Centers for Disease Control. She walked past me on her way to the podium without acknowledging my presence.

She reported that her department had not been able to identify a causative agent for the rashes, although they eliminated airborne bacteria, known viruses, insect-borne diseases, water and air contaminants, plus plant emissions or poisons from the native flora. To justify her job and the money spent, she read from a list several pages long of what we did *not* have. The results were not conclusive, she said, because she and her staff had received little cooperation in gathering data. Even now, affected people claimed they had no rashes. She turned in my direction and pointed to the tie wrapped around my neck.

"It's a hickey!" came from one of the board members, Mrs. Hargrove's son-in-law, I assumed.

Everyone laughed, except Ms. Garcia and me.

Mayor Applebaum called for order.

Ms. Garcia gave more dire warnings about untreated epidemics, drug-resistant illnesses, mutant viruses. And how the government could quarantine the entire village as a health hazard. No one in, no one out.

Again, some listeners fretted. Many looked toward me for the cure. I looked at my watch, wondering how soon we could get out of here. Matt might need help at the vet office. Harris' car might need new upholstery if I didn't get Little Red out of it soon. I hated leaving him in the car, even with the windows cracked, a bowl of water, and a new rawhide chewie. But I couldn't trust him with the cleaning people, and bringing him inside the meeting with me, which was outlawed anyway, made him more of a target for crazy people. Harris' car had tinted windows. He'd made me pull up the hood of my sweatshirt anyway, but Red should be safe. The car was another story.

And I had to talk to Oey. And my mother.

Mayor Applebaum called for the next speaker, another man in a suit, an out-of-town lawyer who wanted permission for his nutcase client to build a new lighthouse on a hill overlooking the bay, right above where the sand was rapidly disappearing. The head of the planning board cited zoning laws, the natural resources chairman referred him to the map of unbuildable wetlands and fragile dunes, Mrs. Ralston had a secretary hand the lawyer a copy of the engineer's beach study that he obviously hadn't listened to, and the village attorney noted that only the federal government could authorize or build a new lighthouse.

The audience laughed again, more cheerfully this time. No disasters, no diseases, just some rich bastard who thought he could build anything, anywhere, simply because he had enough money.

The lawyer shrugged. "I only do what my clients pay me to do. I tried to tell them they were wasting their time."

Voices shouted out asking who.

Privileged information, the lawyer replied, and he couldn't say if it weren't, because everything had been done electronically. No names, untraceable holding companies, and bank codes only. They did pay on time.

Weird. But I could understand in a way. If you were rich enough to buy that tract of land, you wanted privacy. Ditto if you wanted to build a lighthouse. I'd always thought living in a lighthouse might be ideal, as long as it was attached to the mainland, avoiding the need for boats. Of course, in my daydreams, no shipwrecks, hurricanes, or undermining erosion occurred. Lighthouses were secluded, scenic, important. A writer could have important ideas in a place like that.

Mayor Applebaum consulted the notes Mrs. Ralston

handed him and called up the next item on his agenda. I missed the name of the bronzed youngster who stepped to the podium, because my phone vibrated, indicating a text message. I know the signs said to silence all cell phones, but text messages didn't count, did they?

The screen showed a message from Russ, who was monitoring my computer. Several others, including the police chief, also carefully checked their phones, so I knew it had to be bad.

While some of the board members listened to the surfer-type, and some admired or despaired over the tattoos on his bare arms, others read their messages from their laps, under the table.

We'd heard from Deni. He hadn't taken the bribe, or the bait. He hadn't sent his manuscript, just another threat. "Too late, bitch. I heard your mother's a witch. You know how they get rid of them, don't you? Burn, baby, burn."

I wanted to jump up and run out of the meeting room. I had to beg my mother not to come north. Not till we found this monster.

Lou leaned forward to tell me, "We're on it. She'll have an agent with her."

That was not reassuring when someone might be planning to burn up her house or her car. I needed Piet, the fire-damp wizard. I needed the National Guard and a pack of Rottweilers.

Doc Lassiter put a hand on my shoulder. Calm immediately spread from his hand to my racing heart, the way it always did when Doc touched anyone. "She'll be fine. They're tracing the email now. They'll get him this time. Breathe, Willow."

He was right. No one knew where my mother was, not even me. Like the lawyer and the lighthouse dude. No one could say what plane, what rental car, what state she'd be in. And Harris had Mom's house so wired for security a shadow couldn't get past it. Unless, of course, Susan let in another delivery man, one with a bomb. Do not let my cousin go near the house, I sent to Harris.

Next I sent a text to my mother, typing as fast as I could, warning her to beware of unknown messages, strangers, anyone with a match. THREATS, I wrote. SERIOUS THREATS ABOUT WITCHES AND BURNINGS.

She sent back: STOP LISTENING TO YOUR FATHER. BEEN CALLED A LOT WORSE THAN A WITCH.

I turned and whispered to Lou, "Try to convince her the danger is real and to stay where she is for now. And tell her about Carinne."

"Me? Hell, no. I don't even know the woman."

Maybe she'd listen to my father, even if he got things half-assed backward some of the time. He didn't text, and I couldn't step outside to call him, so I sent my mother another message: CALL DAD. WARNINGS? AND NEWS.

She sent back: ALREADY HEARD ABOUT THE ENGAGEMENT. WHAT COULD BE BETTER? TTYL. DRIVING.

She would have killed me, driving while talking. But texting? Good grief! I didn't have to wait for Deni to find her. Some highway patrol car would find her in a ditch first.

Doc Lassiter put his hand back on my shoulder.

Right. She had a dog in the car. She wouldn't take chances. Most likely someone else was driving, or she'd pulled over. I'd call her later, her and my father. I put the phone away.

Right now, my attention switched to the high schooler's complaints that the town had nothing to offer its young people. They'd shut down the skatepark and put in a curfew. The community rec center stayed open only a few nights a week now that it was the off-season, and the high school cut back on sports and clubs, to save money.

Too late I realized that Carinne wasn't listening to his speech; she was wheezing, gasping for air like an asthmatic. Oh, lord, a teenager. I'd thought we'd overcome her anguish of "reading" a younger person by channeling it into pictures so the voices in her head quieted. How arrogant of me to think I'd fixed my half sister in half an hour.

How selfish of me not to think about who might be at the meeting and what effect they'd have on Carinne. All I could do now was thrust a pad and pencil at her. She shook her head. "He's not here. He's not here when he's thirty-seven!" She started crying and holding her hands over her ears.

Jimmie appeared too upset or too frightened to help. He'd turned pale and trembly. I turned to Doc. "Do something!"

He put his arms around a sobbing Carinne, and he and Lou led her out of the meeting room. Monteith followed, looking concerned. I would have gone, too, but I had to stay with Jimmie, who appeared too shaken to move.

The kid at the podium said, "She's right. I won't be here when I'm thirty-seven because there are no jobs here, no affordable houses, no future unless I want to wait on tables for tips and collect unemployment in the winter."

He did not understand. I did, and almost cried. Jimmie had a tear rolling down his cheek, but I did not know if it was for the boy or for Carinne. Then members of the audience started calling suggestions to the teenager.

"You could go to school and learn a trade, Brock. There's plenty of opportunity in the Harbor for plumbers and electricians, tile setters and masons. I had to wait three weeks for someone to come out from Sag Harbor."

Brock made a face. I guess a blue collar was not what he wanted out of life.

Rick from the marina called out, "I'll pay the tuition and guarantee a job for anyone who takes boat mechanic courses."

The kid scowled this time. Grease under his fingernails did not suit him, either.

Someone else said he should study harder. We could use a doctor of our own, and a dentist. A man in back thought he should join the army, serve his country.

No! I almost shouted. He'd never come back from war.

Finally one of the town councilmen asked, "So what do you want to be, a rock star or a world-class athlete? I've heard your band and seen you on the field. Son, you're just not that good. And why aren't you in school now, anyway?"

Brock answered that he was. Coming here was part of his civics project. "Find a cause, Mr. Syragusa said, see if you can make a difference."

"All right," the councilman replied. "You've stated your complaints, but it's easy enough to find fault. What do you propose?"

"We want a park for motorbikes and ATVs. We were thinking of that cliff where the asshole wants to put a fu— Excuse me. Where the rich dude wants to put a lighthouse."

This time I did shout, "No!" I'm no clairvoyant. Maybe my runaway imagination provided the graphics, but I could see this handsome young man crushed under the weight of one of those daredevil, air-polluting, peace-shattering vehicles.

Others also protested. The extreme sports were too dangerous. The village couldn't afford the insurance. The neighbors would have fits. The land was privately owned.

Mrs. Ralston took over when the mayor asked what the boy wanted for the third time. "What else do you want? We can see if there's a way to keep the skatepark open on weekends, and try to find a way to keep the rec center open more hours."

Brock nodded. "With more interesting stuff at youth nights, not just b-ball and Ping-Pong."

"We are not turning the center into a video game arcade."

"Right, but now most courses and activities are for old farts. That is, senior citizens, or little kids. Even Ms. Tate's course last summer had an age limit, and met in the afternoon when everyone over fourteen had summer jobs."

So I volunteered to teach a high-school oriented graphic arts course. "On one condition. You have to take the course." I'd do anything to keep Brock off a death-trap.

He had to think about it, but he agreed. "It's my girl-friend who wants to take a course. She made me add that to my presentation. I guess I'll get to spend more time with her that way, and her parents can't complain."

"Excellent." Mrs. Ralston complimented him. "I'd give you an A for effort. B for results."

He grinned, showing dimples. "I'll get an A+. We knew we'd never get the motocross track. That was a scare tactic."

Looks and brains and charm. The kid had it all, except for a future.

CHAPTER TWENTY-EIGHT

I had a better understanding of the horrors Carinne
must go through every day. I had no idea what to do
about them, except wonder how she hadn't had a
breakdown before this.

Before I could get up to find her, to offer what com-
fort I could or beg Lou to find an answer, the mayor
wandered out, forgetting to close the meeting. Mrs.
Ralston did it, then told the cameraman to shut off the
videotaping. "We are going to have an informal meeting
of the Halloween festival committee, so anyone not involved please feel free to leave."

I was *not* volunteering to help at the witches' sabbath,
so I got up to go. I thought my news should be more
important than trick or treating, but Paumanok Harbor
took its traditions seriously. I'd come back and talk to
some of these people separately.

As people filed out, though, Mrs. Ralston asked if I
might stay behind. "We'd love to hear your ideas, Willy."

That's what I'd come for, so I couldn't leave.

For the sake of the strangers, some who lingered near
the exits, chatting, she explained how everyone in town
took so much pride in having a famous author among
them; they begged to know about my latest book. Besides, she told them, my plots were always so creative, I
was bound to have some notion of how to save the beach

where the festival got held every year, an idea no one
had considered for dealing with erosion. She apologized,
but told the strangers they needn't be bothered with listening to fairy tales. She told Brock to get back to classes,
thank God.

"Right away, Mrs. R."

I didn't need any Royce genes to know that for a lie.
What kid wouldn't extend his official get-out-of-school
pass for the rest of the day? He sauntered out, grinning.

Mrs. Ralston apologized again. She wasn't apologizing for practically shoving people out the doors, but for
the lies.

The police chief clutched his bottle of antacid tab-
lets. Someone else's face turned red, and Rick from the
marina rubbed at his ear. I didn't know how many more
suffering truth-mavens sat at the table or in the audience, but I could work with what Mrs. Ralston had
given me.

I picked my words carefully, not wanting to hurt the
psychic lie detectors more than I had to. They'd be upset
enough to hear my theories. The biggest lie, of course,
was that I'd discuss my work in progress with anyone
except my editor, and that rarely and grudgingly.

The original idea didn't come from me, I started,
which was the absolute truth. I'd developed my sand
people from a mention in Dr. Harmon's fabulous as-in-
fabled bestiary, a book he'd written under the pen name
of James Everett many years ago while teaching creative
writing at Royce University in England. I was honored
to be permitted to illustrate a new edition.

I introduced the professor, Jimmie as he liked to be
called, and made him stand up. He bowed to the council.

When he sat down, I told how he'd described a group
he named Andanstans, belligerent creatures who inhabited seashores and deserts and seabeds, constantly trying to steal the sand from each other's domains.

My grandmother nodded. She'd read his book and
heard some of my conclusions.

"I just drew the people he described." Someone

gagged. Okay, that was not the truth. "Here is what I came up with." I'd brought a sketch of the Andanstans to pass around. "They're very small and impermanent. That is, they can re-form or reconfigure themselves into humanoid shape instantly, simply by pulling together a few grains of sand."

As the story in my head developed, I told the council, the Andanstan character developed, just as it did for all my heroes and heroines and villains. The way I saw them, the Andanstans were fierce warriors, constantly at battle, but with an honor code as strict as West Point's. According to their standards, one theft deserved another in return, one favor deserved one back. The bigger the favor, the bigger the debt owed.

Someone said, "Uh-oh."

"That's right, uh-oh. Say someone needs help and these sand beings come together for once and save the day, or save a ship, for instance. But once the ship is saved, not only are they ignored, unthanked, but they are physically assaulted. Blown up, in fact. The way I'd write the story, which I won't because it's the professor's and I am delighted simply being the illustrator, the Andanstans do not mind the destruction so much as the disrespect. The dishonor."

"Oh, shit." That came from the side wall, where Rick stood, his arms crossed, not rubbing his ear. He knew what I said was true.

I ignored him. "So they steal the sand. When that does not result in a respectful reciprocation, or at least a worthy war, they send rashes to everyone who might have had a grain of sand blow into their eyes or their noses, to get our, that is, their attention. All it needs is a pinprick or a scratch to activate. The rashes are not life-threatening revenge, simply a means of communicating their displeasure, their demand for tribute."

The police chief stopped swallowing Tums like popcorn, but he did not look pleased. My story might be true, but he didn't see any happy ending.

I went on. "It's all about payback. My father tried to tell me."

A couple of people groaned. My father's reputation did not lend confidence to his predictions.

"Bosh!"

Ready to defend my father and his talent, I looked toward the back of the meeting room where the rude sound came from. I hadn't realized Ms. Garcia and the engineer had been standing in the doorway comparing their failed missions. Now she stamped her foot.

"You people don't take anything seriously, do you? I tested the sand. There is nothing dangerous about it. Payback? From imaginary sand people? You'd waste your time listening to this claptrap instead of assisting scientific studies? No wonder this place is on everyone's list to avoid. They told me it was like falling down Alice's rabbit hole, but I didn't believe there'd be a whole village of village idiots."

"It's just a story!" Mrs. Ralston yelled to her as she stormed through the door.

The chief clutched his stomach. The man next to him turned scarlet. Rick from the marina rubbed his ear so hard he rubbed it raw, which caused a rash, which had him pulling his Yankees hat down low so no one could see it.

The marine engineer laughed. "I've heard everything now. Little soldiers stealing the sand. The flu hunter is wrong. You people aren't backward morons. You just like a good joke. Well, I hope you're laughing when your houses fall into the bay. Maybe the little sand guys can bring it back. I can't." He left, too.

"I write fantasy stories," I shouted after him, vehemently, truthfully, and for anyone who didn't know what else I did.

Everyone left at the council's table nodded and urged me on, which meant they were all espers.

Two members of the remaining audience were not: my friend Louisa's husband and an older woman. Dante Rivera had lived his whole life here and had no talent other than making money. He donated a bunch of it, and his time and efforts, to keeping Paumanok Harbor the kind of place he wanted his children to grow up in. Now I heard him tell the older woman beside him, a beach-front property owner, that I wrote good books and won awards.

I smiled at him and made shooing gestures. He smiled, nodded as if he understood what we were about, and escorted the older woman out.

We could all relax now.

The town attorney asked me, "So how can you get these Andywhatevers to give the sand back?"

I ran some of my ideas by them.

Everyone offered a broken cuff link or a single earring, maybe a coin, in case the Andanstans liked gold. Mrs. Ralston took off her gold hoops. "They hurt anyway. Melted down, maybe we could write thank you in the sand."

Emil the jeweler said he had some diamond dust. We could try sprinkling that.

Someone else recalled how ancient cultures and some modern religions used blood sacrifices. He offered his mother-in-law.

We all laughed, but considered how we could get a crowd on the beach to all nick their fingers, so drops of blood dripped onto the sand.

Chief Haversmith asked, "What if that just causes more rashes? I'm finally getting over this one."

"We have to try everything we can think of. We don't know what they like, what could make them happy or improve their lives. I thought of making them clothes, but I don't see how."

"I do." That was Margaret, the weaver who ran a needlework shop. "I have a million quilting scraps and threads. We can shred them into smaller bits and carry them into the tide line."

"Great. They might enjoy all the colors and textures, after seeing nothing but dark sand and light sand. Maybe pink or white sand on some beaches, but not around here. I thought they might like pebbles, but I don't know if they are into grinding rocks into sand."

"And what if they start using the pebbles as weapons?"

I didn't think such insubstantial beings could lift a pebble, unless they worked together the way ants do. They'd built a sandbar, despite their bellicosity, and stabbed Matt with a horseshoe crab's tail.

"They stabbed Matt? What if they figure out how to do their forming thing with heavier materials?" A councilwoman asked. "With pebbles they could be a real physical threat to people."

"Shoot, don't give them ideas," the chief said. "If they like the pebbles, they might start stealing rocks, too, undermining the cliffs entirely."

The professor, who'd been quiet up to now, said, "I propose we meet on the beach and bow down."

Like worshipers? That didn't sit right with anyone.

"No, bow in respect, like Oriental diplomats, or us Brits, to the queen. It's honor they want, as far as I understand, not material items."

"I think we have to try tangibles," I said. "I tried to thank them from the bottom of my heart, casting mental pictures, but they wouldn't listen. They did not even acknowledge my presence. We can't seem to communicate, so we don't know if our gestures have the same meanings in their world. I want to bring you to the beach, Jimmie, to see if your gratitude gets to them. You're one they helped save, after all. They did not react to Moses."

"You mean they helped part the Red Sea?" someone asked.

"No, Moses is Matt's dog, rescued from the ship. Either way, gratitude does not appear to equal a return favor."

Grandma Eve spoke up. "We are not sacrificing our children or our pets. Not even the nasty reporters who try to snoop around the Harbor. But what if we bring them roadkill? Would they know?"

"The Others are usually telepathic, although I could not get through to these. But what if they picked up the image of a car hitting a deer, say? Or read someone's mind. Can you imagine how insulted they'd be then?"

"We've got some talented telepaths of our own. How about getting them to try talking?"

"I already have Oey, the professor's parrot, trying to find out what would satisfy their honor." I explained about the eggs and the favors and the debts. "But sure, send anyone to the beach to try."

"What else?"

I consulted my list. "We could sing to them." The House liked music, when the House communicated with Matt and me. "Maybe play 'Mr. Sandman,' the Beach Boys or the song they play for Mariano Rivera."

"We could have that kid Brock write a rap song dedicated to them."

"Or get the school kids to write praise poems about sand. We could hold a contest where the best ones get carved on the beach."

"I don't know if they can read, much less read English. It's doubtful."

Grandma Eve offered to strew bundles of herbs into the water and along the shore. Someone else suggested wine. Harris volunteered to ask Susan to create a cake in their name, then crumble it in the water like breadcrumbs.

I didn't think they ate the way we did. Besides, give up one of Susan's cakes? "I think the seagulls would get the crumbs. And I doubt the Andanstans would think seagull guano is righteous recompense.

"We have another problem," I explained. A time limit. "Your Halloween festival is held every year at the full moon, isn't it? That's when Oey's eggs hatch and the Andanstans take them home to Unity, along with all our sand."

After a lot of cursing, the consensus was that we should try everything, but try harder to talk to the invaders. Grant might have been able to, but he was in a hospital somewhere. The professor had never spoken with the beings he described in his book, only with Oey. And I felt if the Andanstans had wanted to talk, they would have spoken with me on the beach. "Or sent images for me to visualize. That's what I'm supposed to do, isn't it? They didn't talk to Matt, either."

"About you and Matt . . ."

CHAPTER TWENTY-NINE

I had so much to do and so little time, with so little sleep last night. And I still had a stalker.

They'd delegated me to take charge of the Andanstans and all the efforts to placate them or talk to them. How could I do that when I had to stay hidden away, out of danger?

I met Lou outside when Harris walked me to get Little Red out of the agent's car. I gave the dog some water to hide my mopping at a suspicious wet spot on the seat.

Lou walked us back inside. He reported a trace on the email. Not a name or an address, although they felt they had enough evidence of a serious threat to get a warrant on the server. "But we know he sent that last message from an unregistered smart phone at a coffee shop in Queens. So he's not out here."

Yet.

After Lou explained the new findings, my grand-mother decided we had enough time. Or she cared more about the festival going off than she did about my safety. "So you can take Jimmie to the beach, gather the gold and diamond dust, sing songs, have poetry contests and all the rest. If you keep corresponding with the unpleasant person, Lou can keep track of his whereabouts."

"Fine. Then you deal with my mother."

She pretended not to understand. "Of course I'll see she is informed before the festival."

"Someone will tell her first, then she'll be furious at all of us, from hearing it secondhand."

Grandma Eve looked down her nose at me, hard to do when she stayed seated and I stood in front of her table. "No one will speak of it. I'll see to that."

I believe she could, if anyone could.

"But what are you going to do about that unfortunate Miss O'Dell?" she asked.

"Me? I got Carinne here. You people can fix her." I turned to Lou. "Is she all right now?"

"Yes, the mayor helped her forget about the kid, and Doc helped her relax. Monteith is taking her home. He'll help her sleep."

"Monte?" Jimmie asked. "My godson is liable to smother her cat while she's unconscious."

I didn't think Monteith would go that far, but I didn't think he'd help Carinne do anything but move out.

"He says he can make her sleep so her body recovers from the trauma."

My grandmother turned her scowl on him. "You'd let him drug her? He's no pharmacist or herbalist. I can send something to help."

"No, he doesn't use drugs. No saying how they'll react with a wild talent like hers. He said something about doing yo-yo tricks."

I'd seen his yo-yo, the shiny, spinning silver circles. "You mean he's going to hypnotize her?" I was horrified. After my last experience with an egomaniacal mesmerist who used his powers to kidnap, steal, and embezzle, I didn't trust anything about that particular mental manipulation. Especially not for Carinne, whose fragile personality could not stand much more.

The professor agreed with me. "Monte's good at his parlor tricks, but I do not know about his skill at such a delicate operation. What if he puts her to sleep and cannot awaken her?"

I patted his trembling hand. "I doubt he's that foolish. He knows I'll sic my grandmother on him. And Oey, when she gets back."

"Ah, yes. Oey might have answers."

Lou shrugged. "We can't wait for a broody parrot. We don't have much choice about helping Carinne right now." He echoed my feelings by adding, "She's at the end of her rope."

"Can't you do something?"

"Mayor Applebaum can make her forget, but that won't help the next time she sees a child that's not going to grow up. We can wipe out the talent, but sometimes other stuff gets wiped out, too. Like speech and memory and visual recognition."

"In other words, she could be a vegetable."

"It's not a chance anyone is willing to take."

It better not be. I figured I was Carinne's next of kin, and they'd destroy her brain over my dead body. I must have squeezed Little Red too hard because he growled. Lou got up and took a few steps back. "Grandma, you must know a way to help. Carinne's birth is not her fault. She needs us."

"I'll read some of my research books, but I've never heard of a cure for sorrowful or frightening foretelling. Maybe someone in England knows more."

Lou pulled his chair closer to Grandma Eve, away from me and Red. "I've already sent out the call for assistance. They'll try. And we'll try to keep tabs on the kid she saw today, steer him in safer directions. Monte wants to document everything that went on this morning. That way, he says, he can justify the expenses as necessary research."

"Good for him." Yes, that had a touch of sarcasm. I still felt the new director of Rosehill cared more about the bottom line than about helping people. "But if you keep Brock away from motorbikes, he could drown surfing or get hit by a car or get food poisoning."

"Bad things happen all the time. We'll do what we can. We have to see how unchangeable Carinne's prophecies are, and how accurate. Sometimes a seer misinterprets what he sees."

Grandma Eve made a snorting sound. "Just ask the poor woman's father. The jackass never gets anything right, or not so anyone can figure out."

"I never said Dad was her father!" Between my mother and her mother, only one jackass existed.

"You didn't have to. I was with your mother when you were born. She did not give birth to twins."

"Carinne is two years older. They weren't married."

Another snort. "It wouldn't matter if she were ten years older than you, he never told us about her. Maybe if he got her help sooner . . ."

And maybe if my mother had been easier to talk to, he would have. It was too late for finding fault. "So what happens in the meantime? I wanted to take her around, introduce her to people so she could see she's not the only freak. That is, the only psychic here. Now I don't dare. But you cannot keep her cocooned, or locked away at Rosehill. If you"—I glanced between my grandmother and the man from DUE—"can't help her, she'll be a prisoner in her room there, afraid to see the new students when they come or Lily's grandchildren or the young lawn-mower guys. Jimmie will be her only companion except when a couple of us visit."

Jimmie looked even more troubled. "I won't be around forever, you know."

No one wanted to go there. Lou hurried to say, "I've got a task force working on it, checking for any precedents."

Like my father's mother, who heard voices, too. She never told fortunes, as far as I knew.

Lou rubbed at his bristly chin. "It could take a while. We're spread kind of thin right now. There's a lot of stuff going on."

Trust my grandmother to say, "There always is, when Willow is involved."

"You're blaming the Andanstans and Carinne's misery and Brock's dire prophecy on me?"

"Of course not."

But I know she was. They all were. They always did.

"I'll try to work with the Andanstans, but that's it. I don't know how to save Brock, or how to train Carinne to tune out bad news. Maybe the mayor could teach her to have a selective memory. I can't, and I cannot be the one to tell my mother about her. Not if I have to live with Mom in my apartment while she tapes her new show."

Grandma Eve nodded, but she didn't say anything.

I went on: "She has to know before she gets here. It's only fair, so she doesn't walk into Lily's kitchen and find Carinne there, in front of scores of people, all watching for her reaction. I tried to tell her not to come on account of the stalker, but it's like telling the Andanstans to put our sand back. Or trying to hold one of them in your hand. Dad thinks she'll have apoplexy or something when she sees Carinne, so someone has to warn her."

"I do not see why," Eve said. "Rose loves being the center of attention, my TV star daughter, so let her rant and rave all she wants when she gets here. There's nothing she can do about it, is there? If I call and tell her, she'll fume and fuss all the way here. That's not good for her driving, or her manners at rest stops and gas stations. Or airports if she flies."

I could imagine my mother's road rage through seven different states. And what she'd say to the guards at the security gates when they wanted to pat her down. Not a pretty picture.

Lou rubbed his chin. "We already have an agent on the way to see she gets here safely. He can block her calls. Or slip her a sedative."

Now both Grandma Eve and I gave him dirty looks. "You cannot solve problems by drugging people."

He shot back: "You can keep them from getting arrested."

I thought about it. "No matter how we try, we can't do anything about her broken heart."

The old witch snorted again. "That's a crock, Willy. Not even you with the stars in your eyes can believe it. She divorced the jackass decades ago. She hasn't been pining for him all these years."

I couldn't deny the other men my mother regularly dated, or stayed with. "No, but she rushed to his side when he got sick. And she always wanted to believe him."

"But she never did. She mistrusted his fidelity from the day they wed, and you and that woman proved her right. So, no, she won't be brokenhearted. She'll feel vindicated."

I had to concede the possibility. Mom could gloat with the best of them. Her *I told you so* would be loud and lasting. "I'll stay at Matt's."

"Speaking of that, Rose will be more upset to hear you are not officially engaged."

"Then she'll just have to be upset, won't she? I already tried to tell her, and I am certain your spies have already called to give her the latest update. Maybe besides Carinne, you can get your friends to keep their mouths shut about me and Matt, too."

Lou cleared his throat to interrupt an argument about gossip vs. caring interest that had gone on for at least ten years. "Ladies, we have to talk about the stalker, too. We're getting closer, and we're showing your sketch to where we think he bought the phone we traced. All we need is a name and address and we can scoop him up. Meantime, Eve is right. We need you to stay in touch with him. Keep him communicating."

I hated the idea, but the tech guy, Russ, came in when the chief buzzed him, carrying a clone of my computer already set up with a "compose mail" box. "You've got to respond, Willy, so we can track his whereabouts. The fool shouldn't have switched to his cell phone, even if we can't get him ID'd through it if he used cash and got a prepaid card for it. What do you want to say?"

Uncle Henry came and stood over my shoulder while I reread Deni's last hateful message about my mother.

"Don't threaten him, or he'll take it as a dare to escalate. And don't sound scared. That's what he wants."

"I am scared, and I would wring his scrawny neck if I had it between my hands."

"Not the message you want to send, Willy."

So I typed in: MY MOTHER IS A DOG TRAINER, NOT A WITCH. SHE SAVES ABUSED AND ABANDONED ANIMALS AND WORKS WITH THEM UNTIL THEY ARE ADOPTABLE. RIGHT NOW SHE HAS A GERMAN SHEPHERD THAT WAS KEPT TIED OUTSIDE A METH LAB, A PIT PULL FROM A DOG FIGHTING RING, AND A DOBERMAN PINSCHER SENTENCED TO DEATH ROW ON ACCOUNT OF HIS AGGRESSION.

"Should I add anything else? Like mess with her at your own risk?"

After he chewed a couple of stomach pills, Uncle Henry said, "I think even a moke like this punk can get your message. Good job, Willy. But add some kind of question, to make sure he responds."

"Like how about lunch?"

"I don't think he'll believe you if you invite him over for soup and a sandwich," my grandmother said.

"Not Deni. Me. I'm starving."

"Finish the letter."

I wrote: ARE YOU PUTTING ALL THIS IN YOUR NEXT BOOK? DO YOU WANT TO BE IN MINE?

"That should do it," Lou said, after making sure Russ saved copies of all the notes as evidence. "You'll have Harris and maybe Colin and Kenneth to go wherever you and the professor need to go. I'll stay at Rosehill with Carinne."

The chief said he'd put one of his men on watch at my mother's house until Harris got back. Russ swore he put beepers on my computer and his clone of it to monitor any incoming mail. He also had any phone calls at Mom's house transferred here to police headquarters where someone would be on duty at all times, listening for threats.

Between all of them—the police, DUE, the cyber crimes geeks and the agent left in Manhattan to guard my

apartment and Mrs. Abbottini and the Rashmanjaris—
they really were spread thin, and really were looking out
for me.

Lou brushed my thanks aside. "We're not taking any
chances, especially not until you get the sand back."

CHAPTER THIRTY

I had a posse.

Instead of making me feel safer, the three big men surrounding Jimmie and me and Red brought the danger closer. If Deni were in New York City, I ought to be free to go anywhere I wanted, by myself. If Lou thought I'd be safe, these guys would be off playing golf.

On the other hand, or hip, the outline of the gun at Harris' side did make me stop cowering at every car door slam.

My first stop had to be at my house to get more clothes, not that Matt had a lot of spare closet room or dresser space. I'd lived out of suitcases before.

Harris took the time to check all his instruments and sensors. I checked the phone messages myself. I knew they'd been listened to from here to hell and back, but I still had to listen: my editor's assistant about a copyediting question; a poll taker I had no intention of responding to; the upstairs apartment guys wanting to know about the sublet in Mrs. Abbottini's unit; my college asking for money.

I packed as many clean clothes as fit in the case, and one of Susan's sexy summer nightgowns. I counted on Matt to keep me warm.

Harris found no signs of intruders.

Next I checked on my mother's two dogs, who were

staying at Aunt Jasmine's. Uncle George came home from the farm frequently to walk them, since they couldn't be put out in a pen in the yard, not with Deni's threats. They gave me unenthusiastic tail wags and went back to sleep.

Then we drove into the business area of town, all three blocks of it. I'd wanted Carinne to see Paumanok Harbor at one of its prettiest seasons. The trees still had some color, the village green had pumpkins and mums and bales of hay at every corner, walkway, and lamppost. The streets had easy parking spaces now that the summer crowd was gone. More important, the shopkeepers and passersby had more time and more patience. Carinne could have seen how friendly the Paumanok Harbor people were, how multitalented. I thought that important if Carinne were to live here for any length of time.

People waved and asked how my cousin was. Clerks left their cash registers to say they'd hang posters or put out collection jars for the sand reclamation. Two women handed me gold chains. I handed them to Harris for safekeeping. One of the school board members offered to get the sixth graders to write poems. Bill at the hardware store set the keys to playing *R-E-S-P-E-C-T*, most likely in honor of the Andanstans, but I harbored the warm thought it was for me. Little Red snarled.

Carinne might have been impressed when Joanne at the deli had takeout containers of macaroni and cheese all ready for me and the professor. The perfect thing for mid-October, even the right color, with toasted bread crumbs on top. Jimmie'd never had an American version, so he was delighted. Harris wasn't, when Joanne refused to make him a bologna sandwich on white bread with mustard, and handed him ham and swiss on rye instead. Then he laughed, saying he was only testing her.

She laughed back and teased me about cornering every handsome man in the Harbor.

"But the most handsome one is at the vet clinic, getting a rubber ball out of the Maclays' puppy's stomach."

Which kind of ruined Colin's appetite for his meatball hero.

We sat on benches outside the deli to eat and watch more people go by, many wishing me good luck, others volunteering to help. No one volunteered to talk to my mother, of course. And you could see them biting their lips about Matt, but they showed tact, for once. Or fear of Grandma Eve. I kept my baseball cap on, so no one had to pretend not to see my pink hair.

Janie came out of the hair salon at the side of her house to fetch lunch for her and Joe the plumber at the deli. Showing no tact whatsoever, she pulled my cap off and shook her head.

"Next time, go to a professional."

I put the hat back on.

Jimmie patted my shoulder. "I think it is lovely, my dear. It matches your blushes and a rose that I used to cultivate."

Great. So I looked like a faded blossom. "Thank you, and for being a good friend to me and to Carinne, too." She'd need his gentle companionship more than ever if she couldn't leave Rosehill. No, there had to be a way to help her. I'd find it.

Carinne's existence complicated my life, sure, but I felt sorry for her. And I liked her. She looked like me. She was my sister.

I gazed around, trying to imagine her here in the village, seeing the small town through a stranger's eyes. Not bad.

Until Walter from the drugstore ran across the street and handed me a brown paper bag, then a white pharmacy bag with a tube of something that I doubted was toothpaste.

"If you keep using all these"—the brown bag—"then this"—the white bag— "might help."

How could I even consider staying on in this place, or thinking Carinne might be happy here?

Walter handed a brown bag to Harris. I glared at the bodyguard despite my embarrassment. He was supposed to be guarding my house and the road to Grandma Eve's house and the farm stand. He was not supposed to be entertaining women there, and definitely not my cousin Susan.

Harris looked into the bag and grinned.

Walter handed another to Colin and Kenneth to share. "You can never be too careful."

Jimmie didn't get a bag. "I say, did everyone have prescriptions to fill?"

Walter took a Cadbury bar from his white coat's pocket. "Made in England, so you don't get lonely."

Jimmie beamed. "I've never had so many friends in my life." He waved the candy bar at us on the bench. "I'll share my treat if you'll share yours."

We hustled him to the library.

Mrs. Terwilliger did not have any books for me today. "You're too busy writing your own and helping the town. But here's a printout of the local real estate offerings."

"But I'm not—"

"You will. Talk to him."

I decided she meant I should go talk to the House on Shearwater Street again, where the two homes on either side were back on the market. I silently wished the real estate people good luck in selling either of them.

Jimmie got a book on chess, and the guards got copies of the latest Reacher novel. All without asking.

"Do you have anything I could bring back to my cousin, who is not feeling well?"

Mrs. T didn't ask what Carinne liked, what her usual reading was. She thought a minute, scurried off down the stacks, and came back with James Herriot again, this time for Carinne and the professor to share, and a book about choosing the right college.

"Oh, I don't think Carinne will go back to guidance counseling."

"I do. She needs to stay current."

Carinne might have taken heart at the old librarian's confidence . . . or inside information. She'd appreciate the new library card tucked inside the college book, already made out in her name.

There were mothers with strollers, though. Toddlers coming from story hour. A couple of younger people on the library computers. Twenty-somethings jogging outside.

Thank God Carinne hadn't come to town.

The toddlers reminded me that I wanted to see how my friend Louisa was doing with her new baby, and tell her I'd volunteered to teach that course. I didn't expect her to be at the community center. She managed the arts side of the building, which housed a magnificent collection and gave all kinds of classes. I thought I'd ask her assistant if Louisa was ready for a visit, because I didn't want to call and disturb her if she was resting. I could drop off the wrapped package I'd brought for the baby here, with a message to call me.

There she was, though, with a tiny bundle crosswise at her chest in a sling. She, of course, had either not heard or not cared about my grandmother's caveats. "I love your hair! Can I help plan the wedding? Does it have to be all pink to match? I have the perfect flower girl and ring bearer. They're at school and day care, thank heaven. Oh, and I'd love to meet your new relative. Is she talented like you?"

I knew Louisa meant my books, not the paranormal bit. She herself had no esper aura whatsoever.

I shook my head. Carinne's talent was far from mine, from anyone's here, and potentially harmful. I doubted she could ever be Louisa's friend, or visit the arts center programs and concerts, not if Louisa intended to carry the new baby like a papoose, like I carried Little Red.

The thought made me sad. *I* didn't particularly want to go to many of the cultural activities—Why should I, when I had all of Manhattan's museums and galleries and auditoriums at my fingertips?—but I wanted Carinne to be able to go.

While the professor and the DUE guys looked at the paintings that formed a small part of the building's benefactor's collection, I admired the baby. Out of her swaddles she looked even tinier. I prayed Louisa wouldn't ask me to hold her while she checked the course calendar. I jiggled Little Red, just in case Louisa got ideas.

"After Halloween, I think. The kids get too hyped up about that." And the sand problems would be over by then, one way or another.

"The kids?" she asked. "The whole town goes bonkers, if you ask me. All I'm hearing at sculpture class is talk about that festival. And morning yoga is full of who's bringing what to the women's night before All Hallow's Eve gathering on the beach, then to the big party on the village green on Halloween itself for all the local kids. You know, I've never been invited to the beach."

"I, uh, didn't know it was a private affair. I've never gone."

"But your mother and grandmother run it."

"That's why I've never gone. Why would you want to?"

She unbuttoned her blouse to nurse little Emma. I watched as she gave a Renaissance Madonna's smile at the fuzzy little head at her breast. Then she looked at me with a grim look in her eye. "Because I heard they send out blessings and prayers on little paper boats with candles in them. Because I heard they call on every deity ever known, and more that aren't, to protect the land and all its people. Because they join hands and celebrate women and girls."

I never knew what the witches did on the night before Halloween, just that it used to be called Mischief Night. What she described sounded a lot more appealing than naked old pagan women dancing by moonlight.

Emma finished, and Louisa got her to burp. "And I wish to go because I am a woman who lives here and raises her children here."

I understood. We'd been outsiders together as children in the Harbor. We were summer kids, not locals. We lived in summer cottages, not real houses. Our fathers were businessmen on vacation, not fishermen and farmers who worked here year round. It wasn't just a class thing, because neither of our families was wealthy. It was an "us against them" thing. Louisa and I hung out together because none of the other kids would play with us. We thought they were brats. They thought we were snobs. It was like we were from two different countries, speaking two different languages.

And we never, ever understood why the adults had so many meetings and private gatherings and whispered conversations, or why so many weird things happened in the stupid, boring little town we both despised. Why would ten year olds suspect that the blind postman used magic to sort the mail? Or that the bay constable could control the winds when he needed to, or that crazy Mrs. Grissom really did talk to her dead husband when she walked down the street? Magic existed in storybooks, not real life. So much that went on here was so far beyond our innocent comprehension, our beliefs in how the world operated, that we just ignored the anomalies. The Drurys' lawn never needed mowing? A new variety of grass. The Waskinkis' flowers grew twice as high as anyone else's? Better fertilizer. The rest we disregarded as more adult mumbo jumbo we'd figure out as we got older.

I did. Louisa didn't.

I knew she had inklings. No adult who lived here could be that trusting, that ignorant of how many peculiarities got taken for granted in Paumanok Harbor. So what if she couldn't remember the twenty white mares appearing out of the air at the horse show, or the tsunami that stopped before it reached our shores? She still had to know there was some kind of magic involved, and she had to know she was still an outsider.

But now? Now she had children, kids she wanted to see happy and well adjusted and knowing they were as smart and strong as the boys and girls down the block and in the same school. She wanted her kids to make lifelong friends here, be part of the community. And she wanted them blessed by whatever superstitious, quasi-religious sorcery the women used.

She had every right to be there. More than many, in fact. She'd been the one who influenced the arts center donor to bequeath his collection to the town, along with enough money to build the handsome building. She was the one who made it be more than a sterile museum, but open to everyone, to bring the arts to Paumanok Harbor. She'd managed the galleries and the classes and the recreation center with the seniors and the after-school programs as well, until the job and her family got too big. I knew she and her wealthy husband never turned down a call for help, be it sponsoring the horse show or using Dante's vast computer system to catch the embezzler. I think Dante donated the land for the community center, although that was a closely guarded secret, too. I knew for a fact that he helped Ty Farraday get financing to make Bayview a world-class horse ranch and equine rescue facility.

Yes, they were good, giving people, and yes, their children deserved the same rituals as Janie's grandniece Elladaire, who swallowed a firefly and almost set the whole village on fire. But no, they would not be invited to the secret festivities on Halloween eve.

Unless I took charge. It was bad enough that Carinne couldn't go, not when there'd be so many young people. Maybe I couldn't go either, not if Deni'd be lurking behind the beach grass, or in costume among the crowds. But Louisa and her babies? They had to be blessed, whatever that meant. Enough of this polarized caste-system crap, this hush-hush paranoia. Sure Paumanok Harbor had to be protected from the outside world, and from the federal government, too. But Louisa was a citizen, a taxpayer, a pillar of the community. Between Lou and Grandma Eve and the mayor and the chief of police, there had to be a way. I'd make them find it.

"The beaches are public. You're invited."

CHAPTER THIRTY-ONE

I had another new mission. Just what I needed.

I had a new mental attitude, too. Grandma Eve and her cronies wanted my help with the Andanstans? I'd take a page from the little nasties' book. A favor for a favor. I'm giving up my time, maybe giving up my safety and sanity; the older generation could give up some of their inbred, ancient ways. The world kept changing. Paumanok Harbor had to, also.

I didn't mean for them to go public, inviting supermarket tabloids and undercover documentaries and Roswell-type tourists. I just wanted Paumanok Harbor to acknowledge its other citizens.

R-E-S-P-E-C-T.

I collected my retinue to go take on the sand, then the psychics. Unfortunately, one of my supporters had to sit down. Jimmie was weary and needed a rest after walking through the gallery corridors after the amble through town. He had so much determination to help that I kept forgetting he'd barely recovered from a near drowning and days of being lost. Then he'd had to face his most fiercesome foe in the middle of a hurricane. I also kept forgetting how many birthday candles the courtly old gentleman had blown out in his lifetime.

As we got in the car to head back to Rosehill, he said

he liked my paintings better than any he'd seen at the arts center. He ought to be knighted.

Maybe I'd get Grandma Eve to include men on the beach, not just untalented women and children. Jimmie deserved our blessings, too.

I didn't mind putting off the beach visit till later, hoping Matt could come along with us after office hours. Besides, I wanted to check on Carinne. We pretended to take Jimmie home to get what he called his trainers.

"What you call running shoes or sneakers. Can you imagine me sneaking around?"

Honestly, no.

Lily said Carinne had fallen asleep. I wanted to check for myself. Her public raving could unravel centuries of hidden magic, and I did not trust Lou, DUE, Royce, or Monteith to put her well-being ahead of keeping the secrets. Inviting outsiders to a beach party was one thing. Letting them know we had Pandora going postal was another.

I did trust my mother's cousin, but I tiptoed upstairs anyway. I whispered Carinne's name, and tried the door when I got no answer. It was unlocked, which only went to prove Carinne came from Florida, not Manhattan. She lay curled on the bed, the gray cat next to her on the pillow. I got out fast before Little Red saw a mortal enemy.

I reassured Jimmie, who now had a cup of tea in his trembling hand. When I claimed I had a lot of errands before I went to the beach, he looked relieved at the chance to rest here. I'd come get him later in the afternoon, when odds were better that Oey might appear. Shadows could hide the molt the proud creature did not want Jimmie to see.

Lily nodded in approval.

The new Rosehill director, Monteith, must have a touch of telepathy or precognition because he stayed out of sight, rather than face the lecture I'd prepared on the way over. Like what he could do with his yo-yo. And how he was supposed to guide Carinne, not toss her to the lions.

*   *   *

I found Grandma Eve and Lou and Doc Lassiter shifting papers around in the farmhouse kitchen.

"You're not too busy to listen. Good," I said, setting Little Red down so I could cross my arms over my chest and look belligerent and determined, if not like a pouty six year old. Then I proceeded to tell my thoughts on equality and democracy and brotherhood. I amended that to sisterhood. Then I threw in a few mentions about second-class citizens, bullies, and isolationism, which was nearly impossible in the age of iPads and Ethernet.

"You cannot shut decent people out of public events. To do so fosters hostility, which could have the precise effect you are trying to avoid, namely having people question what goes on here. They are not stupid, simply because they cannot predict winning lottery numbers or find lost people by staring into bowls of water. They'll grow resentful. They'll decide we need a mayor who doesn't forget their names when they've lived here for twenty years, a village board that understands and obeys the sunshine laws, rather than governing the place from this very kitchen table. If you and the mayor and the police chief and Mrs. Ralston keeping ruling Paumanok Harbor like an exclusive country club—read exclusionary in that—there'll be riots in the streets."

Okay, maybe I went too far.

"Or good people will move away. People like Louisa and Dante Rivera, who have done so much for this town. Why should they stay and raise their children here when they'll grow up with inferiority complexes? I finally heard what goes on at the women's night. I heard it from Louisa herself, who heard all about it at the center, so it's not some closely held secret. It's not the witches' sabbath I feared, either, though you might dance naked by moonlight after everyone leaves."

Lou laughed, but Doc Lassiter looked interested. Grandma Eve kept putting stamps on envelopes and ignoring my diatribe.

I spoke louder and pounded the table for effect. Little Red barked, so I had to shout over his noise: "How dare you refuse to bless Louisa's new baby? How could you deny her little girl the chance to launch a paper wish boat and watch until it sinks so she'll know her wish will come true? Are those children any less important than Kelvin's kid whose nose runs when he hears a lie? And while I'm at it, what kind of place permits only women on a public beach? That's not constitutional. It's not even good feminism. It's segregation, that's what. Professor Harmon offered up his very life to save this town. Don't you think he's entitled to take part in its festivities?"

My throat went dry before I could use Montauk's huge St. Patrick's Day parade as an example, where less than ten percent of the marchers, I'd guess, had any Irish in them, unless you counted Irish whiskey and green beer. Doc Lassiter handed me a cup of tea and touched my shoulder. At peace now that I'd said my piece, I sat down and added sugar.

Then I remembered where I was and drank it fast, burned my tongue, poured the dregs down the sink, and rinsed the cup before Grandma Eve could look at the tea leaves in the bottom. Carinne already told my future.

"So what do you think?"

Grandma Eve handed me a stack of stamped envelopes. "I think you can drop the top one at the arts center, the next one at the vet clinic, and give Jimmie his invitation when you go back to get him. The rest go to the post office tomorrow."

I looked. The top one was addressed to the Rivera family.

"You already planned to invite them?"

"And everyone else who can be counted on to appreciate what we do, rather than criticize the traditions. Of course, the mayor will be on hand in case anything occurs that people should not recall. Naturally, we won't permit cameras, cell phones, or recording devices."

Naturally. I didn't win the argument, but I didn't lose either, which was a first with my grandmother, so I felt good. Or maybe that was Doc's touch still talking. Either way, I leaned over and kissed her cheek. She tuttutted and straightened the stack of envelopes.

Then she reverted to the witch I knew and loved: "So we are going to have many more people on the beach, Willow. Two circles at first, men and women separate, so everyone can speak freely, then coming together. Which means we need the sand back. Stop wasting my time and yours. You have less than two weeks."

Maybe the Andanstans would take my grandmother as payment for their help. Nah, they'd just be doing us another favor.

Harris drove me back to my mother's house to pick up the old Outback. He followed me to Matt's, and went room to room before he let me go inside, even though Moses kept watch. I promised to lock the door behind him and call when I wanted to go to the beach. Especially if I had to go without Matt. The stalker might have been in the city this morning, but he could be on the way here now.

On that cheerful note, I tried calling my mother again. She answered, but said she'd call back when she stopped for gas. At least she wasn't driving distracted, or demented like she'd be if I told her about Carinne.

Meanwhile, I called my father. "No, I haven't told her. She's driving north. Do you see any danger to her? Your Danny Boy person made threats. I need to know if the threats are real."

"I can't tell, but I know she'll burst a blood vessel if you let her trip over Carinne on Main Street."

So I had to tell him that Carinne wouldn't be going into the village until we got her premonitions manageable, after what happened with her and the kid, Brock, this morning. "But the Royce people are working on it, which is hopeful." I was more optimistic that Oey'd have advice, but I kept that to myself.

He'd been hoping for better, I knew, but Dad said he was glad I found so many people trying to help. Maybe the yo-yo hypnotist I told him about could work something permanent. "They get people to quit smoking, don't they? They bring back lost memories, too, so maybe the Brit can do the reverse."

"I'll ask."

My first job was bringing back the sand. And staying alive long enough to do it.

"Do you have any new warnings for me, Dad?"

"You know how it works, baby girl, sometimes words, sometimes pictures, sometimes just a feeling like a tickle in the back of your throat. The last touch I had, that Irish guy and Burl Ives were marching in a parade, with a fife and drum band."

"So I'm supposed to look out for a guy with a bag-pipe or a glockenspiel?"

"He's wearing a wig."

"Dad, Halloween is coming. Everyone will be wearing a wig. What kind? What color?"

"I'd tell you if I could! I can't just call it up like ordering takeout, you know."

"I know, Dad. I'm sorry. It's just that I'm worried."

"Me, too. I'll stay home tonight. See if anything comes to me."

"Great. Let me know."

"And you let your mother know."

She called back fifteen minutes later. From South Carolina. She could be here by tomorrow.

"Mom, please take this threat seriously. The dirtbag kills pigeons and beheads rats. He sends filthy drawings. He's so crazy there's no telling what he'll do."

"You're getting me paranoid, Willy. Now I keep thinking someone's listening to my conversations and following me."

"Someone is, Mom. At least they're supposed to be, to protect you. DUE is taking the threats to heart. You should, too. Please stay away from here until they catch the bastard."

"Fine. I'll stop off at the apartment."

"No! That's just as bad. How about visiting Lily's daughter in New Jersey?"

"What's the jackass say?"

Dad said to tell her about Carinne. "Nothing that I can figure out. Burl Ives, fife and drum, and a wig. Oh, and hives and chives and extra wives. He didn't mention the mustang tonight, but he did kind of confirm the profiler's guess that Deni is a boy."

"I can't stay away too long, not with the TV show coming up. And the festival."

"Why didn't you ever tell me the thing on the beach was an earth mother kind of occasion, asking blessings or wishes or whatever?"

"It's also a thanksgiving, so they changed it to the night before All Hallow's Eve generations ago to avoid persecution, but keeping to the full moon tradition. Now the kids can enjoy Halloween, but not get up to trouble with all the women abroad. It's a beautiful celebration, but you wouldn't listen. Now all you listen to is the jackass' drivel. I'm supposed to look out for Burl Ives on a horse? If I catch that fat slob breaking some poor animal's back, I'm calling the SPCA."

"You do that, Mom. Oh, I told Deni you had a pit bull and a Doberman and a Rotty with you, to scare him off. What are you delivering anyway?"

"Two toy poodles and a Maltese. We took them from some conscienceless cretin trying to make designer dogs."

Real scary. "So stay there and find them good homes."

"No, city-ites are more into toy breeds for apartments. But maybe I'll stop by the Greyhound Rescue Center in Philly to help get the racers they took acclimated to domestic life."

"That sounds great. They need you." I didn't. "Just let me know where you are, and I'll let you know when they get this a-hole."

"What about Matt?"

"He already has a dog."

"Don't be—"

"You're fading out, Mom. Talk to you later."

*   *   *

Staying inside with the doors locked couldn't include walking across the yard to Matt's office, could it? I took Moses for protection and Little Red for noise.

The Hargrove woman had decamped, and Marta, the kennel man's wife, already sat behind the counter, looking confident and competent. Two small children played near her feet, crayoning and doing puzzles. Carinne couldn't come here, either.

The kids welcomed Moses like an old friend, and he almost barreled them over trying to lick both at once. Take that, Mrs. Hargrove.

Marta said her mother had a doctor's appointment, but she'd be by soon to take the kids to the playground. The little boy wailed that he wouldn't go, this place was better than any old playground.

With the new income, Marta told me, the children could go to daycare a few days a week, too. She thanked me for recommending her, between answering the phone, making appointments, and reassuring a nervous poodle owner that the doctor would be ready in a few minutes, but Moses would never hurt another animal.

I wasn't so sure about Little Red, so I held him tight and refused her gratitude. Mrs. Terwilliger had been the one to put Marta's name on the list.

Marta promised to make the librarian a bookmark.

A favor for a favor. Repaying a kindness.

Damn.

I handed Marta an invitation to the beach thing. "It's kind of like the annual blessing of the fleet or the blessing of the animals mixed in with thanksgiving."

"I'll say a prayer of thanks for you and the library lady. And Dr. Matt, for sure."

Me, too, when he came out and kissed me and said the poodle was his last patient of the day.

In an hour I was home. Not the pawky little house, not my mother's, but home in Matt's arms. My rock, my island, my lover.

And my listener. He told me about his busy day, no sad stories, thank goodness, and I told him about mine, just like an old married couple. Except my day involved my psychic half sister's breakdown, my appointment as Sand Reclamation Officer, the witches' retreat, my father's prognostications, my mother's disbelief, and my dread of disappointing everyone.

He was certain someone could help Carinne lift her heavy burden, and that I'd get the sand back. I should thank my grandmother for the invitation, he'd be happy to see the town come together, and he'd love to meet my father some day. And the Willingham family is looking for a Maltese to play with the one they already have.

That's what I loved about Matt, one of the things, anyway, besides his smile, his dedication, his strong, gentle hands, his flat stomach, his . . .

I could go on forever, it seemed. Mostly he had such strength, such confidence, that I had to believe anything was possible.

But not in the cold October drizzle. I couldn't drag Jimmie to the beach in this. So I made some phone calls—one to the pizza place for delivery—and we kicked around more ideas of what we could do for the Andanstans to repay their kindness.

We could gather as many Matchbox dump trucks as possible, line them up, and see if the guys could drive them. Or we could make small drag nets out of pantyhose. They might appreciate thoughtful gifts that helped move the sand better.

"Great, unless trucks and nets let them steal it faster."

"Or bring it back faster."

"Maybe they'd like pizza crusts." The dogs sure did.

"So what do you think?"

"Try them all. And beg the parrot to help."

That was my plan, but the storm got worse. And the weather station said it could continue until tomorrow.

So we ate the ice pops Matt kept for Marta's children and made love all night.

Chapter Thirty-two

I had triplets?!!

Holy shit, triplets. That's what my father's six AM phone call told me anyway.

Louisa's baby was the sweetest thing I'd ever seen, and I'd kind of gotten used to cute little Elladaire, the fire-throwing toddler I'd foster-mommed in the summer. I was especially fond of that mental picture Carinne drew of me reading a picture book to a little kid. But three babies, all my own, all at once? "Triplets? Say it ain't so, Dad!"

"That's what I got when I thought about you. Usually I don't have to try, the ideas just come. Dreams, inspirations, who knows? But I did what I said, stayed home all night, no TV, no book, no phone sex. Kidding there, baby girl. But I kept staring at that picture of you I have, from when you came to visit last time. The one with your nose all sun-burned. You sounded so worried. And I wanted to give you as much warning as I could so you'd be prepared."

There was no way in hell to prepare for triplets, unless you were a cocker spaniel looking for a closet and some old blankets. "Triplets?" I know I was repeating myself, but panic clogged my mind. "Never do that again, staying in and staring at an ugly photo. Go out, have fun, I don't care if you go to singles bars or strip joints. Spend your pension on phone sex, it's okay. Watch out for chest pains, is all. But do not dream of triplets!

"And you," I yelled at Matt as soon as I ended the call. "We are never having sex again!"

"Good," he said. "This is killing me."

"Hah! Whose idea was it to go another round?"

"Just living up to Walter's expectations with all those condoms."

"On your rowing machine?"

He groaned, rolled over, and went back to sleep.

I didn't. I couldn't get the T word out of my mind. Triplets. How do you hold three babies at once? How do you carry them for nine months? How soon could I join a nunnery?

Matt's alarm went off in an hour. I pretended to be sleeping so he didn't get any ideas about morning sex, which I could tell he had by peeking between my eyelashes to see his salute.

I was not interested.

He showered, shaved, walked and fed the dogs, then brought me coffee and toast with jam. He sat at the end of the big bed, all fresh and clean, his brown hair curling from the shower or the rain I could hear against the windows. The aroma did interest me, and the coffee smelled good, too. "Is this a bribe?"

"No, this is pure love. I have to be at the clinic in ten minutes. I suppose I could . . ."

"No way, José."

"Okay, but I've been thinking."

"You can still think?" My brain had been turned to mashed bananas.

"Yes, and you were right."

"We're never having sex again?"

"Hell, no. About this house being too small."

"No house is big enough for triplets!"

"Forget about the triplets."

Easy for him to say. He didn't have to juggle a career and the three Mouseketeers. I ate the toast, all of it. If I had to eat for four, I better start now.

"I looked around, and the house really isn't suitable for us anymore. You need a studio and I need an exercise room for when I don't have time to go to the gym. And the view does stink, especially when there's such great scenery around us."

He tossed me the real estate brochure Mrs. Terwilliger thought I needed. "We could look at what's available."

Buy a house? Fill it with miniature Matts? I choked on a crumb. "I'm not ready."

"Well, I am." He reminded me how the practice was growing so fast he needed a partner. He had one in mind, a friend from vet school who liked the idea of being near the beach, the Hamptons, and horses, which Matt did not generally accept as patients because of the time involved in stable calls. His friend sounded eager to leave his current job at a conglomerate veterinary clinic in Jersey for a practice of his own, especially since he'd heard world-famous Ty Farraday was opening a horse ranch here.

"And, yes, I warned him the new ranch might have its own, um, holistic practitioners, but he was fine with that, the newest thing in vet med. He'd be happy at the chance to work with Farraday and his shamans or whatever."

"Ty will be thrilled. I'm sure they can't afford a full-time vet there, or the price for a horse doctor to come so far out. Want me to call him?"

A shadow passed over Matt's face. I guess I shouldn't have reminded him that Ty and I had a personal history. "Or you can. I have his cell number."

He relaxed and leaned over to lick a drop of jelly off my chin. "Not yet. Tarbell and I haven't worked out all the details. The problem is, he can afford a down payment on what a partnership here is worth, but not to buy a house at the same time. And you know what the prices are like out here. So I thought I could rent him this one, at reduced rates since he'll be handling the night duties, and we could find a nicer place of our own."

"I can't afford to buy a house. I'm finally making my city rent and expenses, with something left over for my IRA."

He froze up again. I guess I shouldn't have mentioned the apartment, either.

"I'm not asking you to buy a house or give up your apartment. With the partnership money and rent from here, I can swing a mortgage without going too far into debt."

So then we got into a discussion of chauvinism and male dominance and unequal partners. I did, at least. Matt paced the bedroom and mussed his hair again.

"So we'll put it in my name and you can pay goddamn rent. Your mother should be paying the city rent anyway, if she's going to be using the apartment. And we can sign a prenup, if that makes you happy."

"We're not even engaged! And if you think I'm going to start cooking and cleaning out of guilt that you're paying for the house, or thinking I owe it to you for my share, you're barking up the wrong weeping willow tree, buddy. And I am definitely not going to be your sex slave in return for a scenic view and a writing studio." I wasn't sure about that last, but I put a lot of conviction in my speech.

"Damn, I was counting on starting a harem." Now he smiled, which almost made me rethink the no-sex option. "All I expect is to make you happy. Happy and mine."

"Yours? Like Moses is yours?"

"Wrong word. Mine as in sharing my life. Becoming my wife. Now that I found you, and found how good we are together, I don't see any reason to wait."

Too much, too soon. I loved Matt, I thought. I wanted to be with him, I believed. But a house and babies and forever? Before eight in the morning?

I smiled back, ripped up the real estate brochure and told him, "Okay. I want a lighthouse."

After Matt left, I looked outside, saw the rain, and went back to sleep. Just like a kept woman.

A hot dream got interrupted by my cell ringing. I couldn't find it at first, then remembered tossing it across the room after my father's call. The caller ID came up as my editor, Don Carr.

I started to ask about the weather where he was, but he didn't want to chat.

"There's three dead mice in a takeout container on my desk. They came in a manuscript box, inside a padded manila envelope, left outside the office door with a note that said you told this wacko to send it here."

"I didn't tell him that! But it's good."

"Not for me and my ulcers, the intern who opened the box, or the mice. They have no heads."

"Yeah, that's Deni's style, all right. But it's good he's still in the city. That means he's not here, so I'm okay for another day. You call the police. I'll notify the agents in the Harbor and the man monitoring my apartment."

"Agents? You've got the FBI working on a prank caller?"

"Um, it's a different agency. I can't keep all those initials straight, you know how it is, and they don't think it's a prank. More like malicious intent, maybe connected to some kind of terrorism. Or a serial pervert."

"Hell, you mean the bag might contain poison? It could have blown up or be radioactive? I guess that's why everyone only accepts electronic submissions. The days of finding a great story over the transom are long gone. Some houses won't look at a book unless an agent vets it first. They say it's quality control. I guess it's so if the agent doesn't drop dead, it must be safe to read."

"Unless the agent is the perp. It could be, from some of the stories I hear. Not this time, though. It's a kid, a wannabe writer. Call the police. They're looking for him. And don't tell anyone where I am."

I gave Don Van's number at the police station, even if the publisher's office was in a different precinct. "He'll know who to call. I'm sure someone will be there to examine the package soon."

I called Lou the Lout, who might or might not be bonking Cousin Lily, from her happy laughter in the background, and ruined his day. Good. Then I called

Harris at my mother's house, who might or might not be
bonking my cousin, from Susan's happy laughter in the
background. I bet she was cooking for him, besides. So I
ruined his day, too. Headless mice could do that. I did
not call Grandma Eve and Doc Lassiter at the farmhouse.

My agent was out of town, thank goodness. I'd dedicated one of my books to her, and she'd be easy to find
through her website or literary agency listings. I left a
message telling her not to accept any packages from unknown authors. Stick to electronic submissions but call
the cops if anything looked suspicious.

Since Deni had delivered the latest package before
Don Carr Publishing opened in the morning, I knew
Lou would have someone show my sketch of him to the
super there, the cleaning staff, people in the other offices. But no one would have paid any attention to a
grim-faced, long-haired young man delivering a manuscript to a science fiction/fantasy publisher. So I doubted
that anyone could identify him or say which direction
he'd come from or left to, if he'd taken a cab or walked,
what he was wearing.

I knew it was him. I'd try to find him the Paumanok
Harbor way.

I left Harris on the phone and the computer and took
the Subaru, with its GPS Lou insisted on, so someone
always knew where I was. I was in town, going door to
door.

Joe the plumber couldn't help locate Deni. He stared
at the sketch, but all he saw in the toilet bowl—where
the shithead belonged—was a lot of traffic, no street
signs, no address.

Margaret the weaver could not make a finding brace-
let for me, because I really didn't want to find the bastard. I wanted him found, but by someone else. Someone
with handcuffs and a stun gun.

The Merriwethers had no numbers that might have

helped, a Manhattan cross street maybe. They did come up with a three, as in triplets, which I did not want to hear.

Kelvin at the garage listened to me say the stalker was still in the city. He didn't scratch his big toe, which meant I spoke the truth. Which pinned Deni down to one of umpteen millions. A few less if he lived on Third Avenue or in apartment 3 somewhere. No help at all.

Big Eddie at the police station with his K-9 dog and his nose couldn't help me, although he did wink. I guess the scent of Matt and sex lingered.

I didn't bother with the weather mavens, the aura-detectors, the marksmen, or the fish-finders. Telekineti-cists couldn't help, neither could the smoke disperser. I waved at Micky the gay senser, bypassed the miracle-grow gardeners, the jeweler whose stones talked to him, two best-style experts, a human compass, Mrs. Terwil-liger at the library, the eidetic at the bank, and Aunt Jasmine, expert child wrangler at the school.

Mrs. Grissom's dead husband had nothing to report.

That left the House on Shearwater Street. I brought it a music CD I'd burned in the city and a pot of mums for the front porch.

I felt like Mrs. Grissom, talking to empty air. Luckily, no one came to look at the houses at either side. I guess the House's reputation still scared them off.

No one answered my knock; no one sang to me; no one gave hints about finding the stalker. On the other hand, no one heaved the flowerpot off the porch or tossed the CD back at me when I shoved it through the mail slot.

Discouraged, and having taken enough time from my first priority, getting rid of the sand thieves, I went to fetch Jimmie. I still hoped he could go off in one of his trances and see what the little monsters were up to. And I wanted Carinne to come with us. If we went straight to the beach, we wouldn't encounter any children. School was in session and the day was too overcast and drizzly for anyone to bring younger kids to the beach. Maybe she could commu-nicate with the Andanstans through the voices in her head.

*   *   *

Carinne and Monteith and Lily and Lou were at the kitchen table playing board games.

Here I was, worrying and working my ass off trying to find Deni, trying to reclaim the beach, and trying to solve Carinne's issues, while they might as well be watching Monte do yo-yo tricks. Then I saw they had a Ouija board.

"Hey, does that really work?"

Lou looked disgusted. "No. All we get is the number three."

There was a lot of that going around, damn it. "Where's Jimmie?"

"He's upstairs, fighting that chest congestion again."

Rats. Or mice. "I was counting on him going to the beach with me."

Lou put the Ouija game away. "I think he's hiding. Sounds like he's afraid he won't be any help. That or he's afraid the blasted parrot won't come home with him."

"Oey'll come back when Oey's ready, I hope. Will you come with me, Carinne?"

She shook her head. "Oh, no. I can't. You saw what happened at the council meeting."

I tried to explain how no one would be on the beach, but she wasn't budging.

I thought about her fears and the professor's fears, and how they were choking on them. I might be afraid of a million things—snakes and subways and one-eyed cab drivers and failure and commitment—but at least I lived my life, more or less.

Which reminded me of a big new fear.

"Can you look again at my future? I need to know how many kids I was reading to."

"It doesn't work that way. Nothing will change until my next birthday. Maybe you go to the elementary school to read to the kindergarten. Or the child could be your friend Louisa's baby. Jimmie said your friend was very nice."

She looked away, into the distance, but I heard the sadness in her voice.

"She wants to meet you, too, but it could be too hard on all of you. She has three wonderful kids and I don't know how she'd survive if she knew something terrible would happen to them."

Lord, what if Carinne saw my triplets turned into drug dealers and ax murderers when they were her age? "We have to figure how to control your talent, so it can be used for good stuff again, like getting kids into the right fields. Mrs. Terwilliger thinks it'll happen."

"I sent a note thanking her for the book, but I don't see how. Monte's research hasn't turned anything up."

He'd gone off somewhere, likely to set plates spinning like a circus act. "He's not messing with your mind, is he?"

"That would be an improvement. He's been much nicer, and a big help yesterday. I like being here. I hadn't seen another person in weeks, except Uncle— That is, your father. Again, I owe you so much for helping me."

"Then come with me." A favor for a favor. "See if you can hear the Andanstans."

She sneezed.

"Don't tell me you have Jimmie's cold."

She pulled a tissue out of her pocket. "I'm afraid so."

I was on my own, again.

CHAPTER THIRTY-THREE

I had tiny metal trucks, cut-up old stockings, shredded ribbons and thread, pebbles from Matt's driveway. I had absolutely no confidence in any of my ideas. I also had Moses and Little Red, Harris as bodyguard, Susan as curious cousin. Which meant I had blankets and water bowls and Susan's brownies and thermoses full of hot cider.

I walked the dogs before we hit the sand, thinking of Ms. Garcia and not wanting to piss off the Andanstans worse, literally.

All the rain's runoff might have accounted for extra beach erosion, but it looked more like the little cruds were working overtime. We hardly had room to spread the blankets between the bay and the beach grass. I sat and studied the area.

Harris and Susan kept talking and laughing—flirting—until I told them to shut up so they could listen. None of us heard anything. None of us saw anything. My best hope was Moses, who went for a swim, shook out over all of us, then went to sleep on the blanket beside me, which was now wet on a day already damp and chill. Little Red, who had been guarding the brownies, growled and got up to chase seagulls.

Harris decided he'd better secure the territory, which meant walking back toward the parking area and keeping watch from there lest Deni drive up or come by boat. That's why he needed Susan with him, to cover both directions. Sure. That's why she grinned at me before skipping off.

"He's too old for you. And he'll chase leprechauns and selkies."

She gave me the finger. So I unwrapped the brownies.

I sat and ate and stared for awhile, just trying to be still, leaving my mind open to all possibilities and forms of communication. No one called to me except the brownies.

Then I lay down on my stomach and stared out, my nose almost touching the sand. I tried to project welcome, gratitude, respect, and aiming to please. If a grain of sand moved, I didn't see it.

I lined up the toy trucks. I carried the fabric scraps to the tide line. I placed the pebbles in a neat row and spread out the pieces of pantyhose. And I told the Andanstans I was not littering the beach, but bringing gifts. I explained how the trucks rolled, turning the wheels for them, and how to catch sand in the nylon mesh. I did a mental picture of the scraps and threads used as breech clouts and bikinis. Then I shared some brownie crumbs and related how sharing food, breaking bread together, was a sign of friendship in my world. I told them, out loud and in my head as best I could by double thinking. That is, thinking about what I was saying, what it meant, how it felt, at the same time I said it.

I told them how we all were grateful for what they'd done, how we wanted to do something for them. Without knowing their wants or needs or expectations, these offerings were the best we could come up with so far.

If I felt stupid talking to a vacant house, this was ridiculous. I was happy Susan and Harris were out of sight, although I did wonder how he expected to protect me if he couldn't see me. No matter. The most danger here was losing my mind.

No one talked to me, not even when I called Oey and tried to make the cawing sound she made, then the glub he made when in predominant fish form, or when I pictured them both, flickering between sexes and species. Nothing. I flashed an old picture of the tree with Oey in its branches. *Come, friend.* Nothing.

I was down to singing, and thanking heaven Susan and Harris couldn't hear.

> "Oh, Mr. Sandmen, bring back our sand,
>   Please bring it back
>   as quick as you can.
>   Please turn on your magic runes
>   To help us keep our pretty dunes.

> "Oh, Mr. Sandmen, we'll all come give thanks,
>   if you just help us shore up our banks.
>   Come out peaceful, like I've never seen.
>   We need to talk, so don't be so mean.
>   Please use all your magic skill,
>   to tell us how to repay our bill."

Nothing. Okay, I better not quit my day job.

Screw this. I might be the Visualizer, but I sure as hell wasn't a telepath or an evoker, if such a talent existed, or any kind of snake or sand charmer. Unless my father's hint meant I should bring a fife. Maybe the music teacher at the school could lend me one tomorrow.

Today, before I gave up, I went back to my trusty old sketch pad and marker pens and added curving branches to my willow tree. Now the tree stood with open arms. *Friend*, I thought.

On the next blank page I did the dot-dot-dot thing, forming Andanstans and then the sinking ship they held up. *Brave, kind, smart.* I drew people: me, Matt, Lou, the mayor, and Grandma Eve, all applauding, Jimmie bowing. *Grateful, loving, appreciative.* In case they didn't get the idea, and could read, I put signs in the people's hands. *Thank you.* I drew Moses with his tongue out, giving kisses. I nudged the big dog awake and gave him a dog biscuit so he'd look grateful. Little Red got one, too. *Pets.*

I filled the next page with trucks and nets, bringing the sand back. *Please.* I drew the pebbles and put tiny pickaxes and shell shovels in sandmen hands, making new sand. *You do not need ours.* I drew smiling people on the beach, bringing food, more toys, more pebbles. *Tell us what you want.*

The problem, I decided, lying down again, was that I was too tired to keep the thoughts and the pictures in my mind at the same time. I got hung up on Matt's face, looking serious but kind, and thinking how he'd like Moses' portrait, and how busy he was today and how wonderful he'd been last night. And lighthouses and loving and triplets and partners and . . .

And there they were, while I was in the twilight between sleep and wakefulness, or maybe I was dreaming. I saw them kicking sand over my picture of the willow tree. So much for friendship.

Or peace. They waved the fabric scraps like battle flags, attacked each other with whips made of the threads, and used the nylon stocking I'd so carefully cut into little squares as blockades, then as blankets to smother their brothers. The brownie crumbs became deadly missiles, until Moses leaned over and lapped them up with half a squadron, for all I knew.

They avoided the trucks altogether. Maybe that legend about cold metal being deadly to fey folk had some basis in reality, if I considered this encounter as reality. The troll had no problem, though, kicking over parking meters and fire hydrants with glee.

A crew of Andanstans turned their attention to the pebbles, trying to roll them into a wall formation, but different ones shoved back, so they canceled each other out. Thank goodness the pebbles weighed too much to hurl or they'd be mowing each other down like medieval warriors with their catapults.

Great, I'd brought them more weapons, more instruments of destruction. I gathered the toy trucks before they figured how to run each other over, metal or not.

"Can't you stop fighting long enough to talk to me?"

Seemed not. So I scooped a handful of them up in my hand, most likely breaking a hundred more of their rules of honor. I didn't care. I was tired, angry, frustrated, and chilled. "We need to talk."

I brought them right up to my face so I could see them better and cupped both hands around the captives so, God forbid, none of them fell to the ground and shattered.

They tumbled over each other, pushing, shoving, slapping at whoever was next to them, then trying to climb over each other, all shouting at once, in sounds like glass breaking into a million pieces. I couldn't make out words, so I tried being the Visualizer again. I pictured the willow tree in my head. *Peace, buddies.*

I got back an image of the Andanstans digging around the tree trunk, then shaking their heads. No sand. I broke a branch off, mentally. *Want the sap? A drop of blood? A lock of hair?*

They sent back a scene of them working together for a change, making wet sand into mud to stick the branch back on. Okay, they didn't want a pound of flesh.

I flashed the picture I'd done of them keeping the cruise ship afloat. *Heroes. Thank you.* I showed the happy people on the beach. *We need our sand.* I switched to a different image, of us bearing gifts. *What is it you want?*

Too big.

Too big? They wanted something so big we could never give it?

Then I heard the clacking sound that meant Oey was as frustrated as I was. I looked around and she was perched on the blanket beside me, the fish tail drooping onto the sand, but in my mind, too. In my head, the parrot was glorious, in iridescent colors, with gleaming scales at the split tail end. In actual fact, she still looked bedraggled, dull and patchy. "Welcome, my friend. Are you well?"

She shrugged. "Thtill molting."

I held out my sand-filled hands. "Can you understand them?" It was a relief to my aching head to use real words.

The parrot head bobbed.

"Will they talk to me?"

"Too big."

Ah, *I* was too big. Humans did not exist on the same plane. One shouted word could blow them away, and they refused to work together to form a coherent mental link. The otherworldly fireflies didn't have a big vocabulary, but I could feel their basic fear, trust, need. These guys had one overreaching emotion, obviously anger, but individually they couldn't project it to my mind. Thank God. It must have been Oey translating.

"Do you know what they want from us? I get the bit about honor and returning favors and paying back debts now, but no one has any idea what we can give them to get our sand back."

"Pwethouth."

"Something priceless?"

The little dudes in my hand hopped up and down. It felt like dry raindrops.

Oey clacked her beak and slapped the fish tail against my foot. Yeck, fish slime. "Pwethouth."

"Oh, precious. They want something precious."

Head bobbing from the parrot, less pushing and shoving from the sand. Maybe they were listening to Oey's telepathy, in their own language.

"Pwethouth."

Jimmie must have watched *The Lord of the Rings* with Oey. "That's Gollum's line, but we don't have any magic ring to give you. You guys are the magic ones; we just have traces inside us. We might have enough gold, like in the ring, though. Is that precious enough?" I tried to imagine the sun coming out, sprinkling a shower of gold dust across the beach.

Oey said no and the little guys in my hand, maybe fifty of them, fought to pull scraps of the stocking over their heads

"Okay, no showers of gold dust. What else do we have that you consider precious?"

"Thand," Oey answered for them.

"Yeah, I can see that. So it has to be something *we* consider precious, right?"

Oey fluffed the scrawny chest feathers, as if proud that one of her pets had done a trick right.

I thought about it, and the first thing that came to mind was a portrait of Louisa and her children, especially that little pink bundle she kept pressed against her body. What could be more valuable? What would we never, ever part with? I doubt any of us could survive the sorrow.

"Awwgh."

"Right, no human sacrifices. But, Oey, you are precious to us. Even the Andanstans proved themselves invaluable. Are you asking us to give up our joy in having you come among us?"

I could feel a rash forming on my hands from tiny pricks. Some joy.

The beady parrot eyes looked at me. I felt a shiver up my spine.

"Very well, it's not for us to give you up." That would be like Little Red deciding he'd rather live in California. I thought about what was most important to me, what I would be devastated to lose: Little Red. Matt. My pain in the ass family, even the crazy village. "Are you asking me to leave all of them?"

Now I got a sharp pain in my gut, not from the sand, but at the thought of giving up Little Red. Or Matt, now that I'd found him. The rest of them I could keep in touch with like I did now with my parents, unless the petty tyrants demanded I go into the witness protection plan or something as permanent and complete. But Matt? "Is that what you want? Me to live without love?"

I saw a picture of me, Moses at my side, Little Red asleep on my foot and Matt's arms around me. Oey's wings enfolded us all. I felt warm.

"Petth. Mine."

I sighed in relief. "Thank you. What then? Should I give up my life's work that means so much to me, my drawing and writing?" I could take over as Matt's recep-

tionist, I supposed, or be full-time mother to those triplets.

"Mine. Not thandth."

Okay, I didn't have to sacrifice myself, my loved ones
or my cherished *raison d'être* to save the sand. Something else.

"I'd give you some of Carinne's magic if I could."

"Aawgh."

"That's what I think of her skill, too." I wasn't getting
anywhere with the sand, so I figured I'd try fixing the
sister. "Can you help her? She is miserable now." I tried
to explain about her long-range sight, and the horrors of
Brock and bad futures. I pictured some of the scenes
Carinne might have seen when gangbangers and soldiers turned thirty-seven, if they did.

"Cawwy."

"No, I don't think she's the nickname kind. She's very
serious, burdened as she is."

Oey flapped her wings. They were bare in spots, with
no luxurious, long wing feathers. She did manage to flap
hard enough to blow the sand out of my hand. "Oh, no!
Now they'll be madder than before!"

Oey jumped on where they'd fallen. I had no idea
what that accomplished, but my hand stopped itching.

"Cawwy."

"Carry? I should carry you? Will you let me take you
back to Rosehill and Jimmie? He thinks you don't like
him anymore."

"Thilly Immie. Petth."

"Yes, I know that. You saved his life. You'll always
look after him. But what about Carinne?"

"Cawwy. Cawwy. Cawwy!" Oey shouted.

I finally got a mental picture of her with a parrot on
her shoulder. Oey'd claimed another pet. "Great. But
what good will that do?"

I heard something like a chuckle come from deep in
Oey's chest. "Cawinne thees at Oey age."

"Which is . . .?"

I heard a word that went on and on, but I couldn't

understand the image that went with it. "I guess it's pretty old. So everyone here would be dead by then, and she'd see nothing?"

Oey's head bobbed in satisfaction.

So she wouldn't see tragedies or murders or wretched lives. "But she won't be able to help people, either."

"Fith or fowwu."

Fish or fowl? Which meant she could suffer, or she could be blind to the future, shut off from her personal magic. "But you are both fish and fowl. Both. Can't you help her see the good, without the sadness?"

"Thit happenth."

I knew it well. "But you can't be with her every minute. I know you need to swim sometimes, or go off like now to lay eggs and molt. How will she manage, other than staying in her room at Rosehill all the time?"

She cocked her head sideways, thinking. "Fevver."

"She'll get sick? It's only a cold. Maybe the flu that's going around."

"Fev-ver." Oey plucked at one sad dropping wing.

"A feather will help her when you can't?" I thought of Dumbo, flying with the feather in his trunk. But that didn't end too well, did it? "It will give her the courage to try?"

"Come. Cawwy."

We went down the beach, Oey heavy on my shoulder, that slimy tail flapping against my back. Moses galumphed ahead, Little Red hopped at my side. We reached a boulder and a screen of reeds behind it. There was a nest, in a hole with high sand walls. The Andanstans were on guard, I sensed, united and ready to fend off seagulls or snakes or water rats.

The nest glowed with Oey's lost feathers, with the glittering iridescent colors of the eggs, with an aura even I could see. I sank to my knees to admire all the beautiful colors, the life I could sense within the eggs, the excitement and wonder.

"There are so many of them! And here I worried about having triplets."

Oey stared at me, from the top of the nest. "More petth?"

"Not soon." Then I had an idea. "Maybe Carinne could have one of your babies to help her?"

Oey shuddered and nudged some sand over the eggs.

I understood. Oey didn't share. Besides, the hatchling would be too young. If Carinne saw through its age-view, they'd both have to see infants die.

Worse and worse. The very idea had me shaking and shivering. That or I was catching Carinne's cold.

CHAPTER THIRTY-FOUR

I had a feather, and a fever.

Oey plucked one from the nest for Carinne, one for Jimmie, then, after thinking about it, one for me. I didn't want to ask, though I wanted one of the beautiful feathers more than anything, especially if it could lend a little strength and courage and magic. I needed it. Besides, why should Carinne get one and not me? I know that sounded like jealous resentment, like "Dad likes you better," but I talked to Oey first, and Jimmie saw the parrot first when he was a sickly boy. Carinne had never even met the birdfish. Maybe she wouldn't be able to see the hybrid parts that I could. Maybe she wouldn't see the wisdom and the love.

I clutched all three feathers to me before Oey could change her mind. "Do we owe you another favor now? Will the feather make Jimmie Harmon strong? Will it really help Carinne? Can you come back with me to test if your presence lets her walk through town or come to the festival on the beach? And have you come up with any idea of a courtesy gift for the Andanstans so that we'll have a beach to hold that festival on?"

But the parrot was gone, without giving any answers. I didn't see the sand people anymore, either, just sand, so I headed back toward the blanket, feeling sicker and sicker as I gathered up my stuff. Every step felt like a sledgehammer to the brain, and my sweatshirt was too hot, but my feet were too cold. Shit. I hated being sick and this felt a lot worse than Carinne's sniffles.

Susan took one look at me and said she'd walk back to her parents' house rather than ride in the car. The restaurant had a busy weekend coming up and she couldn't afford to get sick, but she'd make me chicken soup.

Harris had no choice. He drove me to my mother's place, set all the alarms, then drove into town to get whatever Walter at the drugstore recommended, and chicken soup and orange juice from Joanne's.

I took a hot shower, hoping that would warm me, but I only felt weaker afterward. Before I collapsed, I called Matt to tell him I'd stay here. I didn't want to give him the flu.

He laughed. "Do you think I wouldn't have your germs by now? I feel fine."

I wanted my own bed, my own house, and a good night's sleep. Besides, I didn't want Matt to see me all pale and clammy-skinned, maybe sick to my stomach or worse. I had pride too, like Oey.

"Does Harris think you'll be safe there?"

"The place is like a fortress. And Deni is in the city, remember? Besides, I have a feather. A beautiful green one, with yellow and blue and red edges." I had it tucked in the buttonhole of my heavy flannel pajamas, the ones with little monkeys all over. I didn't want Matt to see the jammies, either.

"A feather, huh? Um, sweetheart, I think you're delirious. Get Harris to drive you to the emergency clinic."

"No, it's a real feather. Real magic. I'm not afraid the flu will kill me, for once. You know, turn into some weird mutant bacterial pneumonia, or cause a fever that'll fry my brain cells. I'll be fine."

"I'll come right after work to check. Meantime, take something for the fever, maybe put a cool washcloth on your head. Get some sleep. I'll bring a can of chicken soup as soon as I can get out of here."

My hero.

I took a couple of Tylenols and made some tea, but I couldn't sleep yet, not with so much to do and my energy and ambition slipping away as fast as the sand from the shore. First, I had to cancel the gold collection and the diamond dust preparation, the kids' poems, Grandma Eve's herbs, a bunch of other projects I had the villagers working on. I thought about sending a town-wide email, but I didn't have enough addresses.

I told everyone I could reach, between coughs and sneezes, that reverent gratitude just wasn't going to make it with the sand-nappers. They wanted something precious, priceless, and tangible. Pass it on. We needed new ideas.

"And you need soup, Willy," someone offered. "Sweet and sour egg drop soup is what I always get for a cold."

I thought of the eggs in their beautiful nest. And Oey. Nah.

Someone offered her great-aunt's silver tea service. Someone else a signed Shakespeare folio. A Honus Wagner baseball card that might or might not be counterfeit, a child's first tooth, a signed Tiffany lamp. The judge suggested a green card, so the Andanstans could be legal citizens, or he could get the mayor to give them a key to the city.

"But we don't want them to stay!"

"Oh, right. How about clemency for the theft of the sand? I don't hand that out often, I can tell you."

My eyes were getting blurry and I had to call from a prone position, but I couldn't rest yet. Besides, my stomach didn't feel right. No matter, I had to talk to Carinne.

"How do you feel?"

"Crappy."

"Me, too. I think I caught whatever you have. But how is Jimmie? I'm really worried about him, if he's got this bug, too."

"Yeah, we're all concerned. He refuses to go to a doctor. Says his health plan won't cover it."

"Get Monteith to enroll him with the Rosehill staff."

"There's still a waiting period. But we found a doctor who'll make house calls. And Jimmie swears all he needs is some tea with a dash of whiskey. So far he's finished off two cups of tea and a bottle of bourbon. He seems okay."

"Great. Tell him Oey misses him, and she's looking better. I could see feathers starting to sprout. She'll be coming home soon." I hoped. "And she sent a feather for each of you. If I can't bring them in the morning, I'll send Harris with them."

"That's all right, Willy. We aren't in any hurry to get feathers. Didn't they used to burn them under peoples' noses to wake them from a faint? We're not that bad here, though I think Jimmie's passed out. Monte says sleep is the best thing for him."

So I tried to explain to Carinne Oey's plan to help her situation. How she could walk around with an ancient parrot on her shoulder and never see the horrors.

She wasn't sure about always seeing blanks. Like putting on a TV and only getting static snow. And what could she do?

She could help the professor the way she was doing, or she could go back to being a guidance counselor, as long as Oey was with her.

"Hey, most guidance counselors aren't clairvoyants. I bet you're the only one. And they still help the kids with intelligence and training and caring, if not magic. You're going to be meeting students who are as confused about their talents as you are. Your experience alone should let you empathize and give good advice. And when Oey's not around, maybe the feather will help keep the voices and the panic away."

I could hear her wondering if she should ask Cousin Lily to make me soup.

"It's a special feather, one from the nest. It's better than a fish scale, trust me. This one is beautiful, and I think it's supposed to give you courage to face what you need to do. Or make you feel better, like Doc Lassiter's touch does."

"Do you feel better?"

I couldn't remember when I felt worse. "I don't think I'm dying, anyway."

"Have you been taking Jimmie's cure-all, too?"

No, but I held all three of the feathers in my hand when I made the last call. I did feel a little better. Maybe the Tylenol kicking in. Maybe the tea. Maybe the feathers?

"Mom, I'm sick."

"I'm in Philadelphia. Call your grandmother."

"I did. She's sending over some herbal teas." And most likely chicken soup, if I knew my grandmother. "But that's not why I'm calling. I wanted to warn you, is all. You shouldn't come out here until I'm better. You could catch the bug and miss your first rehearsal. Or you could look pale and sickly." Like I did.

"Hm. I placed all of the puppy mill dogs except for the Maltese Matt said the Willinghams want. Nice people. But there's a lot of work to be done with these new greyhounds at the rescue center. They've never had a toy or gone up stairs."

"Great, you stay there and get them in shape for wonderful new homes. Bye, Mom."

"Wait, Willy. The jackass called."

"Dad? What did he want? Did he have a premonition?"

"He left a message. I guess it's a warning. He said I shouldn't be upset because stress isn't good for a person's health. That he always loved me. That he was never unfaithful to me during our marriage."

Wow. I guess Dad found a feather, too. "What else did he say?"

"That you'd explain more."

His feather was yellow, or was it white they gave to cowards? "I think I'm going to be sick. Gotta go."

I put all three feathers under my pillow and went to sleep. For three days.

I remember Harris coming back with a gallon of soup, a huge bottle of antibacterial soap, and meds from the drugstore.

Matt came to spoon soup into me, and Aunt Jasmine helped me shower. Grandma Eve felt my forehead, declared I'd live, and poured herbal tea down me. Susan moved back in to help poor Harris, who had no idea what to do in a sickroom except drink beer. I think he worried he'd failed his bodyguard job. Susan consoled him.

Mostly I slept. When I was awake, I dragged myself to the sofa downstairs to sleep through old movies on the TV. Harris and Little Red came to some kind of conciliation, because I didn't see blood anywhere. Harris had the can opener, so he became a good guy.

My father kept calling, worried. He didn't exactly sense any immediate disasters for me, only a possible visit to Stony Brook, the nearest big hospital, nearly two hours away.

"Dad," I groaned. "I'm not that sick. And I'm not going to Stony Brook. It's just the flu, so chill. I heard stress isn't good for your health."

"I know. I keep getting a pain in my back."

"Give me a couple of days, Dad. I'm working on it."

"The stress?"

"No, the back thing. You know, the backstabbing, the calling back, the knife in the back. It's payback. If my head weren't so heavy, I know I could figure it out. What's precious to you, Dad?"

"Why, you, baby girl. And Carinne, your mother. My health, especially after the bypass. My good name."

"A thing, Dad. Something you'd hate to give up. A real sacrifice."

"My golf clubs. Did I tell you I bought a set of the same ones Tiger Woods uses?"

Sure, just what the Andanstans needed, after a silver tea set.

I asked Matt, too. He'd been reading on the chair near the sofa, watching me sleep, then half-carrying me back upstairs. He said I was the most precious thing in his life, and he wasn't losing me to any miniscule mineral compounds. He never said how pathetic I looked or how cranky I was about the effing chicken soup or how he missed making love. Yup, my hero.

I had other visitors. Harris didn't like it, having to turn the alarm off for people he didn't know, therefore didn't trust. No one came in, half because Harris had a gun in his hand, half because they didn't want to enter a germ-infested house. Everyone called out good wishes from the porch. They brought flowers and honey and a pumpkin with a smiley face carved into it and a balloon that said Get Well. And more soup. Even Moses was sick of it by now.

I almost wept at the signs of friendship, I was so weak. "Everyone is so kind," I told Matt when he came after work that day.

"Yeah, you're no good to them like this."

So I got better.

The good news was I lost five pounds. The bad news was I looked like a prisoner of war. I went to Janie's and begged. She warned about root damage and brittle ends, but got rid of the pink hair anyway, I looked so pitiful. Now I had my own streaky blonde hair back, and felt almost like myself again.

More good news: Carinne and Jimmie were also recovering. Carinne called to say thank you for the feathers I'd sent over with Lou, but I sensed neither of them was impressed. She said Jimmie had his in a jar on the mantel. She was using hers as a bookmark. No, she hadn't tested it yet. She still felt tired and achy.

I gave her another day.

The bad news was it was Saturday, one week away from the beach ritual. Saturday was also the day when the psi-profiler thought Deni might get out to Pauma-nok Harbor if he had a job keeping him in the city. They hadn't gotten an ID on him yet, but the mice and the threats were enough to slap a subpoena on the original server, who funneled messages—and porn—to overseas servers. The place got shut down, records got confiscated, pornographers got arrested. Sleazebag clients who sent money could be coerced into giving up more information. The FBI was happy, happy enough to search through closed juvenile records for an early sadist with DF initials. The worst news was that someone had hacked into the system and erased files. Russ got to work restoring them, without discussing it with the Feds.

Deni could be here now, blending in with the pumpkin pickers and striped bass fishermen and general Hamptons tourists. We got so much traffic to the farm stand that Harris had Colin and Kenneth take shifts monitoring the cars.

Matt wanted me to move back in with him, but I wasn't ready. I had to get the house in order for my mother, figure out the precious part, and make sure my hair wasn't going to fall out.

By Sunday afternoon I was stir-crazy. I got Matt and Harris to take me to Rosehill, where I browbeat Carinne to experiment. We decided on lunch at one of the clam bars on the way to Montauk. Deni'd never look for me there, and the customers would be strangers.

Lou insisted we take Colin with his superpower eyesight and Kenneth, the danger precog. Lou wanted to watch football Sunday at my mother's house. Monte came, and Doc Lassiter, but Jimmie said he was too weak.

We took three cars, bodyguards ahead and behind Matt's SUV. Monte sat up front next to Matt. I sat in the back with Carinne, both of us with death grips on the feathers. Doc Lassiter had her other hand.

Matt parked, but Carinne wouldn't get out of the car. Matt and Kenneth did, one to get a feel for the atmosphere, one to order takeout we could eat at a secluded beach.

"Can you see?" I asked Carinne, who had her eyes shut tight.

"Fine."

"I mean see futures?"

She opened her eyes and started counting off, starting

with the teenagers on line ahead of Matt. "Ad executive, gas station attendant—Hess uniform. Teacher. Uh-oh."

Doc Lassiter put his hand on the back of her neck.

"What do you see?"

"A wheelchair. A car crash, I think. The girl next to her dies." Her voice rose to an anguished wail that had Harris and Colin and Matt and Kenneth running to surround the car, obstructing her view. "Oh, God."

I wrapped my hand with the feather around hers. "It's okay. You can't do anything about it. Breathe. Do you want to draw?"

She squeezed her eyes so tightly shut she couldn't find the pad with a giant crayon. "No."

I signaled Doc to take his hand away. Carinne trembled, but said she thought she'd be all right, without seeing out the windows. "No voices this time." She quietly wept for the girl who'd died.

"But one lived. And you didn't fall apart. The feather worked!"

Monte took over, reaching back to stroke her hand. "Come on, ducks, be strong. Be like a battlefield nurse. You lose some, but you save a lot more."

Carinne nodded, ready to try again, but everyone's phone, pager, beeper, whatever, started ringing at the same time.

Someone had broken into my house!

No way were Carinne and I waiting at the clam bar. We raced home, sirens and all, calling for backup and roadblocks and warning my grandmother and Susan's family not to leave their houses.

We sped up the dirt road, gravel flying, to see Lou and a woman with a little white dog outside, waving.

I had a relapse.

Chapter Thirty-five

I had to go to Stony Brook after all. Dad had that one almost right.

My mother shouted, "Surprise!" and ran toward the cars, where we were all getting out.

She ignored the men with weapons drawn and rushed to hug Carinne. "How could I stay away when my baby was sick?" Then she saw me.

"Surprise, Mom. That's Carinne, Dad's daughter from before you were married."

She clutched her chest and keeled over.

Dad was almost right there too. "He said she'd have a heart attack," I wailed over the approaching sirens.

Mom shoved a helping hand away. "Not . . . my heart. Low . . . sugar."

"You're diabetic? You should have told me!"

She sniffed around the oxygen mask the EMTs put over her face. "Like you told me about Carinne?"

Stony Brook insisted on keeping her for tests to be sure she had her insulin under control. They recommended rest and no stress.

For her or me? I lost another three days.

Matt got the Maltese to the Willinghams and took Little Red home with him. My poor dog wouldn't know where he lived soon. But he'd be safe. I guess I was too, sleeping in a chair in Mom's hospital room, except when my father called every hour. I shut the door so no one could hear the shouting, crying, blame-naming, and guilt-tossing. And that was before Mom got back from her tests.

I got a crick in my neck, but no further toward a solution to the Andanstans' demands, as Oey saw them. I did get an idea about Deni and Dad's cockeyed premonitions. What if Deni drove a Mustang, instead of riding a mustang? I called it in to Lou, who added it to the file. I couldn't imagine how many Mustangs were registered to a DF, but it might mean something.

Harris and the others ran the plates of every Mustang that drove into Paumanok Harbor. They had the whole police force and all the shopkeepers looking at strangers, comparing young, black-haired men to the sketch I'd done. No one spotted anything while I was at the hospital. No one came up with anything precious that we could part with.

Lou and Grandma Eve picked us up. My mother wasn't talking to me or my grandmother, but she chatted with Lou the whole long ride home. Dogs, Florida, the food at the hospital, her new TV show. When we got home, she sniffed her nose at her sister, who'd cleaned the house, curled her lip at Susan, who'd brought food, dropped her purse on Cousin Lily's foot, who'd brought armloads of get well cards and flowers. Then she demanded the return of her dogs, as if we'd stolen them along with her pride and her trust. No matter that the dogs would be safer at Aunt Jasmine's or be unhappy that they couldn't climb up the stairs to Mom's bedroom, she wanted her dogs, the only loyal creatures on Earth. After labeling the rest of us as traitors, she let Lou help her up the stairs, where she slammed her door.

Oh, boy.

I wanted to go to Matt's, needing to know that someone still believed in me. We'd talked while I was at the hospital, but it wasn't the same. He had a waiting room of sick dogs and cats, though, and I had the whole town counting on me. Besides, I couldn't leave, not when my mother needed me. I couldn't sit in the house, either, pretending I was welcome here. I didn't even have my own dog for company. I had Lou.

"Nice lady, your mother."

Fine. He could stay with her while I went to see if anyone came up with a way to placate the sand guys. It would be easier than placating my mother.

The beach was my first destination, to consult with Oey. I figured I was safe for two days, until the weekend. Deni would be back at work now.

Lou had the police chief send extra police guards with me: Big Eddie and Baitfish Barry. He had others positioned along the road to the farm stand, to keep Mom and her dogs and her house safe.

Barry let out a sharp breath when he saw how narrow the beach was. Not a minnow in range of his fish-finder, either. I saw no sandmen, no nest, no para fish, not even when I rubbed the feather like you would a magic lantern. No genie popped up. No inspiration, either, only the same sick feeling that everything was going to hell in a hand cart and I had no brakes. This was worse than the flu.

I really needed Matt. The cops and the DUE agent had enough couth to wait outside so that Matt and I could have a quick hug between a cat with a cough and a dog with diarrhea.

I whined, too, I admit, about how my mother would never forgive me, and I hadn't even been born yet when the crime got committed!

Matt promised to talk to her. I'd forgotten they were old friends, that she'd been instrumental in getting him to set up an office in Paumanok Harbor. He couldn't wait to see if some of her dog-whispering skills could rub off on him now that he had an aura of esper ability. His admiration and affection ought to soothe Mom. It sure worked for me.

He'd help with my errands as soon as he got done at the clinic, then we'd go relieve Lou. Matt would sleep on the couch if he had to. He was not leaving me alone. We'd been apart too long.

I felt wanted again, and stronger. I had a wonderful

man's affection, and a feather in my cap. Literally. Yankee Doodle, that's me.

Everyone in the village was relieved to see that I was recovered from the bug and my mother was out of the hospital. Time was running out, with the sand. Now if I only had a rabbit to pull out of my hat the way they expected.

We went to the library first. This time Mrs. Terwilliger handed me *Mothers and Daughters* and cookbooks for diabetics. I assumed the cookbooks were for my mother.

Mrs. T related how a young woman came into the library Sunday and asked for my books because she heard I lived here. She couldn't afford the thirty dollars for a temporary library card so she could take them out, though, so Mrs. Terwilliger found her a damaged copy from the paperback trade rack. The girl said she hoped to stay in the Harbor a while, if she could find a job. Then she'd get a library card, first thing.

The librarian wanted to know if Dr. Matt was still looking for office help. She'd get a résumé from the young woman when she brought the book back, as promised.

I'd ask Matt. He might need a temp for when Marta had to take a kid to the doctor or one of them got sick. Right now, I needed to ask Mrs. Terwilliger what she thought was precious.

"Why, books, of course, but they don't do well underwater, naturally. The beach is bad enough, when sand gets under the plastic slipcover and gets in the spine. A library card is perhaps more priceless than any individual book. Read a book, open a mind, I always say. And it's free. I'd issue one to your sand people, but they have to be able to write their names. We can forgo the proof of residency, since everyone knows where they live, but not that."

I appreciated that she readily accepted how I'd seen creatures no one else could see, creatures that couldn't possibly be of our universe. They existed on my word and in Professor Harmon's memory, and they stole our sand. That was enough for her and the other esper villagers.

I got that same trust and the same good wishes at the deli and the grocery store. And the same question about Matt's office help. No one was hiring this time of year, but they felt sorry for the young woman who'd come by on Sunday, so conscientiously asking in every business establishment.

I remembered the girl's voice I'd heard when Deni pretended to be a female fan. This girl had brown hair, though, not the black Mrs. Abbottini had seen on her mugger. She had glasses that Mrs. Abbottini never mentioned. According to Joanne, she did not drive a Mustang, either, but an old rattletrap van. Joanne thought she was sleeping in it. I felt sorry for this kid, but I had more important business right now.

Vincent the barber deemed his family, his skill, his customers, and his community as precious to him. The little bastards were already claiming the Harbor's most valuable commodity though, shovelful by shovel. He'd sacrifice his fancy German Jaguar scissors if I thought that could help.

Walter at the drugstore didn't hand any of us freebies in a bag, to my companions' regrets. I still had some at Matt's house, if I ever got there again. Walter did offer a portrait of his great-grandmother, a truthseer in her day. The portrait still saw. The eyes followed viewers around, and Walter vowed the mouth puckered up in disapproval or gave a slight smile, depending on if a lie was heard. Walter knew the thing was a masterpiece of mentalism, but he'd be glad to get it out of his house.

I doubted the Andanstans wanted a dead divinator either, but I took it because the painting held great magic.

Mr. Whitside at the bank asked if I thought the sandmen would take gold coins with presidents on them. No one else seemed to want them. They were wondrously shiny, so I put one in my pocket.

So it went, all through town, encouragement, but not

a lot of great possibilities. I had a dragon's hoard of treasure, some sentimental, some with appraisal slips. Some making no sense at all, like the free bowling passes. It was the thought that counted.

We went to Rosehill to see what Jimmie thought, now that he felt better.

He took me aside while Lily offered coffee and apple pie. I worried about how pale he looked, how he turned down the pie.

He'd been thinking, he told me. (And drinking, Carinne told me.) He knew what the Andanstans wanted. They'd saved lives. They should have one back. His.

"No!"

"Yes, my dear. You said it yourself. I am precious to you, which I truly do appreciate. But that's about all. Rosehill can get along without me now that Monte shows some signs of humanity. You have all my notes so the book can get done without me, too. And I am old, old and tired, without much to look forward to. What better way to go than saving this lovely place that did so much for me in my dotage? Saving it so my new friends can stay and enjoy the beauties of their surroundings? I found the best bottle of Scotch in the wine cellars here, which I intend to enjoy every last drop of, then walk into the water. It's cold this time of year, you know. It won't take long. I doubt I'll feel a thing, full of spirits almost as old as I am. With luck, the Andanstans will take me back with them and I'll get to see their world again. If not, I have seen it before, which is a memory I shall cherish. That and the friendship of you and dear Carinne."

"No! We need you! And Oey will not let them take you. She thinks you belong to her, she thinks all of us do. I need your help with the book and I need you to stay until it's done, to get the recognition you deserve. I need you to tell stories to the triplets. We'll find another way to save the Harbor. I know we will, if we just keep trying. Promise me you will not do this crazy thing. I'll . . . I'll pour out your liquor, see if I don't." I held his hand, devastated at how frail it felt, how trembly. "Please. I need you."

He patted my hair. "I liked the pink. It made me smile. We'll see. But what's an old man compared to an entire town?"

"We'll find a way. I swear."

So he gave me the bottle to offer the Andanstans.

Carinne stared at me when I went back to the kitchen holding a bottle of booze, so I stared at her, wondering what she was thinking. Her hair was darker than mine now, with the browner roots coming in. Her blue eyes—my father's eyes that we'd both inherited—had shadows under them. She said she'd saved me a piece of pie. And she offered to save the Harbor by being the human sacrifice.

Her life wasn't valuable to anyone, not even her, she said, but the sand people might want it on account of the paranormal power. And look what she'd done, almost killed my mother.

"No, you didn't! And no you can't. Sacrifice is not going to happen! Not you, not the professor, not babies, not pets. I will not let it happen. And your life is so much better already, isn't it?"

She looked toward Monte, who had his computer out. "But what if . . .?"

I dragged her to the backyard. The day had a chill and we had no coats, but I didn't care. A whole squad of gardeners worked on the grounds, wrapping burlap around tender bushes before winter. "Look at the young ones." I handed her my feather to hold with hers, then ordered: "Tell me."

"Gardener, gardener, doctor, drug runner, double amputee." But she didn't flip out. "It hurts."

"It hurts both of you, but you can handle this. You can help him find rehab facilities and vocational training when the time comes. You can help at Rosehill when the students start arriving in January. And Monte can track them and try to change any dangerous behavior. You can save lives, I know it!"

She nodded. She wouldn't drown herself, unless the Andanstans asked for her.

Great. Except all I had to offer them was an Antique Roadshow collection of stuff the sand guys could never use or appreciate.

They might covet the magic. But here the people were magic and they weren't getting any of them. Mine.

By now I was drained. I still had a few more places to visit, without much hope of finding the perfect gift for the beings who had nothing.

Matt met us in town, took one look at me and bought me a hot chocolate, with whipped cream. "You're too skinny." There was magic in those words, too.

He wanted me to go home, I looked so tired. We still had to face my mother, though. I wanted to make one more stop, at Emil the jeweler's place. I wanted to get back the gold we'd collected to return to its owners. And I wanted to check out the stones, with Matt.

"No," I told him. "Not the diamonds. We are *not* engaged. But Emil's stones tell him if a couple is good together."

"We're good."

"But the stones will confirm it." I had to know I wasn't making a mistake.

Matt lost his smile. "You'd believe some cold chunks of rock and a crazy jeweler instead of me? Instead of what we share? What I know you feel?"

"Emil believes I've seen the Andanstan. I believe his gemstones talk to him. And they are always right."

I had a death grip on my feather, anyway, waiting for Emil's pronouncement. He cocked his head to one side, listening. Then he clapped and grinned and brought out a tray of wedding ring sets.

"We're not ready yet."

Matt was smiling again, swearing he'd heard wedding bells. I pulled him away from the rings.

Emil went to get the donated gold jewelry. "No matter. This is the one, Willy. Can't you hear the music?"

I couldn't tell if the stones were singing or Matt was humming. I couldn't keep from grinning, either.

"Don't ruin it, you two. You can wait, but don't wait too long."

No, we wouldn't. I started to glance at the gorgeous engagement rings, for the future, of course, but got saved by the bell, Big Eddie's beeper, anyway. Chief Haversmith had a report of another suspicious package and needed Eddie's nose to check for explosives.

"Where?" I wanted to know.

Harris checked his cell. Baitfish Barry's rang, too. No one looked at me.

Someone said, "Matt, why don't you take Willow back to your place?"

I could hear sirens headed out of town. "Where?"

But I knew.

CHAPTER THIRTY-SIX

I had gold coins, a shifty-eyed painting, a bottle of well-aged Scotch, shaved-off dreadlocks from Leshaun the traffic cop, Mrs. Ralston's Phi Beta Kappa key, a high school all-star jacket, Mrs. Merriweather's lucky panties—don't ask—two eighth graders' ponytails, one track trophy, three free passes to the bowling alley, a furry key chain that wasn't so lucky for the rabbit, my GRABYA award for best graphic book for young adults, and plenty more.

And I had a dead cat.

The two girls cried when they cut their hair off. I cried when I heard about the cat. No one would let me see it, but they did tell me it was wrapped in pages from my book, the dog-eared one from the library, and burned. I prayed the poor thing was dead first.

You know what they do to witches, right?

But a girl had taken the book and asked for work, not Danny Boy.

"No matter," Uncle Henry told me after Matt took the cat away to autopsy. "We've got him this time."

Harris' cameras had videotaped every car that drove past my house. One camera got the rusted van, and a blur of something flying out its window. Another got the license number.

"It's Denis, all right. And your father was close. He

didn't get the car, not the Mustang we kept looking for, but the Mustang is a Ford. Guess your boy's last name? With an E at the end. And guess whose juvey record was missing from the database until Russ recovered it? And whose last known address is an abandoned building?"

"But it was a girl in town last weekend!"

"So he has a girlfriend or a sister. Even sociopaths have friends and families. He's smart enough to know we're looking for your neighbor's mugger, so he brought a decoy. We've got an APB for the car, for him, for a brown-haired female about twenty with glasses. We'll get him this time. Her, too, as accessory."

"You damn well better, Henry Haversmith." My mother pushed forward through the row of police to the chief. "And he better hope you find him before I do. No one tortures an animal in my town. And no one threatens my daughter."

Ah, I was her daughter again. Whew.

Matt came back, gray-faced, silent, and angry. He and I and Mom ate the butternut squash lasagna Susan had prepared, but for once her magic-enhanced cooking couldn't lighten our moods.

The cops and the DUE contingent were looking for Deni's van. So was Joe the scrying plumber, in a rusted bucket. The rest of us still had to concentrate on the missing sand tonight. Tomorrow was the festival. And the full moon.

"You're coming," I told my mother, when she refused to go to the beach after dinner because Carinne would be there. "Maybe you can talk to the Andanstans like you do dogs. And you're the one who insisted I come help, that you and the town needed me. You said honor and responsibility and kinship demanded I take part. Well, it's sure as hell your town and your kin, too. Therefore, it's your responsibility to do everything you can to help."

So we went to the beach, with spotlights and blankets and armed guards and as many psychics as we could gather. I accepted that this had to be the secret, invitation-only conclave I'd protested against. How could we explain to normal citizens that some of their neighbors were about to leave knickknacks and souvenirs on the sand in hopes of reversing beach erosion? People put wreaths in the water as memorials, but a two-hundred-year-old Wedgewood dish?

When Jimmie made his way to the beach, leaning on Carinne, I guided him toward where the nest had been, but not even a feather remained. We both called to Oey, out loud and mentally, me with images in my mind. She did not answer. Maybe she was at sea as a fish, out getting her egg babies prepared for part-time aquatic life.

Several people, including shiny-skulled Leshaun, whose hearing was almost as good as a dog's, thought they heard a strange sound that could have been the Andanstans. No one spotted them.

We laid out all the booty, all the treasures, in a line halfway between the shore and the sea. The beach had gone so narrow that the portrait, lying flat, covered most of the sand. The painted lady looked grim by my flashlight, so I told her she could go home with all the other prized possessions in the morning if the Andanstans rejected her.

One look at what used to be our best bathing beach and Grandma Eve and the five other inner councilwomen present were ready to go home and cancel tomorrow night's seaside ritual. They'd just hold the early All Hallow's party on the green in town. Or move it to after the ragamuffin parade through the village on Halloween itself.

I said no, with more confidence than I felt. This wasn't about the ancient witches' rituals; this was about saving the entire town's future. We could do it.

I placed the gold coin next to the portrait.

Carinne had stayed at the edges of our group, even though no one present was younger than she was. She held her feather so tightly I was afraid it would snap, or she would. She carefully placed a photograph of her deceased father on the sand, not mine, but the man who had raised her.

We waited. And waited. I sat on the cold sand and sketched by the nearly full moon's light and the flashlight Matt held for me. I drew trees, parrots, dotted men, vast beaches with happy visitors.

Jimmie took two steps toward the water. I didn't know if he wanted to reclaim his whiskey or keep walking, but Cousin Lily grabbed him back. She put down a ribbon-tied pack of letters from her dead husband, then brushed away a tear.

Then everyone pricked a finger and spilled a drop of blood among the mementos. We waited another hour, getting colder and more depressed.

What more did these bastards want?

I'd had enough.

I took off my shoes and stood at the tide line. I stamped my foot, cascading the water. I waved my feather and shouted, "It's payback time, Andanstans. We've offered our dearest possessions, and you haven't offered an inch of sand. If it's one of us you want, you can't have them. Or me. I have too much to live for." I thought of Matt and the triplets. They deserved to be born, too. "We all do. Jimmie has to finish his books and Carinne has to help the Royce students. No one is going to drown here tonight for breaking rules we never knew, never agreed to. You're the ones who broke the rules by staying in our world when every other otherworldly went back to, um, the other world." People weren't supposed to know about the existence of an alternate universe but how could they not? Everything they'd experienced in the last six months had to be either magic or miracle. "To Unity."

I shook my fist. "You want more blood? You'll have to get past me. You came because I called for help and your sea god sent you. Oey guided you. I guess you're square with those guys now, so it's you and me. You and me. We're grateful, all right? We'll be grateful forever . . ."

You and me forever.

Oh, hell.

I fumbled under my jacket, my sweatshirt, my turtle-neck, and pulled out the chain I hadn't taken off since my mother gave it to me, the one with the pendant made from her wedding ring. The one inscribed with hieroglyphics from that other universe. *One life, one heart, I and thou, forever.* I'd had it so long I never thought about it anymore. Trying to translate it, Grant said the words held a million meanings, all in mind-speak and history and futures, the way Unity beings communicated.

I pulled it off over my head and held it out. "Is this what you want? Is it precious enough? Or is it a bond of good faith and loyalty?" It hadn't been for my parents, which is why I had it. "If so, yes, you and us, forever, in peace, if you bellicose brats know the meaning of peace. We will not steal from you, and you will not steal from us. If you bring the sand back, we will keep the beach clean and try not to blow any of you up. In return we will help you and your friends if called upon. I swear on this amulet and on my love for these people, this place."

My mother was weeping. So was Grandma Eve at Doc Lassiter's side. Matt put his arm around me, but faced the water. "I swear on my honor and on my love for this woman."

Now every voice on the beach rose up. "I swear on my honor."

I placed my necklace on the wet sand at the water's edge. And I held my breath, expecting a thunderbolt or a tidal wave or a sinkhole opening up beneath my feet, something to acknowledge our presence and reject my oath. Nothing happened.

We decided to leave the offerings until morning, just before the tide would come in again. Colin, with his superior eyesight, volunteered to keep watch, but I saw a picture of Oey in my head, looking pleased. "No one needs to stay. The treasures will be safe. The Andanstans are waiting for us to leave. We're too big."

So we all went home, giving backward glances for what we'd left and lost. Some gave backward glances at me that weren't so fond, as if I'd conned them out of their cherished belongings to sell on eBay.

Matt thought I'd been incredibly brave, standing up to the eldritch beings, standing up to the few espers who doubted me. "That's the sign of a great leader, you know. Getting people to follow you when you don't know where you're going. I am so proud of you."

"That wasn't me. Everyone knows I'm the world's biggest coward. It was the feather."

He kissed me, gently, tenderly. "You're the only one who believes that. I think Oey and the professor watched *The Wizard of Oz* too many times. You're brave and brilliant and see things us poor average psychics can't. And you gave up your pendant, which might have more magic in it than the entire rest of this screwball town."

I automatically reached for it, then felt naked. Which I was, of course, on the couch with Matt under the quilts. Mom was in her room and Harris was in the guest room upstairs with all his electronic surveillance stuff. That left my old room with its two narrow single beds, separated from my mother's bedroom by one thin wall. No way.

Matt leaned over me for his jeans and pulled a little box out of the pocket. I recognized the local jeweler's signature gold paper wrap.

"You didn't! I told you, I'm not ready."

He smiled. "I didn't. Open it. I never thought I'd be replacing what you lost, but it's another sign of love and a promise of forever, if you want it."

The box held a gold chain with a piece of blue beach glass hanging from it.

"I tried to match the color of your eyes, but there's no magic shining through the glass."

Maybe not, but a tiny gold lighthouse charm dangled in front of the glass, framed by the blue of the sea and the sky. Matt helped me clasp the chain around my neck. "I'll try. That's all I can do. I love you."

He meant he'd try to find a lighthouse, the idiot. I said, "I love the necklace and I love you, too. I'll try." I meant I'd bend like the willow tree, so we could overcome the insignificant logistic problems. What did it matter where we lived if we were together?

We made love again, to seal the deal. And to stay awake, waiting for another attack from the stalker, some sign that the next big wave wasn't going to wash over half of Paumanok Harbor.

Sleep was out of the question. Patrol cars kept riding up and down the street, cops on foot called back and forth with all clears; floodlights bathed the backyard. Little Red wanted to sleep on the couch. Mom's old dogs snored.

Maybe sleep wasn't so impossible. Sirens woke us at dawn, but other sounds came, too: church bells ringing, truck horns beeping, someone's car speakers, way too loud.

Then the phones started. And shouts, bullhorns, whistles, engines revving.

"Come to the beach!"

Mom and the big dogs piled into the Subaru, with Matt and me and Moses and Little Red stopping to pick up Grandma Eve and Doc Lassiter in Matt's car. Susan hopped into Harris' SUV, and her parents pulled out behind us. When we got stuck in traffic, cars and trucks trying to park up and down the streets, we got out and ran.

The sun broke through the clouds in perfect time for us to see the beach. A new beach, a glorious beach, the prettiest beach in the world. Surely the widest, cleanest, smoothest beach on the north side of the south fork of Long Island.

A line of driftwood remained near the beach grass and a circle of stones sat in the middle of the sand, waiting for tonight's bonfire. I had no idea how the little guys managed to do all that, but inside the circle, in a shallow depression, rested all the treasures. The pictures, the gold, the medals, the letters, the Wedgewood, all dry and unscoured by sand. People ran to reclaim their mementos, laughing, embracing, almost dancing with happiness.

My pendant wasn't there, not that I expected it. I had a better talisman anyway, all my own. And everyone called me a hero.

The crowd from Rosehill arrived and joined the celebration. But then others came to see what the commotion was all about. They brought their kids to marvel at the sudden reappearance of our beach. Carinne's feather couldn't fix this, not even when I handed her mine.

That's when Oey appeared, seemingly out of the blue. Or the blue water. Mayor Applebaum got busy among the non-talented, urging them to forget the new beach and the bird. Monte did yo-yo tricks for the kids. Or hypnotized them not to notice that the biggest, most splendiferous parrot anyone had ever seen had just materialized from thin air.

Heaven knew what he'd do if they saw the fish tail. Not even Grandma Eve or my mother could see the scales and the split fins, but Matt and I and Jimmie could, and now Carinne could, too. I introduced Oey, who took up a perch on her shoulder. She gave me a thumbs up and a big grin. Jimmie led them away, looking twenty years younger. Monte pocketed the yo-yo and went with them, looking confounded, but willing to follow them anywhere. I guess he'd glimpsed the fish tail.

"Tonight, tonight," my mother was yelling. "Come back to our beautiful beach to say thanks and ask for another year of good luck."

We needed that luck now to find Deni or there'd be no celebrating. Chief Haversmith said it would be too dangerous in the dark, with no way to protect miles of beachfront, or the local hero.

Un-uh. I worked hard to get the beach back for this one night. I wasn't missing it. Lou thought we might have enough men and mentalists to catch Deni before he got to me.

My father didn't see any mortal danger in my future when I called. That was enough for me. "We got the sand returned, and Mom gave Carinne a half-smile when everyone said good-bye. So how's your back now?"

"Killing me. I had to skip my golf lesson and my tennis date. I can't get a doctor's appointment for a week so I canceled the weekend in Miami with Lizzie."

I'd never heard of Lizzie. "She'll wait, Dad. You're worth it."

CHAPTER THIRTY-SEVEN

I had a parrot on my shoulder and panic in my heart. Over fifty women and girls gathered on the beach, and they all looked at me. I kept looking behind me for a stranger with brown hair and glasses, but all I saw was Carinne, sticking close to me and Oey.

Then Grandma Eve called for quiet while Mom and Susan and Aunt Jas handed out small wooden torches dipped in kerosene. Grandma lit hers with a plastic lighter. She came and lit mine next, then tossed hers into the stone fire pit, filled with the driftwood we'd spent an hour gathering.

"Thank you for our own Willow and a good harvest."

"For Willow," others chorused as they lit their torches from the fire, then tossed them into the pit. "And for a good tourist season." "A lucky number." "My son getting into a college I can afford." "My new hip." "My mother-in-law moving to Arizona."

I had a lot to be thankful for. "Thank you for good friends in time of need. And new friends and new family. And for Matt Spenser's love."

I touched my torch to Carinne's, and Oey hopped to her shoulder. "I am thankful to you all for saving my life and giving me new chances."

Mom went next. "I am grateful for family and furry friends. And finally knowing the truth."

Susan raised her torch high. "For good health and good cooking."

Her mom said thanks for Susan and her husband's love and for the children at school.

Louisa thanked the Paumanok Harbor women for welcoming her and her older daughter. Then she gave thanks for her son and new baby girl, who were home with Dante.

We thanked each other, the fire gods, the Andanstans. Some of us silently thanked Oey and the other beings from Unity; some thanked the Earth Mother or whatever divinity they worshiped. No matter. We were all doubly grateful to hear everyone's invocations and know we appreciated what we had, where we lived, and each other.

Mrs. Ralston said thanks for getting her Phi Beta Kappa pin back, so the jerks at the Suffolk County Center knew how smart she was. We laughed, then cried when Janie pushed her niece's wheelchair closer to the fire. Elladaire's mother wasn't all recovered from the fire, but she insisted on coming tonight to thank us for what the community had done for her and Elladaire.

That's why the men had their celebration in the parking lot, so we could weep and hug and act like fools. And so we could enjoy the warmth of the huge fire while they had to stand around freezing on the pavement.

Grandma Eve clapped her hands. "Now let's ask for blessings in the coming year. Wishes, prayers, or hopes, whatever you want. Out loud or to yourself."

Jasmine and Susan took the children aside and helped them write on the paper boats we'd made and stapled to little pieces of wood so they'd float. Then she set a candle in each and let the little girls carry them to the water and set them free after their mothers helped light the candles. We watched the tiny twinkling armada float away while we made our silent wishes.

Not me. I had years of missed chances and wishes to make up. I got the last little boat and drew a picture. Me and Matt, the dogs and a pretty house. Okay, it looked like a lighthouse, kind of. I did not include the three babies; the boat was too small. As I launched it at the water's edge, I also said a prayer to whomever listened for Jimmie and Oey and Grandma Eve and Mom and Dad, my new sister and old cousin, my bodyguards, even Lou. The tiny boat carried a lot of wishes. I watched it drift out, the paper on fire, the wood chip beginning to burn . . . unless that was someone else's boat and mine sank.

It was the thought that counted, Grandma Eve said, the thanking for the past and the looking forward to the future. Like Thanksgiving and New Year's at once. The turning seasons, the turning tide, growing up, growing old, growing relationships.

"Growing the best tomatoes on the east end," someone called out.

"And not growing complacent. May you all go in peace and prosperity and good health and, most of all, with love."

The men came back while we were still kissing each other's cheeks. They made their own toasts to us and all women with hot cider, or what they'd brought in flasks. Then they started cooking hot dogs at the fire, helping the children toast marshmallows. Matt brought veggie burgers for the vegetarians.

He handed me one on a bun. "Funny, I carried one to Carinne first. I thought I could know you anywhere, even in moonlight."

"A lot of people made that mistake tonight, we look so much alike, with the same hair color and blue eyes. But they're accepting her, and she's doing fine with Oey."

"I must have missed the parrot in the dark."

Matt didn't miss much, especially animals. If Oey had gone off to see about her eggs, Carinne could need help. It was hard to see across the fire's smoke or in the shadows, but I thought I spotted her off by herself. I headed in her direction, but she didn't look toward me. She kept staring at the chair Monte had brought for Jimmie to sit on. There was Jimmie telling tales to the two girls who'd cut their hair off for the cause. And there was Monte doing his yo-yo bit for Louisa's daughter. And there was Carinne, with Oey on her shoulder.

But if that was Carinne, who was the blonde woman with my haircut, my height? She had a pad and pencil in her hand, just like me. And she nodded to people who called "Great job, Willy." Or "Nice to meet you, Carinne."

Shit.

I ran toward my friends, yelling for help. Harris came running, so did Matt and Colin and Kenneth, who'd been sticking close to me as soon as the men joined the party.

Kenneth the precog shouted, "Danger!"

Lou stepped away from my mother and drew his weapon.

Harris and Matt both tackled me and tried to shield my body with theirs. I shoved at them. "Get off, you lummoxes. It's Carinne in trouble!"

But we were going to be too late. The third Willow—triplets, damn it—pulled a knife out of the middle of the drawing pad. A knife, like a fife. Knives, like Burl Ives and chives and hives and ex-wives. She aimed it right at Carinne's . . . back. Of course. Damn, damn, damn, Dad!

I screamed, "No, I'm Willow. That's my sister!" Colin had his gun out, so did the police sharpshooter, the chief, and a bunch of others, some unofficial and maybe unlicensed. But they didn't know which way to point, with women and children between them, gray smoke from the fire, and three freaking Willow look-alikes. And the parrot screaming bloody murder, "My petth!"

The girl hesitated, the knife poised in the air. Before anyone could shoot, Monte bobbed his stringless yo-yo twice to get it spinning, brought it back to his hand, then let it fly, so fast it made a silver streak through the night. The heavy yo-yo hit the imposter right in the head just as she released the knife. She dropped to the ground, the blonde wig falling beside her. A blue contact lens glistened in the sand.

We could all see the black buzzed hair and narrow features, the same ones in my sketch of Deni.

Oey flew at him with beak and talon and then barracuda jaws. Boy, the mayor was going to have to work overtime to get people to forget that.

"No, Oey," I hollered. "Don't kill him. He's sick."

My mother stood over the kid on the ground, cowering with his hands over his head. She gave him a solid kick. "I don't care how sick you are, you do not hurt animals. Or my girls."

Then Lou dragged him up and put handcuffs on him. Micky from the fire department helped. "Man, this dude is really screwed up."

"He's gay?" That was Micky's talent, recognizing sexual preferences.

Micky scratched his head. "Nah. I think he goes both ways, in drag or out. They'll love him at Attica."

I almost felt sorry for the sobbing animal who'd caused so much trouble. Almost. I didn't want to go near him, but I had to. "Why?"

"I loved you. You had to be mine. Or nobody's."

"Mine!" This time Oey swooped down and lifted the kid right off the beach and dropped him in the water. At that exact moment a flock of small, brilliantly colored parrots appeared in the moonlit sky and dove after him. Only they resurfaced as a swarm of iridescent fish in the bay, jumping and leaping, churning the water. Deni screamed. So did I.

"No, Oey! No!"

Deni disappeared. So did the fish, the parrots, and the sudden sandstorm that blinded everyone, extinguished the fire, and vanished before we could blink.

Oey came back to inspect Carinne's shoulder where the EMT already had a bandage on the small wound in her upper back. Then Oey came back to where I had my face buried in Matt's chest.

"Mine."

Mischief night was over.

*   *   *

I went back to the city. Mom needed help moving, but not into my apartment. Lou had one that allowed pets, right across the street. She'd stay there and come out to the Harbor on weekends when she wasn't filming in the studio or traveling to locations around the country. I did not ask where Lou would stay.

Susan wanted to sublet my apartment while the restaurant was closed for the off-season. She'd registered for courses at NYU in restaurant management, for when Uncle Bernie retired and she took over the Breakaway. I could always come stay with her when I needed to see my publisher or do a book signing, or when Matt and I wanted to visit the real world.

I didn't think I'd have time. I had so many ideas, so much I wanted to do. I'd finish the professor's book first, of course. He talked excitedly about another one, if the first did well. I had the course to teach for Louisa, a portrait of her baby to paint. And I still wanted to write Little Red's story for children. Then again, Christmas was coming. I loved that season and thought maybe I'd do a YA fantasy about it. I could call it *Yule Tide in the Hamptons*. Or I could write about how hard it was to find the perfect place to live out at the end of the Island. My mother's house was okay for now, with Matt's new partner taking over the one near the clinic, but we wanted one of our own, not the guest house at Rosehill, either, despite Carinne and Jimmie's enthusiastic urging and Monte's not quite as enthusiastic. Dealing with real estate people and zoning rules and mortgage banks could be a story of its own. I'd title that one *Light Houses in the Hamptons*.

Or I could plan a wedding. My father promised he'd come for it, and my mother swore she wouldn't strangle him.

Matt just smiled.

Me, too. I had . . . everything.

Celia Jerome

The Willow Tate *Novels*

"Readers will love the first Willow Tate book. Willow is funny, brave and open to possibilities most people would not have even considered as she meets her perfect foil in Thaddeus Grant, a British agent assigned to look over the strange occurrences following Willow like a shadow. Together they make a wonderful pair and readers will love their unconventional courtship."   —*RT Book Review*

TROLLS IN THE HAMPTONS
978-0-7564-0630-1

NIGHT MARES IN THE HAMPTONS
978-0-7564-0663-9

FIRE WORKS IN THE HAMPTONS
978-0-7564-0688-2

LIFE GUARDS IN THE HAMPTONS
978-0-7564-0725-4

SAND WITCHES IN THE HAMPTONS
978-0-7564-0767-4

To Order Call: 1-800-788-6262
www.dawbooks.com

DAW 170

Gini Koch
The Alien *Novels*

"This delightful romp has many interesting twists and turns as it glances at racism, politics, and religion en route. Darned amusing." — *Booklist* (starred review)

"Amusing and interesting...a hilarious romp in the vein of 'Men in Black' or 'Ghostbusters'." — *Voya*

TOUCHED BY AN ALIEN
978-0-7564-0600-4

ALIEN TANGO
978-0-7564-0632-5

ALIEN IN THE FAMILY
978-0-7564-0668-4

ALIEN PROLIFERATION
978-0-7564-0697-4

ALIEN DIPLOMACY
978-0-7564-0716-2

ALIEN vs. ALIEN
978-0-7564-0770-4
(Available December 2012)

To Order Call: 1-800-788-6262
www.dawbooks.com

DAW 160